A DREAM GONE WRONG

Christianna St. Sebastien has always fantasized about marrying a wealthy nobleman who can pay for her luxurious life in Marie Antoinette's court. But revolution dashes her hopes and sends her fleeing to an English farmhouse far from proper society. And the penniless girl's nightmare is made complete by the amorous advances of a farmer—a man who looks like a Roman god, but acts like a common peasant.

A DREAM COME TRUE

Rude, snobbish, and affected, Christianna is everything Gareth Larkin despises. And he would refuse to have anything to do with her—but she's the most breathtaking creature he's ever beheld. Determined to steal the beautiful aristocrat's heart, Gareth sets out to teach her that the length of a man's title and the size of his fortune are not necessarily his most important assets.

SWEET SUMMER STORM
Amy Elizabeth Saunders

Other *Leisure* and *Love Spell* books by
Amy Elizabeth Saunders:
FOREVER
WILD SUMMER ROSE

Sweet Summer Storm

AMY ELIZABETH SAUNDERS

LEISURE BOOKS NEW YORK CITY

For Lori B.

A LEISURE BOOK®

June 1994

Published by

Dorchester Publishing Co., Inc.
276 Fifth Avenue
New York, NY 10001

Printed in the United States of America.

tim

Part 1
The
Aristocrat

> *. . . She sought, with tempest-troubled gaze,*
> *the skies of her first innocence, now far away,*
> *As travelers who backward turn their eyes*
> *To blue horizons passed at break of day.*
> —Charles Baudelaire

> *Tyrants, cast your eyes on this terrible sight—*
> *shudder, and see how you and yours will be*
> *treated. . . .*
> —Elysée Louslatot, 1789

> *It was of no importance . . . it was the custom*
> *of those days . . .*
> —Pierre Caron, speaking of the execution of
> the Princesse de Lambelle

Chapter One

Christianna St. Sebastien was late—again. She rushed through the quiet, spacious hallways and gilded baroque rooms of Versailles, her heels clattering over the marble floors.

She had consumed an unseemly amount of champagne at a card game the night before and had slept in; now her head ached as she rushed up the wide marble staircase that led to the queen's bedchamber.

The white-wigged guards made scanty bows as they opened the doors to admit her, and she tried to look inconspicuous as she made her way through the throng of noblewomen who crowded the queen's chamber. She pushed through the sea of flowing skirts, taffetas, silks and voiles crowding against each other.

It was considered an honor to attend Marie Antoinette at her toilette each morning, and to watch her select her fans and jewels and shoes, which were displayed for her with all the pomp and ceremony of holy relics carried through a church at a holiday mass.

The ladies of the great court of Versailles stood in the gilt and rose splendor of the room, in careful and jealously guarded positions, according to rank. They glanced quickly at Christianna as she entered, and she was aware of the looks of disapproval that came her way.

Christianna was more than an hour late, and hoped to take her place (in front of Madame Alfort, but behind the Marquesse Pierfitte) unnoticed. To her relief, the queen's face was buried behind a large paper cone, as the hairdresser applied clouds of gold-tinted white powder to the royal coiffure; she appeared not to notice Christianna's stealthy entrance.

"These little rustics," the Marquesse Pierfitte murmured to her neighbor, "they come to court seeking to better themselves, and then they don't have the faintest idea how to behave. *C'est vulgaire.*"

Christianna, whose temper wasn't the best on a good morning (which this was not), glowered at the white ostrich feathers in the back of the marquesse's white wig.

Vulgar, indeed! The St. Sebastiens had been members of the nobility since the time of Charlemagne, and the marquesse was a nobody—a nobody with money.

Christianna's cheeks burned. She wanted to tell the marquesse what she thought, but she was unwilling to call attention to herself—the queen demanded punctuality, if nothing else, from her ladies.

The hairdresser lowered the bellows that he used to apply the powder, his assistant removed the cone that covered the queen's face, and two of the queen's more favored ladies rushed forward to remove the white sheet that protected the queen's gown.

Marie Antoinette's heavily lidded eyes looked around the room, until they stopped on Christianna.

The queen said nothing, simply giving her a cool look down her long nose; but the damage was done—Christianna had been late one too many times, and the queen had expressed her displeasure.

And now, for a while, Christianna would be officially out of favor. Nothing horrible, of course, but not as many invitations would arrive to coveted private dinners and entertainments in the queen's little theater, or picnics at *Le Petit Hameau*, the little peasant village the queen had built for herself.

From the queen's side, Gabrielle de Lambelle shot Christianna a quick look of sympathy, which made Christianna feel better. She almost smiled when Gabrielle touched her golden head with a quick grimace of pain, letting Christianna know that she, too, was suffering as a result of last night's indulgence.

All of the ladies in the room curtsied as the queen rose from her chair, and Christianna's head throbbed as she bent down. The sound of the door closing behind the queen and her entourage seemed unusually loud. The ladies left in the room burst into noisy chatter, like a flock of rainbow-hued birds.

Christianna raised her head and saw that the Marquesse Pierfitte was smiling at her with affected sympathy.

"Too bad, mademoiselle. It seems that things are just not going your way today. I suppose you were out late last night. I understand that when your grandfather was at court he was also given to late-night entertainments."

The chatter around them hushed, and for a moment Christianna didn't trust herself to speak. Everyone at court knew about her grandfather. No, everyone in Paris knew of him. He had been famous for his drinking, whoring, and depravity, and the "theatrical entertainments" that he had presented in his apartments were still gossiped about. People called him the *Marquis Mauvais*, the Evil Marquis.

The marquesse smiled, pleased that her blow had found its mark. She had no liking for little St. Sebastien, with her big blue eyes and pretty black curls, and her haughty ways. Why, everyone knew that the family was poor, almost destitute! The only reason she had come to court was to catch a husband with money; it was common knowledge. And not having any luck, the marquesse was pleased to note, despite her shining curls and lush little figure.

12

Christianna raised her head proudly, an ice-blue ostrich feather from her coiffure moving softly against her cheekbone, and managed a haughty smile.

"I am not my *grand-père*, madame," she answered coolly, and turned her back, tossing her thick black curls over her shoulder.

It was just that sort of arrogance that infuriated the marquesse, and Christianna knew it.

"I suppose that you are off for coffee with Artois again," the marquesse added. "You are wasting your efforts there, my girl. Artois is quite immune to even *your* charms. You are sophisticated enough to know that, are you not? He is a lover of men."

Christianna froze and looked over her shoulder at the marquesse, who was smiling with unkind glee.

The whispers in the room tapered off at the sight of Christianna's cold blue eyes, the arrogant lift of her perfect black brow.

She waited until she had everyone's attention before she spoke.

"And where did you hear that, madame? Perhaps . . . from your husband?"

What had only been whispered had now been said. The marquesse was white with fury, the rouge on her cheeks standing out in stark contrast.

Christianna smiled brilliantly, treating the marquesse to the sight of her dimples, and flounced from the room, pleased with her victory.

* * *

"The marquesse was right," Christianna snapped, sinking into the comfort of her favorite wing chair, looking through her day's letters. "Today is just not going my way."

Here was a bill from her hairdresser, demanding payment within the week, and one must pay her hairdresser first, especially a hairdresser as temperamental as Monsieur Antoine.

And then there was a nasty letter from her dressmaker, saying that all her bills must be paid in full, *s'il vous plait*, and that she would not be allowed any more credit.

And the awful fact was, there was no more money—none at all. Christianna had long since spent the miserly allowance her brother had sent her; and Phillipe refused to understand how expensive court life could be. It was hard enough to find a husband without having to wear last season's gowns.

Why was it so devilishly hard to find a husband? If the men were handsome, they were as poor as she was, or unbelievably arrogant. If they were kind, they were usually boring enough to reduce her to tears. If they were rich, they had rolls of fat and a wrinkle for every *sou*.

"How am I going to pay my bills if I don't find a husband?" Christianna cried out, kicking at the discarded bills that lay on the floor.

Her maid, Therese, gave her an unsympathetic glance from across the room, where she was mending one of Christianna's countless gowns, but wisely kept her opinions to herself.

Christianna moped around the gilt and robin's-egg-blue chamber for a while, reading her invitations to balls and ballets and picnics and soirees, which she put into a tidy pile, and her bills, from the fan maker and dressmakers and *parfumerie*, which she disposed of only a little guiltily.

She changed her dress three times, to her maid's annoyance, at last deciding on the sky-blue silk with the velvet pansies of a slightly darker blue at the shoulder, and at least fifteen yards of fabric in the skirt, which was stylishly gathered and draped in back, and gossamer ruffles of voile around the deep neckline. It was her favorite summer dress; the blue matched her eyes so well. And she had new shoes, blue satin with little curved heels, and sparkling paste jewels on the toes, which were exposed by the shocking new hem length, showing one's ankles.

Unable to decide between going to Madame Alfort's salon or the Marquesse de Guise's for tea (everyone was taking *le thé* these days, mad for all English things) she decided to go visit her friend Artois, who was always amusing and might cheer her up.

Artois was seated at his harpsichord when his valet showed Christianna in, enjoying the sunlight streaming through the open windows and idly running his slender hands up and down the scales. His light brown hair was gathered into a simple queue; his eyes, as light and bright as Christianna's own, sparkled with mischief. He greeted her with a brilliant smile.

"Guess who was here?" he demanded without preamble.

Christianna helped herself to a strawberry tart from a tray on the table, savoring the taste of the almond paste in the crust. "I've no idea," she answered at last. "Who?"

Artois wiggled his brows, a wicked gleam in his blue eyes. "Your future husband."

Christianna felt her mood lifting. Settling herself on the bench next to Artois, she put her fingers on the ivory keys of the harpsichord, enjoying the sound of the sparkling notes.

"Which one?" Christianna's future prospects were a source of endless amusement to both of them.

"The handsome one," Artois answered, trying to keep a straight face. "The Duc de Poitou."

"Oh, Artois!" she exclaimed in disgust. "Really!" She gave an elaborate shudder at the thought of the old, corpulent man. "You're beyond disgusting."

Artois laughed with delight at her response. "Think about it," he teased. "He's rich. Rich, rich, rich. And so wildly attractive and virile-looking. Can't you just imagine . . ."

"No, and I don't want to imagine," Christianna snapped, tossing her carefully arranged black curls.

"You'd be a duchess," Artois said in a tone of mock reverence. "Just think: Then you could hand the queen her shoes in the morning. Or

16

maybe just one shoe. Or maybe that privilege is reserved for princesses of the blood royal. Oh, well, maybe you could hand her a petticoat."

Christianna couldn't help but laugh. Artois thought that the ritual and ceremony of the court was ridiculous and didn't hesitate to say so.

"And then," Artois went on, "you could go back to your lovely husband every night for hours of bliss. Do you think he still can? Can you just picture it? What do you think Poitou looks like in his nightgown? Or even better . . . under his nightgown?"

Christianna shrieked with mingled laughter and horror. "Artois, you're dreadful. Stop it, before I'm ill!"

Artois was enjoying himself. "Can't you just see him, all excited, with his jowls quivering over you? 'Oh, darling. Oh, God, I think I'm going to—' "

"Stop it, Artois! Good God, what am I to do with you? You really are sick. At any rate, the duke isn't interested in me—not as a wife, anyway. I'm too poor for that."

Artois dimpled, and his fingers began to dance over the keys of the harpsichord, playing a sparkling Italian air. "You're too poor for anyone. Perhaps you should just give it up, and become someone's mistress. Now, the Duc de Poitou—"

"Stop it," Christianna warned, banging on the lower keys. The discordant noise made Artois cringe. "And don't even mention the word mistress again. I've guarded my virginity too long to throw it away on a fat old man. Or

17

a fat young man. Or anyone. I'll get a husband, and a rich one, too. Soon," she added, thinking about the bills she had torn up earlier. "Let's talk about something else, Artois. Do you like my new gown?"

Artois leaned back and cast a critical eye over the pale blue silk. "Yes. Very good. Very good. It really makes your eyes look bluer. And I see that Monsieur Antoine did your hair today. But what are those things on top of your head?"

Christianna touched her elaborate curls, piled at least a foot high. "Those are bluebirds. What do you think they are? Monsieur Antoine spent two hours on it."

Artois leaned in for a closer look at the elaborate feathered objects nestled in the shining black curls.

"Hmm. Well, the hair is good, very good. I just don't know about that bird business."

"Never mind," Christianna said firmly. "I like it."

"Maybe without the ribbon. Or maybe just the ribbon. Those birds . . ."

"I said never mind," Christianna exclaimed. "It's my hair, after all."

"It's a little silly," Artois persisted.

She glowered at him; then they both laughed the easy, comfortable laughter of friends.

"Let's try the Torelli piece," Artois suggested, his fingers dappling over the keys of the harpsichord. "You left your violin here, by the way."

"I know," Christianna answered, standing and stretching lazily. The violin was on top of the rosewood armoire, exactly where she knew it would be. She dragged a lyre-back chair across the marble floor and climbed up to reach the instrument, her heels unsteady on the midnight blue brocade of the cushion.

"You'll ruin my upholstery doing that," Artois pointed out, not really sounding as if he cared.

Christianna ignored him, opening the delicate gold filigree clasps of the case and removing the small violin.

She had owned it since she was twelve. Her brother Phillipe had sent it to her from Paris, for her birthday, in a box tied with lavender ribbons; and she had learned to play, at first on her own, and then with a tutor from the nearby abbey.

The violin had been a comfort to her in her lonely, neglected childhood. She and Phillipe had been raised by their grandfather, who was content to leave them in the crumbling old castle near the Auvergne Mountains, under the care of nurses and tutors while he himself lived a merry and depraved life at court. Every now and then the Marquis St. Sebastien would remember that he had two orphaned grandchildren and make a brief, unwelcome visit.

When Christianna was seven her beloved brother Phillipe had departed. She had cried, and screamed at him; but he had gone anyway, anxious to be away from his grandfather's rule now that he had reached the exalted age of eighteen.

After that she had been alone with her nurse and her tutor and Brother Joseph, who came up the mountain road from the abbey once a week to give her music lessons.

He had come unwillingly at first, resenting this intrusion upon his chosen life of quiet devotion, looking askance at the petulant twelve-year-old who was to be his pupil.

She, in turn, had regarded the tonsured young man with suspicion, wondering if he would be as eager to please her as was Nurse and the other servants of the château.

And then Christianna had put her violin into his arms, as gently as if it were a child. His expression had softened at the sight of the instrument: the gleaming rosewood, the perfect varnish, the symmetry and delicate curve of the waist, the silver and ivory pegs.

"This is from Italy; did you know that?" the Brother had asked quietly.

The young man's hushed and reverent tone made Christianna feel as if she was in church. She liked the gentle way he touched the instrument, as if he knew how much she loved it.

"My brother Phillipe sent it to me," she told him. "From Paris. In a box with ribbons."

She did not know it, but the loneliness in her voice was painful to hear.

"Phillipe will come back," she added, "at Christmas. Do you think that I will be able to play something for him by then?"

"Well, that is up to you. If you will work, yes. It is not an easy thing to do."

"I know," the child said soberly. "I've tried, and it sounds like cats fighting."

The Brother laughed softly. "It should not. Not with such an instrument as this. Did Phillipe tell you about this?" At the hesitant shake of her head, he went on. "This is a beautiful violin. It was made in Italy, by a family named Guarneri. Their work is admired all over the world. Each of their instruments has a distinct voice, like no other; a sound all its own, just like a person. Your brother must love you very much, to send you such a gift."

"From Paris," Christianna added softly.

"From Paris," agreed the monk with a gentle smile. He picked up the bow and fingered it gently. "May I?" he asked.

Christianna liked that he asked her permission; she nodded. She sat spellbound as the young man tucked the instrument in the curve of his shoulder and laid the palm of his hand tenderly over the bow. "Like this; are you watching? And you pull the bow; never push. Like this . . ."

The voice of the violin sang softly in the vast emptiness of the great hall: a magical sound of sweetness and clarity, bright and holy sounds that rose up past the dark stone walls, golden sounds that danced above the timbers of the vaulted ceilings.

When the monk stopped playing he saw that the child sat motionless, her blue eyes glowing in her odd, pointed little face, her small hands clasped tightly in her lap.

"It is a voice," she said at last. "It sounds like an angel speaking."

21

The tone was so sincere that Brother Joseph overlooked the little blasphemy. "Will you work?" he asked, and when she nodded, her small, pale face glowing white in its frame of unruly black curls, there was a fiery determination in the round eyes that pleased him. He began to look forward to teaching this odd, lonely child.

When Brother Joseph left that day Christianna had learned three notes. She started to rage at him for leaving so soon, her eyes filling with furious tears, her chin jutting angrily, but Brother Joseph was apparently not as malleable as Nurse where rages were concerned.

"If you shout and stamp your foot at me," he said simply, "I will not come back."

Christianna stopped instantly, horrified at the idea. "*Pardon, Frère,*" she said humbly. "*Excusez-moi.*"

The good Brother smiled with gentle forgiveness at the spoiled child, and was rewarded with a smile that transformed the odd, angular little cat face. She would be a beauty, Joseph realized, when she grew up.

"*Pardonner,*" he said quietly. "Forgiven."

When he returned a week later Christianna had mastered the three simple notes and taught herself the other five in the scale.

And when her handsome brother came to visit at Christmas she ignored the elaborate, pompadoured doll and scented fans and pretty dresses he brought her. To his great surprise, she ran to fetch the little violin he had won in a card game and sent to her, almost as an afterthought.

She had stood in the great hall of the château, where the winter drafts seemed never to leave despite the roaring fire in the huge fireplace, and shouldered the instrument, tucking it beneath her chin tenderly, and played him a simple, but perfect, little air by Mozart.

"What are you thinking of?" Artois demanded brusquely, his mouth full of strawberries and almond pastry. "Are we going to play, or are you going to stand there and stare into space all day?"

"*Bon Dieu*, you're rude," Christianna answered evenly. "I should have gone to Madame Alfort's."

"Madame Alfort," Artois remarked, "is one of those people who think they are terribly clever, only they are not."

Christianna let that pass and came to stand behind Artois, reading the music over his shoulder. "Let's play," she ordered.

Artois ran his fingers up and down the scales. "Fine. But pay attention. Last time we tried the Torelli you butchered it."

Christianna bristled indignantly; then she saw that Artois was teasing, and they laughed together.

The smooth, full sound of the violin sang around the sparkling, baroque notes of the harpsichord, filling the sunlit room. Christianna was happy, content.

She had met Artois within days of her arrival

23

at Versailles, and they had swiftly become friends, going to parties and operas and card games together. Before a year had passed they spent as much time together as they did alone.

He laughed at her sharp tongue and she laughed at his arrogance; he clucked sympathetically over her bills and she listened with awe to the stories of his travels.

Artois introduced her to amusing people and criticized her gowns and sent her flowers and made sure that she attended the right parties; within a year, Christianna was considered one of the court beauties.

It was too bad, everyone said, that the little St. Sebastien girl was poor. It would be hard for her to make a good marriage. And didn't her grandfather have a wicked reputation? Funny, when she seemed almost prudish.

Christianna didn't care what they said. She was in no hurry to marry, so long as her brother paid her bills. She was living at Versailles, far away from the cold and wild Auvergne; away from the cold, damp loneliness of the Château St. Sebastien. Everyone flattered her and invited her places, and when she and Artois rode through the streets of Paris in his open coach, people pointed and said, "There goes Christianna St. Sebastien, the granddaughter of the marquis." Their envy and admiration pleased her.

Throughout her lonely childhood she had longed to be admired and wanted. She had been starved for attention, and now she had it. And if some of that attention took the form of envy and gossip, too bad. Who really cared what anybody thought?

She was Christianna St. Sebastien, one of the reigning beauties of Versailles, the greatest court in Europe, and nothing was better than that. And eventually she would find a rich husband, who could buy her all the gowns she wanted.

"Do you want to play cards tonight?" Artois asked idly.

"No," Christianna replied. She was lying on the blue upholstery of Artois's Chinese-style settee, enjoying the last of the strawberry and almond tarts, watching him try on and discard various waistcoats and fuss with the diamond stud in the snowy lace of his cravat. "I lost all my pocket money last night, and the dressmaker is being a real horror."

"How did you pay for your new things?" Artois asked. "Credit, I suppose."

Christianna grimaced, adjusting the blue velvet pansies at her cleavage. "Yes, I'm afraid so. I didn't mean to, but one must have new gowns. Phillipe will scream when he gets the bills."

Artois adjusted the black satin ribbon that held his hair at the back of his neck and laughed. "And will you promise him to never, ever, do such a thing again?"

"Don't I always?" Christianna asked, and they laughed together.

"I love hot summer nights," Artois said happily. "Shall we go out for a walk in the gardens and see who we bump into?"

"Let's. The gardens are so pretty by moonlight. And we've done nothing but lie around and gossip all day. A walk would be perfect."

Artois decided on a handsome waistcoat of olive and dark gold stripes that made his boyish figure look even more slender, adjusted the falling lace of his cuffs, and rejected the diamond stud as being "too much."

"Very nice," Christianna approved.

"Tasteful," Artois agreed. "Not at all like running around with a bunch of damned birds on one's head."

"*Pédé*," Christianna answered, the insulting word sounding more like an endearment.

Artois laughed at her discontented face. "I certainly am," he agreed. "And don't you forget it, *chère*."

"As if I could," Christianna said. "You're far too kind and well mannered to be anything else."

"We could get married anyway," Artois teased. "After all, you really wouldn't miss what you've never had, would you?"

"Don't be such a pig," she answered. "What a lot of noise in the courtyard," she added, glancing at the open windows. "What do you suppose is happening?"

The sound of shouting and the clatter of horses' hooves could be heard through the tall windows—much more noise than one usually heard on such a balmy evening, when the courtiers were resting before their endless parties and card games.

Artois glanced out, his brow furrowing. "I don't know," he answered, pushing aside the heavy draperies, "But something is . . . look at all the traffic. And troops, as well. There go the king's guard. . . . something is happening . . . I don't like the looks of this, not at all."

Christianna reluctantly left the comfort of the settee and leaned out the window with Artois.

The huge courtyard, flanked by soaring buildings, seemed smaller, so crowded was it with troops and carriages and people. Soldiers, courtiers, and servants carrying trunks and hatboxes were running every which way in a flurry of activity; the glow of a hundred torches and candles bathed the scene with an eerie, flickering light.

"I don't like this," Artois repeated, his intense gaze roving over the frantic scene.

Christianna felt a dark foreboding and murmured a hasty prayer, crossing herself.

There was a sharp knock on the door of Artois's sitting room, and his valet entered with unseemly haste, his wide, dark eyes round with shock.

"*Pardon, monsieur,* but there is dreadful news. The peasants have taken the Bastille and freed the prisoners. They have taken Paris; they say they are going to march on the palace."

Christianna and Artois stood frozen by the window, trying to digest this inconceivable information. Artois's face was stark and white, his eyes blank with disbelief.

"Everyone is leaving," the valet continued.

"They say that the peasants are lighting fires; they are looting the shops." The young man swallowed and bit his lip. "They say they are slaughtering aristocrats."

Christianna and Artois stood silently, the rising noise of the courtyard filling the air around them. Their eyes met, and Christianna began to shake her head slowly. Without thinking, she said the first thing that entered her mind.

"Wonderful," she said. "This is all I need."

She might have been talking about a broken bracelet, or a rip in her gown; and after a long, silent moment, Artois threw his head back and laughed out loud.

"The world is coming to an end," he crowed, "and what do you say? 'This is all I need'! Oh, Christianna, you slay me, you really do."

She laughed with him, shock making it seem funnier than it really was. The young valet looked at them as if they had lost their minds.

"Well," Artois said at last. "Well. I guess we don't have to decide what to do tonight. I'm off."

He was striding to his closet even as he spoke, pulling out clothes and throwing them to his valet, who sprang into action.

Christianna stood frozen by the window, staring in disbelief as Artois and the man emptied drawers and shoved shirts and waistcoats into hastily produced trunks and valises.

Artois grabbed a stack of music from the top of the harpsichord. The Torelli concerto fluttered to the floor and lay there, forgotten.

"Damn, damn, damn," Artois muttered, trying to close a bulging trunk. "I wish I had more cash." His blue eyes raced around the room, stopping sadly at the statue of Apollo that flanked the door to his bedchamber, the sun god's marble robes flowing in an eternal wind. "I shall hate to leave the Bernini," he said sadly.

Christianna found her voice. "Artois! Oh, Artois, what am I to do? Where shall I go? Is everyone leaving?"

Artois stared at her, as if he had forgotten her presence. "I don't know. You could go home to the Auvergne, or come with me, if you like. Is your brother still in England?"

"I think," Christianna answered, trying to keep her voice from trembling.

"Not everyone is leaving," the valet informed her. "Some say that the mob will never make it here, that Lafayette and his troops can hold them off."

Christianna breathed more easily. "That's true, isn't it?"

"Who knows?" Artois cried. "Who knows? I wouldn't take the chance, myself. Come with me, if you like."

"Where are you going, Artois?" Already the room seemed curiously empty, a stranger's room.

"Who knows? Perhaps back to Provence, if it's safe. Or to Italy. Or maybe Vienna. Who knows? Are you coming?"

Artois was genuinely worried; Christianna could see the tension in his face, the set of his straight brows. He sat on the floor, closing an overstuffed trunk. His blue gaze met hers with his typical unflinching intensity.

She liked that about Artois—the way he had of staring directly at people, as if he was trying to see into their minds.

"What will happen, do you think?" she asked at last, totally at a loss as to what she should do.

Artois fastened the straps of his trunk, tightening them carefully while he thought.

"I don't know," he answered at last. "Perhaps nothing. Perhaps the troops will stop the peasants before they even get close. Perhaps it's all wild rumor, but I doubt it."

Christianna glanced at the window, listening to the sounds of hooves clattering across the stone courtyards, the courtiers calling to one another and to their servants—the frantic sounds of an exodus.

"Or," Artois finished quietly, "this could be it. The end. *Fini*. The revolutionaries could take the palace, the army could turn, we could conceivably be slaughtered before tomorrow."

Christianna's eyes were round with horror. "But why?"

Artois looked impatient. "Because they are starving, Christianna. And angry. And here we are, eating pastries and going to operas. Now, what are you doing? You can go to England. Do you know where your brother is? Do you have money? No? I'll lend you some."

"I'm not sure about Phillipe. I have a letter from him, somewhere . . ."

"Or you can go home, to the Auvergne."

Christianna thought of the ancient castle, thirty days' ride from Paris under the best conditions, the cold winds that whistled through the crumbling corridors, the isolation, the loneliness.

"No, I can't. There is nobody there. I don't even know if any servants are there. Phillipe takes care of that."

"Or you can come with me. I wouldn't mind."

"It would cause a scandal," Christianna objected. "I'll never get married if I do that. It's hard enough keeping a good reputation, Artois. If I go running off with a man, I'm doomed."

"Don't be stupid," Artois said. "If the revolutionaries take the palace, your good reputation won't help you."

The valet was carrying out valises, and Christianna could see people rushing through the hallways, loaded with trunks and jewelry cases, paintings and hatboxes.

Artois looked around the empty room, his sharp face quiet and sad, his eyes bright and thoughtful. He smoothed his hair before speaking.

"Are you coming or not? I can't wait much longer."

Christianna thought about her brother Phillipe, far away in England. She thought about her rooms; her pale blue furniture and books and dresses and her collection of Chinese porcelain. She wondered if she should pack everything or nothing. How awful it would be, to have to leave her things. This was her home, the place she had dreamed of living since childhood; Artois was her dearest friend. And he was leaving. Already she felt abandoned, the hollow feeling of loneliness growing in the pit of her stomach.

"I can't go," she answered at last. "I'll stay a while longer, until I'm certain what is happening, and then I'll go to Phillipe in England. He's going to be married there, I think. If you send your valet to my room, I'll give him the address." Her voice trembled; she could feel tears on the edges of her lashes.

"Are you sure?" Artois asked softly, his eyes boring into her.

"Yes, yes, of course. But write to me. Promise you won't forget."

The valet came through the door, shouldering the heavy trunk, his haste betraying his fear. "I'm having the carriage brought around," he informed Artois, his eyes wide and frightened. "It's madness out there. Almost half the court is leaving; but the king and queen say they will stay."

Christianna breathed a sigh of relief. Not everyone was leaving, and if the royal family was staying, things couldn't be that bad, could they?

Artois crossed the room and took Christianna's small white hand in his slender fingers. "I'll write you. But if things start to look dangerous, get out. Better the Auvergne than the Bastille."

"You've never been to the Auvergne," she

answered peevishly, and Artois laughed, as she knew he would.

He gathered her into his arms, still laughing, and hugged her tightly. She leaned her head against his familiar shoulder, trying not to cry on the starched white linen of his shirt.

"Au revoir, Christianna," he said softly, "I'll miss your bitchy temper."

She laughed, because she knew he wanted her to. "Au revoir, Artois," she answered, reaching up to stroke the sharp line of his cheekbone. "I shall miss you. I hope that this madness is over soon, and that everything will get back to normal."

Artois gave her a final squeeze and stepped back, gazing around the barren-looking room, shaking his head as if he could not quite believe it.

"Well, this is it," he announced briskly. "Maybe I'll see you soon; maybe I won't. We'll see what happens." He bent to pick up his valise with a mournful glance at the quiet harpsichord and the marble statue of Apollo. "If you see somebody making off with my Bernini," he added, with a possessive look at the statue, "stop them. Better yet, have it moved to your room. But I want it back, mind you. And don't forget your violin."

Christianna nodded, wiping a tear hastily from her eye, as Artois sent her a bitter smile and moved toward the door.

"Artois," she called, a hard catch in her voice, "I love you dearly."

He looked over his shoulder and gave her a

pleased wink. "Not too much, I hope."

"You're impossible." Christianna managed a laugh, despite the tears in her eyes. "God keep you."

Artois sighed impatiently. "There is no God," he said arrogantly, and Christianna wished that he would sit down for a good argument, and send his valet for coffee and chocolates, and that everything would be as it was before.

"You, too, my friend," he added awkwardly.

There was nothing more to be said. Christianna turned her blurred eyes on the silent harpsichord while the door closed behind him, the sound echoing in the empty room.

She made her way back to her own rooms in a curious daze, the throngs of perfumed courtiers and frantic servants running past her like forest animals fleeing a fire.

She met Gabrielle de Lambelle at the top of the staircase to the queen's apartments. The princesse was leaning on the elaborately carved banister, every golden hair in place, a squirming pug dog under one arm. She was fanning herself and watching the frantic exodus of the aristocrats as if it was a superb evening's entertainment.

She waved at Christianna and motioned her to join her, and Christianna did, feeling oddly indifferent to the noisy crowds rushing past.

"Look at them, will you?" Gabrielle remarked. "Like a bunch of chickens. What a fuss! As if the army would let the mob pass!"

Christianna stared at her friend. "You think they will not?"

"Of course not! Imagine! And all these stupid people will have to come rushing back. Of course it's bad, very bad, freeing the prisoners from the Bastille and all that, but what can an unarmed mob do against the French army?"

Christianna nodded, breathing a little more easily. Gabrielle seemed so calm, so certain.

"Shall we go see the queen?" Gabrielle asked. "She'll be so happy to know that we're staying. She might even forgive you. What are you doing with your violin? Are you going to see Artois?"

"Artois left," Christianna answered, looking down at the violin case in her arms. "He's gone."

"What a rat," Gabrielle exclaimed in disgust. "He didn't even say good-bye. Where is he going?"

Christianna shook her head. "He wasn't sure."

"Oh, he'll be back." Gabrielle smoothed her wide skirts, the pink taffeta whispering under her jeweled fingers, and shifted her frantic little dog to a more comfortable position. "Everybody is being so stupid. This is all so ridiculous. The mob can never take the palace, never."

Chapter Two

October 1789

Only five of us left, Christianna thought. Three short months had passed, and out of all the innumerable women who had once danced attendance upon the queen of France—chamber-maids and wardrobe women, laundresses and princesses, fan makers and duchesses—there remained five of them.

"It's your turn." Gabrielle shot Christianna an annoyed look over the top of her cards. "If you're still playing, that is. Of course, if you'd rather stare out the window, you may."

At Versailles, Christianna remembered, there had been miles of gardens, and halls, and salons, and enchanted little groves with magical fountains. And privacy.

Now that they had been moved to Paris, they were all confined to one floor, and the queen's ladies lived two to a room.

Gabrielle had been much more agreeable before that.

"I'm bored with cards." Christianna tossed her hand face up across the shining tabletop and stared out the window. Rooftops and gray skies were all she saw of Paris, now that she and the others had been forbidden to leave the Tuileries. Once it had been a great palace; now it was a pretty prison.

"You are bored with everything," Gabrielle observed, "and it makes you boring." She threw her own cards down and leaned back, picking at the voile skirt of her frock, which was too light for autumn.

Across the room, Madame Cléry sat in the somber light by the window, working at her embroidery. She looked up long enough to frown at the two younger women.

"You shall both drive me mad if you begin your incessant bickering. Be grateful. Give thanks to God. At least we haven't been arrested."

"Arrested!" Gabrielle threw her hands up, diamond rings sparkling. "Oh, madame! Arrested for what? They can't possibly arrest us! What have we done, after all?"

"We can't be arrested for bickering," Christianna agreed, picking up the cards and shuffling them again.

"What a shame," Madame Cléry muttered,

pulling her silk through her fabric with a fretful motion.

Gabrielle made a sour face.

"Not unless they elect Madame Cléry to the Estates General," Christianna amended.

"It's not the Estates General anymore," corrected madame, her voice betraying her frustration at being subjected to the constant company of irresponsible young women. "They are now the General Assembly, and they arrest whom they choose."

"Impossible," Gabrielle announced.

Christianna wished she believed that. "Have you noticed, Gabrielle, that whenever you say something is impossible, it is sure to happen? It was impossible that the mob would take Paris; it was impossible that the mob would take Versailles; it was impossible that they would force us to the city. And here we are. I wish you would quit saying *impossible*."

Gabrielle glared at her friend; Christianna tapped her foot on the floor, wishing that she had her own sitting room; Madame Cléry exhaled a dragon-sized breath of exasperation.

"If you two wish to spend what may be our last days on earth picking at each other, you may. I think you would be better off praying, but the young these days are absolutely irresponsible." And so saying, Madame Cléry walked to the great carved door, pushing her way past the guard in the hall with a great show of dignity.

"Old dragon," Gabrielle remarked, tossing her golden head.

"She must eat lemons every morning, to keep that sour look," Christianna agreed, and Gabrielle smiled, an ally again.

"I think we're all a little sour," Gabrielle admitted. "Simply from being in each other's company so much. Oh, I wish they would let us leave this place! Why do they keep us here, Christianna?"

Christianna wished she had paid closer attention to politics. All she knew was that the world was upside down, and that they were, to all purposes, prisoners.

"Perhaps they are going to arrest us," she suggested. "After all, they've taken almost everyone else."

She crossed the floor of the little salon and took her violin from a gilded rococo table. She ran her bow lightly across the strings and played a sad, lonely-sounding air.

"How dismal that is!" Gabrielle complained. "You *should* be taken to prison, for depressing me so, Christianna."

Christianna laughed, and immediately switched to a light, easy tune. "That, my friend, *is* impossible. If depressing someone was a crime, we'd have bid farewell to poor Madame Cléry long ago."

Gabrielle's laugh stopped abruptly at the sound of the guards changing out in the hallway, a grim reminder that they were prisoners of the new republic of France.

"Don't think of it," Christianna urged, lowering the bow of her violin. "If we worry, we shall go crazy, Gabrielle."

Gabrielle rested her fingertips against her forehead, closing her eyes for a minute. Then she looked up at her friend, her smile bright and forced.

"Worry, indeed! The only thing that worries me is this: the sheer tedium. Revolutions are boring, Christianna. Worse than a bad dinner party."

Christianna laughed, because she knew that Gabrielle wanted her to.

They arrested Gabrielle three days later, for "crimes against the state," though what those crimes might be, Christianna had no idea.

Gabrielle de Lambelle looked at the arresting officers as calmly as if they were taking her to a ball, her wide-brimmed, feathered hat perched jauntily on her thick golden curls.

"This is stupid," she told Christianna airily, "for the only crime I have ever committed is this: I am going into the rain, in October, and I'm wearing a summer gown and hat. I shall probably freeze."

Christianna didn't laugh.

"I shall be back soon," Gabrielle chattered on, her greenish-gray eyes dancing. "And if not, I shall be in the Concierge with everyone else. I hear that there are some wickedly good card games there." She seemed not to care that she was speaking of a prison, and not a country château.

The arresting "officers" at the door of the delicate salon shifted impatiently, glowering at the two young women in their soft silk dresses, who stood chattering stupidly about dresses and card games.

Christianna lifted a brow at them. She recognized the short one, she thought. He had been a groom, hadn't he? Or a footman, at Versailles. Rough men, who now seemed to think they were running things. And the truly frightening thing was, they were.

"Time to go, you." The one in charge said that, a big brute of a fellow. His tone was insolent, rude. He wanted to frighten Gabrielle; he wanted to insult her by denying her title. "You," when once he would have bowed and said, "Your Highness."

It worked. Gabrielle was frightened. She clutched the striped pink silk of Christianna's sleeve, her eyes darkened to almost gray.

"I shall be back," she repeated almost frantically.

The soldiers were crossing the room, their rough boots dirtying the delicate patterns of the carpets.

"If you should see Artois—" Christianna said, the words hard to speak.

She knew, knew in the bottom of her stomach, that she would never see Gabrielle again, or laugh at her silly affectations. Her heart pressed like a rock against the stiff bones of her bodice, the filmy ribbons of lace and pink silk feeling like a vise.

The men took Gabrielle's slender arms, as if she were a dangerous criminal, and Christianna wanted to laugh at them, to mock them, or to spit at them. If she hadn't been so incredibly frightened, she might have.

Gabrielle's frightened eyes met Christianna's as the soldiers began to pull her back toward the door, and to Christianna's horror, the woman began to cry.

She knows, Christianna thought. *She knows that she is not coming back; we will all die.*

She stared at her friend in mute despair, and even after the soldiers took her from the room and she was alone, with the sound of the rain pouring down the windowpanes, and the indifferently cheerful crackle of the fire, she stared at the doorway that Gabrielle had been taken through, wondering when her turn would come.

Christianna sank to the tapestry seat of a dainty chair and buried her face in her hands. She prayed with all her heart, and said penance for a million little sins.

She bargained and begged and bartered with God, offered a lifetime of poverty, chastity, anything, if only she could get out of this place.

"There is no God," Artois had said, his eyes sparkling with the blasphemy.

"Oh, Artois," she whispered into the empty room, "I hope that you're wrong."

It was at that precise moment that she saw the note, a carefully folded but soiled paper lying behind the door, with a careful *C* inked on it. Christianna tried to remember who had been standing there. She was almost certain it was the short, wiry man, the one from Versailles.

She glanced quickly around the room and, satisfied that no one was about, she rose from her chair and crossed the room, her heels clicking on the smooth marble.

Her heart hammering as she bent to pick up the paper, she leaned against the wall as she unfolded it and read what was written there.

Somebody wants you out. Go to the chapel at ten, tomorrow night. Bring only what you can carry.

The writing was unfamiliar, a crude, sprawling hand, but Christianna didn't care.

Somebody was going to get her out, somebody cared. Phillipe, or Artois, or even that horrid old Duc de Poitou; at this point, she didn't care. She was going, away from her gilded prison, to someone who cared.

She pushed a heavy black curl away from her face and cried with joy and relief.

She burned the letter in the fire and went to her room, eager to begin packing her few possessions.

It never occurred to her to be afraid.

The next day dragged by, and Christianna tried not to think that tonight she would leave. It was hard to behave normally, when all the while she was wondering who had arranged her escape. She felt a little guilty abandoning the queen, who had been so kind to her in the past three months, thanking her for her loyalty in staying when so many others had fled.

Christianna was kneeling by her bed, praying fervently, her rosary beads of crystal and silver filigree passing coolly through her fingers, when Madame Cléry knocked on the door.

"Her Majesty wishes your company," she told Christianna, "and she asks that you bring your violin. It would lift her spirits. She is so worried about the Princesse de Lambelle."

Christianna nodded and rose to her feet, taking her violin case from the table next to her bed. "So am I," she said shakily. "Poor Gabrielle. Do you think they'll put her in the Concierge?"

Madame Cléry shrugged, her mouth forming a bitter line. "Who knows? Perhaps they'll put us all in. Madmen, all of them. My poor queen, her heart is breaking. Poor France."

Christianna slid her rosary beads into the pocket of her gown, comforted by their presence—a reminder that God had not forgotten her, that she was to be rescued tonight.

She looked toward the window as a stream of sunlight pierced the clouds that had shrouded Paris for days, and it seemed that it was a good omen.

"We're all in God's hands now," she said softly, and Madame Cléry sniffed scornfully.

"Desperation makes for piety in the most unlikely persons. Come along, Mademoiselle St. Sebastien. Her Majesty is waiting."

Marie Antoinette was aging rapidly under the duress of her imprisonment. There were dark circles beneath her eyes, and the lines by her mouth were deeper. But she sat quietly and calmly in her graceful little chair and smiled as Christianna played for her.

The dulcet, full voice of the little violin filled the chamber as Christianna played for her sovereign, who had no idea that the soothing melodies of Rameau and Marcello and Vivaldi were farewell songs, Christianna's parting gifts to her queen.

Even as she played they could hear the voices of the crowds that gathered outside the palace, the angry mob that was growing now that the rain had stopped.

They were shouting, as they always did, for the queen to show herself. "Madame Capet," they called her, or "The Austrian woman," or worse.

It was a sound they were all becoming accustomed to, a sound as familiar as the flowing fountains and singing birds of Versailles had once been.

At last Christianna gave up and lowered her violin as the shouts turned into triumphant screams, the unearthly joy of a mob swept away by their hatred.

"What do they want?" the queen demanded frantically, her calm facade at last cracking. "What do they want of me? Must I again exhibit myself like an animal for their amusement? Dear God, what now?" She offered a trembling hand to Madame Cléry, who helped her rise.

"Ignore them," Madame Cléry urged the queen. "They'll stop eventually."

"Or they won't. I may as well satisfy them." The queen spoke in a haggard voice. "Open the doors and I shall show myself once more, and perhaps they will give us some peace."

Christianna set her violin on a gleaming table of inlaid walnut and followed the queen to the gilded doors that led to the balcony. It was a ritual they had been through many times before, and Christianna hated it.

For a few moments the queen would stand silently before the crowds that filled the courtyard, her hands folded and her head lifted with quiet dignity; and they would shout at her, insults and obscenities. They called her whore, murderess, traitor.

The shouting, angry mobs frightened Christianna—the clenched fists, the hate-filled voices, the cruel laughter.

The cold sunlight of October fell across the room as the doors swung open and the queen started to step forward; and then she fell back with a strangled cry.

"Shut the doors; shut them!" shrieked Madame Cléry, and the liveried servants hastened to obey, but not before Christianna saw what had sent Marie Antoinette into a cold faint.

Out in the courtyard, in front of the exultant mob, a crowd of revolutionaries were waving a tall pike, like a flagstaff, in front of the queen's apartments. But there was no flag atop the pole.

It was the head of Gabrielle de Lambelle, her golden hair flowing around the bloody stump of her neck. For a moment her sightless eyes seemed to meet Christianna's.

The balcony doors closed with a bang, but the noise of the bloodthirsty masses filled Christianna's ears in a roaring, evil symphony of darkness, and she let loose a cry of fear and pain as she crumbled to the floor, burying her face in her hands as if she could block out the ghastly image.

She knew that she never would.

"I will live through this," Christianna whispered, trying to stop the tears that threatened her again. "I will live through this."

Her bedchamber was lit by a single candle, the delicately painted clouds and pastoral scenes on the walls looking dark in the dim light, as she carefully bundled the last of her belongings into a valise of heavy tapestried fabric.

Only what you can carry, the note had said. There had been a time when she had required five trunks and ten boxes for a trip, but those days were behind her.

She took only one gown, a simple dress of flowered cotton that she had worn to a picnic at Artois's country estate, one chemise, which would serve as a nightgown, and a change of underclothing. Her ivory-backed brushes, her ebony hairpins, and a bottle of jasmine scent were next.

She had few jewels—a rope of pearls from her grandmother; a pair of diamond and pearl earrings that had been a birthday gift from

Artois; a sapphire brooch that Gabrielle had grown tired of.

Carefully, she put in the letters she had received from her brother last summer, so that she could find him if he was still in England; and then a miniature portrait of her mother, set in a frame surrounded by brilliants.

She studied the face for a moment, so like her own—broad across the cheekbones, pointed at the chin, dominated by large, light blue eyes. She wondered briefly about her, this woman who had given her birth and then died within months. Another Gabrielle—Gabrielle St. Sebastien—who had left behind two children and one tiny portrait to remind them of her existence.

Christianna wrapped the miniature carefully in a pair of embroidered kid gloves and placed it in her valise.

Her crystal and silver filigree rosary beads were next, and she murmured a quick, fervent prayer and pressed the crucifix to her lips before adding it.

There was nothing to do now except wait. On her bedside table the china clock she had brought with her from Versailles ticked slowly.

It was a pretty clock, of delicate porcelain, with painted pastoral scenes of handsome shepherds and buxom country maids. She had won it last summer in a wager with another of the queen's ladies and had borne her prize off with delight to show it to Artois.

He had lifted an arrogant brow at the gilded

rococo curves and idyllic country scenes and pronounced it "a fright."

Christianna smiled at the memory and ran a finger over the cool glass face of the clock. "Oh, Artois, you snob," she murmured, as if he could hear her.

Perhaps it was Artois who had arranged her rescue, and tomorrow they would be eating pastries and drinking too much coffee and haranguing each other and laughing.

Or perhaps she would be with Phillipe, her handsome brother, with his stern face and shining black hair; and he would call her "piglet" and take her to England with him, far away from Paris and the nightmare of this revolution.

For a moment she saw Gabrielle's sight-less eyes, her golden hair stained with blood. Christianna shuddered and pushed the image firmly away.

Five minutes to ten.

She took her cape from the armoire and laid the heavy velvet of dusty lilac around her shoulders, feeling the smooth satin lining of darker lilac against her shoulders.

Outside the open window the October air was cold and damp, fragrant with the scent of burning fires. Christianna wished she could take her blue velvet cape with the ermine trim, but of course that would be silly. Such an expensive garment would mark her as a member of the hated aristocracy.

She took her valise in one hand and her violin

case in the other, running her hand over the soft, fragrant leather.

More out of habit than anything else, she took a final look in the mirror before she left the room and was startled at her own appearance.

Her face looked tight and pinched, her eyes wide and anxious, dilated with fear; an almost fevered stain of red flushed her cheekbones.

She drew a deep, shaking breath and wished she hadn't laced her corset quite so tightly; then she extinguished the candle before she left the room, closing the door softly behind her.

The chapel was silent and dark, a few votive candles flickering their wane lights at the altar. Her taffeta petticoats whispered as she genuflected, the sound loud in the silence of the room.

"Mademoiselle St. Sebastien?"

Christianna turned abruptly toward the sound of the voice, hope and fear rushing through her body and her fingers tightening on the violin case she held against her heart like a child.

A man was stepping from the shadows behind her, and her heart began to hammer wildly. It was one of the men who had taken Gabrielle; the small, wiry one she thought she had recognized from Versailles.

He smiled at her, revealing broken teeth. "I thought that you might come, after what happened to your friend. You're very lucky, you know. The orders for your arrest were to be delivered tomorrow."

Christianna felt sick at the mention of Gabrielle. She tried to speak, to ask questions; but her throat felt tight and pinched.

"Here—" The man reached into the pocket of his shirt and offered her a creased, stained piece of paper. Her fingers shook as she took it from his rough hand.

Her heart leapt with joy as she recognized her brother's handwriting.

Christianna—I am here, in Paris, and am working to bring you out. Say nothing to anyone. Be ready to leave suddenly. Have faith; I will not leave Paris without you.

Christianna wanted to weep with joy, and the eyes that she raised to her rescuer were brilliant.

The man's eyes gleamed back. "Well, Mademoiselle Aristocrat, you're a very lucky girl, aren't you? Very lucky. There is, however, a question of payment. Do you have any gold?"

Christianna shook her head. "Nothing. Not a *sou.*"

Her rescuer snorted in disgust. "Nothing? Horseshit. No jewels?"

Christianna dropped her valise in her eagerness to open it and fumbled around until her fingers felt the rope of pearls. Trembling, she held them out, the perfect spheres gleaming in the flickering light.

She tried not to flinch as the man seized them in his dirt-stained hand. His dark eyes gleamed.

"Good enough. Now, Mademoiselle Aristocrat, you are to follow me silently. We have a four-hour journey ahead of us. It was necessary for your brother to leave the city, and we will meet with him later. You will be traveling in a farm cart, under a pile of hay. You will neither move nor speak until I give you permission to do so. Do you understand?"

Christianna nodded, thinking that she would obey Satan himself, if it meant that she would live.

"Good. I'm afraid that it won't be the sort of trip to the country you are used to, but if you want to save your blue-blooded ass, you won't mind."

He wanted to frighten her, she realized; this ugly little man was enjoying her fear. He relished every sneering, crude word he spoke. She didn't care if he was saving her; she would be glad to get away from this pig.

"By all means," she answered, her voice cool and calm, "let us be off."

His eyes narrowed. "Say 'please' when you speak to me," he snapped. "You are no longer giving orders, mademoiselle. And don't forget it."

He led her toward the back entrance of the chapel, stopping to take a noisy drink from the font of holy water by the altar. Christianna shuddered superstitiously at the blasphemy before she followed him into the cold, clear night.

Chapter Three

England, 1790

"I am not going to New Orleans." Christianna glared across the table at her brother. The waitress serving them dinner set Christianna's glass down swiftly and beat a hasty retreat.

Phillipe St. Sebastien rested his dark head in his hands and sighed. It was a bad day. No, it was a bad year.

The revolution had shattered his life, as well as his country. One day he had been in England, happily in love and planning his marriage, and the next he had been rushing across the Channel to France, hoping to rescue his sister from a war-torn and dangerous city.

For four long months he had lived in the dangerous and bloody city of Paris, disguised as a common wine merchant—not an easy task for a man of his uncommon height and grace, whose every movement spoke of aristocracy. He had paid extravagant sums of money from his rapidly emptying pockets, trying to smuggle messages into the palace to his younger sister.

And then, in October, his messenger had told him that she was gone. Escaped, to God knew where.

Not knowing where else to turn, and guided only by hope, he had made the long journey to their childhood home in the Auvergne Mountains, praying that Christianna would be there.

Like so many great castles, the Chateau St. Sebastien had been burned to the ground and was only a stone ruin when he reached it—but Christianna had been there, living in a rude cottage with her childhood nurse.

She had changed.

The soft, carefree girl who lived only for parties and new gowns was gone. In her place was a thin, brittle creature who jumped at unexpected noises and cried out with terror in her sleep. Her haunted blue eyes pained her brother, even as her tense and temperamental behavior drove him mad.

And after he had risked life and limb to save her and bring her safely to England, she now looked across the table of the crowded inn at him and refused to listen to reason.

Phillipe looked helplessly at his wife, Victoria, silently imploring her for help, but Victoria was happily dividing her attention between her plate of roast beef and the rosy-cheeked infant in her arms.

"How can you even ask such a thing of me?" Christianna demanded. "Phillipe, you promised me that when we got to England it would all be over. You said that I could rest. Phillipe, I've not had a home since I left Versailles. It's been nine long months, and I've been dragged across the mountains and through Portugal and over an ocean—"

"The English Channel is hardly an ocean, piglet," Phillipe pointed out, a weary expression on his handsome face.

"It looks like an ocean, it smells like an ocean, and I'm calling it an ocean," Christianna retorted. "And as for New Orleans, it's on the other side of the world. I can't do it, Phillipe. I'll die; I know it."

Phillipe was more shaken by his sister's words than he liked to admit. She was thin, her wrists as fragile as a child's. Her blue eyes looked too large for her pale, sharp face. By day she was tense and snappish, or flippant and studiously careless. There was a brittle edge to her laughter that frightened him.

At night she cried out in her sleep as she battled with the memories of the revolution. Not once had she spoken to him of those memories, or confided in him about the demons that haunted her.

"I need rest," she said quietly. That was true, Phillipe could see. She was exhausted, and her fingers trembled as she took her glass of wine from the table.

Phillipe leaned forward, his blue eyes bright with anxious concern. "I know you do. But listen, piglet, there's no way around it. We're three English pounds away from poverty, and Etienne has offered me this position. I'm sorry it's in New Orleans, but I have no choice. I have a wife and a child. Where else will you go?"

"She could stay with my family," Victoria said suddenly, lifting her red curls and shifting her sleeping daughter to her other arm.

Christianna stared at her brother's wife.

"After all," Victoria pointed out, "we're on our way there. And there's plenty of room. The country air will do you good, Christianna. And when you're rested and better able to travel we could send for you."

Christianna digested this idea. Rest; a house in the country. She thought of the English country houses they had passed on the way: gleaming white mansions with lush lawns and graveled drives winding through blossoming trees. Oh, to have a bed of one's own, and never have to stay in another inn, worrying about fleas and bedbugs. Maybe she could have her own maid.

"I've already bought passage for three," Phillipe pointed out.

"Then Mary can come," Victoria said, referring to her maid. "She's so good with the baby, and she was dreading having to go home and find another position. Don't be silly, Phillipe.

Christianna will be perfectly happy with my family. They'll love her."

"And if they're like you, I shall love them," Christianna said quickly, smiling at her brother's lovely wife. How wonderful it would be, to be among gentle people and away from this gypsylike traveling. Perhaps Victoria's family would introduce her to some country earl and she could marry; then her future would be secure.

"Then it's settled," Victoria exclaimed in her no-nonsense, English way.

Phillipe looked uncertain.

"Oh, for heaven's sake, don't fuss," Victoria told him, tossing her red head. "Christianna's right—she can't possibly travel across an ocean. She's far too frail. I shall go tell Mary—she's upstairs crying because we're leaving."

"As soon as we have a house," Phillipe told his sister, "I shall send for you."

If Christianna was listening, she didn't respond. Her eyes were far away, dreaming of elegant houses with polished floors and fine carpets and velvet armchairs set in front of marble-fronted fireplaces.

That night, Phillipe was jarred from his sleep by the sound of his sister's cries, anguished and wounded, muffled by the thick walls of the inn.

"Damn," he whispered, fumbling for his breeches in the dark. Next to him, his wife stirred and reached out a warm hand to touch his shoulder. Her voice was husky and soft with sleep.

"What is it, Phillipe? Is it Christianna again?"

"Yes. I'll go wake her, before she screams the inn down."

The room brightened as he lit the candle, casting sharp shadows beneath his cheekbones, revealing the anxiety in his pale blue eyes.

He cast a longing look back at his wife, warm and soft in the feather bed, her hair shining across her pale body, glowing like autumn leaves.

"I'll be back in a moment. And Victoria?"

She made a sleepy sound.

"Don't bother going back to sleep."

"Wonderful," she said, smiling, her eyes still closed.

Another cry sounded from the neighboring room, and Phillipe went without hesitation to wake Christianna, damning the revolution, and whatever had happened to make his sister scream with nightmares.

Jean-Claude was laughing in her face, her pearls clutched in his dirty hand. She could smell the rotten odor of his broken teeth, the dank smell of his greasy hair, the close, stifling smell of the dirty cottage: a smell of cabbages and sour wine and sweat.

"Find her jewels, Raoul. Go through her things."

The words echoed in her dreams; the dark, rough walls of the cottage seemed to press closer, closing her in, and her arms were held, twisted cruelly behind her back.

She couldn't move.

Ugly laughter echoed in her head; Jean-Claude and his brother, their gaunt faces and gleaming dark eyes looked like demons in rough shirts and breeches.

The one named Rauol ripped open the soft leather of her violin case, tearing the gold filigree clasps from their beautiful rivets. The instrument was in his work-roughened hand, its slender neck rudely clutched.

He raised the little violin and brought it down sharply on a greasy table, laughing like a madman as it shattered.

The sound of the breaking strings was like a cry, sharp and harsh. Shards of shining, fragrant wood scattered across the greasy floor and an ivory peg rattled to a stop beneath a rough boot. Christianna felt herself shattering too. Her heart seemed to burst; the room closed in and, as she screamed, a hard fist made contact with her cheek, her head snapping back and brilliant red lights in her eyes. . . .

"Christianna! Christianna, stop it; it's all right."

She came up fighting, as she always did; crying out, striking out blindly.

"Piglet, it's me, Phillipe. It's all right."

She stopped abruptly, her eyes seeming to focus; and she raised a shaking hand to touch her brother's cheek.

"Oh, Phillipe. Oh, I'm sorry. Oh, Holy Mother of God, did I wake the whole inn?" She managed a shaky laugh, trying to still the inevitable trembling that followed her nightmares.

Everything is all right, she told herself firmly. *You are in England now, and you have four new gowns, and Phillipe will take care of everything; and you're safe.*

"No, I think everyone else slept through it this time," Phillipe assured her, but the smile on his mouth didn't reach his eyes.

"Christianna . . ."

"Don't start, Phillipe."

"If you would only talk about it . . ."

"Nonsense. Go away and leave me alone. Or stay and talk, if you like. But not about France."

Phillipe stared at his sister's pointed little face, the bright smile false. She looked younger than her twenty years, fragile in her white nightgown, with her heavy black hair falling around her.

"Christianna," he began, his voice soft, but she was already ahead of him.

"Do we really arrive at Victoria's house tomorrow? What do you think it will be like, Phillipe? Will her family mind me being there? I would so hate to feel like a poor relative."

"If Victoria says that it's all right, I'm sure that it is. They are very kind and good people, I'm certain."

Christianna yawned and settled back into the warmth of her bed. "Inconceivable," she murmured. "The Marquis St. Sebastien, working for a shipping firm."

Phillipe laughed softly in agreement, shaking his long black hair from his tired eyes. "The Marquis St. Sebastien," he admitted with a rueful smile, "is lucky he doesn't have to shovel shit for a living."

Christianna made a face and snuggled comfortably into her pillows, comforted by Phillipe's presence.

"I can't wait to get to Victoria's home," she said with a weary sigh. "I am so tired of traveling, Phillipe. How good it will be, to never sleep in another inn or be around rough people."

Phillipe smiled at his sister and stroked her pale cheek as he stood to leave. "Sleep well, piglet."

He left the candle in the room with her, and Christianna lay awake for a long time, watching the golden flame until it blurred beneath her tired eyes.

When at last she slept she dreamed of Victoria's home, of English country estates with tidy rows of roses along vast expanses of lawn and glittering rooms with cool marble floors and soft, clean carpets.

Tomorrow, she thought, as she drifted off to sleep, *tomorrow my life will be normal again*.

It was not what she had expected.

Christianna stood frozen in the door of the carriage, her eyes wide with disbelief.

"Phillipe," she said, her voice soft, "I think that you've made a mistake."

Her brother seemed not to hear her. He was smiling like an infatuated idiot, his infant daughter held against the front of his waistcoat, as he beamed at the scene before them.

This couldn't be Victoria's home; it was impossible, ridiculous. Christianna stared in horror at the sprawling farmhouse, the thick plaster and dark beams of the walls, the gabled windows shining behind rambling, twisting vines of ivy, the overgrown gardens and gnarled apple trees, the thatched roofs and muddy drive.

This was not the home of an heiress; this was the home of peasants. But Phillipe's wife was walking up the uneven brick path, her face glowing with joy.

Christianna did not see the charm of the low stone fences, the wilderness of spring flowers rioting in the unruly beds, the gently wooded slopes of green pasture, and the freshly planted fields that ran like rich, brown carpets to the foot of the dense forests.

She saw only a common farmhouse, and her dreams of gentility and luxury faded before her.

"Phillipe," Christianna repeated, her voice trembling a little, *"c'est une erreur.* This cannot be the place."

Phillipe turned back, as if to reply, but his attention was diverted as the front door of the house burst open. To Christianna's horror, a screaming horde of redheaded giants appeared, tall, rough men in work-stained breeches with shirtsleeves rolled up over brawny arms.

They surrounded Victoria, shouting with delight, tossing her about like a child and laughing at her elegant traveling costume of green velvet. Victoria was laughing back, seeming not to care when a stubby-legged, long-eared dog came bounding through the bushes and jumped on her, leaving muddy paw prints on her beautiful skirts.

"Phillipe," Christianna repeated, her voice cracking. "Pardon, *mon frère*. Have you lost your mind? Is this a joke?"

Phillipe turned then, and shifted the sleeping baby on his shoulder, an infuriatingly beatific smile on his face.

"No mistake, piglet. And speak English, please. We don't want to be rude."

Christianna sputtered helplessly for a moment. "Rude?" she cried, when she found her voice. "Rude? You came to England to marry an heiress, Phillipe! You're the Marquis St. Sebastien! You cannot marry a . . . a shepherd's daughter!"

"Too late," Phillipe answered, sounding for all the world as if he was delighted about this disaster. "And as for my title, it's not worth much more than a visit to the Bastille. Now do be nice, piglet, or I'll forget to send for you and you can stay here forever."

Christianna gasped several times, wondering if Phillipe had indeed turned idiot. She stared in disbelief as he walked down the uneven path to join the boisterous mob that surrounded his slender wife.

Christianna stood forgotten, half in and half out of the carriage, as the tall, shouting men greeted him. Good God, Victoria had mentioned that she had brothers, but this was not a family, this was an army! Were there six or seven of them? And all of them at least six feet tall, with various shades of red hair glowing in the May sunlight.

And that couldn't be Victoria's father, that silly-looking man with the wispy hair and cracked spectacles, as short and round as his sons were tall and muscled. His shirttails showed beneath his fraying waistcoat as he made his way through the shouting, laughing group, their exclamations of delight punctuated by the dog's sharp barks.

The long-eared hound left the crowd and waddled up to the carriage, staring up at Christianna with round, stupid eyes and an open mouth, happily wagging its tail.

"Good Lord," she said aloud. "You look about as intelligent as my brother."

The dog apparently took this remark as a kindness and tipped over, rolling onto its back and wagging its tail joyously.

Christianna closed her eyes, her dreams of spacious salons and elegant ballrooms and sparkling soirees shattered.

When she opened her eyes she found herself confronting an auburn-haired man.

He stood before her, his white teeth showing in a grin. His moss-green eyes crinkled at the corners and a single dimple showed on his sun-browned cheek. His hands were tucked lazily in the pockets of his worn breeches.

His hair was falling out of the dark, fraying ribbon that bound it at the back of his neck, and he blew an auburn strand out of his eyes before he spoke.

"So, you're Christianna? I'm Gareth Larkin. Come down, girl, and meet the rest of the family. What a toothsome little piece you are! We won't mind having you about for a month or two, not at all."

And with those horrifying words he reached out his sun-browned arms and picked her up as if she were a child, swinging her around as he lifted her easily from the carriage.

He left his hands on her waist for a moment after her feet touched the ground, showing a brilliant grin at her outraged expression. And then, to Christianna's utter disgust, he winked and gave her a quick pat on her derriere.

For a moment Christianna couldn't think of the English words she wanted. She drew several hard, angry breaths lifted her chin, and decided that "stupid peasant" would do very nicely. She was about to say so when the hound, who had been watching with interest, leapt up on her, barking excitedly, staining her new pink skirts with its muddy paws, and almost knocking her off balance.

Gareth Larkin laughed aloud. "There, you see? Even Dog thinks you're wonderful. Come meet Father and the boys."

Christianna promptly burst into tears. It was awful, just all too awful. She wanted a beautiful house and dinner parties and new gowns and a new violin and to be away from peasants—ugly, crude peasants.

And then Phillipe had dragged her across two countries and a sea and whisked her through London so quickly that she barely had time to buy clothes to replace her worn, ugly rags; and then she had thought it was all over. And it wasn't.

"Bloody hell," Gareth said, furrowing his brow, caught completely off guard by this show of feminine hysteria.

"Oh, Gareth!" Victoria exclaimed, rushing down the brick walk, the overgrown shrubberies tangling in her skirts as she pushed the wooden gate out of her way. She rushed to Christianna and folded her protectively in her slender arms. "Whatever did you say, you great booby?"

Gareth glanced guiltily about. Of course everyone was watching: Richard and Daniel and Stewart and James and Geoffery and Father.

"Nothing," he protested.

"He pinched her bum," Geoffery informed them, rubbing his thin freckled nose thoughtfully.

Gareth rolled his eyes at his youngest brother, thinking that eighteen was a little old to be bearing tales.

The exquisite little black-haired girl in his sister's arms cried harder at this, and let loose a flow of French words that seemed to be directed at her brother, who looked less than patient.

"For heaven's sake, Christianna," Phillipe said, "get hold of yourself. And speak English . . . that is, if you've anything civil to say. I'm sure it was meant kindly."

The dainty young woman tore her wide-brimmed straw hat from her head and clouted her brother with it; the heaps of pink silk roses that covered the brim scattered petals into the muddy drive.

Geoffery and Stewart, who at eighteen and nineteen were the youngest of the Larkin brothers, exchanged delighted glances.

"I say, Phillipe," Geoffery observed, "I think you've pissed her off."

"Maybe she's not all there," Stewart suggested helpfully. "A few slices short of a full loaf."

"Shut up, you idiots," Victoria snapped, watching as her new sister-in-law pummeled Phillipe's chest. "She's overtired, that's all."

"What's she saying, Daniel?" Gareth asked, turning to his scholarly brother.

Daniel shook his head in apparent disbelief. "A lot," he answered, pushing his spectacles farther up his nose. "'Ignorant peasants' is about as far as I can follow. And 'horrible dog,' and something about wanting a gun."

"God help us," Gareth muttered.

Phillipe seized his sister's small hands firmly. "Christianna," he shouted, *"cesser! Immédiatement!"*

To everybody's relief, the girl stopped belaboring her brother and buried her face in her small white hands, sobbing as if her heart had broken.

Matthew Larkin stepped through the crowd of his tall, redheaded children, rubbing his ink-spotted fingers together nervously, his round eyes blinking owlishly behind his spectacles.

"Oh, dear," he murmured. "Oh, dear." He laid a gentle hand on the arm of the sobbing girl. "There, there," he said nervously. "No need to take on. I know the boys are a little rough, but I'm sure they meant well. Oh, dear. Please, mademoiselle, don't cry. Really, Gareth is very sorry. I'm sure that he is. Aren't you, Gareth?"

Gareth, thoroughly sick of this ridiculous scene, and resenting the way his father made him feel like a twelve-year-old, instead of acknowledging his thirty years, glowered. "The hell I am," he answered.

At this brusque answer, the black-haired girl dropped her hands from her face and glared at him fiercely, her brilliant blue eyes full of tears. "*Mange du merde, cochon,*" she spat.

Richard, the third oldest son, let loose a short bark of laughter. "I say, Gareth," he exclaimed merrily, "I think she just told you to eat sh—"

"I think we should all go into the house," Matthew interjected hastily. "And find Mademoiselle St. Sebastien a nice cup of tea."

Privately, Gareth thought that someone should turn Mademoiselle St. Sebastien over his knee and beat her dainty behind; but out of deference to his sister's pleading look, he said nothing. After all, Victoria was one of the only sensible females on God's green earth, and he only had one sister.

She must speak to Phillipe, and quickly, Christianna decided. As soon as they were alone. He couldn't possibly have known that it would be like this.

And yet, there he sat, one arm around his wife's shoulders, laughing and talking with these people as if everything was wonderful.

At least the house was clean, she observed, looking around the room. And the food seemed plentiful—no, to be honest, it was delicious. Fresh, good bread and thick, golden soup with tender pieces of chicken floating in it, and sweet, fresh butter and blackberry preserves.

Christianna happily accepted another piece of apple pie and didn't object when one of Victoria's brothers dumped half a pitcher of thick cream over it.

"There," he said. "Pie's no good without cream."

Which one was that? She would never be able to tell them apart. She looked around the long oak table and tried to sort them out.

Gareth, he was the easiest—the eldest son, with the darkest auburn hair and the dimple in his right cheek; and Daniel, the next, with the same clean, strong jawline and dark green eyes, but hidden behind small spectacles, and a gentle way of speaking to her that she liked.

Then there was the one who seemed to look at her as if she had two heads, the one whose long hair wasn't tied back, but fell in wild red curls like a lion's mane. He had a rip under the arm of his stained white shirt. What was his name? Robert? No, Richard, she thought.

And seated on Victoria's other side was James;

he was easy to remember because he was Victoria's twin, with the same tilted eyes and slanting cheekbones.

And the two youngest, who laughed like idiots and ate like starving men; she would never be able to tell which was Geoffery and which was Stewart. It didn't matter, though; she didn't care for either of them.

And Victoria's father! What a bumbler. He had spilled the tea twice, lost his spectacles once, stepped on the dog, burned a hole in his shirt pocket by putting his pipe in while it was still lit. No wonder his sons were so . . . so very unrefined and wild.

Christianna examined the room. There was little wealth to be seen—a shelf of pewter tankards, mismatched chairs, a worn woolen rug in front of the fireplace. The wide planks of the floors gleamed in the evening light, the creamy plaster of the walls reflected the glow from the mullioned windows. If this had been an inn, she would have thought it a clean, comfortable place to spend a night. But never, never would she have thought it an acceptable home.

And she could never stay here, not after Gareth Larkin had handled her like that. She would definitely have to speak to Phillipe.

She looked up and saw that everyone was listening to her brother as he spoke in his clear, accented English.

" . . . March, by the time I was able to reach the Auvergne. And the villagers had burned the castle. Christianna was living with her old nurse, in a one-room cottage. Apparently, she had managed to escape from Paris and made her way there, over two hundred miles."

Gareth Larkin was staring at her in disbelief. "You're joking," he said to Phillipe. "That little piece of fluff? She looks as if she couldn't walk a mile."

Christianna stabbed savagely at her pie.

"How did you manage, mademoiselle?" Matthew Larkin asked politely.

There was a long, waiting silence.

Christianna's fingers tightened on her spoon. She could feel her stomach turning; but when she spoke her voice was light and calm. "I paid a man, a groom from the stables. I gave him my pearls. . . ." *And he took everything else: my earrings from Artois, Gabrielle's sapphire brooch . . .* "And he took me out of Paris, hidden in a farm cart, under a pile of straw. . . ." *He was supposed to take me to Phillipe, but he lied; he took me to his ugly cottage, and his drunken brother.*

Christianna tried not to see it; her mind pushed away the picture of her rosary beads, thrown to a greasy floor and ground beneath the heel of a dirty boot, the crystal beads shattering into a million sparkling splinters. The miniature portrait of her mother followed, the glass breaking over the delicate painted face.

She took a deep breath and swallowed before she continued. "When we arrived at Jean-Claude's cottage we had . . . a difference of opinion—" *He told me that I was going nowhere, and he gave me to his brother, as if I was a prize, and when I screamed they hit me.*

Even now, she could taste the bitter, metallic flavor of blood in her mouth; she could hear the ugly laughter, feel the splinters in her fingers as they clung to a doorframe and were torn away. They threw her onto the hard floor of the back room of the cottage, her head striking the boards with a deafening crack, brilliant red before her eyes. From behind the closed door she could hear Jean-Claude's shouts of encouragement to his brother.

She raised her head and spoke quietly. "And so we parted ways."

I killed him.

I took the knife from his belt as he tried to rape me, and I cut his throat.

She thought she would be sick as she thought of it—how easily the knife slid in, the warm spray of blood that showered the torn ribbons at her bodice, the suffocating weight of the man's body as it slumped over her.

Her hands had been shaking as she forced the shutters of the window open and made her escape into the black night, blind with terror, her gown ripped and covered with blood.

"I traveled for three days, alone—" *By night, half mad with fear, like a creature of darkness in my bloodstained gown and mud and leaves in my hair*— "And then some peasants found me—" *They thought I was dead at first, lying cold and motionless on the road*— "And they took me to their home, and I was ill for a long time. Then the old man, Gaston, took me to the Auvergne.

The castle had been burned; and so I went to my nurse's cottage, and I stayed there until Phillipe came. And he brought me here."

She stared down at her plate. Her food, which had seemed so delicious only a moment before, was making her queasy. She clasped her hands tightly beneath the table, trying to still the inevitable shaking.

She glanced up and saw Gareth's pale green eyes on her, puzzled and thoughtful.

She looked away quickly, forcing a tight smile.

All around her at the table conversation continued, the English words buzzing in her head, making little sense, and she tried to clear her mind, to focus on the present.

Oh, no, they were speaking of the revolution.

"There is only so much injustice that people can bear before they take action," Matthew Larkin remarked. "It was inevitable. Never have a king and queen been so blind to the plight of their people."

Gareth nodded at his father. "Like Nero fiddling while Rome burned. Idiotic, really."

Christianna thought of Marie Antoinette, still the prisoner of her subjects, and her gentle husband, who spoke so lovingly to his children. She thought of the golden, brilliant days of Versailles, of the day she had played her violin for her king and queen and Louis had called her one of the most precious jewels of France. "That's pushing it a little," Artois had murmured, his eyes dancing, and Gabrielle de Lambelle had choked with laughter.

Christianna dropped her fork and glared at Gareth Larkin. "Idiotic?" she repeated. "How would you know? You know nothing about it. They are good, kind people. That is just the sort of remark I would expect from an ignorant peasant."

Everyone looked shocked, as if she, and not Gareth, was in the wrong.

Gareth Larkin stared down the table at her. "And that," he answered calmly, "is just the sort of attitude that caused the revolution. Noble birth does not make for noble behavior, and your idiotic tantrums and foul temper have certainly proven that."

"Gareth," Matthew Larkin said softly, pushing his spectacles up his stubby nose, "please. Mademoiselle St. Sebastien will be here for two months. Let's try and be . . . patient."

Gareth gave her a cool glance, and then turned back to her brother. "Tell me now of New Orleans. What will you be doing there?"

To Christianna's shock, her brother spoke not a word in her defense, simply nodded and spoke to Gareth Larkin as if she wasn't even there.

"A friend of mine owns a shipping company— mainly art, antiquities, that sort of thing; and he needs someone on the receiving end. And everything I had is gone, since the revolution. Etienne offered Victoria and me passage and a decent wage, and I have little choice but to accept. After all, I'm not suited for any other sort of work."

"I don't know, Phillipe," Christianna said coolly. "I think that you should stay here and become the village idiot. I think you'd do well at that, since you seem to have taken leave of your senses."

The auburn-haired lad on her left—was it Geoffery?—gave a bark of laughter.

Christianna glowered at him.

Phillipe rose from the table, his hawklike face set in anger. "Excuse me, gentlemen. My sister and I need to talk."

Phillipe didn't turn her arm loose until they were well away from the house. He sat her firmly on the stone wall that bordered the overgrown gardens and turned on her.

"Good God, Christianna! I have had quite enough of your snapping and sulking and hysterics. Those are good people in there, fine, honest people, and they are my family now, as well as yours. Your arrogant ways may have served you well at court, but that's all over now. We have nothing, do you understand?"

Christianna flinched and turned away, staring out over freshly plowed fields and green pastures, and far away to the wooded hills.

"I don't have the money to take you with us," Phillipe said, biting off each word slowly. "And this is the only place there is to leave you. I will send for you as soon as I can. Are you listening to me? Do you understand? We are asking these people for charity. We are dependent on their kindness."

Christianna blinked hard and stared at her

brother. "I thought . . . I thought it would be different," she offered finally.

"You thought wrong. And you spoke rudely, and I want you to go find Gareth and apologize to him."

"For what?" she cried.

"For calling him an ignorant peasant, for a start. For screaming like a lunatic when he touched you earlier."

Christianna shuddered, thinking of those large hands on her waist.

"You are a St. Sebastien," Phillipe reminded her softly. "Try and behave with a little grace, a little dignity. It is all you have left."

Christianna looked over at the house, the ivy climbing up the walls and the gnarled apple trees with their fluttering pink blossoms, the gabled windows reflecting the setting sun.

It was true. Everything she had and everyone she had loved: gone.

"Very well," she agreed, but her voice was bitter. "You're right, Phillipe. It is all I have left."

She entered the house through the kitchen door and found herself in a large, clean room, with a huge fireplace and brick ovens. Strings of onions and drying herbs hung from the dark beams that crossed the ceiling, and a portly, red-faced woman stood by two enormous tubs of water, her sleeves pushed up to her elbows, scrubbing the heavy kettles as if her life depended on it.

She turned at Christianna's entrance and gave her an appraising look from beneath the starched ruffle of her mobcap.

It was clear that the elaborately arranged black curls and pink silk dress found no favor with her.

"So, you're the sister of the Frenchman, are you?" she asked, and went on without waiting for an answer. "Looks like trouble to me, that's what I said. It's no great thing, marrying some fancy foreigner with a useless title, when our Vic could have had any honest man in the village. But no one here listens to me."

Christianna could see why, since everything she said was so glum.

"Dragging our girl halfway across the world, where she'll be eaten alive by red savages, that's what. And now her brother says he's going too."

"Gareth?" Christianna asked hopefully.

"And who'd run this farm if our Gareth was to go? No, Jamie—our James. Can't bear the thought of his sister halfway across the world. That's twins for you. Never could bear to be apart."

Christianna wondered if all English servants were so outspoken with their betters. She made an effort to smile her most charming smile.

"If you please, where would I find Gareth?"

The woman looked at her suspiciously, as if she was going to ask why. "If he's done with the horses," she answered at last, "you'll find him in the office. That's right off the sitting room, by the front door you came in by." She turned her back abruptly and added over her shoulder, "By the way, I'm Mrs. Hatton, since you forgot to ask. I run the house, and I'll have no nonsense."

Christianna could well believe it.

"Breakfast is at six around here," the straightforward woman added, "and slugabeds are on their own."

Christianna thought with poignant longing of the days when she had slept till twelve, when her maid had fetched her coffee and pastries in little painted dishes of almost transparent porcelain.

"Thank you, Mrs. Hatton," she replied graciously, and received a snorting noise for her well-mannered dignity.

She almost fell over the two youngest Larkin boys as she entered the narrow hall, and the suppressed merriment in their eyes made her wonder if they'd been listening.

"Hello," the freckled one said. "Off to find Gareth, are you?"

They *had* listened then.

"No," she answered. "Actually, I'm on my way to see the king, to ask him if he'll come for tea. Do you think he might?"

Her sarcasm didn't perturb either of them. They fell happily into step behind her.

"Did you really know the queen?" asked the other.

"Not really well, I suppose."

"Is it true she had five hundred dresses?"

Christianna sighed. "No, *I* had five hundred. The queen had five thousand. And four Moorish servants to carry each one, and she beat them, twice a day, unless she was tired. Then she let me do it. Would you like me to demonstrate?"

To her annoyance, they both laughed.

"Sounds like fun," said one.

"Then can we beat you?" asked the other.

Christianna looked from one to the other. "Which of you is which?" she demanded.

"I'm Geoffery," the freckled one answered, "and that's Stewart."

Christianna took note. Geoffery, thin with freckles. Stewart, dimples and a nose that looked as if it had been broken. She tilted her head and smiled prettily. It seemed to have more effect on them than it had on Mrs. Hatton.

"Stewart? Geoffery? Will you do something for me?"

They both nodded, looking thrilled.

"Good! Leave me alone."

She stomped off in search of Gareth, leaving the young men in the narrow hall.

"Damned pretty, isn't she?" Stewart asked, beaming at his brother.

"Damned mean," Geoffery answered. "What do you suppose she wants with Gareth?"

"To tell him to 'go to 'ell,' probably," Stewart answered, mocking her French accent. "Come on; let's go eavesdrop."

"Come in," Gareth called, not lifting his eyes from the papers in front of him. His pen moved quickly over the page before him, and it was only after he heard the door close quietly that he looked up.

His new sister-in-law stood silently by the

door, her wide blue eyes moving quietly around the dark, cluttered room, the battered table that served as a desk, the stacks of ledgers and books that listed the debts and profits and records of the farm, and the open journal in front of him.

At Gareth's feet, Dog wagged her tail, thumping a loud rhythm against the floorboards.

For a moment the girl looked so forlorn and lost that Gareth almost felt sorry for her. Her hands twisted in the folds of her soft skirts, and her eyes seemed to look everywhere but at his face.

"Sit down, if you like," he said shortly, indicating a battered chair across from his desk. He laid his pen next to his journal and blew the ink on the page dry before closing the cover.

She sat gingerly and bit her lip before speaking.

"I . . . I would like to apologize," she said at last. "I did not mean to be rude. I'm very tired, and out of sorts, and . . . it's very kind of you to let me stay here."

A pink flush spread across her broad cheekbones at this last, and Gareth could see that the apology didn't come easily to her.

He said nothing, just watched her. She reminded him of a butterfly trapped in a net. Her thick lashes fluttered nervously over her brilliant eyes. Soft lace fell over her slender forearms, moving delicately when she moved, and her round breasts showed above the stiff bodice of her gown, rising and falling with her quick breathing. She seemed afraid. Of him? he wondered.

"I thought," she said quickly, "that Phillipe had married an heiress, you see. I thought that I was going to live in a great house, with gentle people, and when I saw this place I was . . ." She caught her soft lip between her teeth and seemed to search for the right word.

"Disgusted?" Gareth asked. "That you should have to claim such 'ignorant peasants' as part of your family?"

She blushed.

"You're all very loud," she answered at last, "and big, and I was . . . afraid." She spoke this last word softly, quickly.

"Afraid?" Gareth repeated. "Why?"

The little white hands fluttered in her lap, her eyes darting frantically around the room. "I . . . I don't . . . that is . . . you handled me, monsieur. I don't like to be handled."

Almost at once her demeanor changed. She raised her dark head proudly and sent him a tight, false smile. "What a lot of fuss over a simple apology. Shall we call it done, monsieur? I am so very tired, and I haven't slept properly in a long time. People tend to get a little bad-tempered, don't they, when they're tired?"

"I suppose they do," Gareth agreed. "Very well. I accept your apology." He extended his hand across the table to her.

She hesitated for a moment, and her lashes fluttered nervously before she laid her hand on his. It was a small hand, soft and white, and Gareth closed his fingers over it.

He felt her eagerness to be away and released his grip immediately. She pulled back quickly, the relief obvious on her face.

"Thank you," she said. "I shall try not to be a burden to you while I am here."

Gareth watched her as she rose and almost rushed from the room, her pink skirts whispering.

What an odd, skittish thing she was. Unlike any girl he had ever known, as exotic and graceful as a hummingbird, with her brilliant eyes and quick, fluttering grace.

He sighed, and took up his pen.

From the journal of Gareth Larkin
May the fifth, 1790

Approved the purchase of twenty head of sheep from Everly Farms. Sold two foals to Squire Thornley. Planted hops in north field, plowed under two acres for hay. Paid dues to wool merchant's guild. Mrs. Hatton is hiring another girl for the dairy.

Met Victoria's husband. He seems a good sort. James has asked permission to accompany them to the colonies, or states, I should say.

Phillipe St. Sebastien is leaving his sister under our protection, God forbid.

She is rude, snobbish, and affected. In short, she is everything that I despise in a female. I hope that her stay is a short one.

Gareth sighed again and raked his hair off his broad forehead before putting the pen to paper again.

She is the most beautiful creature I have ever seen in my life.

Chapter Four

Christianna was surprised, when she awoke, at how solidly she had slept. She lay for a few minutes, unwilling to open her eyes, pressing her cheek against the clean linen of her pillow. It smelled of dried lavender, a light, pleasant scent. She stretched like a cat, and sighed aloud.

When she finally opened her eyes she was pleased at the sight of the room she was in. She had only seen it for a few brief moments last night, by candlelight, before she had lain down on the feather bed and succumbed to exhaustion, still in her wrinkled pink silk.

The bed sat beside the gabled window, and sunlight shone gently through the sparkling panes, dappled between the blossoming branches of the apple trees and the glossy green vines of ivy that framed the view of blue sky and rolling hills.

There was a broad, clean sill of dark, polished wood that smelled pleasantly of beeswax, and someone had thoughtfully set a bowl of dried lavender and rose petals there, where the sun warmed them and released their gentle fragrance.

The curtains were of a pristine white cotton, trimmed in simple handmade lace, and likewise, the cover on the bed, which she had been too tired to even cover herself with, was white, quilted in careful patterns, with painstaking vine patterns embroidered around it.

The headboard of the bed was not large, but it was made of a good, solid dark wood, carved with a simple pattern of Tudor roses, and there was a candlestand next to the bed, carefully turned, of the same dark wood, with a fresh candle.

The thick walls and slanting, gabled ceiling were whitewashed and clean, except for the dark beams; her trunk sat in the corner on the polished floor. There was a table with a bowl of water for washing, a few pegs on the wall for her clothing, and nothing more.

"I like it," she said aloud, sounding a little surprised. This was to be her room, the first room of her own in months, and it was clean and sunny, and there were apple blossoms outside her window, and birds in the trees, and it felt good. It was a pleasant, tranquil place.

Christianna rose from the warm hollow her body had made in the soft bed, and washed her face in the cool water of the washbowl, smoothing back the loose strands of black hair that fell around her face.

She judged by the sunlight that it was well into the morning, and the house was curiously quiet. Last night she had drifted off to sleep to the sound of low voices, the heavy sound of booted footsteps going up and down stairs, punctuated by an occasional laugh.

Wondering at the silence, Christianna opened the heavy door to her room and peeked down the empty hall.

There was nobody in sight, just a line of closed doors.

Well, one thing was certain, Christianna decided. She was starving, and she wanted to bathe and change into one of her clean dresses.

Mrs. Hatton in the kitchen had said that breakfast was at six, and it was long past that; but there was sure to be something about, and perhaps Mrs. Hatton would help her with the hundred buttons on her gown, or there might be a maid there that could.

She made her way down the narrow stairs, wondering how Gareth and the rest of those enormous young men managed without striking their heads on the low ceilings.

The kitchen was empty except for the dog, who had her front feet on the scarred worktable in the center of the room and was sniffing with interest at a basket of bread.

"Arreter!" Christianna snapped, and to her

relief the dog paid attention, dropping heavily to the floor.

Christianna regarded the animal with distrust, as she took a piece of the bread for herself. The animal watched with mournful brown eyes as she ate.

"Oh, go away," she said, but apparently the dog understood French better than English, for it simply rolled to its back, exposing its white and brown spotted belly and wagging its tail in a thoroughly undignified way.

Christianna wondered again where everyone was, and then she noticed that the door to the back pantry and yard was open, and she walked out into the brilliant sunlight, hoping to find Mrs. Hatton.

She stopped on the back steps, her piece of bread forgotten in her hand.

A mere ten paces from the door, standing at an old stone well, was Gareth Larkin.

He was shirtless and shoeless, standing amid the overgrown shrubs and vines of the garden, dumping a bucket of water over his head.

It ran in shimmering streams over the bronzed skin of his arms and around his neck and down the strong line of his spine and over the taut muscles of his smooth, broad chest. It plastered his dark auburn hair to his head and neck, and he let out a whoop of apparent delight at the sensation, shaking his head and sending sparkling droplets through the air.

Christianna was rooted to the spot, fascinated. The damp fabric of his tight breeches showed his form from waist to knee, and Christianna thought that he looked like a Roman statue, only vibrant and alive, instead of cold, smooth stone. She forgot that she hated him and stared with wide eyes.

Gareth upended the bucket, let the last of the clear, cold water fall over his face, and turned for the linen towel he'd brought.

He laughed aloud with delight at the sight of Christianna, standing motionless on the steps, her sweet mouth slightly open and her eyes round with shock.

"You're awake," he greeted her cheerfully. "We were starting to think you'd sleep your life away."

To his amusement, she blushed, and turned her eyes away, staring at some uncertain point on the ground.

Gareth began drying himself with vigor. "Are you hungry?" he asked over his shoulder. "Can I help you find something?"

Christianna swallowed hard. "No, no thank you. I found some bread in the kitchen."

"If you mean the stuff you had in your hand, I'm afraid Dog just took it, while you were staring at me."

She jumped, and looked at her empty hand. The dog sat next to her, looking up at her with an anxious expression.

"Stupid thing," she muttered, blushing furiously. To Gareth, she added, "I didn't stare. I was just . . . shocked, that's all."

He sent her a brilliant smile, and he wasn't

that handsome, she thought. His smile was crooked; he only had one dimple.

"As you wish," he said, in an agreeable way. "Everyone went out riding, and Mrs. Hatton took the baby over to her sister's for a visit and a brag. Couldn't wait to show her off. She's a pretty thing, isn't she?"

"Would you please put a shirt on?" Christianna asked abruptly, unable to keep her eyes from straying.

He laughed again. "Left it in the kitchen. Come in and we'll find you something to eat."

He walked close to her as he passed her on the steps, and she reluctantly left the sunshine of the garden and followed him back into the house.

"There," Gareth said, pulling a white shirt off the back of a chair and pulling it over his wet head. He tucked it into the damp waistband of his breeches, and the sight of his large, capable hands performing the intimate task made her blush harder, even though he was decently covered.

"When will everyone be back?" she asked suddenly.

Gareth looked at her. She sat perched on the edge of a chair, looking like a bird that was about to fly away, her hands fastened together in her lap, her eyes looking at the floor. Her cheeks were a brilliant rose color, and her black hair, tousled and tumbling out of its pins, fell heavily over her shoulders and onto the white skin of her well-exposed breasts.

"Christianna," he said, and his gentle tone caused her to raise her eyes. "You don't have to be so nervous around me. I'm not going to put you into a pot and have you for my dinner, though you look very tasty. Now, would you like some butter or honey with the bread?"

She smiled at him, and the sight was so enchanting that he was taken aback and found himself standing like a fool with the crock of honey in his hand. If she had been lovely when she blushed and avoided his eyes, she was doubly so when she looked directly into them and smiled.

"Yes, thank you," she said, and took the crock of honey from his hand.

He took a pitcher of heavy crockery from a shelf and went to the buttery, a cool room off the back of the house, where the casks of ale and wine were stored and the morning's milk stood in clean pans, the cream rising to the top. He filled the pitcher and took it back to the kitchen, where he filled two mugs.

"Mrs. Hatton would have my hide if she knew we were drinking milk with the cream still on it," he told her, sitting across the table from her, and sliding a mug across the oak table to her.

She was stuffing her mouth with bread and honey, and she swallowed before she answered. "Are you afraid of her too?"

Gareth roared with merriment. "Not a bit. She's more likely to bark than bite."

"She seems very fierce," Christianna told him,

and Gareth turned his eyes away from the sight of her licking the honey from her fingers. Good Lord, even her tongue was darling. This wouldn't be an easy two months.

"You should have no trouble with Mrs. Hatton. She likes people who do what is proper, and you seem a very proper little thing. When you're not beating your brother or cursing me in French," he added.

"I was going to ask," Christianna said, setting down the heavy mug of milk, "if there was a *domestique*, a girl in the house. To help me," she explained, at Gareth's blank look.

"Like a maid? Only Mrs. Hatton and the girls that come on Mondays to help in the dairy. Why, what do you need? Could I help?"

She was blushing again, the red staining her little cat's face, the thick lashes dropping over the brilliant eyes.

"Oh, no. I need a girl, you see. To help me with my buttons. I can't do them myself."

Gareth gave a short, startled burst of laughter. "Can't do your own buttons? How did you get dressed?"

Christianna didn't think it was very funny. "The maid at the inn, yesterday, did them. And I slept in my dress last night and I want to get out of it."

Gareth looked very amused. His eyes sparkled dark green, and he raked his hand through his damp hair, off his smooth, broad brow. "Sorry for laughing, but it seems so silly, to have to have help getting undressed at your age. You really are a useless creature, aren't you? Have you ever dressed yourself in your life?"

Christianna decided that she'd had quite enough. "I am not useless!"

"Really? Well, what can you do?"

She looked shocked. What could she do?

"I can play the violin," she exclaimed at last, with a triumphant toss of her head. "I can play as well as any músician. I can play so sweetly that people cry. I can play any music you put before me, and I can make my violin sing like the voice of an angel."

Gareth didn't think that a terrifically useful accomplishment, but the little minx seemed so proud of it that he let her have that point.

"That's something," he agreed. "I'd like to hear it."

The brilliant eyes darkened and the sweet mouth drooped. "I don't have it anymore," she said simply, and Gareth was shocked by the sorrow in her voice. "It was . . . taken from me."

Looking at her, Gareth felt as if she was suddenly very far away. It was as if a veil had dropped over her face, so closed and tight was her expression. And then just as quickly it was gone, replaced by a haughty, cool look.

"What a stupid conversation," she said rapidly. "Let's not speak of it anymore. What very good bread this is, is it not?"

"Yes." Gareth nodded, leaning forward and putting his elbows on the table. "And the honey. The bees at our farm make the best honey in the district."

She smiled, and it brightened her face, made it softer. "Why is that?" she asked. "Are your bees better than any other bees?"

"It's the flowers you grow," Gareth explained, gesturing out at the overgrown gardens outside the mullioned window, where foxglove and verbena and violets and primroses rioted in their clover-filled beds. "They look like a pretty mess, but everything on a farm has a purpose."

Except me, Christianna thought, but didn't say. Useless, he had called her. Odd, how that stung. And when she had wanted to argue she couldn't think of a single "useful" thing she knew how to do. Except for playing a violin that she no longer had.

"May I have more, please?" she asked, holding up her empty cup.

Gareth filled the cup from the pitcher. "You don't have to ask. There's plenty of food."

"*Merci*. It's very good. When do you think Mrs. Hatton will be back?"

"Within an hour or two. Are you really going to ask her to do your buttons?"

Christianna looked worried. "Should I not? I don't want to make her angry, but you see . . ."

She turned her back to Gareth, twisting around in her chair so that he could see the countless buttons, each the size of a pea, secured with little loops of pink silk that ran down the graceful curve of her back.

"I would ruin it," she explained. "And I couldn't fix it. And I don't have a maid to fix it for me."

Gareth made a genuine effort not to laugh. "You know," he suggested at last, "perhaps it's time you learned to do something useful, like dressing yourself and fixing your own gowns. Mrs. Hattton won't have time for it, and there's no other woman in the house. Maybe you'll be stuck in that dress until you leave here. Don't bristle up like a hedgehog; I'm teasing. Turn around and I'll undo your silly little buttons."

She was clearly horrified. "Oh, but you can't! That would be indecent."

"Don't be such a baby. I'm not going to maul you. At any rate, I've seen women's backs before. If you want me to unfasten your buttons, I'll do it, and you can go change out of your dress. Or you can sit in it for another couple of hours and let Mrs. Hatton tell you to do it yourself.

"If you think I'd try anything," he added, "I won't. My father's in his library, just a few rooms away. You could scream, and he'd come running."

He could see the relief on her face. Funny, how frightened she seemed. But she turned her back and pulled her heavy black curls forward over her slender shoulder.

Gareth swung himself into the chair next to her and set about the task of unlooping the little silk cords that fastened the buttons. What an odd, prickly sort of girl she was. Skittish and touchy. When his fingers brushed the skin of her neck she stiffened and shivered.

For some reason it annoyed him.

"What a child you are," he remarked. "You'd

think you'd be very sophisticated, living at the French court, but you're not. I thought you'd faint when you saw me bathing at the well."

Her back looked like pale silk as the buttons released the fabric of her gown, exposing it to his sight. An exotic, flowery smell perfumed her hair.

"Stop calling me a child," she snapped. "I was simply surprised."

Gareth took a deep breath and concentrated on the slippery little buttons. "Surprised," he mocked. "You've never seen a man's chest in your life."

"I have too," Christianna argued, "a hundred times. At Versailles, Artois—" She stopped abruptly, thinking of Artois, who changed his shirt in front of her as casually as he would in front of his valet. "Please, let's not speak of it."

Gareth was silent, respecting the sudden sorrow in her voice. So, she had a lover. It shouldn't surprise him, except that she seemed so maidenly with her blushes and averted eyes. *But of course,* he told himself, *you're not some French nobleman, are you, Gareth? You're a farmer, a stupid peasant.*

The lace of her corset cover showed white against her pale skin—thick white lace of a delicate design against white skin.

Unable to resist, Gareth raised a finger and ran it lightly down her spine, a touch as light as a butterfly's wing.

"Your buttons are done," he said simply, making no move to touch her again.

She rose from her chair so quickly that it fell to the floor with a noisy clatter, and she left the room in great haste.

When she had reached the safety of her room Christianna leaned against the door, her breath coming in rapid gasps.

She should have slapped him; she should have screamed the house down; she should never have let him unbutton her gown.

The fact was, his gentle touch had excited her beyond measure; and watching Artois change his shirt was very different from watching Gareth Larkin washing at the well.

Very different, indeed.

She began to dread the day that Phillipe and Victoria would leave for New Orleans. Of course, it was too late now to do anything about it, she told herself. Everything had been arranged, and even if she changed her mind, how could she explain it?

It was only two months, she reminded herself. Two months wasn't very long. Certainly she could avoid Gareth Larkin for that long.

It sounded so simple.

It wasn't.

He was there every morning, looking at her over the breakfast table, a mocking light in his odd, jade-colored eyes, his crooked smile playing around his mouth.

He seemed to know how embarrassed she was, and worse, he seemed terribly amused by it.

Instead of behaving like a gentleman—which he most definitely was not, she reminded herself—and keeping a comfortable distance, he seemed to make a point of seeking her out, of finding an excuse to touch her. He would squeeze her shoulder when he passed her in the hall, or take her elbow as she tried to pass him in the doorway, or offer his hand when she rose from the table. All very innocent, friendly gestures.

Except for the mischievous sparkle in his eyes.

Christianna kept close to her brother and Victoria, offering to help with the baby—which, in all honesty, she found awkward—or to help Victoria pack her things—which took no time at all—or any other excuse she could find to keep busy.

She felt lost among these boisterous people, with their odd accents and loud voices. They laughed at everything, it seemed, and argued about everything, and seemed perturbed by nothing.

The cool glance and raised brow that used to infuriate the Marquesse Pierfitte sent Richard into gales of laughter; the cold, biting voice that used to send valets and maids scurrying was met with incredulous stares from Geoffrey and Stewart, and later, she heard Stewart doing an infuriating, if accurate, impression of her.

She told herself to think of New Orleans, where she would be before autumn, and dreamed of finding a rich husband who would buy her jewels and gowns and carriages. Then her life would be as it was before the world had fallen apart, and she would never, ever have to deal with these annoying Englishmen again.

Chapter Five

When Phillipe and Victoria left for New Orleans
Christianna felt truly alone. Everyone else
seemed to have their days occupied with sheep
and chickens and cows and fields of sprouting
grain and beds of vegetables.

Mrs. Hatton in the kitchen made it clear
that she needed nobody "hanging about, getting underfoot," and that Christianna was to
expect "no special treatment"; and Christianna
retreated to her room immediately.

She asked Daniel, who seemed the gentlest of
the Larkins, if there was pen and paper to spare,
and she wrote letters to Artois, six identical
letters, and addressed them to French embas-
sies in Rome, Venice, Vienna, and London,
and anywhere else he might be. Even as she
wrote, she knew that there might not be French

ambassadors left in those cities, or that Artois might never have left France alive, but she wrote anyway.

She would feel a little less alone, a little more certain of her place in the world, if she knew that Artois was alive.

Gareth Larkin stood in the bright, cool air of the May morning, surveying the fertile acres around him with a look of satisfaction on his handsome face. His eyes were as bright and clear as jade in the sunlight, reflecting the green of the young leaves of the trees and growing crops.

It had been the warmest spring in fifteen years. The sheep had lambed early, the rows of strawberries were already climbing over their wooden racks, and white flowers were crowding in starry clusters on healthy leaves. There were ten new cows producing for the dairy: fine jerseys that he had bought with the profits from last year's growing season.

A good year ahead, he told himself, walking between the freshly whitewashed, thatched barns. To his right, the sprouting fields of plants stood in tender green rows, berries and lettuces and beans and peas, and two full acres of hops, bright and strong-looking, in the rows of rich brown earth.

The bees had come back, and were industriously humming around their hives beneath the ancient oaks, the barns and woolshed and outbuildings were in good repair, Gareth noted. A well-run, prosperous farm.

The sight filled him with joy and pride, and he raised his face to the morning sun, feeling as alive and strong as the oaks of the wood. His land, his farm, the finest in the county. Let others have their fine cities and towns; there was no more beautiful sight than the growing hops and vegetables in the rich, fertile earth.

He laughed aloud at his own fancy, and turning back toward the house he caught a glimpse of Daniel through the pale green leaves that bordered the road. His brother was riding down the front drive, on his way to his position at Thornley's, and Gareth gave him a shout, his voice echoing through the morning quiet.

"Daniel! Wait a minute."

Daniel turned his chestnut mare easily, and waited by the road while Gareth crossed the gentle slope of green pasture to lean on the stone fence.

The brothers were almost identical with the dappled sunlight falling on their ruddy heads and the strong, clear lines of their faces.

"Daniel, ask Squire if he'll give you a week off for shearing. The wool merchant ought to be around in about three weeks."

Daniel nodded, pushing his spectacles farther up his nose. "Sounds good, Gareth. A lot easier than teaching Latin to Squire's idiot children."

"I'd rather teach Latin to the sheep," Gareth agreed.

"I'd rather teach Latin to Stewart and Geoffery," Daniel said, calming the impatient mare beneath him.

Gareth laughed at his brother, reaching up to stroke the roan's muzzle and fondle her silky mane. "Have you given up, then?"

"Aye, I have. Richard was a quick study, and Victoria and James, but I think Stewart and Geoff are hopeless. They're happy in their ignorant bliss.

"Damn, but you look comfortable," Daniel added mournfully, looking at Gareth's loose white workshirt and faded breeches, torn at one knee and tucked into worn leather riding boots. "There's not much worse, on a day like this, than putting on a frock coat and going off to teach a couple of snotty little bastards. I'd like to strangle them with my cravat."

"You look very scholarly," Gareth said, with a self-satisfied grin.

"Well, bugger you too," Daniel returned pleasantly.

"And when you get back, I'd be obliged if you'd look at the potatoes. There's something ugly on the leaves. A sort of gray color."

"Done," Daniel agreed, and then he looked past Gareth and smiled. "Carpe diem," he called cheerfully.

Gareth turned and saw Christianna hurrying down the brick walk from the house, looking like a fairy-tale shepherdess in her gauzy gown of sky blue and white floral, looped up at the sides to show lace underskirts, and satin ribbons lacing the bodice of the gown over a stomacher of snowy lace. Her black curls bounced over one shoulder as she hurried toward them, her skirts pushing against the overgrown tangles of hedges and green vines.

"Seize the day," she answered Daniel. "That much Latin I remember, Master Tutor." She pushed the wooden gate aside and hurried toward them, her full skirts swaying in an enticing rhythm.

"It's a beautiful morning, isn't it?" she asked.

Daniel looked around and smiled. *"Divina natura dedit agros, ars humana aedificavit urbes."*

Christianna gave this a moment's thought, and then threw up her hands in defeat. "You win. I'm baffled."

"God made nature, man made the cities," Daniel translated.

"You're up early," Gareth commented, "for once."

She ignored him and turned to Daniel, reaching up to lay her hand comfortably on his arm, which for some reason annoyed Gareth. "Are you going through the village on your way? Can you send these for me, please?"

Gareth looked at the stack of carefully sealed letters as Daniel took them and shuffled through. To Artois du Valle, care of Sir Carlo Franchesi, Venice. To Artois du Valle, care of his Excellency the Marquis de Rambouillet, Vienna, Austria. To Artois du Valle, in Rome, and Geneva and London and Florence.

"I'm afraid I haven't the pocket money to post

them," Daniel said. "Have you, Gareth?"

"Bloody hell, do you have any idea what it will cost to send these things?" Gareth demanded.

"No," Christianna admitted, her blue eyes, which had been bright and eager a moment before, clouding with dismay. "No, I have no idea. A lot? It's very important that I find Artois."

She looked so pretty and so dismayed that she hadn't thought of the cost, that Gareth was about to tell her that he would post them later that day; but Daniel spoke first.

"Never mind the cost. I get paid today, and I'll take care of it on my way home."

Christianna smiled a brilliant smile. "Thank you, Daniel. It means a lot to me."

Daniel's handsome face colored, and Gareth wanted to laugh at him for being so easily swayed by a smile. The spoiled little creature had probably never worked for a thing in her life, just showed her dimples and tossed her curls and watched everyone run to do her bidding.

"I'd best be off," Daniel said, tucking the letters into his book of Latin verbs. "I'll check those potatoes when I get back, Gareth," he added, turning his frisky mare onto the road.

"See that you do," Gareth returned, sounding surly.

"Au revoir, Daniel," Christianna called, and Gareth thought how pretty her voice sounded, clear and bright.

She turned to go back to the house, lifting her flowered skirts delicately, and Gareth caught a tantalizing glimpse of lace petticoats and the slender curve of her ankle.

"And what do you intend to do with yourself today?" he asked her. "Hide in your room, sitting on your bum?"

She blushed. "And what should I do?" she asked, her chin lifting. "There's really nothing that I can do, as Mrs. Hatton has been so kind as to point out. It seems that I am indeed— what word did you use? Useless, I think. Yes, that was it."

An apple blossom floated down from the over-hanging tree and landed on one of her fat curls. Gareth's fingers itched to reach out and brush it away, and the urge irked him. Damn her, with her dimples and curvy little waist and ripe little breasts pushing out of her tight gowns.

"Oh, I can think of a couple of things you'd do well at," he said. "But you'd probably slap me if I were to suggest them."

She stiffened and lifted her nose in her most irritating blue-blooded fashion. "Don't be crude," she ordered.

"Well, that's what I am, isn't it? A crude peasant? Fit only to buy your food and post your letters to your lover?" He shouldn't bedevil her like this, he knew; but she had really annoyed him, cozying up to Daniel, trifling with his brother's affections.

"Never mind about Artois," she snapped, tossing a curl over her slender shoulder. "And you didn't post my letters, thank you. Daniel did."

"Aye, and it will take a full half of his pay,"

Gareth informed her. "Doesn't that bother you? Or do you think he'll be thrilled, because you fluttered your lashes and touched his arm?"

Her cheeks turned a brilliant rose. "What a pig you are! I did nothing of the sort. I simply asked, and he said yes, like a gentleman."

Gareth made a disgusted noise. "You flirted with him. You batted your eyes and smiled at him and put your pretty hand on his arm. What else was he to do?"

Christianna tilted her head back and looked at him in surprise. "You're jealous," she exclaimed, sounding pleased with herself.

Gareth flinched inwardly at her accuracy, but simply let out a bark of laughter. "What a vain little thing you are! You're pretty and you know it, and you use it. Daniel may be taken in by that sort of thing, but I'm afraid I'm not. I like my women full-grown, thank you, with a bit of meat on their bones and a bit of backbone. You'd blow away at the first strong breeze."

He spoke rudely; he knew it. He resented this idle creature, with her bewitching, sensuous little face. He resented the fact that she could as easily charm him as she had Daniel, who blushed at her smile like a schoolboy, instead of a man of twenty-seven years.

He was surprised that she didn't snap at him or storm away at his intentionally insulting tone.

"If that was the truth," she said in a tired voice, "I would have died during the revolution."

She turned back toward the house, the curls

that had bounced so jauntily on her way out hanging dejectedly down her back, and he felt a pang of conscience, sorry that he had hurt her.

"Christianna?" he called quickly.

She turned.

"Sorry. Would you like to go for a quick ride before I clean the woolshed?"

She stood, halfway down the garden path, and sent him a cutting look over her shoulder. "For your information," she said in a haughty tone, "I am going to do battle with that dragon in the kitchen and make myself 'useful.' Otherwise, I shall go out of my mind with boredom."

Gareth laughed at the idea of the pretty thing working in the kitchen alongside the formidable Mrs. Hatton, and his eyes shone with bright humor as he watched her make her way up the path, her full skirts whispering with the quick sway of her walk.

Mrs. Hatton accepted Christianna's offer to help with her usual lack of good grace.

"Too many cooks spoil the broth," she said in a grim voice, wiping her plump red hands on her apron.

The good English platitude was lost on Christianna. "I don't need to help with the broth. But I would like something to do. I can hardly spend the next two months sitting in my room."

"Can you use a knife?" Mrs. Hatton asked after a long pause.

Christianna gave a wry smile. "When the occasion demands."

Mrs. Hatton looked less than impressed and

heaved a heavy sigh. "There's a bucket of new carrots out back on the steps. You might as well bring them in and start chopping them. Not too small, mind you, or we'll all be eating mush." She turned her broad back and gave her attention to the fragrant loaves of bread that were baking in the brick oven.

Christianna went to fetch the carrots and wondered why she was subjecting herself to this undignified treatment. *Because you'll go out of your mind with boredom,* she answered herself; but the truth was, she wanted to tell Gareth Larkin to go to hell. His remarks about her being useless and "sitting on her bum all day" had stung.

He didn't like her; that much was obvious. And she didn't like him, either, she reminded herself. He was just a thick-headed, rude farmer, who happened to be blessed with a handsome face and an impossibly beautiful physique.

She found the bucket of carrots and hauled them into the sunny kitchen, wondering why Gareth's opinion should matter to her.

The obvious answer was one that she didn't care to think about—that despite the fact that she had flirted with and teased and been kissed by dukes and princes and the finest young men of French society, there was something about Gareth Larkin that warmed her blood and caused her knees to go weak and her heart to flutter.

She dumped the carrots on the scarred wooden worktable, picked up the heavy knife, and set about them with a determined glare.

By the time she had chopped the carrots—too small, according to Mrs. Hatton—and cut the onions and turnips—too large, according to that same source—and hauled five buckets of water from the well—not full enough, of course—and upset the bowl of custard for today's dinner, Christianna thoroughly regretted her decision to make herself "useful."

Her pretty gown was stained, her hair was falling from its pins, and the kitchen was sweltering in the heat of the day.

Mrs. Hatton greeted each of her new efforts with a raised brow, saying, "Hmmm," which could have meant anything from "Aren't you clever" to "Go fall in the well," and Christianna was hard put to remember her good intentions.

How Artois would laugh, she thought, *if he could see me.*

She pushed a damp curl off her neck and almost laughed herself. Christianna St. Sebastien, formerly of Versailles, granddaughter and sister of a marquis, sweating over turnips in the kitchen of a farmhouse.

She leaned her elbows on the worktable, resting her aching back and arms for a moment.

"All done in, are you?" Mrs. Hatton remarked, sounding happy for the first time that day. She beamed over her ample bosom. "I gather you're finished helping for the day, then."

She said *helping* as if it had been anything but.

"Not at all," Christianna answered quickly, her spine stiffening, meeting the formidable Mrs.

Hatton's gaze evenly. "I was about to ask what was next."

"Hmmm," was Mrs. Hatton's noncommittal but predictable response.

The heavy kitchen door opened with a bang and Geoffery and Stewart entered, their faces shining with a combination of sunlight and work.

They laughed at the sight of Christianna, her tired face and grubby gown.

"Gareth said you were playing at being scullery maid," Geoffery announced, his face dimpling. "We didn't believe him."

Stewart tossed his heavy red hair from his eyes, grinning like an idiot. "Your hair looks better that way," he remarked. "Instead of all piled up like a bleedin' mountain."

"Never mind," Christianna snapped. This was her favorite new English phrase, and a very useful one, too, when it was listened to.

"We brought dinner with us," Stewart announced, and to Christianna's horror he threw a pile of headless chickens onto the table before her.

A warm spray of blood splattered across the bodice of her gown.

She stared down, and the room seemed to sway around her.

The knife in her hand.

The brilliant red sprayed across her gown.

"No." She spoke aloud without meaning to; the word was loose in the room before she could stop it.

Her eyes closed tightly against the sight, but in her mind she saw Raoul pushing her to the floor, his laughter ringing in her ear, his hands on her body, hurting her.

"Are you ill?" she heard someone asking, a faraway voice over the dark roar in her ears, and she forced her eyes open; and slowly, with a shaking hand, she pushed the evil-looking knife away from herself, across the table.

Her vision was blurred, red and then black, and she fell gratefully into the darkness.

From very far away she heard voices, a cacophony of noise, and it took a couple of minutes for the English words to make sense. Something terrible had just happened, but she couldn't remember what.

" . . . just put the chickens down, and thump, there she went."

"Honestly, Gareth, that's all. She said, 'No,' and down she went."

A dog was barking loudly, and someone told it to go away.

And Mrs. Hatton's voice: " . . . ought not to be working in the kitchen, fainting at the sight of a little blood."

"Christ, Gareth, I really didn't mean to; don't look at me like that . . ."

"Thick-skulled asses . . ." This last was murmured very near her ear, and Christianna felt herself being lifted, strong arms wrapping around her, and she was being carried from

110

the room, away from the babble of voices and barking.

She knew that it was Gareth who carried her even without opening her eyes. His heartbeat was loud and strong against her ear, the smell of fresh-cut grass and wind and sunlight was on his skin, and she allowed herself to enjoy the surprising feelings of safety and warmth that his strength stirred in her.

She remembered now—she had fainted in the kitchen, at the sight of the blood splattering across her gown. She must have made a sound, or flinched at the memory, for she felt Gareth's arms tighten around her and he made a soothing sound, the same sort of sound she had heard him make to a skittish colt.

He was laying her on the already familiar softness of her featherbed, with its soft scent of clean linen and lavender. She felt his hand stroke her cheek, and wondered at the gentleness of the work-roughened fingers.

He spoke her name softly, and she opened her eyes with regret, unwilling to leave the soft darkness that surrounded her like a cocoon.

His eyes were very bright and clear, pale green with flecks of gold and gray, and there was no mockery in them; only concern. His hair was loose from the day's work in the fields, falling over his high brow. He took his hand from her face slowly, and she wanted to pull it back.

"Are you ill?" he asked softly.

She shook her head, managing a shaky laugh. "No, no. Just silly. I'm sorry for the fuss."

"What happened?"

"I'm not sure," she lied, looking away from his face. A sharp pain lanced through her head, and she raised a quick hand to touch it.

"You fell on your head," Gareth explained unnecessarily, for she could already feel a lump rising.

"And," he added, "Geoff and Stewart were standing there watching, like a couple of want-wits. Mrs. Hatton thinks she killed you with overwork, and now she feels guilty and says her heart is acting up. Father spilled tea all over *Shakespeare's Works* when he heard."

Christianna's laugh was soft as she pictured this scene, and Gareth looked pleased, the dimple in his tanned cheek deepening.

"Dog had to be put outside; do you hear her howling? And Richard thinks that aristocrats are naturally weak—from too much breeding with their own kind—and that you couldn't help it."

Christianna laughed again, blushing at the chaos she had caused, and Gareth laughed with her, shaking his head with a look of tired resignation.

She leaned back on the pillow, rubbing the throbbing knot on the back of her head. "I don't care what Richard thinks," she said, smiling. "He's got stains on his shirt."

Gareth was looking down at her from where he sat on the edge of the bed, his eyes bright and soft, and suddenly Christianna was very aware of his closeness; and even though her gown wasn't indecently low, she felt as if perhaps it was;

Gareth's eyes seemed to caress her with their steady, bright gaze.

Their eyes locked, and he reached out to touch her head, his fingers moving softly through the black silk of her hair.

"That's quite a lump," he said after a long pause.

Christianna's heart fluttered in a peculiar way, and Gareth's strong fingers lingered in her hair for a moment longer.

"And do you know what I think?" he asked at last, never moving his eyes from her face.

Spellbound by his gentle touch and quiet, rich voice, Christianna shook her head.

"I think," he said, running a soft finger across her lips, a whisper of a touch that caused her to shiver deliciously. "I think that Christianna St. Sebastien lied when she told me she didn't know why she had fainted. What do you think?"

Christianna froze, and then she smiled and tilted her head back in a flirtatious way, gazing up at him through lowered lashes. "As I hear you say to each other so often: bugger off."

The delicate accent made the words ridiculous on her soft lips, and Gareth threw his head back and let out a shout of laughter.

"Do you know what it means?" he asked her at last, his eyes sparkling with mischief.

"The same as never mind, and nobody here listens to that, either. Now leave me alone, to rest my poor head."

"As you wish," Gareth replied, dimpling with

his irritating good-natured smile, and to Christianna's relief, he took his warm hand from her hair and went to the door.

The look that he gave her over his shoulder as he left was kind, and there was a heat behind the serenity of his smile that caused her breath to quicken. When the door closed behind him, her fingers moved to her cheek, where he had stroked it.

She wondered if he had found the touch of her skin pleasant.

She wondered even more at herself, for she found that she was tempted to give Gareth Larkin her body, even after she had killed a man to keep him from taking it.

She tried to pray, but her fingers felt empty without her rosary beads; and it seemed that the harder she searched for the meaning in her shattered world, the less sense it all made to her. And she always ended feeling more alone than ever.

"Mayhap we're supposed to hire a maid, to take her food up to her."

Christianna, who had been about to enter the dining room, froze, one hand on the door.

"Oh, heavens, I don't think we can manage that, can we, Gareth?" That was Matthew Larkin's voice, sounding a little worried, as he always did.

"Richard's just joking, Father."

"Bloody hell, Gareth; have you ever seen anyone so inept? Why didn't she go to the States with her brother?"

"I tried to lend him the money and he refused to take it. You can't blame a man for being proud."

Christianna knew that she should go in to stop the conversation before she heard anything really hurtful, but she stood quietly in the hall, her hand on the slightly open door.

"I think she's very sweet. It's nice to have a pretty face around." This last came from Matthew.

"I think she's ridiculous. The gentry are useless. And the French are worse than the English." Richard again, and Christianna could imagine his fierce face, with his wild red curls hanging around it. It sounded as if he was talking with his mouth full, which shouldn't surprise her.

Geoffery and Stewart began laughing, and one of them said, "Ze blood of ze chickens eez vulgaire. I theenk I will faint."

"Get your damned head out of my plate, you ass!"

"Bon Dieu! Ze chickens are on ze table! Garret, save me!"

Christianna's cheeks burned, and she wished she had stayed in her room. There was a burst of laughter from the dining room, and she heard Gareth's calm, low voice.

"Get off my lap, you jackass." There was a loud thump and the sound of chairs scraping. "Now, listen, fellows, I know that she's a little touchy, and I know that she's as useful as a three-legged horse; but she can't help it. She's never done a thing in her life except her hair. But go easy on her; she's a well-meaning piece of fluff."

Christianna turned around quietly and began her way back to her room, but the next voice stopped her in her tracks.

"I don't believe it! You've got eyes for her, Gareth, don't you?"

"God help us, Geoff, are you joking? No, give me a good, hardworking English girl, like Meg or Janey. Christianna's a pretty thing to look at, but that's all. She might dally with a country man to amuse herself, but she'd never make a good wife. She couldn't lift a finger to do anything without collapsing. Useless."

It doesn't matter, she told herself. *I don't care what that pack of idiots thinks, especially Gareth. And for a minute today, when he touched my hair, I thought he might actually care for me, a little.*

She turned to go up the staircase and almost bumped into Daniel. He stood quietly, his finger marking the page of the book in his hand, and the sympathetic look on his face told her that he, too, had heard her character belittled.

She pushed past him blindly, without speaking, and went to her room.

To her disgust, the dog had made herself comfortable on Christianna's bed and was lying happily on her back, with her white spotted belly exposed and her long ears lying across the pillow.

The stupid animal opened one eye, then closed it quickly, as if to pretend that Christianna wasn't there.

"I don't like you, either," Christianna snapped,

and pushed the heavy animal to the floor.

The dog gave her an injured look with her sad brown eyes and slunk from the room.

It was dark, and Christianna was sitting by the gabled window, listening to the soft night sounds of the country—a horse nickering in the barn, the distant bark of a dog, the cool wind that rustled the leaves. When the knock sounded on her door she was tempted to tell whoever it was to go away, but she answered.

It was Daniel, his spectacles falling down his nose, his dark hair neatly tied at his neck.

"I brought you these," he said, and offered her a book and a folder of papers.

A Study of Englishe Botanicals, Flowers and Herbs For the Garden was the title of the battered book, and in the heavy paper folder were carefully watercolored renditions of plants and flowers, with notes beneath them in a delicate hand.

Monarda Didyma or bee balm, read one. *Mint smell attracts bees, and is beneficial to honey.*

Asperula Oderata, written beneath a leafy plant with tiny, starlike flowers, *or Sweet Woodruff. Used in garlands, it will clear the air. Used on cuts, it will slow bleeding.*

Christianna looked up at Daniel, confused.

"Gareth told me what happened today. And he told me that you were trying to keep busy. I thought that it might be fun for you to put the flowers and herbs in the garden in order. My mother used to do it, and a lot of gentlewomen like to putter about with their flowers."

Christianna looked down at the careful illustrations, the full, ruffled peonies and stalks of lavender, and faded yellow jonquil—daffy-down-dilly, the girlish writing beneath it said.

"You could do as much or as little as you like, and Mrs. Hatton wouldn't be breathing down your neck. And the fresh air and sunshine would do you good."

Borage, Christianna read, *Borago Officinalis. Peacock blue flowers, star shaped. Will lower a fever. Healthful when taken in wine.*

"It's no good being in a house all day," Daniel pointed out. "And it's no wonder you fainted, being in the kitchen on baking day."

"Oh, it wasn't that," Christianna assured him hastily, looking up from the book. "I'm really not that weak, never mind what they said. I just . . . you see, I saw something that reminded me of . . . the revolution."

Daniel said nothing, just looked at her with his clear, pale eyes. He looked very much like Gareth, Christianna thought, and yet different. The bones of his face were finer, his eyes more gray. The calm, kind look on his face reminded her of someone . . . Brother Joseph, who had taught her to play the violin, so long ago, at the ancient castle in the Auvergne Mountains.

"It was the blood, you see." The words came quickly, as if someone had opened a crowded closet; a tightly packed mess spilled out, scattering on the floor. "My friend Gabrielle, she was so silly, and I miss her so, and she's dead. They cut off her head and waved it at us, like a flag; and there was blood in her hair; and I had to go. And then when I did, it was horrible; and I had to . . . hurt someone, and there was a lot of blood. All over me. And then I was lost; sometimes I feel as if I still am. And now Phillipe is gone, and I don't know where Artois is; perhaps they killed him too. I miss him so. Have you ever had a great friend, that truly loved you and always made you laugh? That is why I fainted; it wasn't the kitchen."

She drew a shaking breath and lifted a trembling hand to her mouth, as if she could take the words back. It hurt to say them; it made it real.

Daniel looked shocked, completely at a loss.

"I'm sorry," Christianna said quickly. "I'm sorry. Please don't mention it. Please don't tell the others. I don't want to speak of it anymore."

Daniel nodded, and unexpectedly spoke in Latin. *"Curae leves loquuntur ingentes stupent,"* he said softly.

Startled, Christianna thought for a moment. "Small griefs speak . . ." she translated awkwardly.

"Great ones strike us dumb," Daniel finished. "It's hardest to talk about the things that truly grieve us."

"Exactly," she agreed, relieved that he understood. "And I really don't want to discuss it with anyone else. I would hate for anyone to pity me, or worse, to sit in judgment on me. God and I are doing well enough on that score."

She touched his sleeve, clutching the book to her heart. "I thank you for the book, Daniel. It was kind of you. I'll read it and see if I can busy myself."

Daniel let out a breath that sounded almost like a whistle. "As you wish," he said softly, using the same phrase that Gareth had, earlier that day; and Christianna knew that he would keep her confidences. "If you have any questions, or need help, just ask me. With the flowers, or anything else."

"Good night, Daniel, and *merci*."

She closed the door quickly, the book and drawings still clutched tightly in her hands.

She lay back against the lavender-scented linens of her featherbed and opened the worn pages of the old book.

She read about bee-balm and peonies, violets and larkspur, until the illustrations blurred before her eyes and she fell into a heavy sleep, undisturbed by dreams.

The next morning, she awoke at the first light to the already familiar sound of the cocks crowing. She dressed quickly, ran a comb through her hair, splashed cool water on her face, and made her way downstairs and outside, her new book under her arm.

Only the stupid dog was awake, her tail thumping against the kitchen floor like a drum, her eyes half closed. She lumbered to her feet and followed Christianna into the cool morning.

Christianna stood for a while, watching.

The overgrown flower beds were crowded with weeds, green and tangled; a jungle of vines climbed around tree trunks and over brick walls.

Heedless of her gown, Christianna dropped to her knees and looked closely. The dog pushed against her, and she shoved her away, opening the worn pages of the book and comparing the careful drawings to the spindly, crowded plants before her.

"Chamomile," she murmured, and felt a flush of pleasure as she recognized the daisylike blossoms. *"Anthemis Nobilis."* She studied the faded notes that Elizabeth Larkin had written, many years before, in her pretty, girlish hand. *"A very calming effect when used in tea. Distilled, for rinsing hair. Will take over the garden if allowed."*

"And it has," Christianna agreed.

She moved down the walk, leaves and branches brushing her skirts, and found chervil and costmary and feverfew and fennel, feeling an absurd kind of triumph as she recognized each plant.

She felt much the same way she had the first day she had discovered she could read music, when the jumble of black notes on the page had suddenly become meaningful, forming their own language.

This plant needed more sun; this one needed water; this one thinning.

Here, she would take away the lupines and

let the peonies grow. And there, she would take away the weeds, to give the sweet williams space. She would take the thorny blackberry vines from the roses, and fertilize the delphinums.

She stood in the warming sunlight, listening to the birds calling good mornings to each other in high, clear notes, and breathed the clean, cool smells of the growing plants.

She would create something of beauty; she would astound everyone with her new skill.

She bent over and pulled up a ragged stalk of feverfew, wrinkling her nose at the disagreeable, pungent smell. "Out you go," she announced. "Nothing that smells like you has a place here, useful or not. This is my garden now."

She laughed at herself, talking to plants, and then her attention was caught by a stand of growth that might be hollyhocks, and she clambered over the scruffy border of lavender, eager to begin.

Behind her, Dog wagged her tail and watched the ensuing activity with great interest.

Part 2
The
Garden

Flowers have a mysterious and subtle influence on the feelings, not unlike some strains of music. They relax the tenseness of the mind. They dissolve its rigor.

—Henry Ward Beecher

If I had but two loaves of bread, I would sell one, and buy hyacinths, for they would feed my soul.
—*The Koran*

The heart has reasons that reason does not understand.

—Jacque Bènigne Bossuet

Chapter Six

"I think she's lost her mind," Geoffery said to Stewart as they dumped the buckets of fresh milk into the cooling pans in the buttery.

"I always said she wasn't the sharpest knife in the drawer. This proves it."

Gareth didn't have to ask whom they were talking about.

"What now?" he asked, almost afraid of the answer.

"She's been out in the garden since sunup, wandering in circles," Geoffery informed him.

"When we went out to do the milking she was crawling under a hedge, talking to herself," Stewart added.

"In Latin," Geoffery said, in a tone of foreboding, as if this was proof that Christianna's sanity had, indeed, deserted her.

"Crawling under a hedge?" Gareth repeated, wondering if his brothers were right.

"Aye, and when I asked her what she was doing, she said, 'Following where the sunlight falls.' She's a few eggs short of a custard, Gareth."

"Following where the sunlight falls," Gareth repeated, his brows drawing together. "Are you sure that's what she said?"

Geoffery nodded. "Aye. I asked her what she meant by it, and she said, 'Never mind.'"

"And then when we came back she was out behind some bushes, cursing the blackberries." Stewart dropped an empty bucket to the brick floor with a clatter.

"That sounds sensible enough," Gareth observed. "Blackberries are a damned nuisance."

His brothers exchanged glances.

"Not for 'her highness,'" Stewart objected. "How would she know a blackberry bramble from a potato?"

Gareth shrugged. "Who cares? As long as she's not cursing me, or fainting in the kitchen, let her crawl around in the hedgerows."

"Lost her bloody mind," Geoffery muttered, gathering up the empty milk pails.

"Be that as it may," Gareth concurred, "it's nothing to do with us. I need you fellows in the fields. We can't wait for rain any longer; today we need to load the barrels onto the cart and water the plants."

Geoffery and Stewart looked pained.

"Cheer up," Gareth told them. "We'll all go

down to the Broken Bow tonight and get sotted, if you like."

They cheered up at the mention of their favorite pub.

"I haven't seen Polly for a month," Stewart said. "Now that's my idea of a woman. Tough as an old boot, and ripe as a peach."

"Not like that little madwoman crawling around the garden," Geoffery agreed.

"Oh, leave off," Gareth ordered. "I'll go find Richard and see you in the barn."

Christianna pulled some weeds, threw them over her shoulder, and examined the thin, spindly stems left in the dirt.

"Dianthus Carophyllus," she muttered. "I think. Or bachelor's buttons. We'll have to wait and see."

She took a heavy pair of shears from her pocket and began hacking at some blackberry canes that had twined their way around a spindly, yellowing rosebush. "Die, you ugly thing," she ordered, wincing as the thorns bit into the soft flesh of her fingers. She threw the cut brambles over the mossy brick of the garden walls, stood back, and beamed at her progress.

"Roses," she repeated to herself, picturing the open page of the book Daniel had given her, "must be cut beneath clusters of five leaves, to promote new and healthful growth."

She cut the roses more tenderly than she had the intrusive blackberries, taking care to leave the few branches with buds, examining the flowers that had managed to survive beneath the cloak of brambles and weeds that had covered them.

"A weak and pale rose," she quoted, "is one that has not been fed. The manure of cows or chickens should be placed at the base of the plants and covered with straw."

She wiped a hand across her damp forehead. "That should be lovely," she remarked wryly.

She had begun pulling weeds and unhealthy-looking flowers an hour before, and although it was still morning she was already bathed in sweat. The sun beat down on her back and her hair was tangled with leaves.

She dropped to her knees and examined a stand of ragged leaves, the tall stalks of the plants bending hungrily toward the sun.

"Delphinium Consolida!" she exclaimed triumphantly, peering at the tight buds, which showed a hint of deep blue. "Larkspur! You may stay," she told the plant in a benevolent tone. "I'd like a nice dark blue display, next to the pink roses, *merci beaucoup*. But you," she said, turning a stern face on the more common, spiky lupines that grew beside them, "you go. There are quite enough of your kind about."

Ruthlessly, she pulled them up by their roots, and they followed the blackberry vines over the fence.

"Discrimination of the aristocracy over the vulgar masses," said a voice behind her, and she turned to see Richard and Gareth behind her.

"You go to hell," she told Richard pleasantly, and resumed her work.

He and Gareth laughed.

"What are you doing?" Gareth asked, stepping forward.

Christianna's cry of alarm stopped him, and he looked down at where her dirty finger pointed, to a creeping vine beneath his heavy boot.

"Nigella Damascena," she explained, "or love-in-a-mist. Call it what you'd like, but don't tread on it."

Gareth stared at the delicate, fernlike plant, which looked to him like a weed. "As you like," he said at last, baffled by Christianna's sudden interest in the long-neglected garden.

She disappeared behind a stand of thick, bushy leaves.

"Blues and pinks may stay," her voice said. "And red, certainly. But Callendula Officinalis does not belong in this corner. You'll be too bright; you'll distract the eye. Like carrying an orange fan with a pink gown."

"God forbid that should happen," Richard muttered.

Christianna popped up from behind the leaves, a branch hanging from her tangled hair. "Go away," she ordered. "You're interrupting."

She examined her forefinger, where a thorn had torn the skin, and stuck it in her mouth.

Gareth smiled gently. "Here," he said, pulling a battered pair of leather gloves from the pocket of his breeches and tossing them over the dense foliage to her.

She accepted them without a word, and disappeared into the bushes, like a rabbit.

"Come on," he said to Richard. "There's a revolution happening here, and I think that the aristocrats are winning."

They turned toward the waiting fields, glancing back at the sound of a triumphant laugh.

"Fritilla Meleagris!" Christianna's voice recited. "Checkered lily, will grow to the height of six hands."

By evening, a brick pathway had appeared; the blanket of moss and clover that had hidden it had been carefully scraped away and disposed of. The rows of lavender that bordered it looked thin and scruffy, but they would grow, Christianna told herself, now that the weeds were no longer choking their roots.

The weeds were gone, the tall flowers like larkspur and hollyhocks supported and tied with bits of twine to sharp sticks, driven into the ground, and the earth showed, brown and rich between the plants lucky enough to have survived the day's purge.

Already it looked more like a garden, and less like a jungle.

Sweet williams bordered the front of the bed, their small heads of pink and rose and magenta peeping from their downy beds of soft green. There were also violas, miniature violets of royal purple velvet with a dash of brilliant yellow at their centers. Behind them stood coventry bells, looking like ruffled skirts of pink and lavender clustered on their gray-green stalks, and spicy-smelling gillyflowers of lilac and cream and rich, dark wine—round, ragged disks on their pale, thin stems.

Bellflowers of soft blue and white leaned against the mossy brick wall, and snapdragons—how funny the English word felt in Christianna's mouth, sharp and quick.

She had worked through the day like a woman possessed, pulling the intrusive creeping weed and raggedy dandelions and blackberries, cutting until her hand throbbed, scraping the moss and clover from the bricks until her back ached.

But more than pain, she felt a peculiar empathy with the flowers of the garden, marveling at their will to live despite their neglect; and she wondered at the strength of the dainty blue forget-me-nots and delicate baby's breath, so fragile and yet striving to survive, reaching toward the sun.

Like me, she thought, and found that she wanted the flowers to live; not to show Gareth or Richard and the rest how useful or clever she was, but simply because they were beautiful, being what they were.

By the day's end, Christianna was exhausted. She sat on the cool brick pathway, her back against the sturdy trunk of an overhanging peach tree, unable to move.

Her shoulders ached, her arms throbbed, her back felt as if it might break. Her face had burned; she could feel it without looking, the tight, red heat beneath the layer of dirt and sweat.

Her striped skirts of pink and lavender were stained beyond repair with streaks of black dirt and green moss, and the lace at her bosom and sleeves had been torn by thorns. Her entire body was wet with sweat. She was hungry, but nothing in the world could have induced her to move.

She closed her eyes and imagined the garden as it might look in a few weeks—tried to picture bursts of color and beauty where the tired and yellowed leaves now stood—but even that required too much effort.

"Are you dead?"

She opened her eyes with considerable effort and saw Gareth standing before her, an amused smile on his face. His hands were slung comfortably in the pockets of his breeches and his full-sleeved white shirt was open at the throat, showing the smooth muscles of his chest. Behind him, the rays of the sun warmed his hair to a fiery red.

"Go away," she said, her voice sounding more exhausted than angry, and she closed her eyes again.

His footsteps retreated and then returned, and Christianna opened a suspicious eye.

He set a wooden bucket at her side and offered her a dipper of water.

She accepted it gratefully, and drank it without stopping, the cold, clear water from the well sliding down her parched throat like ice.

"You've done well," he said, mild surprise in his voice. "I didn't think you'd get so far in one day."

Christianna smiled.

"I'll send Geoffery and Stewart up the tree tomorrow," he said, "and have them cut back the branches. You'll need more sun here."

"I hate the sun," she muttered.

Gareth laughed, showing his strong white teeth. "Your face is red. Where it isn't covered with dirt, that is."

Christianna closed her eyes, and when she spoke her voice was faraway and dreamy. "At Versailles, I had my own bath. It was covered in porcelain, painted with rosebuds and lilies; and whenever I wished my maid would fill it for me and put half a bottle of jasmine scent in the water. I never had to wash from a bowl, or haul buckets of water upstairs."

"But the maid did," Gareth pointed out.

Christianna thought of that. "Poor Therese. And half the time I forgot to pay her."

"It's a wonder she didn't leave," Gareth said, and there was no sympathy in his voice.

"And after my bath," Christianna went on dreamily, "she would do my hair, and help me with my gown, and I'd go to operas and ballets and dances. Or I would just go to see Artois; we would have supper, and sometimes I'd play my violin." She hummed a soft, poignant melody, remembering the golden notes of music that had filled her life. "Albinoni," she explained.

"So pretty. How I miss the music. And Artois. I wonder if he's dead."

Gareth said nothing, and after a few minutes he left.

Christianna let the soft evening breeze play over her face, watching the golden light of the spring twilight fall between the branches of the tree.

Gareth returned. "Here," he said gently, and he took her hand and pressed a cake of soap into it. "Mrs. Hatton's best. Lavender and primrose oil."

Christianna raised it to her nose and inhaled the soft, clean scent. She looked up at Gareth and saw that he had a linen towel in his hand.

"If you can walk," he said, "I'll take you to the lake for a bath. There's nothing like a bath in the woods after a hot day's work." He laughed aloud at the expression of mingled longing and suspicion on her face.

"I'll turn my back and keep watch for you. Don't be such a baby. It's cool and clean, and you smell like a piglet."

"Bugger off," she muttered, but she offered him her hand and let him help her up. She followed him from the yard and across the green fields and into the green wood, her aching body unable to resist the idea of soaking in cool, clear water.

The grass of the pasture was drying in the sun, and it smelled sweet and fresh. The sheep looked overdressed in their thick winter coats, Christianna thought.

She laughed with delight at the sight of the lambs and the way they half-hopped, half-skipped around their stodgy elders.

"How can they bear it: jumping about so, in this heat?"

"Just like children," Gareth answered, flashing his white grin. "Hot sun or ass-deep snow, it's all fun."

He leaped easily over the low stone fence that bordered the field and extended his hand to Christianna. She followed with less ease, her heavy petticoats and cumbersome skirts weighing her down.

"Silly clothes," Gareth remarked. "When our Vickie lived at home she went about in James's breeches half the time."

Christianna could see why. The heavy, boned bodice of her gown was cutting into her ribs; her layers of petticoats felt like weights around her damp legs and her back felt slick with sweat.

She followed Gareth into the woods, welcoming the shade with pleasure.

"Cow path," he explained, leading the way along the uneven trail.

Christianna was too tired to answer.

"It's not far," Gareth added, "and when you get out of the water you'll feel wonderful."

"I'd rather lie on my bed and have a maid fill a tub for me," Christianna grumbled. "That's what I think is wonderful."

Gareth gave her an exasperated look. "Sorry, your highness. Mayhap you should just be happy with what you have."

Christianna glared at him. "What do I have?" she demanded.

"Apart from a bad temper and an arrogant manner?"

She said nothing.

"You have your life. You have a solid roof over your head, and food to eat, and a brother who cares for you, and a stupid dolt for a brother-in-law who's taking you for a nice cold swim when he could be drinking beer at the Broken Bow. Though why I am, I couldn't tell you. You're the most ungrateful little wench I've ever had the misfortune to meet."

They stood on the path in the dense green forest, glaring at each other for a moment, until Gareth turned his back and walked ahead.

Christianna gathered her dirty, cumbersome skirts in her hand and followed his long-legged stride.

"You don't like me, do you?" she asked after a minute.

Gareth looked over his shoulder, a puzzled look on his handsome face.

"You're not very likable, are you?" he answered. He turned his back and kept walking.

Christianna thought about that. Likable? Had it ever mattered if anyone liked her or not? For some idiotic reason, she felt hurt.

"Pig," she muttered, taking care not to be heard; and that made her feel a little better. She lifted her nose proudly and stumbled over a root in the path, breaking the little curved heel from her stained shoe.

"*Merde, merde, merde!*" she swore.

Ahead of her, Gareth laughed.

"Did you step in some?" he asked. "I told you it was a cow path."

"Never mind," Christianna snapped, and hobbled after him on her broken shoe.

Chapter Seven

The lake was small; the water looked cool and green and inviting. Tall trees and feathery ferns surrounded the soft banks, glowing in the golden sunlight.

Christianna inhaled the cool scent of the water, and the dusty, spicy scent of the warm leaves.

"It's pretty," she said to Gareth as she stepped over a fallen log. Twigs crackled beneath her feet.

He smiled. "Yes, it is. Even if it isn't a porcelain bath, with lilies and roses."

Christianna stood awkwardly for a moment, fingering the cake of soap.

"I'll head back up the bank," Gareth offered, seeing her dilemma. "And I'll keep my back turned."

"See that you do," she said sharply, her cheeks flushed with heat and embarrassment.

He heaved an impatient sigh. "For God's sake, you really are full of yourself. Do you think that you're so damned beautiful that I brought you here to ravish you? You're not my sort; you're too small and skinny, for one thing, and too sharp-tempered, for another. I like my women soft and sweet."

"Good," she snapped, her eyes narrowing. "Go away."

Despite his promise not to look, Christianna hid behind some bushes to undress, her cheeks burning. With a quick look around to assure herself that nobody was in sight, she slid down the grassy bank and into the water, clutching the bar of soap in her grubby hand.

She sighed aloud with delight as the cool water covered her body, washing away the sweat and dust of the day. No, this wasn't at all like a porcelain bath; it was better.

She waded in up to her neck, laughing with delight as the soft mud squeezed between her toes, soothing her tired feet. She splashed water onto her face and felt the coolness of it against the sunburned skin of her nose and cheeks.

She felt weightless, buoyant. Even her hair floated, the dark strands moving around her neck and shoulders like liquid silk.

She let her arms float up and felt the throbbing pain of her day's exertion subsiding, drifting away into the cool green depths of the lake.

The air was full of birdsong: sweet, high notes like a flute. Fingers of golden light reached between the trees and sparkled on the water, and the cloudless sky above looked like a dome of blue above the circle of trees.

Christianna felt like a nymph, a tree sprite in an enchanted wood. She had never felt anything as heavenly as the touch of the limpid water against her skin; she had never felt so light and euphoric.

The softly scented soap felt like silk against her bare skin; she filled her hair with the clean lather, scrubbing her scalp vigorously before dunking her head.

She laughed aloud as she emerged, shaking her head, sending crystal droplets flying across the surface of the water.

"Are you having fun, then?"

Instinctively, her hands moved to her breasts, even though they were covered by the water. She looked over her shoulder to see Gareth sitting on the bank, his teeth showing in a broad white grin.

"Turn your back," she called, her face hot, a panicky feeling in her stomach.

"Don't be stupid. I can't see a thing. And even if I could, it'd be nothing new." He glanced down at the pile of her discarded clothing and picked up a beribboned garter, examining it with a good-natured smile, touching the white lace and pink silk rosette. "Pretty," he remarked.

Christianna glared, her good mood vanishing.

"You look like a wet kitten," Gareth added,

dropping the dainty frippery back onto the pile and turning his attention back to her.

"Thank you very much. Now go away."

"How's the water? Cold?"

Christianna wondered if he was hard-of-hearing, or just enjoying her discomfort. She decided it must be the latter. "The water is fine, thank you. Will you turn your back?"

"Truth be told, I was thinking of coming in."

Genuinely panicked, she sputtered for a minute. "Don't you dare!"

"Why not?" he asked, laughing. "There's enough room, I think."

He pulled his shirt over his head as he spoke, and Christianna's heart fluttered and started thumping wildly against her ribs. He wouldn't; he simply couldn't. She looked wildly about, but there was nowhere to go except back toward the shallows.

She began backing up into the deeper water, and suddenly the ground was gone; there was nothing beneath her feet.

She flailed wildly, reaching for something solid. But there was nothing there, and the water closed over her head.

She tried to cry out, and water rushed into her mouth, choking her. Instinctively, she tried to draw air, and swallowed more water. She splashed wildly, and for a second, light appeared through the darkness and there was air.

She choked, and tried to breathe and immediately went down again, into the murky green. Her lungs ached and her hands grasped at nothing; she wondered fleetingly which way was up.

Her lungs felt as if they would explode, brilliant lights were bursting in her eyes, and she felt her body sinking down, deeper into the endless expanse of blackness.

Something seized her waist with a terrifying grip and was pulling her; she fought against it, arms and legs lashing out helplessly against the relentless pull.

And then she broke the surface into the blinding brilliance of the light, and she was choking, coughing water and gulping painful drafts of air; still trying, in her terror, to pull away from the tight grip that clutched her body.

"Stop fighting; I've got you. Stop fighting or you'll go under again. You're out; it's all right."

It took a moment for the words to register.

"Stop struggling and breathe."

She sagged with relief as she realized that Gareth was holding her, and her hands instinctively grasped his shoulders. Blindly, she coughed and sputtered, her ribs heaving painfully as she drank in air.

He pounded her back. "Good, that's right. Slow and steady. Don't gasp so, you'll faint. Try to relax, and breathe slow and deep."

Shaking, she tried to obey.

Her vision cleared, and the pounding in her head subsided; then she realized that she was naked, clinging to this man like a vine, her arms and legs wrapped around him tightly, her bare breasts pressing against the warm skin of his chest. She froze.

"Good," he murmured, and the pounding on her back was replaced with a soft, slow stroking. "Lord, you gave me a fright. Jumped in with my breeches on. You've got a lot of fight for such a little thing."

His skin was warm against her, and she felt a soft thrill, a gentle wave of heat moving through her body. His voice sounded as gentle as the soft lapping of the water.

"Are you better? Got your breath back?"

She tried to speak, but her throat felt tight; a strange, full pressure that had nothing to do with the water she had swallowed. The gentle hand on her bare back felt like velvet, and she shivered.

"Christianna?"

She couldn't speak. Her nipples tightened and throbbed against the warm skin of his chest, and she was painfully aware that her legs were twined around his hips, the very center of her tightly against him. The cool water moved between their bodies, touching every inch of her skin.

Wondering at her silence, he put his strong fingers beneath her chin and tilted her head back to look at her face.

Christianna stared back, unable to look away as his expression of concern turned to puzzlement, and then, slowly, gradually, awareness.

"Oh, Lord," Gareth murmured as his eyes took in the sight of her flushed cheeks and glowing eyes. "Oh, Lord." His hand moved across her cheek like silk; his rough fingers moved to her parted mouth.

Unable to stop herself, she closed her lips over his finger and tasted warm skin and lake water.

She could feel his breath quicken, a sudden tensing of his muscles. His heartbeat was loud in the quiet of the forest.

He looked down at her and took his fingertips from her lips and traced them along the line of her cheekbones, smoothing a wet black curl back from her face.

It seemed forever that they stayed there, locked together, with the cool water sparkling around their waists.

And then Gareth smiled at her, a gentle, soft smile, and his eyes glowed, cool and green in his tanned face.

"You want me," he said softly.

He said it as calmly as he might say, "The sky is blue," or "It might rain today."

Christianna wanted to die of shame. And even though her body was clinging to his and her heart was pounding like thunder and her breasts were throbbing against the hard breadth of his chest, she lied.

"No, I don't," she whispered. Her voice quavered with the lie, and she drew a deep breath and was about to repeat herself when his mouth covered hers.

If he had been rough, she might have found the strength to pull away; but his lips touched hers with the most incredible sweetness she had ever felt. Warm and rich, with a gentle persistence, until she felt herself lifting her mouth for more, opening to him; and when his tongue met hers the smooth heat of it made her cry out, softly, deep in her throat.

He pulled her closer against him, and his mouth trailed to her neck and his breath was hot against her ear.

"The truth," he whispered.

The truth was that she was trembling with unspeakable feelings, that she thought that he was beautiful, strong and golden from the sun, with shimmering drops of water rolling down his arms; and she wished with all her heart that she was a simple country lass whose virtue meant nothing to her.

"I want you to let me go," she answered, the words taking an enormous amount of effort.

He laughed softly. "The truth, I said."

His hand was on her breast, gently teasing the hard bud of her nipple against his palm; and she quivered at the sensation and gasped.

"Is it so hard, then, to say it?" His voice was low and soft. "You want me. It's a simple enough thing to say."

"I don't." Her voice sounded strangled, and he laughed again.

"What a stubborn little thing you are. Lie until you choke, if you wish; but bodies don't lie, Christianna. You opened your mouth to me like a starving kitten; and here," he said, his finger circling her nipple till it tingled and throbbed, "your lovely little breast isn't lying. Your body knows what it wants."

It did, she thought, almost crying with the indignity of it. Her traitorous body was clinging to him, pulling closer to his touch, her breasts lifting to his hand as her spine arched back.

Easily, he shifted her weight over his arm and bent his head to take her aching nipple into his mouth. His lips were firm and strong, his tongue hot and damp against the sensitive bud. An almost unbearable heat rushed through her body, and she moaned, tossing her head.

At the sound, he pulled her almost roughly to him and took her mouth again, his tongue stroking hers with a fevered, velvet heat.

He stopped only when he felt her hands in his wet hair, pulling him closer and deeper into the kiss.

"Lie to me again," he whispered, his breath hot against her cheek, "if you can."

Christianna couldn't speak. His hands were on the round curves of her derriere, pulling her against him in the limpid water of the lake; and she realized that she was pressing against the hard length of his shaft, with only the thin fabric of his breeches between them.

She wanted to tell him to put her down, to stop this and leave her alone; and at the same time she wanted to feel his back beneath her palms, to tell him to kiss her again, to tear away the fabric of his breeches and let him fill the aching need of her body. His mouth was on her neck, raining soft, fiery kisses against the tender skin.

"Tell me that you want me." His voice was gentle but insistent. One of his hands was stroking the soft curve of her thigh, and Christianna trembled, even as her body answered him, moving toward his touch. Hot tears trembled on her lashes; her mouth quivered against the clean, warm skin of his shoulder.

His mouth sought hers again; he bit her lip gently, as if he was tasting her; and she cried out into his kiss as his hand slipped onto the soft black mound between her legs.

She was lost. Nothing had ever felt as sweet and exquisite as the firm fingers that stroked her, softly and expertly. She was senseless, caught up in the pulsing, tingling thrills that chased through her body; sparkling, swelling waves of fire.

Shamelessly, she writhed against the insistent heat of his fingers, closing her eyes against the sunlight that sparkled over their bare skin. When he began speaking softly in her ear it only inflamed her more, even as his fingers teased and stroked the soft pink petals of flesh; and she opened to him, like a rosebud unfurling in the sun.

"That's right; that's good. Aah, yes, what a beautiful girl you are. You're wet for me; do you feel it? God in heaven, you're so sweet. . . ." His breath flowed like fire against the tender skin of her ear; his voice was husky and low. His fingers stroked her, firm and quick.

"Don't fight it, sweetheart; just let go. . . ."

She did. A wild cry rose from her throat,

a primitive, animal sound. Her body shook with white-hot spasms, wave after rolling wave of heat.

Her pulse was like a drumbeat in her ears; her fingers gripped his shoulders and hot tears flooded from her eyes as she collapsed, shuddering, against the smooth golden skin of his chest.

"Sweetheart . . ." He was stroking her face, kissing the salty tears that poured down her cheeks.

She shook with shame and anger and disgust at her own animal behavior, and pushed his hand away from her face.

"Batard sale!"

Gareth's handsome face was blank with shock at the fury in her voice. He shook his head, flinging the dark, wet strands of hair from his eyes. "What?"

Christianna turned away from his clear, troubled gaze, folding her arms over her white bosom. She was still trembling. She felt exposed and humiliated, and she wanted to strike him.

"Christianna, sweetheart . . ."

"Don't call me that! Stop calling me that! You bastard; you stupid, filthy bastard!" She was choking with rage and shame. She struggled to get loose from his grip.

He took her shoulders and pulled her roughly against him, turning her face up with a cool hand.

"Stop it. Stop it right now, do you hear?" He didn't raise his voice, but there was no mistaking the anger in his eyes. "What the hell is wrong with you? Are you crazed?"

"Let me go." Her voice was cold, her cheeks burning.

He laughed, but it wasn't a happy sound. "What, drop you in the water so that you can drown? Calm yourself and tell me—what is wrong? I didn't force you, for God's sake; you were having fun—"

She twisted her head away, humiliated.

"Aah. That's it, then." He was silent for a moment, and Christianna froze, afraid of what he would say next.

"You bloody little snob."

She glanced up through the curtain of wet black hair that covered her face, and stopped at the cool anger on his face.

"You bloody little snob," he repeated slowly. "You can't bear it, can you? If I were an earl or a prince, well, that would be a different story, wouldn't it? You'd be laying your pretty head on my shoulder and cooing in my ear. But you can't bear the thought that you've been twisting and crying on the hand of a bloody peasant, can you? Like any common little wench would."

Christianna didn't know what to say, and her face burned with shame.

Gareth stood silently for a moment, his eyes bright with anger, his generous mouth set in a hard line. He lifted her in his hard arms and carried her toward the shore, where he dumped her abruptly in the shallow water.

"Get your clothes on and go home, little girl.

And don't come trifling with me again; because the next time you look at me with your big blue eyes and press your pretty white tits against me you'll get more than you bargained for. I'm no damned courtly fop to play your games with."

No, he wasn't that at all, Christianna thought, watching him stride back into the water. He looked like a pagan god, with his long, wet hair clinging to the hard muscles of his shoulders and the sunlight dappling over the long, smooth line of his back.

She sat where she was, wiping her tears of rage and shame away with a trembling hand, until he plunged into the water with a mighty splash and began swimming away with long, even strokes.

She struck the surface of the water with her fist, and the resulting splash was only mildly satisfying.

Her grubby gown felt wretched against her clean skin as she dressed, and she swore under her breath as she made her way back through the quiet forest. She wondered how she could ever face him again.

"Monsieur Larkin?"

Startled, Gareth looked up from the ledger before him, and his pen scattered droplets of black ink over the carefully noted columns of figures. He sighed and dropped the pen with a deliberate motion.

"Come in, then."

She entered the room like a royal princess, her head held high and her expression cool and haughty. She had dressed carefully, he noted, in a gown of lavender silk. The stiff bodice of the gown pushed her breasts up, round and soft-looking above the starched lace of the square neckline. She had pinned her hair high, in an elaborate design of thick curls that cascaded over one smooth shoulder.

She didn't look anything like the grubby little creature who had followed him from the garden earlier. She was an aristocrat, impeccably cool and correct.

He pointed to the battered chair that sat opposite his desk, and she sat with a graceful turn, her skirts whispering, her hair shining in the candlelight.

He said nothing, just sat and waited for her to speak.

She cleared her throat. "I . . . I find that I am no longer able to live here."

Gareth nodded, trying not to smile at her formality.

"Very good, then. Where will you go?"

She raised a dark brow. "New Orleans, of course. To my brother. It seems the only possible thing to do."

Gareth nodded agreeably, and picked up his pen. "Very good. Very sensible of you. Have a nice trip."

He bent over the ledger, and the room was silent, except for the scratching of his pen against the paper.

"Monsieur Larkin?"

He looked up and smiled at her. "Well?"

"I thought . . . that is . . . I don't really have the money for the passage."

"I see. Well, it's a damned long way, and I can't say that your swimming is quite good enough to get you there. You do have a bit of a problem, don't you?"

"Can you lend me the money?" She spoke quickly; he could hear that the words were difficult for her.

"I see. I take it, then, that I'm of sufficient social standing to lend you money, if not for . . . er, other things."

He enjoyed the red that stained her pale cheeks, and the way her soft lip caught between her teeth.

"Yes," she answered softly, not meeting his eyes.

"Christianna?"

She looked up swiftly, her hope plainly written in her anxious blue eyes.

"No."

Her composure faltered, her dark brows drew together, and her mouth tightened. "Why not?" she demanded.

Gareth leaned back and stretched lazily. "Because it suits me not to."

Her face went white with rage. "I cannot live under this roof any longer!"

"There bloody well isn't anywhere else for you to go."

"She could go to Uncle Alden's cottage."

Gareth and Christianna turned toward the door in one swift motion.

Geoffrey and Stewart stood there, their eyes bright with interest.

"She bloody well cannot," Gareth objected.

"It's not under this roof," Geoffery pointed out.

"Please, who is Uncle Alden?" Christianna asked.

"He won't bother you; he's dead," Stewart explained cheerfully.

Gareth sighed. "I said no, and I meant it."

"Who the hell made you the bloody king?" Geoffery demanded.

"Yes, who the hell made you the bloody king?" Christianna echoed.

"Don't swear," Gareth told her sharply.

"She can if she wants to," Stewart told his older brother. "I like the way it sounds. 'Oo the ell made you ze bloodee king?' "

He and Geoffrey laughed like idiots.

"How much did you drink?" Gareth asked impatiently.

"A little," Geoff replied, and, "Enough to float a boat," Stewart said, at the same time. They exchanged quick glances.

"A little boat," Stewart hastened to add.

Gareth rested his head in his hands for a moment.

"Bloody fools," he muttered. "You do remember, I hope, that we start shearing tomorrow?" he asked pointedly.

Stewart belched, and Christianna cringed.

"Why's her highness want to leave?" Geoffery demanded.

"Probably your breath," Stewart answered.

"Probably your belching," Geoffrey returned.

"Polly missed you tonight," Stewart informed Gareth, wiggling his eyebrows. "She said to give you a kiss."

"I wouldn't, if I was you," Geoffrey told Stewart. "He's in a foul mood."

"Haven't you got something to do?" Gareth asked pointedly.

"No, not a thing. Why is Christianna leaving?"

"She isn't."

"I am," Christianna argued, her chin jutting obstinately.

Richard stuck his head in the open door. "Where is she going?" he asked, chewing on a piece of chicken. Behind him, the stubby-legged dog watched, her eyes fastened longingly on the food.

"She's going to live in Uncle Alden's cottage," Geoffery replied. "Hello, Dog. What a good old girl."

"She isn't," Gareth snapped.

"Well, there are worse dogs . . ."

"Not the dog, you twit. Christianna is not going to Uncle Alden's cottage."

"I will if I choose to. Who is Uncle Alden?"

"He's dead, I told you. Crazy old man."

"Then he won't mind at all if I use his cottage."

"Stupid bitch," snapped Richard; and everyone stared at him with shocked faces. "Dog, not

154

her highness," he explained, and they all looked down at the dog, who was swallowing his piece of chicken, bones and all.

Stewart and Geoffery burst into loud laughter.

Gareth rose abruptly. "Out! All of you, out! Not you," he added to Christianna. "You sit your bum on that chair, and don't move."

"What the hell is wrong with him?" Richard demanded.

"Ee theenks ee eez ze bloodee king," Stewart answered, his imitation of Christianna's accent drawing a glare from her and guffaws from Geoffery.

"Out," Gareth repeated, and his brothers listened, and made their exit with a great deal of noise.

Gareth slammed the door behind them and turned back to his chair.

Dog had climbed into it and was pretending to sleep. Gareth tipped the chair, and she hit the floor with a loud thud. She slunk to Christianna's side and leaned against the lavender silk skirts with a mournful look.

"Now," Gareth said, "let's sort this out. Uncle Alden's cottage is across the west pasture, by the foot of the hill, and it's not fit for anything but mice. It's old and dirty, and I use it to store traps in."

"Move them," Christianna said. "As for the mice, I'm sure that they won't be half as annoying as you and your brothers."

Gareth glared at her. He raked his hair from his high forehead. "Don't give me orders. If you want the traps moved, move them yourself. I've better things to do than wait on you like a bloody lackey."

"Then I may go there?"

"And what will you eat, your highness?"

Christianna looked crestfallen. "I hadn't thought of that."

"Ah, the little details. Well, your brother left you under our protection; I won't let you starve."

"Fine. I shall take my meals here, and pay you back by finishing the gardens. I have no intention of being in your debt."

Gareth sighed. "Christianna, if you're so damned set on keeping away from me, yes, go. But spare me the high-handed going-to-tea-with-the-duke dramatics. I know why you're going, and so do you."

Her face turned pink and she lifted her chin. "Oh, and why is that?"

Gareth smiled and took up his pen, dipping it into the ink.

"Because you want me," he answered simply.

Her arched brows drew together and her eyes looked daggers at him. "Go to hell," she snapped, and rose from her chair, her skirts hissing as she left.

With a sad look, Dog followed, her nails clicking across the wood floor.

Sweet Summer Storm

From the journal of Gareth Larkin
May the fifteenth, 1790

Watered the east fields. The crops will do badly, if there isn't rain soon. Shearing starts tomorrow; have hired five extra men to help.

The strawberries will be ready in a week, almost a full month early. Daniel has found some sort of bug on the potatoes, but doesn't know what.

Christianna has started putting Mother's gardens in order. She is stronger than I gave her credit for.

I find myself watching her, and I wonder if she is aware of how incredibly lovely she is. She is one of those women who is made for love; and it is impossible not to think about it when she is around.

Is it conscious, I wonder, or just second nature to her—the way she sways her hips, the way she moves her head. Her lips are like ripe berries, and I find myself wanting to kiss her as she speaks.

She's as ripe as a peach, but will not allow herself to give in to her "base" desires. I would like to tumble her down and give her what she so badly wants, but there will be greater pleasure in making her admit it—if she ever will.

God help me if I ever loved her.

Chapter Eight

Christianna dreamed that night—vivid, sharp dreams, where every detail assumed painfully bright clarity.

She was in the woodland lake again, floating and turning with the skill and agility of a sylph. The water flowed around her like sparkling fingers, warm and twinkling like a million diamonds in the sunlight.

The trees around the lake seemed to glow and move with life; their lush green branches seemed to whisper to her, beckoning her with their strength. Leaves glowed like emeralds against the impossible azure-blue brightness of the sky.

Christianna floated through the water with a speed that could never be achieved in the waking world, and she wondered if this was what it would feel like to fly, to feel the sky rushing past her.

"Say that you want me," Gareth whispered as he rose from the water. He was radiant, his skin glowing like gold, his eyes shining with the same brilliant green of the leaves of the trees, his hair wet and dark, dripping over his shoulders.

The water of the lake carried Christianna against him, lifting her with a magical force. She didn't resist, but went willingly and ran her hands over the warm skin of his chest and his flat stomach.

The trees seemed to shimmer and bend toward her; the sunlight was impossibly bright and hot, and Gareth's voice was rich and warm by her ear.

"Say it," he whispered, and Christianna clutched him tightly and felt as if his strength and energy were pouring into her.

"I want you," she said, and the words were clear and strong. She felt no shame or hesitation as she spoke, and it seemed that the words gave her an almost magical strength, like the power of a spell or an incantation.

"But you're useless, you know," Gareth said. "You really don't belong here, do you?"

As he had in reality, he carried her toward the shore and tossed her away from him; but when she hit the water she slid over the top of it and realized that the landscape had changed, as landscapes often do in dreams.

She was sliding on ice, a vast, empty expanse of cold. The lake was frozen and had grown in size to the proportions of a sea, a surface of mirror-smooth ice as far as the eye could see. Far away, the trees stood, barren and laced in white frost in the glittering, blue-gray landscape.

The wind was moving around her with a lonely cry almost like the sound of violin, and the tree branches clattered against each other.

Christianna wished that she had her blue velvet cape; and there it was. Suddenly, she was back at Versailles, on a winter day long ago.

The canals that ran through the grounds had frozen over, and everyone was buying or renting horse-drawn sleighs to race across the sparkling ice.

This is better, Christianna told herself, and she laughed with joy as she snuggled in the elegant sleigh next to Artois.

On his other side, Gabrielle leaned forward, and Christianna remembered clearly how lovely she had been that day, in a smart little jacket of white velvet trimmed with priceless black mink. Diamonds sparkled like snowflakes in Gabrielle's golden hair beneath the gossamer veil of her hat.

"Well, ladies," Artois said, "is this silly enough to please you?" He waved his hand to indicate the luxurious sleigh, the sparkling brass footwarmers at their feet, the glittering bells that bedecked the matched white horses.

Christianna laughed aloud, as she had on that magical December day of three years ago. "Drive," she urged Artois; and he flicked the reins lightly over the horses' backs and the sleigh coasted over the frozen canal with delightful speed.

Daringly, they sped past the other courtiers in their luxurious conveyances, the cold wind and the brilliant sun of the day staining their cheeks red.

Artois shouted with delight as the horses picked up speed, and Gabrielle began to laugh; Christianna joined her as they flew along, the sleigh bells ringing and the runners hissing, the horses' hooves clattering over the road of ice before them.

Faster and faster they went, and the sleighs of more cautious courtiers hurried out of their path, sometimes with indignant shouts and words of reproval.

All along the banks of the canal people had gathered to watch the rich at play, and Christianna could see people pointing at them, admiring and envious of the trio, their youth and beauty and wealth. The snow sparkled in the sunlight, like the diamonds in Gabrielle's hair, and the air felt crisp and invigorating as they sped along.

When Artois at last slowed the horses they were all three breathless with exhilaration and laughter, and Christianna and Gabrielle collapsed, giggling, against Artois's shoulders.

In her dream, Christianna remembered the elegance of his greatcoat of dark cashmere with the silver filigree buttons at the sleeve, the lace of the cravat at his throat as white as the snow.

"We're very badly behaved for such an elegant threesome," she proclaimed, exactly as she had in reality.

Gabrielle, still laughing, made a dismissive gesture with her finely gloved hand, and Artois said, "That's what makes it so much fun, isn't it?"

"I'm so happy to be back," Christianna said, and there was a strange shifting of focus in her dream. It was as if she was back in the past, on the day of the sleigh ride, and yet she remembered all that was going to happen in the future.

"I'm glad you're back too," Artois said, suddenly serious. "But things have changed; do you see it?"

Christianna looked around at the sparkling landscape, at the rich sleigh and bells shimmering on the horses, at the frosted trees and the rosy, happy glow on Gabrielle's face.

"No, it's exactly the same as it always has been," she argued. "Nothing has changed, Artois."

"But look," Artois said impatiently, "just look, will you? This is driving my valet mad. . . ." As he spoke, he was untying the white lace of his cravat, his gloved fingers moving with his characteristic haste as he pulled the fabric from his throat.

His head rolled from his neck and fell into the snow, as if the fine lace of his cravat had been the only thing keeping it attached.

Christianna wanted to scream, but her heart

was blocking her throat, and she couldn't utter a sound.

She awoke with a start and stared at the gabled ceiling of her room at the Larkins' farm.

The gray light of early morning was just starting to fill the room; the house was still silent.

Trembling, she sat up in her bed, a shaking hand pressed to her lips, the images of her dream still painfully vivid in the silent room. She could clearly see Gabrielle's dimpled cheeks, glowing in the cold winter day. She could see the heavy silver embroidery on Artois's velvet cuffs; hear his voice and the quick, sharp way he had of speaking that other people often found rude, but that she found so amusing.

Outside her window, a cock crowed, and the sound seemed mournful in the cool, early morning darkness. Her dream seemed so close, so real, that she almost expected to see snow outside the window instead of the greens of spring.

Christianna suddenly felt very alone and lost; and she realized that even if Artois was alive, he was as lost to her as Gabrielle.

"I can't bear it," she whispered, and her heart seemed tight, as if there was a fist in her chest.

Her mouth twisted into a hard, tight line, and she cried quietly into her pillow, grieving for the friends who were lost to her forever, grieving for herself, and for the empty, aching sorrow of knowing that she was very alone, in a world in which she had no place. It seemed that she might die of pain, and that nothing would ever be right again.

Her body was stiff and sore from her work in the garden the day before, and her fingers ached as she laced herself into her dress of pale blue. She moved quietly down the staircase, out into the garden.

It was cool in the garden, and quiet. Christianna was surprised at the changes she had wrought. Already the flowers looked healthier, as if they had grown in only a night. She bent down and ran a finger over the lavender, breathing the delightful fragrance. The aroma seemed stronger in the early morning, she thought.

A rosebud had opened slightly, revealing tightly furled petals of a deep pink, and she wondered what it would be like fully opened.

She walked slowly from one plant to another, thinking of nothing but the shapes and colors of the blossoms and how the dew clung to them, sparkling in the pale sunlight—the deep magenta of the tiny sweet williams, the pale, dusty pinks and deep red velvet colors of the rosebuds, the true, brilliant blue of the bachelor's buttons.

"Look at this," said a quiet voice behind her, and she turned quickly.

It was Daniel, dressed for farm work in a rough, full-sleeved shirt and worn breeches, instead of the neat frock coat and carefully tied cravats he wore to teach Latin.

"You're up early," he said. "Did you come out to admire your work?"

Christianna nodded, not without satisfaction. "It looks better, doesn't it?"

Daniel smiled, his eyes roaming around with approval. "Very much so."

Christianna warmed to his approval. Daniel had such a calm and gentle manner that it was impossible not to feel comfortable with him.

He set down the empty bucket he was carrying and reached out to pull a leaf from a rosebush, showing her the yellow bumps beneath it. "Rust," he said. "When you see it get rid of the leaf quickly, before it spreads."

Christianna studied the leaf carefully, nodding.

"Are you well?" Daniel asked, looking with concern at her reddened eyes. "You look like you've been crying."

Christianna flinched and was about to tell him to mind his own business; but he looked so kind and his concern seemed so genuine that she decided to answer him honestly.

"I was." She studied a clump of foxglove, the purple bells with the spots of black and white inside, and drew a deep, painful breath before finishing. "I was dreaming that I was back at Versailles, on a sleigh ride with Gabrielle and Artois. It seemed so real. . . ."

Daniel nodded, saying nothing.

"Sometimes," Christianna continued, "I feel as though everything is fine, in an odd way. None of it seems real—as though Gabrielle hadn't been killed, as if Artois could walk through the door and say, 'Let's have coffee and try that new piece by Mozart'; as if I had never cut a man's throat."

If Daniel was startled by that, he didn't react. He simply stood quietly. "And the rest of the time?" he asked at last.

Christianna bent down and grasped a small weed that had escaped her notice. "The rest of the time," she said, and her throat felt tight and closed. She pulled the weed savagely before she finished. "The rest of the time I feel like my heart might break. Truly, literally break. Sometimes I feel like the loneliest woman in the world. I hurt so badly, and I don't think it will ever go away. It comes and goes in waves. A million times a day I think, oh, that will make Artois laugh, or, wouldn't Artois have something to say about this, or Gabrielle would die before she would wear a bonnet like that one."

Her eyes stung with hot, unshed tears. "And I know that I will never see them again."

"Perhaps not," Daniel agreed softly. "But you're very young, barely twenty. And you will have other friends who love you."

"Not much chance of that," Christianna said, managing a wry smile. "I'm not a very likable person."

"Bull," Daniel said agreeably. "I like you, and the boys like you, in their stupid way, and Gareth likes you."

Christianna snorted, a thoroughly ungraceful sound. "Bull," she echoed, her cheeks reddening at the mention of Gareth's name.

Daniel laughed. "Truly. You're an admirable person. You're very strong and brave. Did you really kill a man?"

He said it as though it were not the most horrible crime in the world.

"I had to," Christianna said. "It was terrible. A terrible, ugly thing. But I had no choice."

"Of course you didn't. I would not have thought otherwise."

They were quiet then, listening to the birds in the trees and the soft sounds of the animals stirring in their barns, and Christianna reached out and laid her hand on Daniel's arm.

"Thank you," she said softly, unsure of why she was thanking him. For listening, perhaps. For not being appalled that she had killed someone.

"Think nothing of it," he answered, and reached out to pat her hand before taking up his bucket and moving toward the well. "Shearing day," he informed her. "Work starts early today. We'll be having people over to help. A whole houseful. It's like a party when the work's done."

Christianna nodded, and turned her attention back to the flowers, selecting a few forget-me-nots to wear in her hair, delighting in their brilliant, pale blue.

For a few minutes, she had forgotten about her resolve to leave the house and move to the cottage, but the sound of Gareth's voice calling a greeting to his brother jarred her, and she turned back to the house, determined to carry out her plan.

The kitchen was a hive of activity. Mrs. Hatton was already putting pies into the oven and cutting thick slices of ham and cooking eggs. Geoffery and Stewart and Richard were drinking tea and arguing about who could shear the most sheep, and the dog was waddling to and fro, trying to steal food and getting under everybody's feet.

Matthew Larkin sat at the table, an open book before him, seeming blissfully oblivious to the noise around him as he drank his tea, his wispy gray hair standing on end.

"Are you really moving to Uncle Alden's cottage?" Richard demanded, noticing Christianna standing by the door.

"I am," she answered.

Mrs. Hatton looked over her broad shoulder and gave a snort of disbelief. "Be running back as soon as you see it, I shouldn't wonder. Dirty place."

"Then I shall clean it. What will I need, please?"

Mrs. Hatton waved a wooden spoon at her, like a weapon. "Now look, my girl, this is a busy day for me, and everyone else here. I've no time for your silliness. We've got guests arriving and three meals to cook and no time to teach you how to use a broom. The best thing you can do is try not to get underfoot, thank you. I've no time for nonsense."

Christianna bristled and was about to answer, but everyone's attention was distracted by the sound of horses arriving.

"Here we go!" Geoffery announced, standing up. "Let's go after the sheep. Where's Gareth?"

"Somewhere," answered Richard, speaking around a mouthful of ham. "Probably already working."

Christianna stood, forgotten, as they clattered out the door and called greetings to the arriving friends and neighbors.

Ignoring Mrs. Hatton's disapproving glare, she took a cup of tea and a warm piece of bread and retreated out the door into the sunshine.

The yard was full of people, mostly strange men, shouting greetings to each other.

Gareth was standing by the door to the barn, speaking to Daniel and two strange men, and there was a girl next to him, her arm linked comfortably in his.

Christianna felt a quick, ugly stab of jealousy.

This woman was everything she was not. She was strong and tall, with an impressive display of bosom showing over the top of her tightly laced bodice. Her white cap seemed to serve no purpose other than to display her thick, golden hair. Her cheeks glowed with good health, and she was laughing at something Gareth said—a full, husky laugh that commanded attention.

When she saw Christianna she said something to Gareth, and he laughed and gave her shoulders a quick squeeze.

Christianna stood stiffly as the girl walked

toward her, her striped skirts of red and yellow swaying, her golden braid shining in the sun.

"I'm Polly," the girl announced. "From the Broken Bow. And you're Christianna. The boys were in last night, telling me about you. What a dress! Is it French?"

Christianna looked down at her dress, the sky blue ribbons and thick white lace. "No," she answered, "it's from London."

Polly looked disappointed. "Oh. I did want to see something from Paris."

Christianna didn't quite know how to answer that. So this was Polly, who had told Stewart to send Gareth a kiss. She looked the type. Her eyes sparkled with mischief; her freckled face was alight with curiosity.

"Tell me," Polly said, "how do you like living here? I wish my brother would dump me at the Larkin farm. I wouldn't get much sleep; that's a fact. Wouldn't know where to start!"

When Polly laughed her round breasts looked as if they might burst out from her bodice. The simple fichu, a triangular scarf of thin lawn that was tied over her shoulders, did little to veil her ample charms.

Christianna was taken aback by Polly's frank earthiness and the blatant desire that shone in her green eyes as she watched the Larkins moving about the yard, unsaddling and stabling the horses of their guests.

"Look at that," Polly said. "Aren't they the best?" She gave a little whoop of delight and put a hand over her heart, as though to still it.

"Fairly makes me weak in the knees, it does. A girl would be lucky, to catch herself one of them."

Christianna didn't like the way Polly smiled at Gareth.

"Do you think so?" she asked coolly.

Polly's merry smile showed. "What, are you mad? Look at them!"

Christianna looked at Gareth, standing in the center of a circle of men. He stood at least a head taller than anyone else, his auburn hair gleaming in the sunlight, his full, loose shirt tucked into tight, worn breeches that showed the long, muscled length of his legs.

The men he spoke to listened to him with looks of respect and admiration.

"Aye, he's a fine one," Polly breathed. "The best of the lot. What I wouldn't give to be in your shoes. This is a fine farm, full of hot young men. I'd love to live here."

Christianna blushed. "I don't," she said curtly. "As a matter of fact, I intend to leave today. I would go to New Orleans, to my brother; but Gareth won't lend me the money."

"Leaving?" Polly cried, her freckled face incredulous. "Whatever for? Where are you going?"

Christianna ignored the first question. "Gareth told me that I might go to Uncle Somebody's cottage."

"What, Uncle Alden's?"

Christianna nodded.

Polly shook her head. "Why?" she demanded,

as if she had a right to know. "It's a dirty little place. At least it was the last time I saw it. Cobwebs all over the ceiling."

Christianna didn't want to know what Polly had been doing there that she remembered the ceiling. "I haven't seen it yet," she admitted. "I was going to ask Mrs. Hatton to let me use some soap and . . . whatever you need to clean a room."

Polly moved aside as Geoffery and Stewart passed, carrying a keg of beer. "Save some of that for me," she told them merrily. "I've the day off and I intend to have a fine time."

"Can't wait," Stewart answered, showing a white grin.

Polly tossed them a flirtatious smile and turned back to Christianna. "Have you ever cleaned a cottage before?" she demanded, casting a suspicious eye over the delicate gown of flowered lawn, the white lace underskirts exposed by the elaborately ribboned gathers of the full skirt.

"No," Christianna said, "and I don't think Mrs. Hatton will be very helpful. She doesn't like me, I think."

"She doesn't like me, either," Polly said with a wicked grin. "The old witch."

As if on cue, the back door opened with a bang and Mrs. Hatton appeared long enough to dump a pan of water, send a suspicious glare in their direction, "Haruumph" loudly, and disappear back into the house.

Polly's husky laugh rang out, and after a

moment Christianna joined her.

Across the yard, Gareth looked in their direction, and he seemed slightly worried.

"Come on," Polly ordered, linking her arm in Christianna's. "I'll help you with the cleaning, even though I think you're crazy for leaving. I'll bet Victoria left something here that you could wear. You can't clean in a dress like that."

"But Mrs. Hatton said that I wasn't to get underfoot," Christianna protested.

"Then she'd best give us what we need, so we can get out," Polly said cheerfully. "You'd be all day, cleaning that place alone. You don't want to miss the party, do you?"

Christianna really didn't think that she'd be missing much, but Polly seemed so enthralled by the idea that she declined to say so.

"Let me tell you," Polly said, with a conspiratorial wink, "when that Gareth has a few beers, he's some fun."

Christianna looked alarmed. What did Polly know, or was she thinking of herself?

"You're right, Polly. I wouldn't want to miss the party. And . . . *merci*, Polly."

Polly hooted with laughter. "*Merci*," she repeated. "Listen to you! I'd bet that accent drives them wild."

"Would you look at that?" Stewart remarked to Gareth, watching Polly and Christianna walking toward the house, arm in arm. "I didn't expect her highness to care for our Polly."

Gareth watched the two girls as they put

their heads together, and Polly's full, husky laughter floated across the sunlit yard, followed by Christianna's softer, more hesitant laugh.

"What do you suppose they have to talk about?" Stewart asked curiously.

Gareth looked a little worried. "I shudder to imagine," he answered. "Come on, fellows; let's get those sheep under way."

He cast another look over his shoulder at Christianna and Polly, the gleaming black curls next to the bright golden head, before he turned back to his work.

Chapter Nine

Polly pushed open the dilapidated-looking door of the stone cottage, and her upturned nose wrinkled with disgust.

"Good God," she announced, peering into the dusty depths of the room. "If I were you, I'd turn around and run."

Christianna leaned around Polly's shoulder, and her heart sank.

The single room was dark and musty, dust motes floating in the sunlight that streamed through the open door. There was an old cot, covered with some disreputable-looking blankets, a pile of rusty, evil-looking traps, heaps of mysterious and unsavory-looking rubbish, and a few stray fishing poles.

Everything was covered with at least an inch of dust.

Christianna looked over her shoulder across the soft green meadow at the Larkin house, which suddenly looked very large and clean and comfortable.

"No," she answered, setting down the heavy bucket of water she had lugged across the west field. "Not after what we had to go through with Mrs. Hatton. I'll roast in hell before I go back and tell her I can't do it."

Polly laughed. "I don't blame you. The old witch." She leaned the broom she carried against the wall and dropped her buckets of soap and rags next to them. She tucked her golden braid beneath her cap, pushed her sleeves up above her sturdy forearms, and tightened the strings of her borrowed apron.

Christianna followed suit, trying to look as capable and determined as Polly, even though her shoulders already ached from the long walk with the heavy bucket.

"The first thing to do," Polly announced, marching into the musty room and surveying the dirt as though it was an enemy, "is we haul all this rubbish out of here. Then we burn it."

Christianna followed. There was a blackened fireplace littered with broken glass against one wall and a shuttered window opposite. She brushed the cobwebs from the window, pushed it open with a good deal of effort, and struggled with the heavy shutters.

Polly joined her, and when they succeeded in forcing the stubborn shutters open, more light and air poured in.

Christianna stepped back and wiped her blackened hands on the voluminous folds of Mrs. Hatton's apron, which almost wrapped around her twice.

"It looks even worse in the light," she said, looking around. "Where do I start?"

Polly kicked at a broken stool. "Anywhere. Let's just get rid of it all."

Trying not to look at it, Christianna picked up an old kettle in one hand and a fishing pole in the other.

"And you can tell me about France while we work," Polly added. "Did you really know the queen? Did you really have five hundred gowns?"

"Yes, and no," Christianna answered, smiling at Polly. "Not even near five hundred."

Polly looked disappointed.

"But I did have a good many," Christianna added hastily, "and my friend Gabrielle had a hundred. And shoes to match each one."

"All French," Polly sighed. "Fancy that."

Christianna wanted to point out that it was France, after all; but Polly seemed to have a high regard for things French, in the same way that Mrs. Hatton had a suspicious disregard for them.

"All French," she agreed. "And her own hairdresser, and five little pug dogs. Each one had a diamond collar."

"Diamonds on bloody dogs!" Polly shrieked with dismay; and Christianna had to admit that it sounded a little stupid.

"I'd knock those hairy little dogs over and keep their collars for myself, if I ever saw such a thing," Polly added, and Christianna, who had felt much the same from time to time, laughed aloud as they set to work.

By noon, the cottage was empty of everything but the bedframe, and Christianna and Polly were on their hands and knees, scrubbing floors and walls with Mrs. Hatton's thick brown soap. The lye in the soap stung Christianna's blistered fingers, but it was very effective in removing the dirt and grease.

"Pearls and roses in your hair," Polly said dreamily. "I'd love to see an opera. And what did Artois give you for your birthday?"

"Earrings," Christianna answered softly. "Eight diamonds on each one, and a big fat pearl teardrop hanging down. As big as my fingertips." She straightened her aching back for a moment and flexed her stiff fingers before gripping the heavy wooden scrub brush, and bending over the floor again.

"Diamonds and pearls," Polly echoed. "Did you let him at you?"

"Did I . . . oh! Oh, no. Nothing like that. He wouldn't have. Not in a million years."

"Hmmph," Polly remarked in a suspicious tone. "Sounds like a funny sort of man, if you ask me."

Christianna smiled, watching Polly dump more water over the floorboards. "But a good friend."

"I guess," Polly said. "Eight diamonds. I'd like to find me a nobleman to set me up and buy me earrings. I'd give him a tumble he'd remember, that's what."

"Artois didn't want a tumble,'" Christianna explained. "He . . . well, he didn't like women. Not for that."

Polly looked shocked. "What a waste," she commented. "Did you ever try?"

"Oh, never! He'd have been horrified."

"Funny sort of man," Polly repeated. "Though he did give you diamonds. That's something."

They worked in silence for a while, and then Polly stood up and tossed the dirty scrub water out the door.

"This is about as clean as it'll get," Polly declared. "What do you think?"

Christianna thought that she'd never scrub another floor again as long as she lived. She ached from head to toe, and her hands felt tight and sore and stung from the strong soap; but she had to admit that the cottage looked good.

The creamy plaster walls were clean and bright. Polly had scrubbed the window with vinegar until the diamond-shaped panes sparkled and the floorboards were smooth and pale, bleached with the strong lye.

"It's lovely," she proclaimed, struggling to her feet. "I thank you, Polly."

Polly looked pleased. "Nothing of it," she shrugged. "It was nice to spend the time. Most women don't like me, you know."

Christianna could see why. Polly was pretty

in a golden, overblown way that men loved, and she knew it. She made no bones about her lusty appetites, and apparently didn't see any reason to deny herself. "They ask," Polly had confided, "and I can't help meself. I've a soft heart."

"Now," Polly said, "we take those old traps down to the house and Gareth can tell us what he wants done with them, and then we move your things up and we're done."

"You can talk to Gareth," Christianna said quickly. "I don't want to."

Polly turned around, her eyes lighting up with curiosity. "Is that so? Why is that? Is he the reason you don't want to stay in the house?"

Christianna stood up awkwardly, trying not to trip on the too-long skirt that Polly had appropriated for her, and removed the plain white cap from her head, shaking out her curls. "Perhaps," she admitted.

Polly seemed delighted. "Tell!" she demanded. "What happened? Did you—"

"Polly! Is that all you ever think of?"

"Mostly," Polly admitted cheerfully. "And it doesn't take a lot to figure it out. The way you were watching him and the way he looked at you, and you being so eager to get away that you'd spend the day cleaning a hellhole like this. Did you?"

Christianna sighed. "No, Polly, I can't. You see, my brother is going to send for me, as soon as he can; and when I get to New Orleans he'll help me find a rich husband. If I want a good marriage, I have to stay . . . untouched."

Polly shrieked with horror. "You mean to say you *never?*"

Christianna blushed. "No," she said abruptly.

Polly shook her head, her eyes wide with wonder. "How can you not? I'd die, meself."

"Never mind," Christianna answered. "Shall we get those traps down to the house?"

Polly nodded, but didn't take the hint. "That's why Gareth won't lend you the money to get to New Orleans, I'd bet. He wants to keep you here, for himself."

Christianna considered this. "I don't think so. He doesn't like me."

Polly snorted. "What's liking got to do with it?" she asked in a brusque tone. "But I'll tell you what—if you really want to get passage to New Orleans, come down to the Broken Bow and we'll put you to work. Nothing like having a bit of money to call your own. Me, I don't like to depend on others."

"I don't either," Christianna agreed.

Christianna followed Polly out into the bright afternoon, and they gathered up the heavy traps and made their way back to the house.

The sheep were crowded into the sheepfold, bleating piteous cries as they awaited their turns.

The men were working quickly, laughing and teasing each other about their skill, or lack of it, as they went about the shearing.

Gareth and Richard were the fastest, the most skilled shearers. They lifted each sheep up to the makeshift wooden table beneath the shady trees, and Daniel and Stewart held the frightened animals still as their brothers wielded the long, heavy shears.

They worked quickly and skillfully, the long shears moving close to the sheep's skin, beneath the fleece. The fleece, when properly cut, would fall away in one smooth, even piece, and Geoffery would rush it away to the barn, where they would be bundled and sorted for the wool merchant.

Christianna was fascinated by the quick pace of the routine, the easy rhythm. The men had all abandoned their shirts during the heat of the day, and everywhere she looked strong arms and bare backs glistened in the sun.

Look at him," Polly whispered in her ear, nudging her arm. "Just look."

Christianna looked at Gareth as he sweated in the sunlight—the smooth, glistening muscles of his chest, the lean, hard line of his stomach. His arms moved with an easy grace as he sheared through the heavy fleece of the animal before him. There was not an inch of spare flesh anywhere on his hard body, and Christianna felt a flush of heat as she watched the movement of his lean hips. She looked away. "Stop it, Polly."

"What are you afraid of?" Polly demanded, taking off her apron and adjusting her bodice to better show her impressive cleavage. "Take that apron off," she added. "I'll tell you what you're afraid of: giving in. Silly girl. You should just try it."

Christianna blushed, but she took off her

apron and made an attempt to tame her black curls. "Polly, I couldn't. My brother will arrange a marriage for me, and I—"

"Piss!" Polly exclaimed with a derisive look. "If I've been a virgin once, I've faked it at least ten times. Don't you know anything?"

Apparently not, Christianna thought, wondering how such a thing was possible.

"Geoffery," Polly called, and Geoff tossed the fleece he was carrying to another man and trotted across the grass to them, jumping over the wooden rails of the sheepfold.

"What's about?" he asked cheerily, wiping the sweat from his thin face. His gray eyes moved with curiosity from Polly to Christianna. "Look at you," he exclaimed, taking in Christianna's simple skirt, the full-sleeved blouse beneath the tightly laced, sleeveless black bodice. "You look like a regular girl. Aren't those Vic's old things?"

Polly tucked her arm beneath Geoff's, and Christianna was surprised at the change in her. She sparkled; she moved like a cat.

"Geoff, we need your help. Will you?"

Geoffery nodded, without question.

"Good. You're the darlingest. Go get a cart and help us move some things to Alden's cottage."

Geoff glanced back at the shearing.

"Thank you so," Polly added, and she leaned forward and pressed her lips to Geoffery's sharp cheekbone. He colored and smiled stupidly.

"What are we moving?" he asked obediently.

"Oh, just a few things," Polly said sweetly. "A

clean mattress, a table, a chair, Christianna's things. A barrel of water, if you can. Oh, and Geoff—find a place for those old traps over there, will you?"

Geoffery trotted off toward the barn, and Polly cast Christianna a smile of triumph. "There. That was a snap."

Christianna laughed. "Polly, you're a gem. I couldn't have lifted another finger without collapsing dead on the spot."

"You're just not used to hard work," Polly said kindly. "Come on; let's go get something to eat while Geoffery does the rest of the work."

"Are you sure you won't come down to the house, just for a bit?" Polly asked.

Christianna shook her head. "No. I'm far too tired, truly, Polly." She picked up a candlestick and set it on top of the scrubbed mantelpiece, next to a glass of pink rosebuds and ivy that Polly had taken from the garden.

The little cottage bore no resemblance to the dusty cave it had been that morning.

Geoffery had put the feather mattress from Christianna's room onto the scrubbed wooden frame after Polly had expertly tightened the supporting ropes. Christianna had made the bed herself, with the lavender-scented linens and blankets from her room at the farmhouse.

A small table, a chair, a washbowl, and a candlestand transformed the room into a simple but habitable place.

Christianna's trunk stood at the end of the

bed and she opened it, digging through her few belongings. If only she hadn't lost all of her things when she had left Paris. Phillipe had tried his best to replace her wardrobe in London, but time and money hadn't allowed for much.

"Here, Polly," she said at last. "Take these, please. For your help."

Polly reached out and took the offered objects—a little cap of heavy Venetian lace and a matching fichu of gossamer voile, trimmed in the same heavy, silken lace.

"Truly?" she asked, touching the cap with a reverent finger, her freckled face blank with surprise. She touched the finely sewn seams, the lifelike clusters of pink silk roses at the side.

"Of course," Christianna said. "It will suit you."

Polly went to the pilfered looking glass they had taken from the house, and discarded her own simple cap and scarf, turning slowly to admire herself in the new.

"Thank you," she said awkwardly, and Christianna was surprised to hear a catch in her voice. "I . . . I've never owned anything so fine. I feel like a duchess."

Embarrassed to find her small offering received with such gratitude, Christianna said nothing.

"Are you sure you won't come back to the house and see the party?" Polly asked again.

"No," Christianna repeated. "I think I'll stay here and rest. I really am exhausted, Polly. I've never worked so hard in my life."

"Suit yourself," Polly said. "All the more men for me." She laughed her husky laugh, tossed her golden head, and went toward the door of the cottage, where she stopped suddenly. "May I come back and visit you again?" she asked quickly. "It's so nice to have a friend."

Surprised, Christianna nodded. "Of course," she answered, and she felt a warming in her heart. "You're right, Polly. It's very good to have a friend."

She sat on the stone steps of the cottage for a long time after Polly left, watching the sun turn the sky gold and rose and crimson and the field darken.

From the house, she could hear much shouting and laughter, and an occasional burst of song. She wondered if Gareth would notice her absence. Probably not. She was an annoyance, an intruder.

She closed her eyes, listening to the crickets, a thin, reedy sound. A sudden crackling in the underbrush made her jump, her heart pounding with fear.

She gave a startled laugh as Dog appeared, her white-tipped tail wagging, a full loaf of bread in her mouth.

"You stupid animal," Christianna said aloud. "Did you come all this way to plague me?"

Dog sat on the hem of her skirts and leaned heavily against her knee, not seeming to care that she was unwelcome.

Christianna was too tired and stiff to push her away. She leaned back against the doorframe and rested her hand on Dog's solid back.

The animal sighed, dropped her loaf of bread, and rested her large nose on Christianna's knee, gazing at her with adoring brown eyes.

"Stupid thing," Christianna repeated, but continued to stroke the warm, sleek back and, after a few minutes, she began to take comfort in the solid, warm presence next to her, and fondled the long, silky ears.

They sat together in the darkening night and watched the moon rise over the wooded hills, listening to the sounds of the crickets and the distant merriment. Every now and then the dog or Christianna sighed, until the quiet sounds of the country night lulled them to sleep.

Gareth sat in the silence of the house, taking note of the day's work in the farm ledger. A good, full day's work. They'd make a fine profit.

"Gareth?" He looked up to see Geoffery in the doorway.

"Horses in? Everything locked up?"

"Aye, and everyone's gone. Stewart's finishing up in the dairy."

"Thanks." He turned back to his work, the pen scratching over the paper. "Oh, Geoff—have you seen Dog?"

"No, not today. Some dog—won't help with the sheep."

Daniel stuck his head in the door, looking worried. "Gareth, Christianna's gone."

Gareth looked up, startled. "Gone where?"

"I don't know. I went to her room and it's empty."

"What were you doing in her room?" Gareth demanded sharply, and Daniel lifted his brow in quiet reproach.

"Taking her a book, if you don't mind."

"She's at the cottage," Geoffery said helpfully. "I helped her move in. Polly helped her clean it, and it looks grand."

Gareth sighed and rested his head in his hands. "That stubborn little twit," he muttered.

"She really hates you, Gareth," Geoffery added none too diplomatically. "Told Polly that she's going to New Orleans if she has to swim. Do you want another beer?"

Gareth looked up from his ledger at the half-empty mug before him. "No. I've had more than enough, and so have you."

"Why did she leave?" Daniel asked quietly, tucking his book beneath his arm.

Gareth met his eyes without flinching. "I don't think it's any of your concern. Maybe because she's an arrogant brat who doesn't want to soil her hands by coming too close to the peasants. Bloody useless gentry."

Daniel leaned his tall frame across Gareth's desk. "I'd like to remind you that our mother was also 'bloody useless gentry.' As for it not being any of my concern, you're wrong. Christianna is as much my concern as yours. More, maybe."

"What the hell does that mean?"

"What the hell do you know about her?" Daniel asked. "Did you ever think that she has reason to mistrust us? Did it ever occur to you that she's genuinely suffering?"

Gareth was quiet for a moment, startled by the quiet anger in Daniel's usually tranquil eyes.

"Suffering?" he asked after a moment. "Why? Because she doesn't have a maid to dress her and fetch her shoes for her?"

"It's not like you, Gareth, to be so hard, or stupid. Do you think she just walked away from a revolution unscathed? As to why she's suffering, if she chooses to confide in you, she may. I'll not break her confidence."

Gareth shut the ledger with a sharp bang. "I didn't realize that you two were so close."

"I didn't realize that you'd react like a jealous ass."

Geoffery stared at his brothers in dismay. "I think you're both acting like asses," he remarked.

"Piss off," they exclaimed in unison.

"It's true. If she wants to live in Uncle Alden's cottage, who cares? If she wants to go work at the Broken Bow with Polly, who cares?"

"She *what?*" Gareth burst out, his eyes darkening.

Geoffery flinched. "She mentioned it. Said she wants passage to New Orleans, and you refused to lend her the money."

"Why is she so eager to get away, Gareth?" Daniel asked again. "What's happened between you?"

"Mind your own damned business," Gareth said rudely. He left the room abruptly, his boots echoing over the wooden floor.

"Touchy bastard, isn't he?" Geoffery remarked.

Daniel pushed his spectacles to the top of his head and gave his youngest brother a tired look. "Bugger off, Geoff."

"Bugger you too," Geoffrey replied, assuming an expression of injured dignity. "I'm going to find Richard and Stewart and see if they'll have another beer. You and Gareth are both touchy bastards. Must be getting old."

When Gareth approached the cottage at the foot of the wooded hill he was greeted with a low growl.

He stopped and peered ahead into the darkness. "Dog? Is that you, girl?" he asked softly, and heard a tail thump in response. "Stupid animal," he muttered. "Growling at your own master."

His eyes adjusted to the darkness as he moved forward, and he saw Dog leaning against Christianna's side.

She was sleeping against the frame of the open door, her head leaning against one shoulder, one arm around Dog's sturdy back. Dog regarded Gareth with a suspicious eye, leaned her nose against Christianna's knee, and went back to sleep.

Gareth stood silently, watching Christianna for a minute. She was sleeping solidly, her dark lashes fanned against her pale cheeks. Her bosom rose and fell with her breathing, a soft and enticing motion.

Gareth moved quietly around her, blinking with surprise as he entered the dark cottage. It smelled of soap and fresh air and, faintly, roses. He searched his pocket for a flint, struck it, and lit the fresh candle that stood on the mantelpiece.

She had worked, and worked hard. The place had changed from a dingy, rubbish-filled room to a light, clean space. He wondered how she had gotten the table and chair up from the house. There was a stack of books on the table, and a sheet of paper, half covered in writing.

He picked it up, frowning at the foreign words, wishing that he had paid closer attention to his lessons.

Mon cher ami Artois . . .

He laid the paper down, suddenly aware that he was intruding. He walked to the open door and looked down at Christianna. Her face was very soft and peaceful-looking. A smudge of dirt was across one cheek; the hand that lay across her lap was blistered and red. For the first time he noticed that she was wearing one of his sister's old dresses—a battered, homespun skirt of moss green over a full-sleeved white chemise, and a plain black bodice, tightly laced.

He stood in the doorway for some time, staring at the crescent moon suspended over the dark hills, listening to the night song of the woods, the crickets, and the soft breeze moving through the trees.

When Christianna spoke it startled him.

"No," she said clearly, and when he glanced

down at her he saw that she was still sleeping. Her hand twitched a little and rose, and then fell back to her lap. Her eyelids flickered lightly and then were still.

At her side, Dog sighed contentedly, scratched at a flea, and then lay quietly.

Gareth stepped quietly around them and sat on the low stone step, watching her. So, she thought she might work at the Broken Bow. He tried to imagine her carrying heavy mugs of beer, or seizing a drunken man by the arm and shoving him out the door, as Polly did. The thought made him smile.

On the other hand, she was just stubborn and contrary enough to do it. He had laughed to see her pulling brambles and weeds in the garden, and she had done it. He'd been sure that she would return meekly to the house once she had seen the state of the cottage, and here she was.

And looking like the work had almost killed her, he told himself. She hadn't stirred, not even when Dog growled, nor when he had stepped over her and walked about the room.

She made a slight sound and, as Gareth watched, a tear slid out of the corner of her eye and slipped down her cheek. It stopped by the corner of her soft mouth, shining softly in the darkness.

What did she dream of that made her cry in her sleep? Perhaps her lover. Perhaps her home.

"It's as much my concern as yours," Daniel had said. What in the devil did he mean by that? What was she doing, keeping secrets with Daniel? What confidences had she shared with his brother?

Gareth thought about the moment in the lake, when she had looked at him with her eyes hot and brilliant and hungry. How she had quivered at his touch, and the way she had pressed her silken body against him . . .

He grew hard at the memory, and felt a flush of anger. *Don't forget,* he told himself, *how she took her pleasure and turned against you, cursing you.* "Filthy bastard," she had called him, her soft mouth bitter with rage.

"You're mad, Christianna St. Sebastien," he whispered. "And you're driving me mad, as well." He blew a stray lock of hair from his eyes and sighed. "Mad or not, I'll not leave you to sleep out here. You'll be half frozen by morning. Move, Dog." He rolled the heavy animal off Christianna's skirts and stood up, lifting the sleeping girl easily in his arms. Then he carried her into the quiet cottage.

Chapter Ten

In her dream, Christianna stood outside the cottage in the French countryside. The October night was cold, and the air smelled of smoke.

"Where is my brother, monsieur?"

Jean-Claude smiled at her, showing his broken, blackened teeth. "In time. Now we must see my brother."

She shivered in her heavy cape and hesitated. Her violin was clutched against her heart, the soft leather warm from the heat of her body.

"You said that you were taking me to my brother."

"Get in the cottage, Mademoiselle Aristocrat, before we're arrested. It's dangerous for your kind to be about; or had you forgotten?"

Gabrielle. Her sightless eyes, the blood in her thick golden hair.

"No, I haven't forgotten." *She stepped forward, stumbling in the rutted drive, the mud that was beginning to freeze. The ground was hard beneath her soft shoes; a layer of frost sparkled in the wan moonlight.*

The door of the cottage was opening, and panic surged through her body. Don't go in there, run away, anywhere; don't go in the door—

She came up fighting, a strangled cry choking her, twisting away from the hands that held her. A strong arm was clutching her shoulder; her wrist was seized in a fierce grip—

"Christianna! It's me, Gareth!"

She froze. Her heart was thundering, and for a moment she couldn't breathe. Then, slowly, the real world came into focus.

The smell of soap and clean air, and the smell of grass cooling in the night air. She saw the glass of rosebuds that Polly had put on the mantelpiece, perfect and pink in the circle of golden candlelight. The letter to Artois, half written on the table—*My dear friend Artois, today I decided that you were dead; but I am writing to you anyway*...

And Gareth, smelling of sunlight and warm skin and fresh air, holding her tightly against the rough fabric of his shirt, his heartbeat clear and strong in the quiet night, his breath coming quickly.

She tried to stop herself from trembling, but it happened, as it always did when the nightmares came. She shook wildly, her legs and hands trembling as if with cold.

She knew that if she tried to stand her legs wouldn't support her; so she simply closed her eyes and waited for the shaking to subside, as she knew it would.

"Damn." Gareth's voice was a husky whisper. "Are you ill?"

"No." She shook her head and made a weak attempt to laugh. "I'm sorry."

"Don't be." He made no move to put her down; just stared into her face with his green eyes dark, almost frightened. "What was it?"

"Nothing." Too much. Too much to explain, too painful to say it out loud.

"Bloody frightening nothing, if you ask me."

She said nothing, and after a minute he carried her across the small room and laid her on the bed, still watching her carefully. He pulled up the worn wooden chair and sat next to her, his long legs stretched out comfortably, his hair dark in the soft light from the candle.

He was quiet for a while, and Christianna envied his tranquillity, his calm silence. He smiled at her, his teeth white in the tanned gold of his face.

He leaned forward and took her hand, turning it over in his own and touching the reddened, blistered surface.

"What have you done with your soft white hands, my lady?" he asked softly, and the single dimple in his cheek deepened.

Christianna was grateful that he had changed the subject and glad of his company in the silent cottage, where her nightmare seemed so close and real. He was real, and earthy, so far removed from the world she had known before.

"I moved your bloody traps," she said, "and all the rest of the garbage that was in here."

"Very nice," Gareth said. "The boys will be heartbroken." He made no move to release her hand, and Christianna was glad of the steady warmth. It was a comforting feeling.

"Why will they be heartbroken?" she asked, not wanting him to leave. There was nothing worse, after a nightmare, than to be alone, with nothing to distract her from the ugly memories.

"Well, this cottage is where they lure the local girls. There's not much privacy in the house."

"I noticed," Christianna said. She made a face. "I'm glad I burned the blankets."

Gareth laughed softly. "Did you? I'm not surprised. You've worked hard today."

"Polly did most of it," Christianna confided. "She's very strong, isn't she?" Gareth's callused fingers were warm and strong over her hand; his thumb was circling softly in the palm of her hand. A warm, pleasant tingle was radiating from his touch. Christianna swallowed and tried to remember what they had been talking about.

"We missed you at dinner tonight. It was jolly. Lots of company; lots of beer. Shearing time is grand. Now there's not so much to do, except watch the plants grow."

"I was too tired," Christianna explained. "And I really didn't feel like . . . like I belonged. All I seem to do is get in the way and cause trouble."

He smiled. "You do cause trouble. Even when you're not there. Daniel was demanding to know why you've left. What shall I tell him?"

Christianna blushed. "Anything but the truth," she suggested.

"That sounds simple, doesn't it? But it isn't. I've never lied to my brother before, and he's never kept secrets from me. And now I find that we're doing just that."

"Tell him what you like," she said. "Everyone thinks the worst of me anyway. What does it matter to me?" Her words were flippant and bitter. She pulled her hand from Gareth's and looked away from his bright, soft gaze.

"Geoffery tells us that you're thinking of working at the Broken Bow. I don't think you'll like it. I can't see you working around a bunch of drunken sots."

"Polly thinks I can. She says that I'll make a lot of money. Perhaps enough to pay my own passage to New Orleans. And it isn't any of your affair, anyway. Why should it concern you?"

Gareth tipped his chair back and appeared to think about that. "It concerns me," he said at last, "for different reasons. For one, your brother left you under our protection, and I don't think that he'd care to have you hefting beers in a public house. For another, I don't think you'd like the company, and I don't mean Poll. Bar wenches aren't exactly treated with respect, sweetheart. They're pinched and kissed by whoever feels like it. And lastly, I wouldn't like it."

Christianna's heart skipped a beat, and she looked closely at his face to see if he was teasing her.

"Against my better judgment," he added quietly, "I find that I care about you—bad-tempered or not. God knows why. Perhaps I'm a glutton for punishment."

His quiet words sent her pulse racing, and she felt a warm glow. *I care about you.* Simple words. How strange that they would touch her so, make her heart quiver like the strings of an instrument—a soft, vibrant hum.

She looked up at Gareth and saw that he was studying his fingernails with great interest, his handsome face shadowed by the candlelight.

"Well." He tipped the chair forward and gave her a quick, almost sad smile. "I should go. I just came to see how you were, and you were sleeping on the stoop. Thought I should bring you in, or you'd wake up frozen and in knots."

She didn't want him to go. She didn't want to be alone in the cottage, she told herself. *No,* she corrected herself, *you want him to stay, and touch your hand again, and look at you with his green eyes. You want him to kiss you, you imbecile.*

She thought of being in the lake—her breasts full and aching against his chest, her legs wrapped around his strong hips, his tongue against her own.

A rush of heat sped through her, and she felt her cheeks warming; her lips seemed to tingle.

Who would ever know? "If I've been a virgin

once, I've been a virgin ten times," Polly had said. How was such a thing done? Polly would know.

Christianna drew a quivering breath and looked up at Gareth. He was still sitting quietly, his eyes on her, a thick strand of hair hanging over his high forehead.

"Stay." She spoke the word quickly, so quickly that it was barely there.

Gareth startled and leaned forward slightly. He watched her lowered lashes, the slight tremble of her mouth, the sudden, hot color that stained her slanting cheekbones.

"Oh, Christianna." He sighed and tipped the chair back. "Stay? Just like that? Stay?"

She was blushing furiously.

He looked at her carefully, without blinking. "Why?"

Christianna hadn't expected that. Such a simple question, but what could she say? Silently she answered, *Because you're good, and gentle; and when you look at me with your soft eyes I feel like I've been healed. Because you're so alive and strong and real, and it takes me away from the past. And I think that maybe, if you loved me, I would be whole again.*

Ah, she could never say such a thing! She shrugged and said aloud, "I don't know. Does it matter?"

Did Gareth look disappointed by her answer? He studied his fingernails again, then looked up at her with a quick, soft smile. "I suppose not. You surprised me, that's all. Stay, her ladyship says. Do you think that's wise? For your sake?"

"I don't care," she retorted, exasperated. "Must you always be so kind? What does it matter to you?"

He laughed at that, a good-natured, loud laugh. Christianna looked down at the blankets and bit her lip.

"Why should I stay, Christianna?" His voice was gentle and teasing.

She glanced up at him through her lashes. His eyes were bright and warm.

She knew what he wanted her to say. Well, damn him, he would have it, and then some. She leaned up on her elbow and reached her hand out and laid it against the warm skin of his neck and stroked it. She looked directly into his eyes and spoke.

"I want you."

"Ah. That's hard to say no to." His voice was husky, a low whisper. "But do you mean it? I seem to remember that yesterday you called me a filthy bastard, and cursed me roundly for touching you. And left me with a battering ram in my breeches that could've knocked down walls."

She blushed to the roots of her hair. "I mean it."

He leaned over her and kissed her slowly, taking her lower lip between his and teasing it with the soft heat of his tongue until she felt herself growing breathless.

"Prove it," he whispered.

She lifted her head, unsure of what to do. Prove it? Did he mean for her to seduce him?

He leaned back and tipped back his head and smiled his lazy, calm smile.

Christianna hesitated only for a minute. She rose from the bed, crossed the floor to the open door, and closed it firmly, dropping the bolt into place.

"As you wish," she said, and wondered if he recognized his own words. If he wanted her to seduce him, she would.

She tried to remember everything she had heard about seduction. She wasn't completely without knowledge, she told herself. At Versailles, the ladies discussed their lovers and affairs as casually as they discussed their gowns.

She went to the candle and was about to extinguish it, but Gareth spoke abruptly.

"No. Leave the light. If you're going to do this, I want you to know that it's me. You'll not hide from me in the darkness and pretend that I'm some handsome nobleman from your past."

Christianna gave a short, startled laugh. "Is that what you think?"

He said nothing, just cocked a brow and smiled.

She swallowed, and her hands fluttered helplessly. "Very well."

He leaned forward, his elbows resting on his knees, and rested his chin on his hands. His eyes were bright with interest, and she felt like a mouse in a trap.

"Well?" he said. "This is something new to me. How do noblewomen seduce their lovers, Christianna?"

She drew a deep, shaking breath. "Madame Alfort," she answered lightly, "had herself carried into her lover's dinner table, naked, on a silver platter, wearing only grapes. And the diamond bracelet he'd given her."

Gareth's brows shot up. "Sounds expensive."

"Oh, it was. Her husband was furious."

"I should think he would be."

"Not about her lover: about the cost of the silver, for the plate. And the servants, to carry it. And the Marquesse Alvârre paid a troop of dancers to perform a ballet, completely without clothing. I understand that it was very effective."

"I can imagine."

"It's not so terrible, after all, to take a lover," she said quickly, hoping to convince herself. "Everyone does, after all."

"Do they? Then by all means, go ahead. Far be it from me to stop you."

Christianna had imagined her first night of love would be very different than this. She took a deep breath and crossed the room and stood before him.

"I'm not sure of how to go about it."

He laughed softly. "I would imagine that seducing a peasant isn't all that different from seducing a lord, minus the silver platters and naked ballet dancers. Why don't you just kiss me?"

She bent over and touched her lips to his, and her breath caught at the heat, the softness. Hesitantly, she stroked his lips with the tip of her tongue and tasted the warm, salty flavor of his skin, and the surprisingly pleasant taste of beer.

He reached up and pulled her to his lap, and took her mouth beneath his, his strong, work-roughened fingers playing along her cheek and moving beneath her hair.

Heat flowed through her veins, sparkling and fast, and she put her hands in his hair, pulling his mouth closer over hers. His tongue played inside her mouth, a hot insistent stroking.

She felt his hand at her breast, loosening the laces of her bodice and slipping inside the loose neckline of the chemise. He touched her nipple lightly at first, and she felt it tingle and stiffen between his fingers.

She quivered at the sensation and felt herself growing warm and damp, and she pressed herself more tightly against him.

"Sweet." His whisper sent a thrill through her, and his mouth trailed to the soft hollow of skin at the base of her throat. "You taste like strawberries and roses."

She was breathless, and her mouth felt empty without his.

He raised his head and placed a firm hand beneath her chin, raising her eyes to look into his own.

"You'll not turn me away again, will you? You'll not push me away and call me names and look down your nose?"

"No," she whispered, and her voice quivered in the quiet room, like the dying note of a harpsichord.

"Undress."

She felt her cheeks burning, though with shame or desire, she wasn't sure. She stared at his face, at the smooth, high brow, and his strange, pale green eyes, and the strong, clean line of his jaw. Strong, like him. Honest and open; nothing hidden.

She bent her head and began pulling the thin laces from her bodice, then shook it from her shoulders. She stood on shaking legs and unfastened the heavy green skirt, then let it fall to the floor. She pulled the thin white chemise from her shoulders, and it followed with a faint whisper.

She stood proudly and pulled the pins from her hair and let it fall, thick and curling to her waist. The cold air of the room and the heat of Gareth's gaze caused her to shiver.

"Christianna," he whispered, and ran his hands over the white skin of her stomach and the swell of her hips, and up over her ribs. His sun-bronzed hands looked very dark against the white of her skin.

Her nipples throbbed when he reached up to cup her breasts in his hands, the rose-colored buds aching beneath his touch.

"God, but you're lovely. All pink and white . . ." His hands were sliding over her waist, reaching behind her to her derriere, running smoothly over the round curves.

"Beautiful," he murmured.

He leaned forward and pressed his mouth to the soft skin of her stomach, to the curve of her

205

hip. His hair brushed over her skin as he pulled her toward him, and his lips trailed over the swell of her hip and around to the tender skin of her derriere. She quivered at the sensation, and her hands grasped his shoulders as she steadied herself.

Without another word he stood and began undressing. He pulled his shirt over his head and tossed it aside, revealing the sun-bronzed skin of his chest, strong and taut and smooth. He took the dark, frayed ribbon from his hair, and it fell over his shoulders, giving him a wild, almost barbaric air.

He smiled almost impishly at her wide-eyed gaze as he undid the twin rows of buttons that ran down the slender lines of his hips, and he disposed of his breeches and boots with an easy grace.

She looked, and looked away again quickly, almost frightened by the heat of her hunger, her desire to reach out and touch the hard, long length of him.

He seemed not at all ill at ease with his own nakedness, and he moved to the bed with a comfortable motion, shaking his hair back from his eyes.

"Come here, my lady," he murmured, and held out his arms to her, "And teach me the ways of the gentry."

She moved into his arms as easily as if a wind had tossed her there, and felt for the first time the incredible sensation of bare skin against bare skin, from neck to foot—like the feeling of warm velvet caressing her body.

His mouth covered hers again, this time with a strength and insistence that shook her, and she felt as if their skin was melting together.

His hands moved hungrily and quickly over her body, lingering at her breasts, tangling in her hair, pulling her body closer to the hot, smooth shaft that pressed against the very center of her with an almost unbearable heat.

"My own," he whispered when his mouth left hers, and a hot thrill rushed through her at the sound.

She ran her hands over his chest and his arms, marveling at his strength, at the feeling of hard muscles beneath warm skin, intoxicated by the scent of his body and the rich taste of his mouth.

She buried her hands in his hair and felt the silk of it in her fingers; her body wrapped itself around the strength of his with an instinct as old as time.

She moaned aloud as he rolled her beneath him and his fingers sought the secret places between her legs, sliding easily into the damp heat.

"Christianna." His voice was rough and low, and she opened her eyes, unwilling to leave the dark, swirling sensations that surrounded her.

She was startled by the pale light that shone in his eyes, the hunger, the desire. His breathing was rough and ragged.

"Tomorrow," he whispered, his eyes burning into her face, "tomorrow you may hate me, and curse me if you wish, but this night, you're mine."

She tried to speak, but she was beyond words. She lifted her mouth to his, her body writhing beneath him with a dark hunger.

Without warning, he drove into her, hard and fast and strong, filling her completely.

Her cry was lost beneath his shout of triumph.

For a moment, she thought of how peculiar it was, how strange it felt, a stretched, aching fullness.

And then he took her mouth beneath his, and the honey-sweet warmth rushed through her again, and her arms pulled him to her body.

They were one, her softness and his strength, moving in a rhythm and movement sweeter than any music that had ever been written, a brilliant harmony of heat and light.

His heart was pounding against hers; her legs were twined around his; their mouths met again and again, hungry and seeking.

Her hips writhed against him and he filled her over and over again, and she was lost in the sensation, a roaring light that lifted her higher and higher, a heat that flooded her body like sunlight. The taste of his skin, the sound of his breath, the whisper of his hair against her cheek . . .

He half lifted her from the bed and pulled her body tightly against him, a strong hand gripping her derriere. She clung to his shoulders and felt herself opening wider to the heat and strength.

Thrill to the most sensual, adventure-filled Historical Romances on the market today...

FROM ⬛ *LEISURE BOOKS*

As a home subscriber to the Leisure Romance Book Clu[b] you'll enjoy the best in today's BRAND-NEW Historica[l] Romance fiction. For over twenty years, Leisure Book[s] has brought you the award-winning, high-quality author[s] you know and love to read. Each Leisure Historica[l] Romance will sweep you away to a world of high adven[ture]...and intimate romance. Discover for yourself all th[e] passion and excitement millions of readers thrill to eac[h] and every month.

Save $5.⁰⁰ Each Time You Buy!

Six times a year, the Leisure Romance Book Club brings you four brand-new titles from Leisure Books, America's foremost publisher of Historical Romances. EACH PACKAGE WILL SAVE YOU $5.00 FROM THE BOOKSTORE PRICE! And you'll never miss a new title with our convenient home delivery service.

Here's how we do it. Each package will carry a FREE 10-DAY EXAMINATION privilege. At the end of that time, if you decide to keep your books, simply pay the low invoice price of $14.96, no shipping or handling charges added. HOME DELIVERY IS ALWAYS FREE. With today's top Historical Romance novels selling for $4.99 and higher, our price SAVES YOU $5.00 with each shipment.

AND YOUR FIRST FOUR-BOOK SHIPMENT IS TOTALLY FRE[E]
IT'S A BARGAIN YOU CAN'T BEAT! A Super $19.96 Value!

⬛ **LEISURE BOOKS** *A Division of Dorchester Publishing Co., Inc.*

Get Four Books Totally FREE— A $19.96 Value!

PLEASE RUSH
MY FOUR FREE
BOOKS TO ME
RIGHT AWAY!

Leisure Romance Book Club
65 Commerce Road
Stamford CT 06902-4563

AFFIX
STAMP
HERE

A dark roar filled her ears; sensations of silver and lightning were blazing through her body, each one sharper and brighter and hotter than the last, until she heard her own voice in a wild, rough cry of blind passion, and around her, the world shattered in brilliant arrows of sensation.

Gareth's answering groan reached her through a dark, rich haze, and she felt him shudder and felt the throbbing pulse of his climax deep within her body.

He said not a word to her afterward, just gathered her against his chest and kissed her face tenderly, raining gentle kisses on her eyelids and cheeks and mouth, and stroked her hair with an almost reverent touch.

And Christianna, shaken and exhausted by the depths of the passion they had shared, and feeling almost as if she had been touched by some healing magic, fell asleep thinking what a blissful and marvelous thing it was to have a warm, strong body in one's bed, and to feel cherished.

She had never felt so alive; she had never felt so much a part of the world. Outside the open window the crickets sang, and the breeze rustled the leaves of the trees, and Gareth's heart beat a steady rhythm beneath her ear. Was this what it felt like, to be loved? If so, it was a magical thing, the best thing in the world.

She slept with a peacefulness she had never known before.

Chapter Eleven

She was sitting at the battered little table by the cottage window, writing, the rose-colored light of early morning falling over her dark hair.

She was the first thing Gareth saw when he opened his heavy eyes, and regret stabbed at him.

Damn, what had he done? *Take care of my sister*, Phillipe had said. Gareth was relatively certain that he had taken care of her in ways that his brother-in-law would not approve of.

He had always been respected as a man of his word, and justly so. When he spoke to his neighbors or his brothers, they listened with respect and trust. He thought of Daniel, and the way his brother's eyes glowed when he spoke to Christianna.

And she had simply held out her white hand

and said, "Stay," and he had stayed, losing himself in the silken touch of her hands, the heavy black curls that moved like feathers over his skin, the hot, sweet grip of her, tighter and sweeter than any woman he had felt before. . . .

And now, very simply, he felt guilty.

He watched her silently as she wrote, unaware that she was being watched, her pen scratching over the paper, her bottom lip caught between her teeth. She smiled at what she had written, a soft, tender smile, and smoothed her hair back from her face.

She was dressed in the same pink silk she had worn the day she had arrived, and the stiff bodice straightened her spine and arched her shoulders back in the proud, graceful posture that the ladies of the aristocracy shared.

"Are you writing to your lover?"

She looked up, startled. It obviously wasn't the greeting she expected.

"I didn't know you were awake," she said at last, a deep rose color flushing over her cheeks.

"I wake before dawn. That is, I usually do."

She seemed at a loss for words, and her hands fluttered quickly, in that butterflylike way she had. Her cheeks were brilliant; her eyes dropped to the table.

Embarrassed, Gareth thought. Ashamed of what she had done, taking a hulking farmer to her dainty bed.

"What are you thinking, sweetheart?" he asked, keeping his tone light. "That you've sullied yourself? That you should never have asked?"

She stared at him with brilliant eyes, and her hands tightened. For a quick moment, she looked as if she might cry, and then a cool, brittle mask descended over her face.

She shrugged, as if it was a matter of indifference to her.

"You sound as if you're sorry. Should I not have asked?"

"No, you shouldn't have. And yes, I'm sorry."

Her back stiffened; her blue eyes looked cold. Again, she gave a careless shrug.

"I don't really care, monsieur. After all, nobody will ever know. We hardly move in the same circles, do we? I'll just go on to New Orleans, and my brother will arrange a good marriage for me, and everything will be as it was before."

She turned away abruptly, smoothing back her hair. Unbound, it looked too heavy to be supported by her slender neck.

Gareth cursed himself for the unexpected twist of sorrow that he felt when she spoke so casually of her future husband.

"Of course," he agreed. "How else could it be? You've had your pleasure, your little adventure. Tell me, my ladyship, how does a farmer compare to your fancy French lover?"

She stood up from the table, and only her clenched hands betrayed her anger. "I really wouldn't know, and I find this conversation very boring. Forgive me, monsieur, but it seems very crowded in here." She bent with a graceful motion, picked up his boots, and hurled them to the bed. "I'll thank you to be gone when I get back."

Gareth laughed at her icy dignity as she opened the cottage door.

"Cheer up," he suggested. "Mayhap your brother will send your passage soon, and you can wash your dainty hands of us and move on to better things."

Dog was still sleeping on the cottage steps, her bulky body blocking Christianna's way, and she looked up reproachfully as Christianna gave her a none-too-gentle shove with her foot.

"Go to hell, Monsieur Larkin," Christianna said over her shoulder. Failing to dislodge Dog, she stepped over her and started down the path toward the house. Gareth noticed that the pearl-sized buttons that trailed down her back were buttoned unevenly, and that she had missed two in the center of her back. For some reason, the sight touched him.

Dog gave Gareth a disdainful glance from her sad eyes, struggled to her stubby legs, and waddled off behind Christianna, wagging her white-tipped tail.

"Stupid dog," Gareth muttered, rubbing his forehead. To hell with Christianna, he told himself. She'd asked for a tumble, he'd given it to her, and if it made her feel better to act as if she'd been insulted, let her.

If he hadn't had so much to drink, he never would have agreed to it. He'd come here with the intention of setting her straight and ended up in her bed, seduced by her soft beauty. "It's not such a terrible thing," she had said. "People take lovers all the time."

Aye, perhaps they did, Gareth thought, but she was by far the sweetest creature he'd ever held in his arms, damn her arrogant ass.

"Forget it," he said aloud, swinging his legs out of bed and reaching for his discarded breeches. He dressed quickly, hoping that nobody had noticed his absence. He turned back to the bed, to take his boots from where Christianna had thrown them, and stopped cold.

The sheets were stained with pale smears of blood. Virgin's blood, he thought, with a sinking feeling. It couldn't be, and yet . . . He thought of her incredible tightness, her cry when he had rudely entered her body. "I'm not sure what to do," she had whispered when he had told her to seduce him. It had never occurred to him that she was innocent.

"Oh, hell," he muttered. "What have you done, you great oaf?" Best go find her and apologize, and hope that her brother wasn't prone to dueling.

Guilt was a new sensation to Gareth, and he found that he didn't like it. Not one damned bit.

A quick walk through the barns told him that his brothers had already been up for a while, and he felt another pang of conscience at missing the morning chores.

He went toward the house, stopping at the

well to splash cold water over his face and rinse his mouth, when the sound of laughter caused him to look over toward the garden where Christianna had been working.

For a few minutes, he stood watching.

Geoff and Stewart had made good on their promise to cut back the branches of the old peach tree, and sunlight filled the corner of the yard. Someone had dragged in an old wooden bench, and there, sitting comfortably between Daniel and Geoffery, was Christianna, one of Mrs. Hatton's aprons covering her dress, the battered leather gloves he had given her lying in her lap.

Stewart and Richard and Dog were all reclining on the sunlit brick walk; everyone was drinking tea from thick mugs and laughing at something Stewart had said.

Richard reached into a bowl in front of him and offered Christianna a handful of early strawberries, which she accepted with a smile.

"At Versailles—" she began, but Richard interrupted.

"Let me guess—at Versailles you only ate strawberries from solid gold plates, and they were vastly superior to our poor English berries."

She tossed a stem at him and made a face. "What a rude creature you are! I was going to say, at Versailles the strawberries never tasted so good. Why is that, do you suppose?"

"*Fabas indulcet fames,*" Daniel answered. "Hunger sweetens everything. And we're all hungry for fresh berries, since it's been so long since we've had them."

"You should have a trellis," Stewart said, pointing at the side gate. "Right there, over the path, to get the ivy out of the way. Like a little door. There used to be one, didn't there?"

Daniel nodded. "Years ago. And a swing, in the peach tree."

"Aye, there was," Geoffery exclaimed. "Isn't that how you broke your nose, Stew? Someone pushed you out on your head?"

"Vic did," Richard said, and a burst of laughter rose from the group.

"She reminds me of your mother."

Gareth hadn't heard his father approach; he looked over his shoulder, startled, and then back to the scene in the garden, where Christianna was bending to stroke Dog's ears.

"You're joking," Gareth said, trying to see the resemblance between Christianna and his tall, redheaded mother.

"No, not a bit," Matthew answered, lowering his spectacles to his round nose and tucking the small book he carried into the torn pocket of his waistcoat. "Not to look at, I mean, but in her way. The way she moves among the flowers and looks at them as if they were children. She has a gift for gardening."

"She's nothing like Mother," Gareth said shortly.

"I beg to differ. Your mother was a gentle-woman, and when she first came here she was as lost as a lamb. The first thing she learned to do was tend the flowers and herbs, and it touched something in her soul. Like our little French guest. I shall hate to see her go."

"She doesn't belong here," Gareth said abruptly. "She hasn't the strength to live this sort of life."

"Your mother—" Matthew started to say.

"There are some that say Mother didn't have the strength either," Gareth retorted. "And if she'd been a strong, country-bred woman, perhaps she'd be here now, instead of lying six feet down in Reverend Finkle's churchyard."

Matthew looked shocked, and Gareth regretted his bitter words. "I'm sorry, Father," he said softly.

"Oh, dear," Matthew muttered. He took his spectacles off and wiped them carefully on a spotted handkerchief, which seemed to do more harm than good. "Pneumonia," he said, after some thought, "is no respecter of rank, my boy."

Gareth said nothing.

"As to the rest, you seem a little harsh toward our guest. One would almost wonder why. I think she's a joy. It does my heart good to see someone tending my Beth's gardens again. Sometimes I wonder if I did her an injustice, taking her away from the life she knew."

Gareth hated to hear the quiet sorrow in his father's voice.

"But," Matthew finished, "if I had not, I would have missed her every day of my life. At least I had twenty years of happiness before

217

my heart was broken. And that, my boy, is better than having thrown it away with both hands."

Across the yard, Christianna's silvery laugh rang out as Geoffery and Stewart began wrestling over the last of the strawberries.

"Don't bleed on the gillyflowers," she cried, in tones of mock horror, and they straightened up with exaggerated care.

"It doesn't apply," Gareth told his father sharply. "She's not like Mother, and there's little point to this morose conversation."

Matthew smiled and gave Gareth an infuriatingly knowing look. "As the Bard said, love is blind. . . ."

"Bugger the Bard."

Matthew raised his brows and turned back toward the house, already taking his book from one pocket and patting the others in his eternal search for his spectacles.

"On your head," Gareth said automatically, and smiled at his father, who lowered his spectacles over his eyes and walked away, already lost in the pages of his book.

"You should move some of these flowers up to the cottage," Daniel told Christianna, "so you have something pretty to look at."

"Can it be done, without killing them?"

"Yes, of course. I can help you, if you like."

"You should get rid of the lavender," Geoffery told her. "Stinky stuff. Let those little pink things grow."

"Dianthus Minora," Christianna said, following his pointed finger. "Sweet williams. No, I like the lavender very much."

"Stinky stuff," Geoff repeated, tossing his long hair from his eyes.

"Have we all quit working and taken to all-day tea parties?"

Christianna flushed at the sound of Gareth's voice and bent to pet the dog, unable to meet his eyes.

"Enter the bloody autocrat," Richard greeted his brother. "I didn't see you at the barn this morning, your lordship."

Gareth ignored that. "The fleeces need counting and bundling, the horses are going to fat, and the books need tallying."

"He's getting old," Geoffery confided to Christianna. "Makes him cranky, doesn't it?"

She managed a weak smile.

"The books are for me," Daniel announced, standing and stretching. "Your garden is lovely, Christianna. I thank you for it."

"Geoff and I'll take the horses out," Stewart announced. "Do you ride, Christianna?"

"Very well—in a carriage," she admitted, and the small joke she made at her own expense was greeted with a noisy round of laughter.

"That's not a problem; we'll teach you later."

She nodded, and pulled on her oversized gloves, bending to pick up the small trowel she had left on the path.

"I'll count fleeces," Richard said in a dismal tone, "if you lazy beggars help me bundle them."

Geoffery and Stewart agreed, and they left the garden, arguing in good-natured voices.

Daniel touched her shoulder lightly before leaving, and she smiled up at him before turning back to the tangle of weeds and vines before her.

She felt more than heard Gareth standing behind her, and she tried not to think about him. Finally he knelt next to her and put a hand over hers.

"Christianna—"

"Go away."

"I need to talk to you."

"Never mind. Go away. Bugger off."

He sighed and took the trowel from her hand and tossed it away. "I wish you wouldn't swear."

She looked at him, and a hard lump rose in her throat at the sight of his gentle expression, his handsome face.

"You swear. Your brothers swear. I feel like swearing, and so I shall. Piss off. Bugger off. Kiss my ass—"

"I did," Gareth said simply, "and it was as soft and sweet as a new peach."

She almost choked, and couldn't think of an answer. Her face burned, and she finally said, "Never mind," and tried to rise to her feet.

Gareth caught her arm. "No. I won't leave. Now sit down and talk to me."

She sat, and stared at a clump of moss growing between the bricks of the path. She took a stick and began poking at it.

"You were a virgin, weren't you?"

She thought about lying, changed her mind, and gave him a curt nod.

"Damn it. Why didn't you tell me?"

"If I had, would you have stayed?"

"You know damn well I wouldn't have."

She met his eyes and wondered at the suppressed anger there, and the sadness. "What possible difference could it make?"

He looked exasperated. "A lot. Contrary to what you think, I consider myself an honorable man, and I would never have done such a thing had I known."

"And now you're sorry and you're afraid I'll go crying to your father, or to Daniel, and you'll be forced to do the honorable thing and save my reputation by marrying me. Believe me, Gareth Larkin, I have no intention of allowing such a thing. Do you really think that I'd trap myself into a life in this place?" Her words were bitter and sharp. In truth, she had dreamed of it. When she had first opened her eyes and found herself sleeping next to Gareth, his warm, strong body wrapped around her, she had dreamed exactly that. She imagined him opening his eyes and smiling his lazy smile and saying, "Stay." Fool, she told herself silently. She pulled a weed with a ferocious gesture, avoiding Gareth's eyes.

"I see," he answered quietly.

"And now that I've eased your mind, I'll thank you to leave me alone. Go chase your sheep around, or whatever it is you do."

He sat quietly for a few moments, and then

rose to his feet, his tall shadow falling over the tangled ivy and roses.

"As you wish," he said, and Christianna sat unmoving until she heard him leave.

"I don't care," she whispered, and tried to think of New Orleans and new gowns, and the handsome, rich men her brother would introduce her to.

After a few minutes she cried, and the stupid dog lumbered over and thrust her sorrowful face into Christianna's and licked at the salty tears.

"You idiot animal," Christianna said, but she wrapped her arms around the sleek, bulky body, and it made her feel a little better.

For three long weeks they maintained an uneasy truce. Gareth avoided speaking to Christianna; she concentrated on the garden.

She woke every morning to the sound of birds singing and, dressed in one of Victoria's old dresses, she would hurry across the sunny pasture—the cows no longer frightened her— and make her way to the kitchen, where she would take breakfast with Matthew and his sons. Gareth, she noted, took care to be absent.

She found that she was growing very fond of Matthew, and she loved the way he greeted her with a new quotation of poetry or wisdom each day, and told her how pretty she was, and admired her efforts in the garden.

She fell into the habit of knocking on his door and reminding him to eat at noon, or else he would stay buried beneath his books and papers full of accounts of Roman ruins and Greek philosophies and emerge each evening more muddled than usual.

Stewart and Geoffery built her a trellis, and Daniel showed her how to train the roses to grow up onto it. He suggested that she pull up the ivy that mingled with the rose vines, but she liked the way the deep green leaves looked and refused, electing to trim the wayward vines instead.

With a habit that had been carefully cultivated over the past year, she refused to allow herself to think of anything unpleasant.

Instead, she concentrated on her garden and, to her amazement, it was thriving. Fed and watered, the roses began to bloom, climbing over the brick walls in fragrant sprays of pink and red, warm next to the brilliant blue of the larkspur—the same deep blue as a summer night, the same blue as the velvet cape she had worn—had it only been a year ago?—at Versailles.

She routed the weeds and watered the gillyflowers and pulled the dead blooms off the tall, ruffled peonies and chased Dog, who had a passion for rolling in the violets, out of the beds at least three times a day.

She gave up trying to make any fashionable display of her hair, and began wearing it in a simple braid that hung down her back like a rope.

To her surprise, she found herself looking forward to the evenings, when the chores were done and everyone would find a reason to wander to her garden. Geoffery and Stewart and Daniel and Richard were all impressed with the lush, blooming flowers, and their praise warmed her.

Their teasing, she found, was kindly, and she began teasing them back. Her laughter came more easily, and for the first time since the revolution she felt as if she belonged.

Every evening after dinner she would make her way back to the stone cottage at the end of the forest, Dog waddling behind her with her long ears swaying, and she would bolt the door and sleep an exhausted sleep.

"She wants to go to church," Geoffery said to Stewart, looking worried. They were in the barn, with the sunlight slanting in, lighting the dust motes that danced above the hay they were pitching.

"Damn," Stewart answered. "That's no fun at all. Did you ask if she'd rather go fishing?"

"Aye, and she laughed. Said no; the time had come."

Gareth, sharpening a scythe on the heavy grindstone, tried to ignore his brothers.

"Says she needs to go to confession. Isn't that a Papist sort of thing, Stew? Can Vicar do that?"

"Confession for what? What's she done?"

"Who knows? Trampled on some violets, maybe."

Geoff and Stewart laughed like fools, and Gareth gave them a sharp glance over his shoulder and sprinkled more water on the grindstone to keep the blade of the scythe cool as it sharpened.

"Well, I'm not going to church," Stewart announced. "You take her."

"What, and leave you to go fishing alone?"

"I'll take her," Gareth said, testing the hone of the blade against his hand.

Geoff and Stewart looked at him as if he had lost his mind.

"She'd rather go with one of us. Or even Richard. Nothing personal, Gareth, but she really can't stand you."

Gareth raised his brow. "Is that so?"

"Not that she's said so," Geoffery hastened to assure him, "but every time you come around, she shuts right up and gets that pinched look. Like she did when she first came here."

"She doesn't look like that anymore," Stewart pointed out, sounding pleased. "She's getting all rosy from being in the sun. Less like a bloody princess and more like a real person."

"She's even got herself a paying job," Geoffery added. Stewart gave him a sharp look.

"She does, does she? And where might that be?" Gareth asked. He sounded more abrupt than he had intended to, and Geoff looked nervous.

"Where what?" Geoffery asked, studiously stupid.

"Her paying job, idiot."

"Don't know a thing about it," Geoff lied in a cheery tone.

"No, he doesn't know a bloody thing. Don't worry about her, Gareth. If she wants to go to church, I guess Daniel could take her. She's very fond of him. They're always off somewhere, blabbering together."

Gareth felt a little sick. "They are?"

"Aye, they're as thick as thieves. Mrs. Hatton says that maybe Daniel will marry her, and then she'll be able to stay."

"The hell he will," Gareth burst out. The words were loud in the quiet barn. His brothers looked startled.

"Never mind, Gareth; I'll take her to church if she wants to go."

"I'll go too," Stewart said. "Who cares for fishing?"

"You do," Geoff replied, looking confused.

"Both of you go fishing," Gareth said, in a tone that forbade argument. "I'll take Christianna to church, if that's what she wants."

He stalked from the barn, and Geoff and Stewart exchanged worried looks.

"Now he's crazy," Geoff observed. "What do you make of that?"

"Eee theenks ee iz ze bloody king," Stewart replied, tossing his hair in exaggerated imitation of Christianna.

They both laughed and decided to go fishing.

Chapter Twelve

Church was not at all what Christianna expected. To begin with, she had hoped that Stewart or Geoffery would take her, and instead, Gareth had appeared at the front gate, looking very stern in his fine frock coat, with his thick hair neatly tied at his neck. She almost changed her mind about going, but there was no real way out of it.

She had dressed so carefully, and suddenly she felt ridiculous, from the way her rose-laden hat dipped over her eye to the way her flounced hem showed her satin shoes.

And they had walked, two ghastly miles, in silence. Well, not exactly silence, but their conversation was limited to stiff observations on the weather and other such stupid things.

The church, too, was very different from what

she had expected. There was no Mass, no blessing of the Host, none of the familiar incense, the mystical-sounding bells ringing.

She thought of the last time she had been to church with Artois—he went only when there was particularly good music—and they had sat beneath the gilded, vaulted ceilings and heard a choir, two hundred voices strong, rising and falling in the vast cathedral around them, filling the air with sounds so brilliant and majestic that it seemed that they already might be in heaven.

And here she sat in a little stone church with only two stained-glass windows, next to a brooding man with whom she had slept, and who now treated her like a stranger.

All around them country neighbors were straining their necks to get a good look at the Larkins' new sister-in-law, and the even more unusual sight of Gareth Larkin attending church.

Geoffery and Stewart were right, Christianna decided; Reverend Finkle was an old windbag. Gareth had informed her, on the way there, that English clergymen didn't hear confessions. That rankled her as much as the off-key singing of the church choir.

She watched the vicar, with his thin, pinched face, and tried to imagine saying to him, "Father forgive me, for I cut a man's throat." No, she didn't think that would do at all. He would probably faint.

It was not what she had wanted. She wanted

the familiar ceremony, the holy mysteries. She wanted to unburden herself in the dark confessional and receive absolution, to hear the priest murmur, *"Pax tecum,"* peace be with you.

She focused on the stained-glass windows and felt like a child trying not to fidget. She tried to say the litany of the Blessed Virgin to herself, but had trouble remembering if "health of the sick" and "refuge of sinners" came before or after "gate of heaven" and "morning star."

Besides which, all that "Mother most chaste" and "Mother undefiled" business made her feel not a bit better.

She was very relieved when it was all over, and she made her way quickly out the door, past the stares of the local villagers, not waiting to see if Gareth was following.

"Now that," Gareth said cheerily, "is what I'd call a fine waste of a good morning."

Christianna glanced at him as he fell into step beside her. "Then why did you go?"

"Why did you?" he asked evenly.

She thought for a while as they walked down the dusty road, beneath the shade of the overhanging trees. "I thought it would do me good. I thought that the vicar might be more like a priest. I thought that I might be able to confess, and that God might forgive me."

Gareth laughed softly. He had already discarded his cravat and frock coat, and they hung negligently over his shoulder. "And did God forgive you?"

"Don't be stupid," Christianna answered. "I

haven't even confessed. That old windbag wasn't a proper priest."

Gareth was very quiet again, and they walked down the road together, each alone with his thoughts.

"I don't think I even believe in God anymore," Christianna said suddenly.

"There we part ways," Gareth answered cheerfully, his dimple deepening, "for I most certainly do."

"Don't joke when I'm blaspheming."

"I'm not. Not a bit. But I don't think you need some fellow in a frock to hear your confession, and I certainly don't expect to find God standing at old Finkle's right hand."

Christianna looked sharply at him. "Where does one find God, then, if not in church?"

Gareth smiled at her. "I think in the earth. I think the fact that the sun comes up and there are stars at night and that things grow every year is enough. Every little flower in your garden is a miracle, in a way. Every growing thing is. What does one need, after all, that the earth can't give you? Evidence of God, in my opinion."

Christianna thought about that. "It sounds sensible," she admitted.

"Think about it," Gareth said. "Is there anything you need that you don't have? Really need, I mean. Not things like twenty gowns and maids to draw your bath and silk fans and that sort of stuff. But is there anything you've lost that you really can't live without?"

She thought for a very long time. "I suppose

not. I would like . . . I would like to have my violin." She looked at Gareth to see if he was laughing, but he wasn't. "I miss music."

"You sing," Gareth argued. "I've heard you singing in the garden."

"How dreadful," Christianna cried, truly embarrassed.

"You sound lovely," Gareth assured her.

Christianna stopped and watched a lark winging across the vast blue sky. "It's not the same. My violin was perfect. It made perfect sounds. Like an angel speaking."

"You grow perfect flowers," Gareth pointed out.

Odd, how much that cheered her. She forgot about her violin immediately. "I do, don't I? Have you seen how well everything is doing? The poppies are coming; I'm so excited. Are they red, I wonder, or white, or the mixed sort? And the roses are doing so well. Even Mrs. Hatton loves them. By next year they'll be beautiful."

"By next year," Gareth said quietly, "you'll be gone, and the whole garden will go back to weed."

Christianna felt a cold, sinking sensation. She made a weak attempt at a smile. "What kind of flowers will grow in New Orleans, do you suppose?"

Gareth shrugged. "Is it true," he asked abruptly, "that you intend to work at the Broken Bow?"

"Yes. I thought it would be nice, to have a little money."

"I don't care for the idea."

Christianna shrugged.

"If I were your . . . brother, I would forbid it."

"But you're not. You're not my brother, or my father, or my lover, and you have no right."

"Haven't we been through this before?"

Christianna blushed, thinking of the way that conversation had ended.

"Look here, Christianna, you really shouldn't. It's not a good idea. It's not a nice place."

Christianna tossed her head. "For your information, I have been there already; and it isn't that horrible."

Gareth looked so surprised that she laughed.

"You never! When were you there?"

"Richard and Stewart took me there, to visit with Polly and to meet Mr. Tubbs. He's the owner, you know."

"I know who Tubbs is," Gareth said impatiently.

"And as Daniel would say, *Stet pro ratione voluntas*. It's my decision, and the argument's over."

"Don't go quoting my brother to me; that's all I need. What does Daniel say about this?"

"Do you want me to quote him or not?" Christianna had never seen Gareth so agitated, and she found that it pleased her very much.

"I can't believe that Richard and Stewart took you to the Broken Bow," he went on, as if she hadn't spoken. "They ought to know better."

"They did," Christianna admitted, "but I talked them into it."

"I'll bet you did," Gareth said, sounding decidedly displeased. "I'm surprised Geoffery and Daniel weren't in on it."

"They were," Christianna said, laughter bubbling up again. "You and Daniel were teaching Geoff to do the books."

Gareth stopped in the road, looking at her as if she had told him the world was coming to an end.

"Damn it!" he exploded, and Christianna jumped.

He stomped over to the edge of the road, kicked at a tree, stomped back, looked around, and went to kick the tree again.

"Everybody says how sensible and calm you are," Christianna observed. "I don't think so."

"I am," Gareth shouted. "I've been bloody calm my whole bloody life. And do you know why? I'll tell you why. Because you weren't prancing about my bloody farm causing trouble, that's why."

Christianna adjusted the pink silk ribbons that hung down from her hat and waited for him to quit shouting. It struck her that a month ago his anger would have sent her scurrying away in fear, but now it amused her more than intimidated her.

"What am I to do?" he demanded. "You've bewitched my father; you've bewitched my dog. My brothers are lying to me, just to please your selfish whims. Bad enough they lounge about staring at your bloody flowers half the day—"

"Oh, they do not."

"Like a bunch of besotted fools. And your bloody brother carried my sister halfway across the bloody world to be eaten alive by a bunch of red savages—"

"Now you sound like Mrs. Hatton," Christianna observed, trying not to smile but unable to resist needling him further. "Except for the 'bloody this' and 'bloody that.' Geoffery thinks that your temper is getting bad because you're getting old."

"I'm thirty," Gareth shouted, "and I am not bad-tempered." He stopped and took a deep breath, and when he spoke his voice was low and calm. "I'm not bad-tempered and I'm not old."

"As Daniel would say . . ." Christianna began, but Gareth cut her off abruptly.

"If you quote some bloody dead Roman at me, I'll not answer for my actions."

Christianna thought about laughing and decided against it. She gave an eloquent shrug and continued up the road.

Gareth fell into step beside her. "Speaking of Mrs. Hatton," he said, sounding more like his calm and tranquil self, "Geoffrey and Stewart were saying that she hears wedding bells."

Christianna wrinkled her brow. "Is it her ears?"

"Is it what? Oh, no. It's an expression. It means that she hopes that you and Daniel might get married."

Christianna glanced up at Gareth to see if he

was teasing. He wasn't. "Where did she get an idea like that?"

"I thought you might know. Geoffery and Stew tell me that you two are as thick as thieves."

"He's kind to me," she answered. "And I can talk to him. That's all."

"And what do you talk about?"

About France, she answered silently. *About how it felt to kill a man, while his brother laughed at you from the other side of a door. Things I never want to say to you because you might despise me.*

"Just things," she said with a vague shrug.

"And what does Daniel say about the Broken Bow?"

"He thinks it's nice, that I have a friend. He thinks that it's good for me to spend time with Polly."

Gareth gave a sharp laugh. "I don't. Polly is . . . a little free with her favors. I wouldn't like to see you picking up her habits."

Christianna fixed Gareth with a lifted brow and the same cool stare that used to throw the Marquesse Pierfitte into a rage.

"And you call me a snob! How dare you criticize Polly. It's almost funny, considering what I've learned from you."

That gave him pause for thought, Christianna noted with satisfaction. She looked up the road and saw Dog plodding toward them, her tail wagging joyously, her tongue hanging stupidly out of her mouth.

"As to my working in the Broken Bow: *omnia*

mutantur nos et mutamur in illis—all things change, and we change with them."

She hurried toward Dog, who rolled over in the dusty road and wagged her tail.

"I hate bloody Latin," Gareth said in a tired voice.

"Listen, Christianna," he called, but she ignored him, rubbing Dog's fat belly and cooing at her in the ridiculous voice that women use when speaking to animals.

She didn't look up until his shadow fell over her.

"I'm not joking, and I'm not trying to be a tyrant. But I simply won't have you working in the Broken Bow."

She tilted her head back and gave him a stern look from beneath the wide brim of her hat, her dark brows drawing together.

"You keep saying things that aren't so. You say you haven't a bad temper and you bellow at me. You say you aren't a tyrant and give me orders. And you have no right to do so."

"The hell I haven't."

"The hell you have. And now we're back at the beginning again."

Dog, lying on her back in the dusty road, looked from Gareth to Christianna and back again with an anxious expression.

Christianna settled back on her heels and gave a sigh. "Listen to me: How would you feel, Gareth Larkin, if you woke up one morning and your farm was gone? Sheep, cows, chickens, everything. Right down to the last stone?"

"I don't follow you."

"That's because I'm not finished. Be quiet, and listen. Suppose it happened. And then suppose that your brother—Richard or Daniel, it doesn't matter—suppose they took you somewhere that was unlike anything you'd ever known. Suppose they took you to King George's court and left you there. They said, 'Here, Gareth; here is where you live now.'"

"I'd leave," Gareth answered. "And maybe beat their asses up and down the street."

Christianna threw her hands up. "You aren't listening, Gareth! What if you couldn't leave? What if you had to stay there? And every day you had to deal with politicians and ambassadors and intrigues and such, and you had no idea what you were doing. To have everyone looking at you and saying, 'He doesn't belong; he's useless; he's dependent on our charity. He's nice to look at, but that's all.'"

Gareth was silent for a moment, watching her. Her cheeks were pink, her eyes bright.

"And then, someone tells you that there *is* something you can do. Something that will let you feel as if you belong. You could hold your head up, have a little something of your own again. Would you let anyone forbid you from it?" She was bristling like an angry kitten.

"No. I guess I wouldn't," he admitted. He settled down across from her on the road and reached out for her hand, clasping it firmly between his own. "Christianna, you have me wrong. I don't want you to feel as if you have nothing. I don't want you to feel like a poor relation. I simply worry about you, and your safety. What if you were walking home and some drunken bastard decided to follow you? Could you protect yourself?"

She flinched, and her mouth tightened.

"You couldn't, sweetheart. You're as little and soft as a lamb. I'd never forgive myself if something happened to you."

She turned her face away and stared out over the green hills, her expression tight and unreadable. A gloss shone over her blue eyes, and Gareth wondered if she was about to cry.

"That's not fighting fairly," she said softly. "I'd rather you bellowed and stomped around in circles. Instead you call me 'sweetheart' and speak to me in a lover's voice. That's not fair."

She reached up an unsteady hand and moved a pink ribbon away from the brim of her hat.

"It is fair," Gareth answered. "It is. And I am your lover, if you want to be honest."

"You're not!"

He raised his brows. "Then what do you see it as, Christianna? What would you call it? I've kissed you; I've held you in my arms; I've made love to you. You welcomed me into your body, I spilled my seed in you, and you slept next to my heart. Doesn't that make me your lover?"

"No! No, it doesn't." A red stain flushed across her cheeks and tears gathered on her lashes. "It means that once, and by your own word, against your own good judgment, you bedded me. People do that all the time; animals can do that. That's not what a lover is!"

"Then what?" Gareth asked quietly.

"A lover is someone who cares about you—who dreams of you and wants to be with you and thinks highly of you. Someone who admires you and talks to you. Not someone who sleeps with you once and thinks himself well rid of you."

There was sorrow in her voice, bitter and sharp. Gareth reached out and placed a firm hand under her chin, turning her face toward his own. The sunlight sparkled on the tears that clung to her lashes.

"Listen to yourself, Christianna. Now think. I do care for you. Very much. And I admire you. Not just because you're beautiful, though you are that. I admire the effort you've made to fit in, and the care you show to Father and the others. And as for thinking myself well rid of you, I don't. Damn it, girl, do you think that once was enough? If I had my way, I'd move you back into the house and into my bed, and I'd make love to you every night, in every way I could think of."

She sat perfectly still, staring at him with round eyes. A warm breeze fluttered the pink ribbons of her hat and whispered through the green leaves above them.

"And if you think you must work at the Broken Bow, go on. Give it a try. But I'll be there every night to take you home. I'll not let you wander the roads alone at night, do you hear?"

The small hand beneath his own trembled a little, and she nodded.

"Thank you, Gareth," she said softly. "I thank you, very much. It means so much to me."

"I can't think why," he answered with a quiet laugh.

"Oh, it does! I would like to feel more a part of things, as if I were able to take care of myself. It's so awful always to feel left out and different. I feel as if I don't belong anywhere."

"That's bloody silly. You belong to us. You're part of the family, like it or not."

She looked at him with a curious, pained expression, as if she didn't quite believe him.

"You belong to us," he repeated, and he reached out and drew her toward him, holding her tightly against his chest.

For a moment she resisted, her shoulders stiff and unyielding beneath his arm; and then she gave a soft sigh, and her slender arms wrapped around his neck and she lifted her face to his.

He kissed her gently, his mouth moving against the warm, silken skin of her cheeks and forehead and over her eyelids, where damp, salty tears still clung to her lashes.

When their lips met she made a soft sound in her throat, and her body seemed to melt against his, with a heat as warm and luminous as spring sunshine.

They broke apart as Dog gave a furious bark and butted her head between them, clambering onto Christianna's lap· and wagging her tail furiously.

"Stupid animal," Gareth muttered, giving her an affectionate shove.

Christianna laughed softly and looked at him with dazed and brilliant eyes. "Come, Gareth, she's telling us to have a care for our reputations. We've shocked her, sitting and kissing in the road."

"Reputations be damned," he replied, but he stood and offered Christianna his hand, and helped her to her feet.

"Shocking behavior," he teased, "for a gentlewoman of good family."

"But just the sort of thing one would expect from a bar wench," she retorted, blushing and straightening her hat, which was sliding down the back of her head.

Gareth reached out and took one of her thick black curls in his hand, sliding the silk of it between his fingers, his hand trailing lightly over the skin of her bosom. "I like this bar wench," he informed her. "I like her all too well. Perhaps you should ask Daniel to see you home safely tonight. I don't know if I trust myself that much. A long walk under the stars on a deserted road might prove too tempting, sweetheart."

She laughed and met his eyes with a merry look. "I think I'll take a chance, Gareth Larkin. As our friends the Romans used to say—"

"Don't say it!" he cried with a pained look. "Whatever it is, say it in good plain English. Daniel is bad enough; I don't need you picking up his bloody awful habits."

She laughed aloud at his plea but said nothing,

and they made their way in silence down the sunny lane and back to the house.

For the first time in days they were comfortable in each other's company, and they looked at each other with soft, wondering eyes.

"You came," Polly cried, her freckled face breaking into a delighted smile. "Wait just a half moment and we'll get you started."

Christianna untied the ribbons of her bonnet, watching as Polly expertly maneuvered her way through the crowded pub, her capable hands full of heavy mugs.

The air of the room was thick with the yeasty smell of ale and the odor of roasting meat; the tables were crowded with the local farmers, who, Sunday or not, gathered at the tavern each night to compare notes on crops and sheep and the prices the London buyers were offering.

Polly's husky laugh sounded as she moved through the room, tossing her golden head flirtatiously at one man, slapping at another's hand, and grabbing empty mugs from a deserted table on her way back.

"Here's how it's done," she announced as she reached Christianna. "Ask them what they want, go get it from Tubbs, and give it to them. Simple enough. And don't let anyone give you any crap."

Christianna joined in Polly's easy laughter.

"And what if they do?" she asked.

"You call me," Polly explained, "and if I can't throw him out, Tubbs can."

She laughed again as she offered Christianna an apron.

"Then we try to close up as early as we can," she added, "so we can get out of here at a decent hour. Maybe sit down and have a pint or two ourselves."

Christianna didn't care for ale but didn't say so.

"You take all the tables from here to the wall," Polly instructed. "We'll start you slow."

The work wasn't hard, Christianna thought. The local farmers were, for the most part, kind, and tolerant of her slowness. "That's Larkin's Christianna," they said when introducing her to newcomers, and the local villagers all nodded respectfully and asked after Matthew and his sons and spoke admiringly of the farm.

"Never been a farmer like that Gareth," commented one old man. "That's a son any man could be proud of. That boy could throw horse crap in a mud pile and it'd grow."

"You're doing so well," Polly commented, passing her with an armload of steaming plates. "You've toughened up a bit since the first day I saw you. You're a damned good worker."

Was it the words themselves or Polly's bright smile of approval that warmed her? A little of both, Christianna thought. *I can work, I'm not helpless.*

She laughed when some drunken fellow across the room groped at Polly's curved waist and Polly tipped him out of his chair with a firm push.

"Just like that," Polly called merrily over her shoulder, as if the whole scene had been for Christianna's benefit. "Never let anyone push you around."

"Nobody'd dare," commented Tubbs, filling three pewter tankards and shoving them across the bar to Christianna. "You're from the Larkins, and there's no man in the district wants those boys breathing down his neck. Those boys adore you, they do. You should hear them when they come in—Christianna did this, and Christianna did that. Half expected you to walk on water when Polly brought you here."

Christianna stared at him, and a warm, contented feeling spread through her. "Truly?" she asked.

She wondered why this bit of gossip should make her so happy and suddenly realized that for the first time in her twenty years, she felt as if she belonged to a family.

The more boisterous customers of the establishment were raising their voices in a well-loved barroom song, and without thinking, she sang along on the final chorus, her pleasant soprano ringing out across the room. Whistles and laughter greeted her when she was done, and she laughed aloud with pleasure.

"That's Christianna from Larkin's," she heard someone say, and the words were pleasant to her ears.

She and Polly were taking what Polly called "a breather," standing at the bar and resting, when the door of the inn opened to admit some latecomers.

"Hell's bells," Polly muttered, "just what we don't need."

Christianna looked curiously at the newcomers—a young gentleman who could have stepped off the streets of London or Paris, fashionably dressed in an elegant frock coat, his somberly suited valet, and another aristocratic young man with a carefully styled white wig and a carefully folded cravat.

"Who are they?" she asked, curious at Polly's disapproving tone.

"That brown-haired one in the blue coat, that's Master Giles, Squire Thornley's oldest, and he thinks he's the bloody lord of the manor. That other fellow, don't know him, but he looks full of himself. These young lords, they think it's funny to mingle with the peasants and look down their noses." Polly gave Christianna a rueful smile. "Always thought that someday some great lord would come in here and take one look at me and carry me off to be his ladylove. But the fact is, most of 'em are snotty pups, like these."

Christianna looked over at the young gentlemen, who had settled themselves at a table. Their valet was flicking at imaginary dust on the table with a white handkerchief, his face sour with disdain.

"As if the damned table wasn't clean enough," Polly said with a look of disgust. "I'll take them, if you like."

Christianna was about to tell Polly to never

mind, but Polly was already on her way to the table and inquiring in a brisk voice as to what they wanted.

The brown-haired young man looked at Polly with scorn.

"To start with, Polly, I'd rather the new wench served us. We've already had our fill of you."

His words were rude and cutting, and there was a double meaning behind them that caused Christianna's cheeks to flame. So, this was Squire's son, whom Daniel taught Latin, to prepare him for his years at the university. Daniel was right; he was an arrogant brat.

His eyes were fastened on her with cool interest. "Come here, wench," he said.

Christianna took a deep, calming breath and approached the table with her nose high.

"You're new here in the village, aren't you?" the arrogant young man demanded.

"I am," she answered, her tone equally proud. "I'm staying with relatives until I join my family in New Orleans."

The young man looked startled. "French, are you, wench?"

The word *wench*, Christianna decided, had a very unpleasant sound, especially when spoken in such haughty tones.

"This must be the little froggy that's staying with my Latin master's family," Giles Thornley remarked to his friend. "One hears rumors . . ." He turned back to Christianna, and she found herself wanting to slap the arrogant white face. "There are a whole mess of your kind over by Ashby, at the old Notleigh estate. Madame Alfort, and some others."

Christianna drew a quick, sharp breath. "Madame Alfort? I know her. She is here? In England? And others?" Her heart was racing. "What others? Do you know their names?"

The young man leaned back in his chair, his eyes alight with interest. "I might," he admitted.

Christianna wanted to shake him. "Well, who are they?"

He smiled at his friend, who was watching the scene with an amused smile. "Perhaps we can make a trade," Giles said. "I tell you what the names of the froggies at Notleigh are . . . and you agree to warm my bed tonight, wench."

Christianna froze, and then a wave of fury rushed through her. It seemed suddenly very quiet in the room.

"And you," she answered in icy tones, "you will remember, sir, that my title is not wench. I'm the sister of the Marquis St. Sebastien; when you address your betters, you grant them their titles. Perhaps you need someone to tutor you in manners, as well as Latin."

The young man was swelling with fury. His pale face flushed red, then white.

Somewhere in the room, a loud snort of laughter sounded.

"You foul-tempered little bitch," the young man began.

Christianna very calmly grasped the back of his chair and tipped him onto the floor, as she had seen Polly do earlier that evening.

She turned her back and began to walk away, but Giles Thornley grabbed her wrist and swung her around.

"How dare you?" he spat. "How dare you? I shall have this establishment closed. If ever you dare speak to me like that again, I shall beat you within an inch of your life. You impudent, foul little bitch—"

"Stop there, Thornley."

Christianna turned to see Gareth behind her, his eyes glowing cold, his mouth set in a firm line.

"Take your hand off her or I'll rip your arrogant head off your shoulders." His voice was calm and clear, but there was no doubt that he meant what he said.

Giles didn't move. His eyes narrowed, and a muscle twitched in his jaw.

"I'll do it," Gareth said, very softly. "And tell your dandy friend to put his sword away. There's only two of you, and there's not a man in this room that won't back me."

Christianna stood frozen until Giles released her arm. She stepped away from him, her heart hammering in the watchful silence of the room.

"Get out," Gareth said to the furious young gentleman. "And forget about that foal I was going to sell you. Keep away from our land and away from our Christianna."

Giles looked around the room and met the cold stares of the local villagers and farm folk.

"I know who you are," he announced, "and I'll not forget."

"Good," Gareth answered in a pleasant voice. "See that you don't."

"I've been sacked, as Polly says," Christianna announced, crossing the dark innyard to where Gareth waited on horseback.

"You sound sad," Gareth commented, sounding surprised.

"I am. It was fun. Everyone was kind, and I felt as if I belonged. As if I had a place."

Gareth was quiet for a few moments; and then he leaned down from the saddle and took her fingers in his.

"You have a place, Christianna. Come home."

She tilted her head and watched the moonlight play across the sheen of his hair and the strong, clean lines of his face.

He lifted her to the horse and settled her comfortably in front of him, his strong arms wrapping comfortably around her, his long legs resting easily against hers.

He guided the horse skillfully onto the dark road, and after a few awkward moments she leaned back against the solid warmth of his body and breathed the scent of his skin and listened to the sound of his heart.

"Thank you," she said. "For stopping Giles. I really was frightened."

"Were you? You didn't look it."

"Maybe I'm not quite right for tavern work," she admitted.

"That's the truth," Gareth agreed.

They rode along in silence for a while, and Christianna tried not to think of the closeness of Gareth's body, the feeling of his arms around her, the strength of his thighs against hers.

It was impossible.

Apparently, it was impossible for him, too, for after a few minutes he gave a heavy sigh and lowered his mouth to the soft curve of her neck. She turned to him eagerly.

When he stopped the horse and carried her to the quiet darkness of the trees she went willingly, and returned his burning kisses and caresses with a hunger that shook her.

"I want you," she whispered as she felt the hard length of him enter her body, and when he shuddered and plunged into her hot grip she felt a joy and triumph that she had never known before.

Part 3
Midsummer

Come live with me and be my love,
And we will all the pleasures prove
That hills and valleys, dales and fields,
Or woods or steepy mountain yields.
—Christopher Marlowe

The lotus leaves which heal all wounds lie in thy hands. Oh, be thou kind to me, while yet I know the summer of my days.
—Oscar Wilde

As the apple tree among the trees of the field, so is my beloved among the sons . . .
—The Song of Solomon

Chapter Thirteen

Gareth was pitching the dirty hay from the horse stalls when Daniel came into the barn and tossed his books of Latin verbs to the ground, followed by his neat frock coat. He took a pitchfork and began working beside his brother.

"Aren't you off to Squire's today?" Gareth asked.

Daniel cast him a rueful smile. "I've already been, and now I'm back. I've lost my place. Been told not to return."

Gareth sighed. "I suppose we should have expected that. I'm sorry you lost your place, Daniel."

Daniel smiled. "No great harm. Giles is an arrogant young bastard, and I won't miss him. Did you really threaten to kill the boy, Gareth?"

"Nay. Well, I told him I'd tear his head from his shoulders."

"That might do it," Daniel observed thoughtfully. "Why?"

"He laid hands on Christianna," Gareth answered, taking an armload of clean straw and scattering it across the floor of the stall. "He cursed her, and was threatening her."

Daniel looked shocked.

"It's my duty to protect her," Gareth added.

Quis custodiet ispos custodes? Daniel asked quietly, turning away to discard some dirty straw.

"Which means?"

"Who will guard the guards?"

Gareth looked sharply at his brother. "And what do you mean by that?"

"What do you think I mean? If you're protecting Christianna, who'll protect her from you? Do you think I can't see what you're doing? It's very obvious."

"Is it? And what if it is?"

"Will you marry her?"

Gareth laughed. "Don't be so simple, Daniel. She'd never have me. As soon as her brother sends her passage, she'll be out of here like the wind. She intends to have her fun and be on her way. Marry some rich Frenchman and live happily ever after, with fifty gowns and twenty maids, I shouldn't wonder."

"You jackass." Daniel moved on to the next stall and began mucking it out. "You don't even know her."

"And you do?"

"Aye, I think so."

"Keep out of it, Daniel."

The two brothers stood and glared at each other, until a low rumble of thunder distracted them.

"Rain," Gareth exclaimed, a relieved look breaking over his face. He strode to the barn door and examined the darkening sky. "It's about time."

Daniel stood behind him, watching the approaching clouds. "You should marry her, Gareth."

"God's blood, you're starting to annoy me. Who made you the keeper of my conscience?"

"It's not you I'm concerned with. It's Christianna. I'd not like to see her hurt."

"I'm not hurting her, you jackass," Gareth snapped, feeling guiltier than he wanted to admit.

"If you want to amuse yourself," Daniel fired back, "why not one of the local girls?"

"Because it doesn't suit me," Gareth replied. "Leave off. Isn't there something you have to do with yourself, or do you just intend to follow me about and moralize?"

"You should marry her," Daniel repeated. "Love conquers all, and *nos cedamus amori*. We should yield to it."

"One day," Gareth said in a tired voice, "I'm going to pick up your book of Cicero and clout you with it."

"It's Virgil, not Cicero," Daniel answered calmly. "And it's true."

Gareth regarded his brother with a lifted brow,

and then burst into merry laughter. "Daniel, you tire me. Now listen: Christianna would scream and faint if I ever suggested marriage. She made it very clear that it's not part of the game." That hurt, more than he would ever admit. "Remember how she told us about Marie Antoinette's little peasant village, and how they'd dress up as country maids and wander among the sheep? Sheep that were bathed every morning and had satin ribbons tied round their woolly little necks? That's what this is to Christianna— a pretty, silly little farm. It may amuse her to dress in Vic's old clothes and play at being one of us, but she isn't, Daniel. She never will be."

Christianna stood outside the barn wall, where she was filling a bucket with old manure to put around the base of the roses. She had started toward the barn but stopped short at the sound of Gareth's voice.

"She may play at being one of us, but she isn't. She never will be."

Oh, how that hurt. Did he know how she longed to be one of them; how she loved him?

No, and she'd never be the one to tell him, she decided. This was insane, this whole affair. And if he came to the cottage door tonight, she'd tell him to take his green eyes and warm hands and go home.

She turned abruptly on her heel and lugged the heavy bucket back to her garden. She took her spade and attacked the earth savagely, turning it over and working in the fertilizer until she lost herself in the sights of the ruffled pink peonies and the brilliant purple of the foxglove and the crisp, pungent scent of the lavender. After a while she felt calm again, and the ache in her heart subsided.

When the first raindrops fell they surprised her.

She stood in the garden for a while longer, watching the thirsty earth drink the rain in and marveling at the cool smells that rose from the ground, and the sweetness of the rain-scented roses, and the way the sparkling droplets clung to the velvety petals and deep green ivy. It never occurred to her that she was getting wet until a window in the house banged open.

"I have heard," Richard remarked, "that the gentry aren't smart enough to come in out of the rain, but I never thought to see it proven in my own yard."

Christianna laughed up at him. "Look," she demanded, pointing to where the roses hung over the brick wall, like lush swags of pink and green and scarlet. "Aren't they beautiful with the rain on them?"

"I guess," Richard said, doubt showing on his face. "Come in and get a cup of tea." The heavy window banged closed. Christianna thought about it and found that the idea of sitting in the warm kitchen and drinking tea and having a friendly argument with Richard was a pleasant prospect.

That night at dinner she thought that if she hadn't overheard Gareth's words in the barn, she would truly have felt like part of the family. She laughed at Stewart and Geoffery and listened patiently while Matthew discussed the effects that the Greek philosophers had on modern-day society (which she really didn't find very interesting) and told Richard to go put on a clean shirt. Richard told her that he wasn't listening to anyone who dragged buckets of manure around in rainstorms, and everyone laughed at that. "Some people," Mrs. Hatton told Richard, "just don't know about roses, and you're one of them," and Christianna was delighted to hear Mrs. Hatton defending her.

She found herself blushing whenever she felt Gareth's eyes on her, warm and approving, and she tried not to think about the hours they had shared last night, under the moonlit trees. She wondered if anyone else noticed her blushes and her inability to meet Gareth's gaze, and that made her even more uncomfortable.

To her relief, everyone was more intent on tomorrow, which was the day of the midsummer fair in Ashby. It seemed that this was the day when the first crops of young peas and strawberries and beans and cheeses from the dairy went out for sale to the London merchants.

"It's more than that," Geoffery informed her. "It's wool merchants and horse traders and weavers and jugglers. It's a bloody lot of fun, for being work."

"If the rain stops," Mrs. Hatton added, in a dark tone.

"It will," Gareth assured her, and his eyes were

bright as he turned to Christianna. "Of course you'll come, won't you?"

At that moment she could no more have said no to him than she could have flown, she was so happy to be asked, to know that he wanted her company. "Of course I will," she answered, and when she saw how much her answer pleased everyone she felt again the warm sense of belonging.

And later that night, after she had changed into her nightgown and pushed Dog off her clean sheets, she heard footsteps approaching the cottage and knew it was Gareth. She opened the door to him before his feet sounded on the first step.

He smiled his gentle smile at her and held out his arms, and she went to him without a word and lost herself in the touch of his warm hands and the scent of his skin. The rain thundered down outside the cottage and poured in rivers down the small window, while inside the fires of their bodies sparkled and flamed together in the golden glow of the candlelight.

"Wake up," Gareth whispered.

Christianna opened her eyes to darkness. Was it the middle of the night? She snuggled in closer to the heat of Gareth's body, twining her legs around him, half lost in the memory of their passion and the rich, sweet dreams that had followed.

"None of that," Gareth said, laughter in his

voice. "Don't you know what day it is?"

Christianna buried her face in his neck and kissed the warm hollow of his throat.

"God help me," Gareth murmured, and she felt him growing hard against her. "Leave off, sweetheart, or I'll never get out of bed."

"Good," she whispered, and boldly, she reached out to grasp him in her hand and guide him into her body, already hot and wet for him. He rolled her body beneath his and held her tightly against his chest.

"Nice." His voice was heavy and warm with sleep, and his mouth sought hers as he began to move in her slowly, with a hypnotic rhythm.

She almost wept with pleasure at the sweetness of it, the rightness, and she wished that it could always be like this; just the two of them, every night, every morning.

His mouth felt like fire moving around her neck and ears; his hands moved like silk across her skin, stroking and teasing her until she ached and wrapped her legs around his, writhing against the heat of his body, arching desperately against him.

"Stop." His voice was husky in the darkness; his hands grasped her hips, stilling them. "If you move again, I'll be undone."

He moved away from her for a moment, his tall shadow barely visible in the dark room. His hands moved over her hips, warm and strong, and she quivered like the taut string of a violin beneath his touch.

His fingers moved between her legs, stroking

the soft curls, playing between them until she gasped.

"Sweetheart . . ." His breathing was ragged, dark with passion. "Let me show you something. . . ."

With an easy movement, his mouth descended to where his fingers had lately been, his breath hot and intoxicating, his tongue flowing like fiery satin over the tender cleft.

Instinctively, she tried to move away, heat flooding her face; but his arm reached up to grasp her waist, pulling her back toward him.

"Don't be embarrassed," he whispered, his hand stroking her thighs. "Never be embarrassed with me. You're as sweet as honey."

And then again, the heat of his mouth, tender and burning against her, the feel of his hair, falling like silk against her thighs.

All the feelings that had been coursing through her body were now centered in the tender petals that lay beneath his mouth, poignant, sharp thrills of heat that flicked at her.

He kissed her tenderly, gently. His mouth sought the small, hidden bud of her most tender place and closed over it, while his tongue circled it, hot and quick, until her fingers reached to his hair, pulling his mouth closer.

His hands slid beneath the curves of her buttocks, lifting her hips from the bed and closer to his mouth as he feasted upon her sweetness, gently rocking her against his tongue as it stroked and teased and suckled at the very core of her, until passion and fire blinded her to all sensibility and she shattered with a piercing cry.

Brilliant light and swirling darkness pulled her, her body arched and quivered, tossing from side to side.

Then he pulled her to him and entered her throbbing body and rode her wildly and fiercely, while she trembled with aching pleasure. Her hips rose to welcome him, the drumbeat of her pulse matching his long, hard thrusts.

She called his name into the darkness and felt him throb and spill his seed deep in her body with a low gasp of pleasure.

"Sweetheart," he whispered, collapsing against her, and he kissed her, the musky taste of her own passion against her lips.

They held each other tightly as their heartbeats slowed and their breathing steadied.

"Such a way to wake up," he murmured into her hair, and she laughed softly into the darkness.

"Such a time to wake. Is it midnight?"

"Nay; almost dawn. And the fair at Ashby's today. We'll start loading things, grab a quick bite, and be gone by six."

He was already moving as he spoke, climbing from the bed, fumbling around in the dark. He tried to light the candle and knocked something down with a crash.

There was a short yelp from the darkness.

"Dog, you idiot. What are you doing here?"

Christianna smiled. "She lives here."

She laughed at the sound of the dog's tail thumping against the floor.

"She's lying on my breeches," Gareth said, "and I know I've flint in my pocket. Move over, you great hog."

A spark struck, the room flared into brightness, and Christianna blinked as Gareth lit the candle.

From the floor, Dog blinked her soulful-looking eyes, rose to her squat legs with considerable effort, dragged her sleek brown body across the floor, and tried to climb up onto the bed.

Christianna laughed and pushed her away, her hair spilling over her shoulders and into her eyes. "Get down, fat Dog."

She glanced up at Gareth and blushed at the warm, appreciative look in his eyes as he watched her.

"Christianna St. Sebastien," he whispered, "you're the most beautiful creature I've ever had the pleasure to lay eyes on."

She lowered her head and scratched the soft hair behind Dog's long ears, smiling with warm delight.

Gareth dressed quickly, his skin glowing gold in the candlelight. "I've got to get to the house and get moving before they notice I'm not abed," he explained. "When you're dressed come down and help if you like."

Christianna felt a surge of pride, that she would be asked to help. It was a much better feeling than being called useless.

"Wear something pretty," Gareth added, showing his white teeth in a quick smile as he pulled on a boot. "All the girls dress up a bit for the fair."

He leaned over and ran his hand across her bare shoulders and reached down to touch a soft breast.

She shivered with pleasure. "That won't convince me to put on clothes."

He laughed at her softly. "Hot-blooded little wench. Get dressed, then."

She sat up in bed and surveyed the gowns hanging on the wall. What did one wear to a country fair?

"Definitely not the pale blue and white," she mused aloud. "When I wore it to church everyone stared at me."

"They stared not because of your dress," Gareth pointed out, "but because you crossed yourself and curtsied when you came in. Nobody's ever seen a real live Papist in the church, I'd guess."

Christianna blushed and laughed with him.

"We'll see you in a bit," he added, and bent to kiss her quickly before going to the door and lifting the bolt.

"Come on, Dog," he called softly, but Dog closed her eyes and leaned against the bed, pretending to sleep.

He gave a quick smile, shrugged, and hesitated in the open doorway, his eyes locked with Christianna's.

For a brief moment he seemed as if he was

about to speak, but he simply cast her a quick smile and went out into the darkness, closing the door behind him.

I love you. He had almost said the words aloud, Gareth realized.

Fool, he told himself. *You're a fool for even sleeping with her; you'd be a greater fool to offer her your heart. And for what? To have her cast you aside as soon as the first opportunity to leave presented itself?*

He thought of how she had looked when he had left, sitting with the tangled sheets wrapped around her pale body, her cheeks glowing like roses, her black curls tangled and brushing over the gentle curve of her waist.

He knew that the wise thing to do would be to keep himself safely at a distance, and keep his heart and pride intact. He also knew it would be impossible.

He walked quietly up the kitchen path to the house, relieved to see the windows dark, and entered the kitchen quietly, feeling like a thief in his own home.

Daniel was there, already dressed, stirring the ashes of the fire and making ready to add more wood.

He glanced up at Gareth and said nothing.

Gareth hung an iron kettle on a hook over the fire and stood back, waiting for the water to heat. He pulled a wooden chair up to the brick hearth and sat heavily, watching his brother as he fed the fire. The kitchen was quiet, except for the crackle of the flames as the dry wood sparked and caught.

"The rain stopped," Gareth offered at last.

Daniel gave him an impatient glance. "Well, aren't you an observant fellow?" His voice was cool, disapproving.

Gareth sighed and stretched. "Look," he said after a pause, "she's not a child, Daniel. She's . . . well, she's not a child."

"She's twenty," Daniel informed him.

"Fine, she's twenty. I knew that."

Daniel gave him a doubtful look.

"I did. I knew that. And that's not the point. She knows what she's doing, and I know what I'm doing, and I wish you wouldn't try to make me feel like a toad for it."

"If the shoe fits," Daniel suggested, pulling a chair up to the hearth and stretching his long legs toward the fire.

"Bugger off. What would you do in my position?"

"Marry her," Daniel replied, without hesitation.

"I would too," Gareth exclaimed abruptly.

Daniel looked up, startled.

"If she'd have me, which she won't. And I don't need you to remind me of the fact, so let it be."

Daniel smoothed his hair back from his high forehead, deep in thought.

"Very well," he agreed. "I've no reason to doubt that you're speaking the truth, because you always do. But are you sure that the truth is absolute, or simply what you perceive the truth to be?"

"Bloody philosophy before sunrise," Gareth remarked, kicking at Daniel's chair.

"I think," Daniel continued, "that Christianna cares for you more than you suspect."

"What, has she said so?"

"Not in so many words," Daniel admitted. He studied the fire for a moment. "She said . . . that you are so good that she couldn't bear it if you thought badly of her."

"What the hell did she mean by that?" Gareth asked, wrinkling his brow.

Daniel shrugged. "You don't strike me as being particularly good." He stared at the fire for a minute. "Coal is more efficient," he added, changing the subject abruptly.

"Dirty stuff," Gareth commented. "Give me clean wood any day. And wood is free."

They sat quietly for a few minutes, watching the flames dance off the brick walls.

"Listen," Gareth said abruptly. "What if I was to woo her? Supposing that I gave it my all, and tried to win her hand before her brother sends for her? Would you quit looking at me as if I was a pillaging Viking?"

Daniel's smile was genuine. "Aye, that would please me. I expected nothing less of you."

"The final decision, of course, is Christianna's," Gareth pointed out. "I have a hard time believing that she'd be willing to spend the rest of her life feeding chickens and making butter."

"You love her," Daniel remarked, as if that was

the final word on the matter.

"God help me," Gareth muttered, "I knew she was trouble the first time I saw her."

Daniel laughed, and Gareth went to find the tea. "Go wake the others," he called, "and let's start loading the wagons. We'll want to be in Ashby by eight."

"I'm going to take my share of the profit," Geoffery announced, "and buy a new horse. If there's one that catches my eye."

"There always is," Gareth pointed out. "What will you do with yours, Richard?"

They were loading the last of the fleeces onto the long, low farm wagon. It was already crowded with bushel baskets of strawberries and early peas and young carrots and round, waxed wheels of cheese from the dairy.

Richard stood for a moment, studying the sky before answering. The clouds had cleared and the trees and fields sparkled beneath the morning sun, clean and fragrant from the rain.

"I'd like to go to sea one day," Richard finally admitted. "I'll save my money to that end."

"For heaven's sake," Stewart remarked, "that's the first I've heard of that."

"Unlike the rest of you yahoos," Richard retorted, "there are some things I like to keep to myself."

"Are we loaded, then?" Gareth asked, checking the harnesses of the sturdy Welsh workhorses that pulled the weight of the wagon. "What happened to Christianna?"

"Off in her garden," Geoffery answered. "Said she'd be right back."

"I'll fetch her," Gareth said, "and we'll be off."

She was standing by a pink climbing rose, carefully tying a cut rosebud into the ribbon of the lace cap that she wore.

Gareth stood watching her, thinking how much she had changed. When she had arrived she had been thin and white, and sharp-looking. She had startled at every movement, tensed at every teasing word. He remembered how she had taken over an hour, every morning, to pile her hair into the elaborate coiffures of the French fashion, and how stiffly she had moved in her stiff gowns.

How different she looked now, in her full-sleeved white blouse beneath her simple black bodice, her skirts of pink and lavender stripes. Her hair hung in a single braid, thick and glossy, down her back. Her cheeks were bright and rose-colored in the morning air, and her face was rounder and softer than it had been when she arrived.

"Ready to go?" Gareth asked.

She looked up, startled, and smiled. "Yes, thank you. I just wanted to dress up a bit. Flowers are like free jewelry, aren't they?"

"They become you," Gareth told her. "You look wonderful. I like your hair like this, instead of towering over your head. It looked like your little neck couldn't hold it all. Silly, wasn't it?"

Christianna laughed. "Oh, it was much worse

in France. Monsieur Antoine came to do my hair every morning. One day he put three yards of pearl beads in it. And feathers. And one day, blue birds, building a nest of ribbons . . ."

"What are those things in your hair?" Artois demanded, peering with disapproval at the feathery blue objects. *"It's a little much, isn't it?"*

"Don't think of it," Gareth said.

Startled, Christianna looked up and found his eyes on her, soft and sad.

"When you think of France," Gareth said quietly, "your sweet face pinches up, as if you were in pain. You look as if your heart might break. I tell you what—today, I want you not to think of it. For one day, forget you were ever there; pretend that you've lived in Middlebury all your life. What do you think?"

She smiled up at him, with such a radiant look that it took his breath away.

"I like it. I intend to have a nice day and see the sights and visit with Polly. I was going to ask around and see if I could locate Madame Alfort, but I won't. I'll leave that for another day."

"Was she a good friend of yours?" Gareth asked. He had heard rumors regarding the French aristocrats who had recently moved to Notleigh Manor by Ashby.

Christianna shrugged. "Madame Alfort," she said, quoting Artois, "is one of those people who thinks that she's terribly clever, but she's not. No, not a dear friend; just someone I knew. It doesn't matter. I'd rather spend the day with you."

Gareth looked surprised, and then his smile

showed, warm and pleased. "Fancy that," he remarked.

He leaned toward her, as if he was going to kiss her, until Mrs. Hatton's strident voice spoke.

"Some people," she said, "should be tending to business instead of lolling around making sheep's eyes at each other."

Gareth jumped back, looking like a guilty child who'd been caught at some mischief.

"That's more like it," Mrs. Hatton snapped, her broad face showing disapproval. "Now don't you forget to bring back figs. And cinnamon, if you can remember it. And get some new milk pans from the tinker, if your mind isn't too busy thinking about what you shouldn't be thinking of."

Christianna wanted to laugh at Gareth's obvious discomfort.

"And you, miss," Mrs. Hatton added with a stern look, "you keep away from gypsies. We've trouble enough around here, I shouldn't wonder."

Christianna blushed and assured Mrs. Hatton that she had no intention of going anywhere near the gypsies.

"Hmmph," was the predictable reply.

"Let's be off," Gareth said quickly. "It's a long day ahead."

"And don't let your brothers come back in their cups," Mrs. Hatton called after them. "Drunk as seven lords, last year. I never heard such a noise."

She stood in the garden, watching as Gareth

helped Christianna up onto the seat of the farm wagon. Daniel climbed up next to her and took the reigns.

"Trouble," was Mrs. Hatton's cryptic remark. "That girl is nothing but trouble."

Chapter Fourteen

The Ashby Fair was held in the center of the village. Tents and tables crowded the common green and spilled over onto the streets. Crowds of country folk, in their Sunday best, jostled and shouted greetings to their neighbors. A group of country musicians played a lively air on their flutes and fiddles, the sound barely audible over the noise of the crowds and the bleating of sheep and the nickering of horses.

Christianna noticed again how the local folk called out to the Larkins, and spoke respectfully to them, and admired the fine, clean fleeces and baskets of berries in the wagon.

"That farm was nothing till you took it over," one old man told Gareth. "You've a touch for the earth, son. Not like your father. No head for farming. All he could grow was sons."

Gareth laughed. "Aye, but he did that well."

"And is this the girl who set Squire's son on his ear? Heard all about that. Is Giles making trouble for you?"

Christianna flushed under the old man's scrutiny.

"He can't," Gareth answered. "We own that land, free and clear, and if Giles knows what's good for him, he'll keep well away from us."

Christianna turned away, watching the crowd of people. A group of acrobats were stringing a rope between two poles and calling to the crowd to wait and see the famous rope dancer, who had performed for the king himself. The crowd greeted this announcement with derision but waited about anyway.

Stout farm women mingled with rosy-cheeked lasses; children and dogs ran about excitedly, enjoying the sunshine and fresh air, and men shouted at each other and asked about the weather and the crops.

Where was Polly? Christianna climbed onto the wagon to get a better view and stopped suddenly, her heart giving a sickening lurch.

Jean-Claude was standing by the rope dancers. She stared in horror at his wiry frame, his dirty dark hair.

How could it be? For a moment she was standing in the dirty, dank room in France, and his brother was tearing open the bundle of her possessions—the portrait of her mother, the earrings from Artois, the letters from Phillipe—

274

I am getting married to a wonderful woman, her name is Victoria Larkin, and she's from a town called Middlebury, about two days' ride from London. . . .

"Christianna? Are you ill? You look green . . ." Daniel laid his hand on her shoulder.

She looked back to the crowd, and the man turned briefly in their direction.

It wasn't Jean-Claude, after all. She let out her breath with a long shudder. "I thought I saw . . ." She glanced at Gareth, but he was busy showing a bundled fleece to a well-dressed merchant and hadn't looked her way. "I thought I saw Jean-Claude," she said quickly. "The brother of the man I killed. But it wasn't. Just someone who looked like him."

Daniel helped her down from the wagon. "Take a deep breath," he suggested. "Better?"

Christianna gave a weak smile and steadied her knees. "Oh, yes. That was stupid of me, wasn't it?"

"No, not at all. You look terrified."

"I was," she admitted.

"Don't think of it," Daniel told her. "The chances of him knowing where to find you are nil, aren't they?

"As good as," she agreed. Even if Jean-Claude had read the letters from Phillipe, he wouldn't have the means to follow her to England.

"Look, here comes Polly."

Christianna followed Daniel's gaze, and there was Polly, her golden hair gleaming down over her well-exposed shoulders, her waist tightly laced above her full skirts, her freckled face alight with pleasure.

"There you are," she called. "What a day. Come on, Christianna, let's go see the gypsies and have our fortunes told."

Christianna laughed at the idea. "Mrs. Hatton told me to stay well away from gypsies," she protested.

"Old witch," was Polly's answer. "Bugger that. Gypsies are the most fun. Last year one told me I'd marry a duke and have eight children. Fancy that!"

"That doesn't say much for the gypsy's predictions," Richard commented, passing by.

"Well, I did meet a duke," Polly argued, "and a damned armful of fun he was. Didn't marry him, though," she added, with a mournful look. "But who knows? Maybe he'll be back."

"Here," Gareth said, pressing a handful of coins into Christianna's hand. "You go with Polly and see the gypsies, and buy yourself some new ribbons or something. I'll take care of the wool and catch up with you in a bit."

"I'll go too," Geoffery chimed in. "Gypsies have some fine horses sometimes."

"Most likely stolen," Gareth added. "Mind you don't get taken, Geoff. They drive a hard bargain."

"Thanks, Grandfather," Geoffrey said in a sour tone.

"Come on—" Polly grabbed Christianna's arm— "let's go have some fun. I just love the fair. Have you seen the rope dancer? Her dress is all spangled and cut right up to here. . . ."

Christianna laughed at Polly's enthusiasm and happily followed her into the crowd.

"Guess who was in the Broken Bow last night?" Polly demanded. "Giles Thornley, that's who. Drunk as a fiddler's bitch and looking for trouble. You really took him down a peg, Christianna. He'll not forgive you for it."

Christianna tossed her head. "Who cares for Giles Thornley? He's only a squire's son, after all."

"My goodness," Polly exclaimed, her eyes sparkling. "Only a squire's son, is he? If I'd known that, I'd have wiped me boots on him when he came in! Fancy being that far beneath us grand folk!"

Christianna joined Polly's laughter. "Oh, Polly, you know what I meant."

"I'm just teasing. Look, Christianna, there are the gypsies! Don't you think black-haired men are handsome?"

The gypsy wagons were on the edge of the crowd, brightly painted with designs of red and yellow. Dark-haired children with bare feet played among them, and their mothers, gaily dressed in multicolored skirts and gold jewelry, called to them in unknown words.

"I'll be over here," Geoff announced, pointing to a group of swarthy men and fine horses. "Mind you don't sell your souls."

"Oh, give over." Polly laughed.

An old gypsy woman rose from the steps of her wagon and beckoned to them. "Come to have your fortune read?" she called in a singsong voice. "Don't be afraid; come over here."

Christianna hesitated, and then stepped forward.

"You wait," the old woman told Polly sharply. "This is not for your ears."

Polly shrugged, undaunted, her eyes already sparkling at a black-haired man with a brilliant scarf around his neck. "Suit yourself," she said cheerily.

Christianna followed the old woman into the dim wagon and sat across from her at a small table. Hanging fabrics of brilliant colors covered the walls, fringed and embroidered in heavy silks. Candles flickered in the spicy-smelling room, casting a mysterious glow over the scene.

To Christianna's surprise, the old woman leaned over, and her spotted, gnarled fingers moved over Christianna's head, feeling the shape of her skull, the bones of her face.

"Aah," the gypsy said, sounding surprised. She sat down and held out her hand.

Christianna placed a few coins in the thin hand and the woman looked pleased.

"First," the gypsy said, "we pray. You must ask the Holy Mother for her guidance."

Hoping that the Holy Mother in question was the same one that she had been praying to her whole life, Christianna shut her eyes and obeyed.

"Now," the old woman said, "take these cards and mix them well."

The deck was large and awkward in Christianna's hand.

"Larger than you're used to," the gypsy said. "But at least you won't be losing your earrings and pearls at my table, or spending money that you should be paying to your dressmaker."

A chill ran down Christianna's spine. How did this woman know that she had gambled her jewelry and money a hundred times? She was dressed as simply as any country maid; she didn't look like anyone who had owned jewels.

"Shuffle again," the gypsy ordered.

Trying to calm her nervous hands, Christianna obeyed.

"You have nothing to fear," the gypsy said, taking the cards into her own weathered fingers. "Except the truth."

Christianna stared, fascinated, as the woman began to lay the cards down in a mysterious pattern. Strange pictures, painted in soft colors, stared up at her.

"This," said the woman, "is you. Today." She pointed at a card: a man and a woman in flowing robes, holding golden cups, facing each other. "You're in love, aren't you? Lucky girl."

Christianna didn't answer.

"And here," the woman said, "this is what went before."

Christianna stared at the picture on the card: a hooded figure seated in a boat, surrounded by swords.

"You've come a long way, haven't you? Not an easy journey, but what is? You take an easy journey, you get nowhere. This wasn't just a trip across a sea; it was a trip into a new life. And here you are. Do you want to go back to the old life?"

Christianna thought of Versailles: the glittering, golden days of pleasure and careless laughter.

"Silly girl," the woman muttered. "What did all that gold get you?" She pointed to another card, a castle tower, flames shooting out of the windows and screaming people falling. "That. Grief and despair. Any castle built on the misery of others will fall. Maybe you didn't build the castle, but you lived in it, like a silly bird that didn't know it was in a cage until the cage burned. But you flew, didn't you? And where did you land?"

She pointed to another card, a woman with a shining crown of stars, surrounded by fields and flowers. "In peace and plenty. You've learned a lot. Some people wait all their lives for such happiness. Will you keep it?"

"Will I?" Christianna echoed, her voice soft with surprise.

"Don't ask me," the woman snapped. "I tell you what I see, but the decision is yours and God Almighty's. You have a choice coming up. Look at this card. It's the card of the Fool. Do you see how careless he is? Staring off at the stars, while he's about to walk over the edge of a cliff. When the time comes to make your choice think carefully, for you can never undo what you have done."

Christianna stared at the card, at the glowing youth, unaware of his danger.

"You know that already. You've already done something that can never be changed, haven't you? What have you done, pretty thing, that haunts you at night?"

Christianna stared with horror at the woman.

"And if you had it to do again, what could you do that would be any different?" the woman demanded. Her dark eyes bored into Christianna's round blue ones, knowing, watching. She sighed.

"I'm not trying to frighten you. If you had done this thing and not felt grief, you would be a monster. But there comes a time when you must forgive the past. Lay it to rest. Nobody else would judge you as harshly as you judge yourself. Who do you think you are? God can forgive you; can you not forgive yourself? Or are you greater than God?

"And here," the woman said, a knotted finger poking at a card. "Here is how those around you see you. Discontented, yet unable to leave. And why is that? Is it because you cannot? Or is it that you don't really wish to? Perhaps you should let someone know what you feel, else they judge you wrongly."

Christianna stared at the woman, half fascinated, half afraid. "What will happen?" she asked, and her voice quivered a little. From outside the open door of the wagon she could hear Polly's husky laugh, and Geoffery's merry voice above the sounds of the fair, but the sunlit day seemed very far away.

"What will happen?" the woman repeated, sounding very aggravated. "What will happen? Why am I even wasting my time with you?" She threw her hands up in a gesture of contempt, her gold bracelets clattering. "I told you once, now listen again. You will have a decision to make. What will happen depends on your choice."

Christianna stared at the woman's dark, wrinkled face, and then down at the cards on the table. The mysterious renditions of stars, swords, and clouds told her nothing.

"The final card," the woman said, and flipped over a card from the deck.

It was a picture of a woman, seated between two columns, a crescent moon balanced on her head, strange runic symbols around her.

"What does it mean?" Christianna asked, her heart pounding.

The gypsy's eyes watched her, dark and knowing. "Not too much more than I've already told you. This card can mean many things. It could be you: the woman you could be. It could be a fate undecided. Or it could be that fate is at work, unseen by your eyes. Something hidden, someone whose influence is at work, but not yet known to you. Be ready for it when it comes."

Christianna waited, but the old gypsy said nothing more. She swept the cards off the table and into a neat pile, her bracelets sparkling in the dim light.

"That's all," the woman said, her tone sharp. "Go back to your garden and think about it.

Now send your friend in here, so she can ask me when she'll get married, and how rich her husband will be."

Startled again, Christianna laughed softly. "And will she marry a rich man?"

The gypsy offered her a short smile. "You ask a lot for a few pennies. Here is your answer. There are those whose lives are rich in gold, and those whose lives are rich in love. Which one are you, *petite* mademoiselle?"

Christianna rose uncertainly, her hands quivering slightly, anxious to get back into the sunshine.

"Forgive yourself," the woman called after her, "but don't forget. There is always a lesson to be learned."

"What a bunch of twaddle," Polly announced when she emerged from the gypsy's wagon. "I wish I had my pennies back and could buy a new ribbon."

"I'll buy you a ribbon, Poll," Geoffery offered, rising from the grass where he and Christianna waited.

Polly smiled and tossed her golden hair. "Will you, Geoff? That's sweet of you. You Larkin men . . . too damned charming for your own good."

Geoffery looked pleased with himself.

"And I want to see the rope dancer," Polly added, "don't you, Christianna?"

"Very much," Christianna agreed, not really caring.

Geoff said that they should go there first, and Polly accused Geoff of wanting to peek up the rope dancer's dress.

"As if I could help it," Geoffery retorted, "when she's ten feet over my head."

They stopped and bought pies full of nuts and apples from a vendor, and then made their way back to the merriment of the fair, Christianna casting a look back at the gypsy camp.

"Are you enjoying the fair?"

Christianna looked away from the acrobats, who were balancing on the taut rope above the cheering crowd, and smiled at Gareth.

"Yes, I think."

He rested his hand on her shoulder, and she blushed at the warmth his touch created.

"Come with me," he suggested. "I've got to go round to the tinker's and get Mrs. Hatton's pans."

"And figs," Christianna reminded him. "Don't forget her figs."

"Go on," Polly told her, her eyes dancing with interest. "I'll see you later."

Christianna followed Gareth through the crowd, her heart fluttering when he took her hand in his firm grasp.

He seemed in no hurry, and he stopped to look at all the merchandise displayed—fine bolts of fabric and tables of herbs and curing medicines for every conceivable complaint, cider presses and barrels, and spices and oranges from far-off places.

They stopped to watch a puppet show, and Christianna laughed at the sight of the puppet father dropping his hideous baby, and his puppet wife clouting him with a club.

Gareth stood behind her, a warm hand on her waist, more intent on her enjoyment than the show before them.

"Bought you a present," he told Christianna, and he pressed a bottle into her hand.

Curious, she removed the stopper, and the rich smell of jasmine rose from the bottle. Delighted, she looked up at him. "It's my very favorite scent," she said softly, as pleased as if he had handed her jewels.

Gareth looked awkward. "You mentioned it once," he said, and bent down to whisper in her ear. "I couldn't find you a maid to pour it in your bath. Do you suppose I might have that honor?"

She laughed, her cheeks flaming, her blood racing at the thought. "I think so," she answered, "since Therese isn't to be found."

"Probably off looking for the wages you didn't pay her," Gareth teased. He looked ahead through the crowds. "Now look here," he exclaimed, "those are some damned fine plows."

Christianna followed his long-legged stride through the crowd, though she didn't really care about plows. Gareth, however, seemed enthralled by them, and spent a great deal of time talking with the merchant selling them.

Christianna wandered to the next stall and

looked over the displays of ribbons fluttering in the sunlight, like rainbows of silk, and finely knit laces, white and delicate, carefully displayed against black fabric. She was about to turn back to find Gareth when the high, clear sound of a violin caught her attention.

She turned abruptly and made her way through the crowd, where a man had several violins laid across a table.

"Did you make these?" she asked him.

The man stroked his grizzled beard and nodded proudly. "Aye, mistress, that I did. Learned it from my da, who learned it from his. As fine a fiddle as you'll find."

She reached out hesitantly and ran a finger across the four strings of the nearest one. "A fiddle," she repeated, thinking how comical the English word sounded.

"Pick her up, if you like," the man added. "They're fine, sturdy things. Last a man his lifetime."

She picked one up, then another, feeling the light weight of the hollow wood, smelling the fragrant smell of the oil that polished their bodies, seeing the strings stretched with precision over the bridges.

"I had a violin once," she told the man. "A Guarneri."

"Foreigners," the man replied contemptuously, unimpressed. "Give us a tune, then, sweetheart." He offered her a bow.

Christianna took it from him, hesitating for a moment.

It had been so long! Her fingers felt awkward as she tucked the instrument onto her shoulder, and her hand trembled a little as she raised the bow.

She pulled the taut bow across the strings, smiling at the sound, rich and true. She ran up the scale and down again.

"It's a fine instrument," she told the man.

"I told you that," the man replied. "Give us a tune."

She closed her eyes and played. Sweet and lilting, the baroque notes of Vivaldi sounded. Awkwardly at first, and then with growing strength, the sounds filled the air, rich and golden and almost painful in their beauty. The notes danced around her ears and into the cloudless blue sky above her. True and clear, vibrating through her fingers and shoulder, filling her with joy.

It was over too quickly, and she was startled at the appreciative whistle of the fiddlemaker and the boisterous applause of the crowd that had gathered while she played.

Gently, she put the instrument back on the table. It was almost painful to leave it. Her fingers lingered for a moment, touching the violin softly.

"Did you hear that?" the fiddlemaker demanded of the crowd. "Never heard the like. Now, mistress, you should buy that. Made for you, it was."

"I'm sorry. I can't." She backed away from the table, feeling, for the first time in weeks, keen

287

regret that she had no money of her own.

"That's a damned shame," the man replied. "A sorry shame. Anyone can do that, they should have a fiddle."

"They should, indeed." It was Gareth who spoke, and Christianna stared at him. His eyes were on her, sorrowful and knowing, his handsome face serious as he took in the sight of her longing expression, the thin mist of tears that covered her eyes.

Before she could speak he stepped up to the table, and spoke quietly to the fiddlemaker. Then he soberly counted out four precious gold coins.

"You can't," she whispered, pulling at his sleeve.

He gave her a quick smile. "Stop me," he said, and put the instrument into her arms.

Amazed, she stared down at it, at the shining wood, the graceful curve of the waist, the carefully measured frets.

And then, not even caring that she was watched by a crowd of people, she threw her arms around Gareth's neck and burst into tears.

"Foreign," she heard the fiddlemaker explain to someone, as if that accounted for her peculiar behavior.

"Damned fool thing to spend your share on, if you ask me," was Richard's comment when he saw the instrument.

"Nobody asked you," Gareth said easily.

Christianna sat on the edge of the empty

wagon, the instrument across her lap, her eyes shining with pleasure. Her shoes were discarded on a pile of straw; her hair was coming loose from her braid.

"Maybe you could learn to play something jolly," Stewart suggested, "like 'Sally from our Alley,' or 'The Goldsmith's Wife.'"

"Philistine," Daniel remarked. "I like Christianna's music very much."

"You could have had a horse for what that cost," Geoffery informed her.

"There's an idea. I could take it back, if you like," Gareth suggested to her, "and buy you a horse."

She shrieked with horror and clutched the fiddle to her heart. "Don't even say such a thing," she cried. "Don't even think it."

Gareth's eyes sparkled at her. "Are you certain?"

She wished that they were alone and she could kiss him again.

"I'm for a pint," Richard announced, surveying the empty wagon with a look of satisfaction. "Anyone else?"

"That's me," Polly announced. "My favorite part of the fair. And there's dancing later. I do love to dance."

"I'm starving," Gareth put in. "There's a fellow selling roast duckling, over to the other side of the green. Anybody else?"

Christianna climbed down from the wagon and placed her violin carefully in a bed of coats and straw.

"Do you think anyone will steal it?" she asked.

"No," Richard answered. "Who'd steal a silly thing like that? If it was a horse, or something worthwhile . . ."

"Never mind," she told him. "You just don't understand the value of it."

"That's something," Richard announced, "her highness telling me I don't understand the value of money."

Gareth picked up the fiddle and bow and tucked them carefully beneath his arm. "I'll carry them for you, so you don't have to worry," he offered.

Daniel fell into step beside her and Gareth as they went in search of the roast duckling.

"Everything smells wonderful," Christianna announced. "I must be starving too. Is it my imagination or do I smell coffee?"

Gareth tilted his nose up and sniffed the air. "I think so. Do you want some?"

"More than anything."

"This way, I think," he said, and took her hand, pulling her through the crowds of vendors and merchants, who were busily packing up their wares for the evening. "I think it's over by the bakers."

"Are you happy?" Daniel asked her, as they made their way across the crowded green.

Christianna looked up at him and at Gareth, as they walked on either side of her, their identical auburn heads glowing in the evening sunlight, their green eyes shining at her.

"I think," she announced, "that I'm as happy as I've ever been. Ever. I've got a garden full of roses, and a dog, and friends, and plenty to eat, and a violin to play. What more could I possibly want?"

And I feel loved, she added silently, *and safe*. France was a lifetime away, another world. She realized with a start that she no longer had nightmares. When had they stopped? She tried to remember the last time she had dreamed of the revolution and, after a moment, remembered that it was the day she had started her garden— the night that Gareth had come to the cottage and she had asked him to make love to her. It was as if his gentle hands and soft words had driven the demons from her nights.

"You are so good," she told him suddenly, not meaning to speak aloud. "You have been so kind to me."

Gareth looked down at her, startled and pleased. His crooked smile was tender and embarrassed. "How could I not be?"

"Now this," Daniel said, "is too much. For weeks you two snap and scowl at each other, and now we're being subjected to all this cooing and sighing. As Virgil would say—"

"Never mind," Christianna exclaimed, and "Bugger Virgil," Gareth said at the same time.

Daniel affected an offended look, and they were all laughing, when a voice in the crowd caught Christianna's ear. She froze, suddenly silent.

" . . . *au charme vieillot. C'est bon, n'est pas?*"

Gareth raised his head, his eyes moving quickly over the crowd.

"You don't have to go looking for your Madame Alfort," he said softly. "I'd guess that's her, over by the bakeshop."

"Where, where?" Christianna demanded frantically. She stretched on her toes, trying to see over the heads of the crowd, her hand gripping the white fabric of Gareth's sleeve.

"Right there, in that carriage. Here . . ." He gripped her easily around the waist and lifted her from the ground, resting her weight against his hip. "There, can you see her?"

Christianna stared. It was Madame Alfort and the Comte Du Bretonne, sitting in an open carriage. How strange they looked, among the crowds of simply dressed villagers, in their embroidered silks and laces, their powdered hair. Madame Alfort wore a hat covered with silk flowers and ostrich plumes, her white face shielded from the sun with a dainty parasol.

"Do you want to go speak to them?" Gareth asked. Christianna tightened her grip around his neck.

"I should," she said. "It would be rude of me not to."

How peculiar it felt, after all this time, to see someone from Versailles. Madame Alfort had not changed a bit; she appeared untouched by the revolution. It was as if no time had passed at all, as if they had been magically transported here from another world.

Madame Alfort was laughing at something the

comte had said, waving her graceful hand in its delicate lace mitt and leaning forward in the carriage to accept a cup of coffee from someone beside the carriage. . . .

A slender man, his light brown hair tied in a neat queue with a tasteful black ribbon, his white cravat perfectly tied, silver filigree buttons shining on his waistcoat of azure blue . . .

"Artois!"

Her cry was half strangled; her heart leapt and raced.

Gareth and Daniel stared at her in shock as she half jumped, half tumbled from Gareth's arms. She stumbled as she hit the ground and pushed through the crowd ahead of her, almost blinded by the hot tears that filled her eyes.

"Artois!" Her cry of joy carried through the crowd clearly this time; and the man by the carriage turned, his thin face still with shock, his eyes scanning the crowd quickly, bright with intensity.

"Artois!" She was crying out loud, hot tears spilling over her cheeks as she pushed people ruthlessly out of her way.

Artois stared at her in disbelief for a moment, the cup of coffee in his hand spilling over the white lace of his cuff, and then he threw his head back and gave a shout of joy that would have carried over three fields.

And suddenly she was in his arms, crying against his immaculate shirtfront, breathing the familiar clean linen smell, hardly daring to believe that he was real, that he was alive, that he was here.

"You're alive," he cried.

Christianna laughed with delight as they stood back from each other, her hands gripped within his tight grasp.

"Your hair is turning gray," she said, unable to think of anything else.

Artois's eyes were brilliant, his sharp cheekbones flushed with color as he stared at her. He reached out to tug her heavy braid and touched her damp cheek, staring at her simple gown, her bare feet.

"You look awful," he said at last, trying not to smile, which was impossible. "Simply dreadful. What have these English done to you? You look like a goosegirl."

Christianna threw her head back, laughing. "Oh, Artois. Oh, Artois, how I've missed you."

Artois gathered her in his arms again, tears showing in his eyes. "I've missed you too, my friend."

Gareth stood in the crowd, Christianna's forgotten violin in his hand, watching as she embraced the elegant aristocrat again and reached up to touch his shoulder, her eyes brilliant. Her voice reached him, the foreign words tripping over each other like rushing water, sparkling and bright.

Daniel laid his hand on his brother's shoulder, his eyes quietly searching Gareth's face.

Gareth looked at him quickly with a quiet, rueful smile. "Well," he said at last. He stopped and cleared his throat and brushed a lock of hair from his high forehead. "Well," he said again. "I suppose that's that. Shall we bother waiting?"

"*Respice finem*," Daniel advised. "Don't jump to conclusions, Gareth."

"She knows where to find us, if she chooses," Gareth answered. "If she pleases."

He looked across the crowds at Christianna, her eyes dancing with happiness, oblivious to everything and everyone but the elegant nobleman at her side. She reached up to touch his cheek, and the tender familiarity caused Gareth's heart to turn over with a sickening lurch.

"So," Daniel said thoughtfully, "there is Artois, *redivivus*. I really didn't think he was still alive." He turned to his brother, but Gareth was gone.

Chapter Fifteen

" . . . and then I spent a month in Venice," Artois added, "but it was tiresome. The Italians can be so . . . *Italian*."

Christianna choked back a laugh. "They can hardly be anything else, can they?"

"I suppose not. Listen to that music," he went on, switching subjects abruptly, as was his habit. "Simply dreadful, isn't it?"

Christianna frowned, looking across the crowded village green. Torches flickered in the darkness; ale was flowing freely, and a group of country musicians was playing a lilting folk tune.

"I don't think so. It's pretty, in a way."

Artois rolled his eyes. "Bad enough you lost your place at court, bad enough to lose your money and wardrobe, but it would seem you've lost your taste as well."

"Snob," Christianna retorted, with a smile.

They sat on the back of the farm wagon and watched the villagers dancing for a few minutes.

"Will you come and stay at Notleigh with the rest of us?" Artois asked. "Madame Alfort and the comte would love to have you. And you remember Suzette and Lucien Bértin, don't you? They are there, as well. They're a little common, but rich, rich, rich. And who else is there . . . let me see—"

"Never mind, Artois. I'll come and visit someday soon, but I'm happy where I am."

Artois looked baffled. He looked as if he was about to argue when Richard strolled up to them and offered them two heavy tankards of ale.

"Are you still drinking beer with the rest of the common folk?" he asked. "Or shall I have the boy go fetch some wine?" He turned with an affected look on his face and snapped his fingers at Geoffery, who was standing by the horses and talking with a pretty young girl. "Oh, boy!" he called in imperious tones.

Geoffery glanced over with a disdainful look and spit on the ground. "Call me boy again and I'll take off your head and shove it up—"

"Stop it," Christianna ordered. "You're absolutely impossible, Richard. Of course we shall drink beer."

Richard chortled at his own wit and held out the heavy mugs. Christianna took hers and drank heartily.

Artois, she noticed, gave a grimace and an

elaborate shudder after tasting his, and she was surprised to find herself a little annoyed by it.

"Well, Artois," Richard went on, a mischievous look in his eye, "what do you think of our quaint little English peasant customs?"

Artois lifted a brow. "They're not so different from French peasants, really. Or Italian peasants, for that matter. They just have worse accents."

Richard laughed aloud at that, and belched.

"Don't be rude," Christianna told him, and Richard gave an elaborate bow.

"Whatever her highness commands," he replied, and wandered back into the crowd.

"This is your brother-in-law?" Artois demanded. "Good heavens, Christianna, are they all that awful?"

"Richard's not awful at all; he just likes to tease. He's really very kind."

Artois looked doubtful.

"Truly, Artois. They all are. Look, there is Daniel; he teaches Latin. Or at least he did, but they let him go. It was my fault, really, because I had a little fight with the·squire's son when I was working in the Broken Bow."

"You were doing what, where?"

"Working, my friend. Don't look so horrified. As far as taverns go, it's not so bad. Goodness, Artois, are you choking?"

"No, I'm dying of shock," Artois replied. "Are you sure you won't come to Notleigh? I can't believe these ruffians sent you to work in a tavern."

"They didn't force me; I chose to." Christianna looked into the crowd and saw Gareth. He was standing by Polly, his arm linked in hers in a familiar way. She felt a quick, unreasonable stab of jealousy.

As if he felt her watching, he turned and met her gaze without smiling.

"Gareth," she called, beckoning to him, "come meet Artois."

He hesitated, and then strode through the dancers, his hair glinting auburn in the torch-light.

He offered his hand to Artois and shook it briefly.

"So, this is Artois. We've heard about you incessantly."

"Not incessantly, surely," Christianna argued. "Artois, this is Gareth."

There was an awkward silence, and then Polly raced up, her striped skirts swaying. "What, aren't you dancing, Christianna?"

"No, not yet. Polly, this is my friend Artois, the one I told you about."

Polly's smile sparkled at them. "What, the same Artois who gave you diamond earrings for your birthday?"

"The same," Artois agreed.

"Fancy that," Polly remarked. "And here you are at Ashby fair. Are you not dancing either, Artois?"

"I don't dance," Artois answered, and Christianna noticed for the first time that he sounded a little pompous.

"Well, I bloody well do," Gareth said suddenly. "It's about as much fun as two people can have with their clothes on. Come on, Poll, let's have a whirl."

He took Polly's arm and pulled her into the crowd. Christianna looked away as Polly whispered something into his ear and he threw his head back, laughing.

"What a surly fellow," Artois remarked.

"He usually isn't," Christianna objected, her eyes following Gareth and Polly. Daniel stepped between them and led Polly off into the dance. Gareth laughed and shrugged and went to get another beer, draining it in almost one gulp.

"Tell me again about Phillipe," Artois ordered. "What possessed him to leave you in this place? Was he out of his mind?"

"I thought so at the time. But now—" She stopped abruptly as a local girl danced by in Gareth's arms, her curly head tipped back, her expression bordering on adoration as she gazed up at him.

"What?" Artois demanded. "What are you staring at, Christianna? Shall we go and see if we can find some wine? This English beer is enough to kill me."

"I like it," Christianna protested, tearing her eyes away from Gareth and the curly-haired girl. "Tell me about Notleigh, Artois. Who else is there?"

They sat on the back of the wagon, with the sounds of flutes and fiddles and singing around them, and they talked of France, of who had lived and who had not, and who was still lost and who had surfaced in what countries.

When Geoffery and Stewart arrived to hitch up the horses and return home Christianna made Artois promise to visit her the next day.

She climbed into the wagon, leaning against a pile of straw with her new violin clutched in her arms, and waited for Gareth to return.

They waited for over an hour, and then Daniel made the decision to return home without him. "Likely he's off having a pint somewhere," he reassured Christianna.

It didn't make her feel a bit better.

Chapter Sixteen

Mrs. Hatton greeted Gareth's appearance in the kitchen with a contemptuous glower.

"After I told you not to let your brothers come back in their cups. And there you come, almost dawn, drunk as an earl."

Gareth offered her a sickly smile, trying not to wince at her strident tone. There was no point in denying it; he had gotten blissfully, stupidly drunk.

"Sleeping till noon," Mrs. Hatton added.

Gareth examined a half-finished cup of tea on the table, decided it looked safe, and tossed it down his parched throat.

"Eat and drink till midnight, piss and moan till noon," Mrs. Hatton observed, very uncharitably, to Gareth's mind.

"Where is everyone?" he asked. Where is

Christianna? was what he meant. The last time he had seen her, she had been sitting on the back of the farm wagon with Artois, laughing adoringly at him, her black curls resting comfortably against his shoulder.

Mrs. Hatton gestured to the back door. "Where is everybody? Up to no good, that's where," she replied ominously, and turned her back, concentrating on the beef she was salting.

Gareth stepped out onto the worn stone stoop, wincing as the brilliant sunlight blinded him. Looking around, he saw Geoffery and Stewart leaning against the wall of the house, and Daniel standing between them, a put-upon expression on his face.

Gareth started to speak, and Geoff and Stewart gestured at him to be silent.

Christianna's voice was speaking, somewhere around the corner—speaking French—and a deeper voice answered her.

Stewart and Geoff looked at Daniel.

"She said," Daniel murmured quietly, "that it's not too bad, when you get used to it. He said that she looks like a . . . something. I don't know."

"What the hell are you doing?" Gareth demanded.

Stewart and Geoffery shushed him.

"She's telling him about her garden," Daniel whispered, cocking an ear toward the garden, "and he says . . . 'Too much lavender. Get rid of it.'"

"I don't believe you're eavesdropping like this," Gareth said softly, glowering at his brothers. He sat down on the stoop and waited to hear more.

"He said that she can't be happy here. Impossible. 'It could be worse, but not much.'"

"Bugger him," muttered Geoff.

"I can believe this of Geoff and Stew," Gareth remarked, "but not you, Daniel."

"He can't help it," Stewart said cheerfully. "We're blackmailing him."

"Over what?" Gareth demanded.

"Ssshhh," Geoffery hissed. "What are they saying now, Dan?"

"Artois is saying that she should come with him, and he can take her to New Orleans. Maybe go to Vienna first. He says . . ."

Gareth stood up and tossed his hair from his eyes with an impatient gesture.

"Enough," he said quietly. "Enough. We've all better things to do, I think. Let's quit this assing about and get to the fields."

"You're pretty this morning," Geoffery commented. "Smell like a brewery too."

Gareth didn't answer as he stalked toward the barn, his face dark and tense.

"What the hell's wrong with him?" Stewart demanded.

"Get to work," Daniel told him, and followed Gareth.

"Bullshit," Geoff said cheerily. "Let's go for a ride."

Stewart grinned. "Done," he agreed.

Christianna offered Artois a cut rosebud, which he carefully placed in his buttonhole.

"And Phillipe just dumped you here?" he demanded, with his usual lack of tact. "No money, nothing?"

"He didn't *dump* me. I wasn't strong enough to travel."

Artois looked doubtful. "You look strong," he observed. "Healthy, very healthy. You might even be getting a little fat."

Christianna bristled with indignation. "Fat! I am most certainly not fat!"

Artois, delighted with her reaction, cast a critical eye at her figure. "A little, maybe."

"You're so rude. I'm just not wearing corsets, that's all."

"It's that goosegirl look," was Artois's comment. "The latest thing. Lose your figure, stop doing your hair, throw a little dung on your shoes, and voilà—the latest fashion."

"It's comfortable," Christianna told him. "You can't garden in silk gowns."

Artois laughed at her lofty tone and looked around the sunlit garden. "I can't picture you crawling in the dirt. It's funny, isn't it?"

Christianna smiled. "I suppose. But it's a wonderful thing, to put one's hands into the earth and make things grow. Very calming. It makes me feel so much a part of things."

"It's that eternal return thing," Artois agreed. "That cycle of life sort of thing. You know, everything growing and dying and returning. That thing."

"Exactly," Christianna told him.

"And," Artois added, "it gives you something

to do. After all, what else would you be doing, stuck out here in the middle of nowhere? Have you been bored out of your mind?"

"Oh, no. Never bored. I'll hate to leave when Phillipe sends for me. I wish I could stay forever."

Artois looked very surprised. He leaned forward, staring into her face, his eyes bright and blue and intense.

"Ha!" He gave a bark of laughter, so sudden and loud that Christianna jumped.

"What? What is it?"

Artois grinned, his eyes sparkling with mischief. "Oh, Christianna. What have you been doing here to amuse yourself?"

"What? I've been gardening, I told you, and just . . . living." To her dismay, she was blushing.

"And what else?" Artois demanded merrily. "Look at you blush! My dear Christianna, you are the most abysmal liar. No wonder you don't want to leave! You're finally doing it, aren't you?"

"Don't be so rude; I am not—"

"You are! Look at your face! Oh, this is rich. This is really rich. Which one is it? The scholar, or the one with the wild hair?"

"Certainly not! Artois, how awful you are."

"The surly one?" Artois persisted.

"Gareth is not surly!" Christianna snapped.

"Gareth," repeated Artois, in a tone of mock reverence. "Is that his name? Tell me, when did this start?"

"You know," Christianna said, rising and walking over to the gillyflowers and pulling some dead blooms off, "when I thought you were dead I actually cried. Buckets of tears. Oceans of tears. And now I can't imagine why. What a terrible tease you are!"

Artois laughed, undisturbed. "No wonder you don't want to leave. 'I don't want to go to Vienna, Artois; I'd hate to leave my garden.' For God's sake, Christianna. I almost believed you. No wonder the man was glaring at you last night."

"Was he?" Christianna had been so delighted to see Artois that she hadn't noticed.

"Right up until he left."

Christianna frowned.

"Is it serious?" Artois asked. "I mean, is it all just fun, or do you love him?"

Christianna was silent for a while, looking at the bright blue blooms of the larkspur, the velvet magenta of the sweet williams, the deep, rich plum of the violets.

"I love him," she admitted, her voice quiet.

Artois looked delighted.

"But," she added hastily, "he doesn't love me. He desires me, but he doesn't love me. He thinks I'm vain and silly."

"You are vain and silly," Artois pointed out.

"I am not. *Bon Dieu*, you're awful. I may have been vain and silly once, but I'm not anymore. Truly I'm not."

Artois looked doubtful.

"Well, perhaps just a little vain. Oh, never mind. It doesn't matter."

"I suppose not," Artois agreed. "After all, what if he did love you? He'd ask you to marry him, and then you'd be stuck on this farm, growing flowers for the rest of your life; and that would be—"

"Heaven," Christianna finished softly. "It would be wonderful. But it's not going to happen, so I'm not going to think of it. I'll just stay here until Phillipe sends for me, and then I'll go. But until then, I intend to enjoy myself."

"Is it that good?" Artois asked, adjusting the white lace at his cuff.

Christianna gave him a withering stare and then laughed at his teasing expression. "Better," she admitted, "better than good."

"First the revolution, now this," Artois remarked. "The world really has come to an end, hasn't it? Tell me, Christianna, did you do it in the straw? Or in the sheep pen? Or out in the field with the cows watching?"

"Stop it, Artois! What am I to do with you? You really are dreadful, you know. Simply dreadful."

Artois dimpled. "I am, aren't I? It's part of my charm."

Christianna tried to look cross and failed miserably.

"I've missed you so much," she told him. "Even though you're such a pig."

Artois looked pleased. "I've missed you. Now, show me your cottage. I can't wait to see this bower of bliss."

Christianna laughed. "Very well. You'll laugh. It's as simple as a convent cell."

"But much more lively, I'd imagine," Artois added.

Christianna raised her brow at him, and he laughed at her indignation as he followed her from the garden, out beneath the shady trees and across the green pasture.

"Has Artois left?" Daniel asked when Christianna appeared in the kitchen that evening.

"He just did. Do you like him? Isn't he funny? My sides hurt from laughing so much."

"Like a couple of lunatics," commented Mrs. Hatton, looking up from the piece of beef she was roasting over the fire. "Laughing about God knows what."

"He liked your cheese," Christianna told her hastily. "He was very impressed with it."

"Hmmph." Mrs. Hatton responded with a dark look over her broad shoulder.

Daniel closed his book with a smile and raised his spectacles to the top of his head. "Yes, Artois is very amusing. Are you happy?"

Christianna settled happily on the bench next to Daniel and leaned on the table. "Happy. Yes, yes, I am. How wonderful, that we both should be alive. And to think that he was at Ashby all this time." She thought about how strange life was, that Artois had been only a few villages away from her all the times she had been writing to him, grieving for him, wishing that she could tell him about

Gareth. "Have you seen Gareth?" she asked abruptly.

Daniel nodded. "Out in the fields, working."

"Sulking," Mrs. Hatton corrected.

Daniel offered Christianna a swift smile and a shrug. "Perhaps you should go speak to him."

"Perhaps I should," she agreed, rising from the table.

She found him in the easternmost field, standing in the hops. They grew in thick vines, climbing up their poles and twining over the stout lines of string, forming lush, narrow corridors of green, taller than a man's head.

He was leaning on a hoe, staring off into the sky. The evening sun warmed his hair to a fiery glow and warmed his skin to a burnished gold. He didn't appear to hear Christianna as she approached down the soft dirt path until she spoke.

"Gareth?"

He turned and smiled a quick, sad smile. "Where is Artois?"

"Gone back to Ashby, for the night. What are you doing?"

Gareth looked at the hoe in his hands. "Fighting weeds. What do you think I'm doing?"

"Staring off into space."

"That too," he agreed. "Watching the hops grow."

Christianna looked at the vines growing over her head, and could almost believe it.

"Have you come to say good-bye?" he asked abruptly.

Startled, she gave a quick laugh. "And what makes you think I'm leaving?"

"Aren't you?" Gareth asked, his voice betraying none of the sorrow he felt. "Off to Vienna, and then to New Orleans, with your blue-blooded sweetheart?"

"Where did you get that idea?" Christianna demanded.

"Geoffery is the world's greatest eavesdropper. You should know that, by now. No secrets in this house."

Christianna frowned. "Geoffery doesn't speak French."

"No, but Daniel does, and Geoff blackmailed him into translating. With what dirty secrets, I can't even imagine."

"No wonder your father hides in his study all day," Christianna observed with a rueful laugh. "This is a madhouse."

"Well, you'll be leaving soon, won't you? And then you won't have to be bothered with us."

"You really are annoying me," Christianna said. "In the first place, either Daniel's French isn't equal to his Latin or Geoffery is spreading false rumors. And Mrs. Hatton is right; you're sulking."

Gareth blew a lock of hair off his forehead. "What, you're not leaving with Artois?"

"No, I'm not." She watched his face carefully, trying to see his reaction, but she saw nothing more than his typical tranquil thoughtfulness.

"He asked you, didn't he?"

"Well, yes. Would that bother you?" *Say*

yes, she thought; *ask me to stay. Tell me you love me.*

Gareth shrugged.

The careless gesture struck Christianna like a sharp slap. She felt her face tighten; then she gave a quick, bitter laugh.

"No, I'm not leaving. I told my brother I'd stay here until he sent for me, and I'll stay. After all, it shouldn't be too much longer, should it?"

"Not if you're lucky. And then you're off to find a rich husband. What does Artois think of that? Isn't he rich enough?"

Christianna laughed. "You're jealous, and you shouldn't be. Artois and I are perfectly unsuited."

"Balls," was Gareth's answer.

Christianna wrinkled her brow. "Balls?" she repeated. "What do you mean by that?"

"Nonsense," Gareth explained. "You two are perfectly matched. Anyone can see it. The way you look at each other, the way you laugh together, the way you touch his arm . . ."

"Balls," Christianna echoed. "You're jealous. He's my friend, that's all. Mrs. Hatton said you were out here sulking, and she was right."

Gareth gave her a sharp glance. "Christianna, if you choose to think so, suit yourself."

Christianna turned her back and pulled a leaf off a hop vine, examining the yellow, papery cones that grew on it. She sniffed at the pungent smell.

"They're called catkins," Gareth told her. "Used for making beer."

She threw it to the dirt, shrugging. "Will you

miss me when I leave?" she asked.

Gareth was quiet for a long time. "Some things," he admitted. *The way your shoulders feel beneath my arm; the way your hair smells of lilacs; the sound of your voice; the way you sigh in your sleep and twine your body around me.* "And you?" he asked. "Are you looking forward to going?"

Christianna swallowed and lied. "Oh, yes. It will be so wonderful to be in New Orleans, and live in a fine house, and have a maid again. And to buy some new gowns, and to be among people who speak French . . ." She drew a deep breath, trying to think of what else she could say, and suddenly she thought of the gypsy, sitting in the dark wagon, her knotted finger resting on a card.

"This is how others see you . . . discontent, yet unable to leave. Because you can't, or because you don't want to? You should tell them, else you be misjudged . . ."

"No," Christianna said, and the truth hurt to speak. "No, I don't really want to go. I hated it here when I came, but that's changed. You don't know how lucky you are, you and your brothers. Never to be alone, always having someone to talk to, somebody who cares for you. I've been alone all my life, ever since Phillipe left home. I was eight years old, and I've been alone since. Except at Versailles, where I had Artois and Gabrielle. But they weren't family. It's not the same. You have your land and your home, and you all know what life will bring you. . . ."

Her voice trailed off. "It's funny, isn't it," she said, "that I should be envious?"

Gareth stood for a moment, surprised. "No," he answered, in his low, calm voice. "No, it's not funny. Not a bit. I didn't know you felt that way."

"It doesn't matter," Christianna said, shrugging.

Gareth laughed softly, an impatient look on his face. "I hate that," he said. "Do you know, I really hate that. Anytime you don't feel like speaking the truth, you toss your head and say, 'It doesn't matter,' or 'Never mind.' Isn't it simpler to tell the truth?"

"Not always," Christianna admitted.

Gareth looked taken aback, and then he laughed again, reaching out to tug the end of her braid. He curled the ends around his fingers, smiling. "That may be so," he agreed, "but it does matter. It matters to me."

His eyes were on her, cool and green like the leaves around them.

"Come here," he said, and opened his arms.

She went to him and leaned against him, and his arms pulled her tightly against his chest. She leaned her cheek against the soft faded linen of his shirt, and felt his heart beating against her cheek, and smelled the warm scent of his skin.

"I waited for you last night," she confessed. "But you didn't come."

His hand was in her hair, moving across the black tendrils by her face. "I thought you might have company."

"Only you," she whispered. "And that, Gareth, is the truth."

He looked at her face, wondering what he would do when she left. He thought of her in New Orleans, safely married to some faceless, elegant Frenchman, who would buy her all the things he never could, and take her to his bed every night and fill her with his seed. "For now," Gareth corrected. "For now, it's only me."

She stared up at him, her hand touching the strong line of his jaw, tracing the shape of his mouth. "I don't want to think of anything else," she confessed.

"As you wish," he said softly, and his eyes searched her face before he bent and covered her mouth with his own. Only the sound of the wind rustling through the vines around them intruded.

She closed her eyes and felt the heat of his mouth, the teasing, soft feeling of his tongue as it moved silkily against hers; the familiar warm rush of desire that flowed through her body.

"Ah, what you do to me," he murmured, pulling her body closer against his. His lips moved beneath her ear, hot and velvety against the tender skin of her neck.

"We should go back to the house," she whispered, her voice quivering. "Mrs. Hatton is making roast beef."

"I'm not hungry for roast beef," Gareth told her, his hands traveling down the length of her back and tracing the curve of her buttocks. He pulled her hips against his, and she felt the hardness of him pressing against her.

Her hands moved over his arms, feeling the muscled curves of his shoulders, the tense strength of him. He rocked against her, and she felt her body quiver hungrily in answer.

"Gareth . . ." Her protest sounded feeble even to her own ears. "Gareth, we can't. Someone may come."

He silenced her with a kiss, demanding and swift, his mouth taking hers with a fierce hunger that left her breathless.

Her heart raced; her breasts ached against the tightly laced bodice and she felt the telling dampness between her legs, a hot thrill of hunger.

"We can't," she repeated when his mouth left hers.

He laughed quietly, his hands tugging at her skirts, lifting them over her bare thighs. "Can't?" he repeated. "Can't? Oh, but we can."

She gasped as his hands sought the soft black pelt between her legs and moved into the warm dampness.

"Liar," he murmured, nuzzling the fragrant skin of her neck. "You want it as badly as I."

Christianna clung to his shoulders, hoping her legs wouldn't collapse beneath her as his fingers moved swiftly and surely over her, seeking and finding the hidden places of her body.

His mouth covered hers again, stilling her words of protest. His tongue moved in her mouth, hot and fast, echoing the rhythm of his fingers, until all thoughts of caution fled her mind. Heat flowed through her veins, like sweet summer wine, dark and rich. She moaned softly into his kiss and didn't object when he lowered her to the soft, furrowed dirt and pushed her skirts up to her waist.

He loosened his breeches and guided her hand to his shaft. A ragged sigh escaped him at her touch, the grip of her soft palm against the warm, rock-hard length of him.

"This is indecent," she murmured, but the words were spoken softly, lovingly; and her eyes glowed up at him as he stretched his body over hers.

"This is perfect," he whispered back, his lips grazing over her forehead and across her cheeks. His fingers tugged at the laces of her bodice and pulled the soft fabric of her blouse away. She blushed to think of the wanton picture she presented, her breasts bare to his gaze, her skirts around her waist, tumbled in the dirt beneath the lush walls of verdant vines, with the evening sun golden and bright across their bodies.

He entered her body slowly, teasing her with just a little of his length, until she arched beneath him, driving the rest of his hot hardness deeply into her soft passage.

His rough palm thrilled her as it moved over the aching buds of her nipples as he began to move in her; slow, even strokes caused her to arch beneath him, her hips moving to match the motion of his own.

She inhaled deeply, her face pressed into the hollow of his shoulder, breathing in the scent of musky sweat and clean hair, and the pungent smell of the hops that grew around them, and the fresh, clean smell of the rich earth beneath them.

Her hands moved across his back and over the tight muscles of his haunches as he plowed into her body, possessing every inch of her, driving harder and harder with every smooth, hot stroke.

His breath was ragged against her ear. "Tell me," he whispered, his voice dark and husky, "tell me you want me."

She quivered at the sound and raised her hand to his cheek, her eyes drinking in the sight of his face, the glow of his half-closed eyes, the sunlight that fell across the line of his jaw.

"Oh, yes. Oh, I want you. More than I've ever wanted anything . . ."

Her words seemed to inflame him, and he tossed his head back, his hair flowing like a stallion's mane. He hooked his arm beneath her knee with an easy motion, opening her wider to his body, and he thrust into her almost wildly, with an increasing hunger.

She welcomed his thrusts with joyous abandon, her body twisting and arching to meet him, all sense of modesty long forgotten, until she felt the blazing, quivering thrills of ecstasy that she longed for. She cried out, her voice sharp and wild beneath the sky, her heartbeat racing.

He raised himself up on his arms and thrust into her again, his eyes closed, his face raised to the sunlight, before she felt the rush of wet heat that poured into her body, the shudder that coursed through his tall frame.

He kissed her hungrily, his mouth moving over her cheeks, her lips, her neck; and she kissed him back, her breath shaking, feeling dazed.

"Oh, Christianna . . ." His voice shook a little, but his smile was bright and hot as he gazed at her. "Ah, if you could see yourself, all rosy and glowing." He bent down and took her soft breast into his mouth, his tongue flicking at her nipple, his lips sucking gently at the stiffening bud. "Wanton," he murmured. "Hot little thing."

Blushing, she gathered up the fabric of her bodice, pushing him away with a husky laugh. "I am," she admitted, struggling to sit up. "But it was you that made me that way."

He moved off her obligingly, pulling his breeches over his lean hips. He sent her a devilish smile as he tugged her skirts down over her legs, his dimple showing.

"In the dirt, my lady," he teased, trying to sound shocked. "How could you?"

"How could I not?" she asked, her fingers still trembling as she tightened the laces of her bodice.

"Let me," Gareth urged, and he took the thin ribbons in his fingers, threading them carefully through the bound holes and tightening them. He dropped his mouth to the hollow between her breasts and placed a soft kiss there before tying the ribbons.

"You've got dirt in your hair," he said, shaking her braid.

"I'm not surprised."

They sat quietly for a few minutes, sheltered by the twisting green vines around them.

"I'm glad you're staying," Gareth told her suddenly, reaching for her hand. "You're right; I was jealous. Stinking jealous."

Tell him, she thought; *tell him you love him. What harm could it possibly do?* She took a deep breath and started to speak. "Gareth—"

"There you are. What the hell are you doing, sitting in the dirt?" Geoffery appeared at the end of the row, his lanky shadow falling over them.

Gareth dropped Christianna's hand, and it fell to her lap, looking curiously empty.

"Sitting," Gareth answered calmly.

Christianna blushed at Geoff's searching look.

"Funny place to sit," he observed. "Do you know what's happened?"

"What?" Gareth asked, trying not to sound impatient.

"There's dirt all over your back," Geoffery informed Christianna, raising an inquisitive brow.

"I know that," she answered, sounding snappish.

"What's happened, lack-wit?" Gareth asked.

"It looks like she fell," Geoff suggested.

"No, not what's happened with Christianna. You came looking for me and asked if I knew what's happened. Are you going to tell me?"

"Oh! Oh, that's right. The cows have taken out the fence, and they're off down the road toward the village."

"Damn!" Gareth exclaimed, jumping to his

feet. "Why didn't you say so?"

"I bloody well just did," Geoff replied, sounding insulted. He gave his brother a curious stare and walked away.

"Can I help?" Christianna asked, rising to her feet.

"No, that's fine. Cows are stupid; it shouldn't take long."

"They were smart enough to take down the fence," Christianna remarked.

Gareth laughed. "I guess they were." He looked after Geoff's retreating back and pulled her toward him, planting a hot, swift kiss on her mouth. "I'll see you after a bit. Stay awake tonight; I'll be there."

She nodded. "Tonight, and any other night," she whispered. His eyes lit up and his teeth flashed as he grinned. She watched him as he raced across the fields after Geoffery, his hair shining like autumn leaves over his broad shoulders.

"Until Phillipe sends for me," she reminded herself, and the thought made her heart ache with a sharp, quick pain. "You have all summer," she told herself sternly, and that made her feel better.

She straightened her skirts and brushed the dirt from her hair as best she could and walked back to the house with as much dignity as she could muster.

Chapter Seventeen

It was the most glorious summer in Christianna's memory. Artois, who visited every Sunday, told her that it had been just as hot and beautiful in France—hotter, even—but Christianna didn't remember it.

Perhaps, she thought, she just hadn't taken the time to notice things—the way that dew sparkled in the morning, the furry coats of bumblebees, how the air sweetened as the summer wore on and the grass began to dry. It all seemed new to her.

"That's because you're in love," Artois informed her, rolling his eyes and making it sound ridiculous, which didn't bother Christianna at all. She was far too pleased with life to let little matters perturb her.

Her garden had grown into an enchanted

place, and the air was rich with the smell of roses and the sweet woodruff that grew like airy green clouds starred with white. The rich, sweet scent of the pale checkered lilies (guinea-fowl lilies, the Larkins called them) wafted through the hot air like a rich perfume, with the sharper, more pungent smell of lavender beneath it.

"It's enough to make a body dizzy," was Mrs. Hatton's opinion, and that, Christianna knew, was as close to a compliment as she was going to get from those quarters.

"Too many colors," was Artois's comment, and Christianna threw her hands up in exasperation and demanded to know exactly which colors were too much?

She loved them all, the deep wines and pale pinks of the roses, the butter and peach shades of the tall lilies, the brilliant azure and midnight of the larkspur. The thought of removing even one carefully nurtured blossom appalled her, and she told Artois so, in no uncertain terms.

"Fine," he answered. "But those violets rioting next to the red poppies are too much. It gives me a headache."

Christianna learned to ride, on a tired old mare with the preposterous name of Lucifer, which didn't suit the pale, spotted old thing at all. Geoffery ran circles around her on his high-spirited coffee-brown steed, and laughed at her awkward progress; Stewart suggested that she stick to gardening.

"Balls," she told them loftily, and they screamed with laughter and told her that it didn't mean *nonsense*, exactly.

Enlightened, Christianna searched Gareth out and found him in the south barn, sharpening scythes on the whetstone, getting ready for haying-time.

"When you define a word for me," she told him in indignant tones, "please be so kind as to tell me *exactly* what it means."

Gareth looked up at her, his eyes crinkling at the corners as he smiled. "Why, what have you said?"

"Balls," Christianna informed him, her cheeks reddening. "I've been saying it when I wanted to say 'nonsense,' and Geoffery and Stewart think it's very funny."

Gareth turned the crank of the grindstone thoughtfully and watched the steel blade of the scythe sing against it. "It is a little funny," he pointed out, his eyes dancing.

"Not to me," Christianna argued, and Gareth laughed at her and laid the scythes aside and pulled her into the feed room, kissing her until she was dizzy and laughing.

She lost count of how many times they made love—in the cool green woods, in the dusty toolshed, in the quiet loft of the south barn on a pile of warm, fragrant straw, and countless nights in her cottage, on the cool, lavender-scented sheets, with the soft breezes of the summer nights wafting through the open window, cooling their sweating bodies.

Christianna felt that she knew every inch of Gareth's body as intimately as she knew her own. She watched him with hungry eyes as he moved around the barns and fields with his easy, long-legged stride, the summer sun shining on his golden shoulders as he repaired stone fences and ripped up blackberry brambles and cut wood.

She spent an entire afternoon watching him with a three-year-old colt, a young and untamed creature. It pulled and fought against the unfamiliar harness and lead, its silky black mane tossing against its cinnamon-colored neck. Gareth spoke to it in his quiet, low voice, as gently as if it were a baby, never letting go of the rope, coaxing the skittish animal with sweet young vegetables. By the end of the day, the colt would trot obediently around the pen in even circles and follow Gareth to the watering trough, the lead line slack in his hand.

To Christianna, it seemed nothing short of a miracle, and Gareth seemed godlike. He laughed when she told him this, with his soft, easy laugh, and told her she would make him conceited if she didn't stop.

Mrs. Hatton began entrusting Christianna with errands to the village, and she went gladly, Dog following faithfully at her heels; to the miller's for flour, to the draper's for linen, to the cobbler's, to pick up the fine leather boots that the Larkins wore through so quickly. Christianna took advantage of these times to visit Polly, who was always delighted to see her, and show off a new ribbon or trinket that her latest admirer had given to her.

In the evenings she played her violin, delighting at the sweet, mellifluous sounds as they floated beneath the starlit skies; and it seemed to her that there was a new richness and fullness in her playing.

And July ripened into August, and the green and red blackberries began darkening on their thorny canes; the only troubling thought in her mind was that one day soon she would get a letter from her brother and have to leave for New Orleans.

It came sooner than she would have liked.

Polly brought the letter up from the village, on a brilliant day in early August. She and Christianna had planned to spend the afternoon together, making over an old dress of Victoria's, and Christianna had walked down the lane to meet her.

The ancient apple trees that bordered the road were green with leaves, their twisted branches heavy with ripening fruit, and wild daisies grew in airy bunches along the dusty road. Christianna was resting in the shade, leaning against the stone fence when Polly came into sight, a brilliant green ribbon around the end of her golden braid, her freckled face flushed with the heat.

"It came," she announced, pulling a battered letter from her pocket.

Christianna stared at the wrinkled packet in dismay, and her heart seemed to plummet. She made no move to take it from Polly's outstretched hand.

Polly gave her a sad smile. "I know. I wasn't too happy about it."

Christianna took the letter reluctantly and shoved it into the pocket of her apron without looking at it.

"Look at you," Polly exclaimed, her attention diverted from the unwelcome letter. "Take that apron off! Don't you care what you look like?"

Christianna laughed at Polly's dismay. "Who's going to see me?" she asked.

Polly shrugged, her husky laugh joining Christianna's lighter one. "You've got me there. Aren't you going to read your letter?"

"Maybe later. What would be the purpose? I know what it says." Christianna swallowed. Two months ago she would have sold her soul for this letter. Now she'd do anything to have it disappear.

Polly nodded, shading her eyes with her hand as she stared down the road. "Look at that, would you? Bloody toffs."

Christianna tilted her head, following Polly's gaze. Down the slope of the lane, where the road turned to the village, Giles Thornley and a few of his friends were riding by, their horses kicking up the dry dust of the road. Giles and his cronies looked very genteel and overdressed in their expensive riding coats and hats.

Giles stopped at the crossroad, hesitated for a moment, and then turned his horse up the road, riding toward Christianna and Polly. His friends followed.

"What is he up to?" Polly demanded.

As Giles grew closer, they could clearly see the mocking smile on his face. Instead of riding past he drew his horse in close to them, so close that Christianna stepped back from the dangerous-looking hooves.

"What have we here?" he asked, looking over his shoulder at his friends, who rode up to meet him. "A couple of tavern sluts, taking the afternoon air? Or looking for a bit of fun, perhaps?"

"D'you know the pretty things, Giles?" A young man with a tall riding hat beamed at them and received a cool stare from Christianna.

"Know them? Why, of course. That's our dear Polly, from the Broken Bow. And as for the other, she's the little frog staying with my old tutor and his family."

Christianna lifted her chin and offered her most eloquent sneer.

"Poor Master Thornley," she commented to Polly—if she had been carrying a fan, she would have given it a languid wave—"he has the most abominable time remembering his manners. I suppose it is understandable, given that he is only the squire's son." She addressed the young man with the ridiculous riding hat. "I'm Lady Christianna St. Sebastien, lately of Versailles and the Auvergne."

The young man looked startled, and hastily doffed his hat, bowing in his saddle.

Giles glared at him. "Don't bow to her, you idiot. She's a lying little frog, is what she is. 'Lady,' indeed. Have you ever seen a lady dressed

328

as a milkmaid, wearing a stained apron?" He laughed at his own meager wit, and his friends, after hesitating, joined in.

"Bloody toffs," Polly muttered under her breath.

"Don't let them offend you," Christianna told her friend, tossing her braid as loftily as if it was a pearl-and-ribbon-laden coiffure. "One can expect little better from commoners with pretensions to gentility. What is this Master Thornley, after all? The illustrious descendant of wool merchants?"

Thornley's pale face turned brilliant red. His friends, he knew, were of more genteel backgrounds than he, and it was something he didn't care to be reminded of.

"And what are you," he retorted, his lips tight, "the illustrious descendant of a barroom whore? How much, little frog, to get you to lift your skirts?" He moved his horse closer to the two young women as he spoke, forcing them farther off the road.

"Get down off that horse, Thornley, and I'll show you what I think of your bloody offer," Polly challenged, her eyes darkening. Her hands were on her hips, her chin thrust out.

Christianna affected a yawn. "Don't trouble yourself, Polly. Giles is really not responsible for his words. You can take the lower classes and dress them up and buy them little titles, but you really can't breed the vulgarity out of them."

"I say, Giles," one of his cronies remarked, "I

think you've been set down by the milkmaid. What an amusing surprise."

Giles sputtered, his eyes filled with hate. Christianna raised her brows, and fixed him with a cool stare.

After a moment he turned his horse and started back down the road, and his friends started after him, chuckling.

"What a horrible young man," Christianna said, her face hot with anger.

"You really put him in his place," Polly agreed. "Oh, Christianna! You can sound like the worst snob in the world! Fairly took the wind out of his sails!"

"Good. I think he's a pup."

"I think he's a pig," Polly rejoined.

"If Gareth had been here, he wouldn't have been so brave," Christianna added.

"That's a fact. Not that you needed help. You've got a mean mouth, Christianna."

"It's from having been at court for so long," Christianna admitted. "If you aren't a little mean, people tear you to pieces."

"If he'd have gotten off that horse, I'd have torn him to pieces," Polly grumbled.

Christianna laughed, and she and Polly started back down the lane toward the Larkin house.

Christianna thought about the letter in her pocket and rejected the idea of opening it. Instead, she tilted her head back, thinking about the blue sky and the brilliant green leaves and the wildflowers that grew along the road.

"Look, Polly. Aren't those little daisies pretty?"

Polly looked, and then smiled, her attention diverted. "Now that's a sight I'd much rather see," Polly said in appreciative tones. "Hayingtime, is it?"

Christianna looked out over the fields, nodding.

Gareth and Richard and Daniel were moving through the field of golden grass, swinging their scythes in a swift, easy rhythm, slicing swaths of sweet-smelling hay. Stewart and Geoffery followed behind, spreading the cut grass with heavy pitchforks. All of them had discarded their shirts, and the sun beat down on their glistening backs and bare chests.

Christianna leaned on the stone fence again, relishing the sight of Gareth's bronzed back and the motion of his shoulders and arms, the rippling muscles in the sun.

Beside her, Polly heaved a sigh. "Grand, aren't they? Like a bunch of bloody gods."

"Richard's too skinny," Christianna said critically. "And Geoffery's too young."

"Picky, aren't we?" Polly teased.

A rabbit suddenly leapt up in front of Daniel's scythe and hopped away, startling him. His brothers laughed at his surprise as he jumped back, and for a few moments their work ceased. Stewart took his pitchfork and raced after the poor rabbit, threatening violence.

"Poor bunny," Polly remarked.

Gareth was wiping the sweat from his brow with an old handkerchief, and he spotted them standing by the road and waved, sending them a brilliant smile.

Christianna waved back. The letter tucked in her apron pocket weighed on her mind, and her smile felt weak.

"What will you do?" Polly asked, as if she had heard Christianna's thoughts.

"What can I do?" Christianna asked.

"Throw the letter away. Burn it. Better yet, trade in the passage for money and buy a new dress. Yours are looking just awful."

Christianna glanced down at her pale blue skirts. The lace was ripped and mended, the patterns of flowers and vines faded and worn.

"A new dress wouldn't help," she told Polly.

"A new dress always helps," Polly objected. "At least if you're miserable, you look good."

Christianna smiled at Polly's advice.

"Listen," Polly said, leaning against the fence, her eyes suddenly serious. "I don't want to change the subject, but I've got a little news of my own."

"Good or bad?"

Polly sighed, twisting the ends of her braid around her fingers. "That depends, I guess." She gave a wan smile. "I've got a bun in the oven."

Christianna raised her brow, confused.

Polly stood, waiting expectantly. "Well?"

"Should you go home and take it out?"

Polly looked appalled, and then let out a roar of laughter. "God help us, if only it was that easy! No, listen—I'm caught, expecting, pregnant. I'm going to have a damned baby."

"Oh, Polly! Oh, my. What will you do?"

"Tell the father, I guess. I've been so damned good this summer; I never thought it would happen. But I got a little drunk at the fair and so did he, and things just happened. . . ."

Polly gave an embarrassed shrug. "So, if I tell him, and he believes me, maybe I'll get married. Could be you'll be calling me 'Mistress Larkin' before long."

Christianna stared, an awful suspicion dawning on her. She was remembering the night of the fair: sitting with Artois, watching the country musicians, and seeing Polly dance by in Gareth's arms, laughing, her face flushed and rosy.

"Oh, Polly . . ."

Polly was staring out at the hayfield, her face pink with shame. "I didn't mean to trap him. But you know how he is, about always doing the honorable thing. And what else am I to do?"

Christianna felt sick, and a hard lump rose in her throat. She swallowed, and then a fierce rage rushed through her and she found her voice. "Polly, how could you! How could you?"

"It's those green eyes of his," Polly offered feebly.

"Green eyes be damned! You know that I love him . . ." Christianna thought she might choke with fury. Tears smarted in her eyes.

Polly whirled about, her jaw dropping. "What the devil are you off about? I thought it was Gareth you were mad for!"

Christianna froze and stared at Polly. "What?"

Polly tilted her head back and let out another

merry roar of laughter. "God help us, Christianna! I'm bad, but not that bad! Do you honestly think I'd be diddling your sweetheart behind your back?"

Christianna blushed, weak with relief.

"You did! Shame on you. No, it was Daniel."

Christianna stood still with surprise, and then laughed. "No! Daniel? I can't imagine . . ."

Polly looked indignant. "What's so bloody funny about that?"

"It's just that he's so solemn, and good . . ."

"Damned good," Polly agreed, her good humor restored. "Do you think he'll believe me? He wouldn't half be a bad catch. What do you think? Mistress Larkin . . . I like the sound of that."

"I do too," Christianna agreed. Polly's position suddenly seemed more enviable than disgraceful. If only . . . She raised her head abruptly. "Is there any way to . . . to get a bun in the oven? To try, I mean?"

Polly's brows shot up. "What, you mean on purpose, like?"

"Exactly."

"Christianna St. Sebastien! You little schemer," Polly said, a note of admiration in her voice. "You mean you'd get yourself with child, just to stay here? When you could go see the world and get a rich husband, and have maids and carriages and fifty silk gowns and diamonds?"

"I would," Christianna answered firmly, her pointed chin lifting.

Polly laughed and pushed at Christianna's

shoulder. "Go on . . . you're mad!"

"I would! I swear it!"

Polly shook her head, letting her breath out in a low whistle. "Fancy that. Most girls would do anything to avoid it. Childbirth is a messy thing. And then you've got a child."

"I want one," Christianna said recklessly. She tried to imagine herself as a mother, and met with no success. It was much easier to picture Gareth with a baby . . . his gentle hands holding a black-haired infant against his chest, his soft eyes glowing with pride. The picture decided her. "Oh, Polly, just imagine . . . Why didn't I think of it before?"

Polly threw her hands up in dismay. "Wouldn't you rather have diamonds? Operas? Get married in a cathedral?"

"No," Christianna admitted, her eyes sparkling a brilliant blue.

"Do you even know any babies? Ever held one?"

"Well, just Phillipe's daughter, and I didn't pay much attention. But Gareth could show me, I'm sure. He knows how to do everything."

"Well," Polly sighed, "if you're sure . . ."

"I am, I am. Do you know of anything I can do?"

Polly laughed. "How often are you going at it?" she demanded.

Christianna blushed.

"Every day?" Polly demanded.

"Twice, at least," Christianna admitted. "Or

335

three times, if we can. Polly! Stop laughing! Isn't it enough?"

"God, yes! You'd think it would be. Now, my sister Nancy, she has three, and she says you stand on your head."

"Stand on your head?" Christianna repeated.

"The minute he's done . . . you know. You roll right out of bed and stand on your head."

"I can't do that! Imagine! Gareth would think I'd gone mad!" Christianna began to laugh at the idea. "Oh, Polly! Isn't there anything more . . . *dignified* that could be done?"

"If you want to be dignified," Polly told her, "you bloody well keep your skirts down. Dignified! Can't say as there's much 'dignified' about it."

Laughing, they turned to go back toward the house.

"If it's marriage you want, and he won't speak," Polly said, after a few minutes, "why don't you just ask him? He sets such a store by speaking the truth. And it sounds a good deal easier than having a baby. You're bound to get one anyway, the way you're going."

Christianna gave a startled laugh. "You mean ask him to marry me? Oh, I couldn't. I just couldn't. What if he said no? I'd die."

"Has he told you he loves you?"

Christianna's head bowed. "No."

"Have you told him?"

"No. I couldn't bear it if he didn't feel the same."

Polly looked disgusted. "As if! You and your

bloody pride. It's perfectly plain to everybody else that you two are in love."

"Nobody knows," Christianna argued.

"Go on! Everyone's known for weeks! Geoffery found out and told Stewart, and that was the end of that secret. Whole bloody village knows."

Christianna felt her face flame. It must have looked as red as it felt, for Polly shrieked with laughter.

"What, you thought you two were having at it three times a day and going all dove-eyed at each other and nobody would know? Go on!"

"Never mind," Christianna exclaimed. "Stop laughing, Polly! I mean it! Come help me do something pretty with my hair. What should I wear, for heaven's sake?"

"What, are you leaving town?" Polly demanded, her face still pink with laughter. "Now that everyone knows that you're a fallen woman?"

"No, don't be silly. I'm going to propose to Gareth, and I want to look nice. If I'm already without shame, what have I got to lose?"

"It sounds a mite more dignified than standing on your head," Polly agreed, pushing open the front gate. She stopped to admire the roses that grew over the stone fence. "Pretty. This house looks more like something, now that you've done the gardens. It's a pretty house, isn't it? Big."

Christianna looked at the sprawling farm-house, the lush ivy growing up the sturdy plaster walls, the dark beams and shutters, the diamond pane windows that shone in the sun, the fragrant and rainbow-hued flowers that crowded along the stone foundation. It looked sturdy, and inviting, and welcoming. Watching, Christianna thought of the day she had arrived.

Either the house had changed or she had.

Mrs. Hatton appeared at an upstairs window and stared out at them, a suspicious look on her broad face. Her mouth pursed with disapproval, and Christianna could imagine her saying, "Hmmmph."

"Old witch," remarked Polly. "Come on; let's go get something cold to drink and do your hair. I wouldn't half mind some plum wine."

"Mrs. Hatton won't approve," Christianna pointed out. "But I think it's a wonderful idea. It'll get my courage up. Let's go in the back door, get it from the buttery, and go do my hair."

"Sounds good to me," Polly agreed. "Better get two bottles, while you're in there." Christianna led the way through the gardens, stopping to pick some pale pink rosebuds on the way.

"You look like the May queen," Polly pronounced, twisting a black curl around her finger and dropping it over Christianna's shoulder. "Sweet and innocent." She laughed at that and winked, stepping back to admire her work and stumbling over Dog. "Move your lumpy arse," she snapped, pushing Dog out of the way with her foot.

Christianna laughed at Dog's injured expression and bent to stroke her silky ears. "What a beautiful doggy you are. Like a great big sausage. What a pretty sausage."

"Oh, sit up and quit fawning over that dumb beast. Look, drag that curl over more, so it hangs in your cleavage. Like so . . ." Polly pulled the curl over, demonstrating. "Men like that. Can't keep their eyes away from it."

Christianna adjusted the lace at the decolletage of her lavender silk gown and nodded. She looked around the cottage for her glass of wine and, failing to find it, picked up the bottle and took a healthy swallow.

"Pretty," Polly observed ironically.

Christianna shook with laughter, imagining what she must look like—the aristocrat in her silk and lace, dainty mitts on her hands, roses in her hair, swigging wine from the bottle like a street urchin. "Balls," she answered airily, taking another drink. The sweet summer wine slid down her throat, cool and fruity, working its soothing way through her veins. She sighed and held the bottle up, surveying it carefully.

"This," she told Polly, "is divine. I shall have to send a servant around to Mrs. Hatton's tomorrow, with my compliments."

"Listen to you," teased Polly. "Getting in your cups already. Now stop being silly. You don't want to go off and propose to Gareth half drunk, do you?"

"No. I want to be all the way drunk, so I don't die of shame."

"You're well on your way," Polly observed

cheerfully, stifling a laugh. "Stand up, and let me button your gown."

Christianna rose, the heel of her shoe tangling in her lace petticoats. She pulled it loose, ripping the lace, and made an effort to look dignified.

"God help us," Polly muttered, her strong fingers working the buttons of Christianna's gown. "You're wobbly."

"It's because I'm wearing corsets for the first time in weeks," Christianna explained carefully. "I can't breathe as well as usual, and it's making me a little light-headed."

Polly laughed her husky laugh. "If you say so."

Christianna reached for the wine bottle, closed her fingers around its slender neck, and raised it to her lips.

"If you dribble on that gown, I'll scream," Polly announced.

Christianna set the bottle on the table with exaggerated care. "I don't dribble," she retorted. "*Bon Dieu,* you're as rude as Artois. You're supposed to be making me beautiful, not insulting me. If Therese had spoken to me like that, I'd have dismissed her. Sent her to the kitchens."

Polly laughed, undisturbed. "And if I'd been Therese, I'd have knocked you flat on your ass."

Christianna joined Polly's laughter. "It wouldn't take much effort, about now," she admitted. "Oh, Polly! What am I doing? Half drunk, going off to ask a farmer to marry me. Oh, God, what if he says no?"

Polly considered that for a moment. "Don't think about it. Here, have another drink."

Christianna did, and calmed down immediately. "How do I look?"

Polly surveyed her with a critical eye, and then reached out to affix a pink rosebud more firmly against a black curl. "Perfect."

"This is it," Christianna announced. "I'm off. I'm doing it. Here I go . . ."

"Go, then," Polly cried, "and quit babbling."

Christianna raised her chin with what she hoped was icy dignity. "I never babble," she announced. She tucked the bottle of wine under her arm and swept through the cottage door.

With a distrustful look at Polly, Dog lumbered to her feet and followed.

Polly walked to the cottage door and watched them as they crossed the soft green pasture— the elegant young woman in her expensive silk, her black curls swaying, and the stubby-legged hound following devotedly in her footsteps. As Polly watched, Christianna stopped abruptly, raised the bottle of wine to her lips, and took a long drink before continuing.

"God help us," Polly remarked to the empty room, "by the time she finds Gareth, she'll be drunker than a fiddler's bitch."

She laughed to herself, picked up a discarded ribbon, and tidied the room before she left.

Chapter Eighteen

It was almost evening when Gareth called to his brothers to stop their work in the hayfields. Even though the hour was late, the heat of the day had not abated; the fields shimmered and waved under the sultry August sun.

The first day of haying was done, the field leveled and the cut grass spread in the sun to dry. The next day it could be raked into windrows and loaded into the hayrack, a long, light wagon that would transport the golden, sweet-smelling stuff to the barn.

As they did every year after working in the hayfield, the brothers immediately ran for the cool green woods, and the cool, shaded water of the lake.

They stripped their clothes off their sweating bodies and entered the water with a good deal

342

of splashing and shouting. They wrestled and dunked each other like children, whooping with delight as the cold water revived their aching muscles and sun-browned bodies.

It was more than just a bath in the lake; it was a time-honored tradition among the brothers, a joyous end to the first day of early harvest, a reward for a season of work well-done.

Gareth slipped beneath the surface of the water in order to avoid Stewart, who had advanced on him, splashing great, sparkling waves of water with his arms flailing like a windmill.

He swam in the dark, cool depths and emerged a safe distance away, shaking the wet hair from his eyes and laughing. A movement on the shore caught his eye, a flash of lilac color against the green leaves.

Christianna. She sat somberly on a fallen log, her silk skirts carefully arranged. Her black curls were piled high over her pointed little cat face, dressed with pink roses and spilling over her slender shoulder.

As usual, Dog had accompanied her, and was sniffing at the water with great interest, her tail wagging.

Christianna seemed not at all disturbed by the fact that his brothers were frolicking naked in the water. Indeed, she hardly seemed aware of it. She simply sat, hands folded patiently, her eyes fixed on Gareth with a serious and unfathomable expression.

Geoffery spied her at that moment, for he

gave an indignant shout, sinking into the water to his neck.

"Turn your back, for heaven's sake. We're bare-arsed naked."

Christianna turned her steady gaze away from Gareth for a moment, fixing Geoffrey with a cool stare. "I can see that," she replied coolly.

The lake, which had been echoing with noise only a moment before, seemed oddly quiet. Gareth watched his brothers exchange troubled looks as they all sank a little deeper beneath the concealing surface of the water.

"Well, go on, then," Geoffery urged.

Christianna acted as if he hadn't spoken. She very carefully reached to the ground next to her, picked up a dark green wine bottle, and, to Gareth's surprise, put it to her mouth and drank. She looked at the bottle for a moment after she was done, looking a little surprised.

"You know," Stewart remarked, "every time I think she's doing well, she goes off. She's just not quite all there."

"I don't think it's a matter of sanity, quite," Richard argued. "It looks more like inebriation."

Gareth was inclined to agree.

"What?" Geoffery asked. "Are you saying she's drunk, Richard? Christianna, are you drunk?"

She looked up from the wine bottle and appeared to consider the possibility. "Be quiet," she said at last, raising a lofty brow at Geoff. "I don't speak to naked men. Especially skinny ones."

"I'd say that you're in entirely the wrong place, then," Richard pointed out.

Christianna stood slowly, with a great show of dignity. "You be quiet too. You're skinnier than he is."

Richard looked offended. "Be that as it may—" he began, but Christianna cut him short, turning her attention back to Gareth.

"Come out of the water. I need to speak with you."

Gareth smiled at her, and exchanged a quick look and shrug with Daniel, who was treading water next to him.

"Are you sure?" he asked. "I mean, if you don't speak with naked men . . ."

"Don't be funny. Come out and speak to me." She took another drink from the wine bottle, held it at arm's length, and gave it an annoyed frown. She attempted to throw the offending object, but the bottle landed almost directly at her feet.

"She's off the deep end," Stewart muttered.

"Always was," Geoff agreed.

Gareth dissappeared beneath the surface of the water and emerged closer to the shore. He watched Christianna for a moment, wondering at her odd behavior, her flushed cheeks, her determined gaze.

"Are you well?" he asked.

"Glorious. Divine. *Merveilleux. Fabuleux.* Come out and speak to me."

Feeling a little silly, slightly worried, and all too aware of his brother's eyes upon him,

Gareth waded out of the water, grabbing his breeches off some shrubbery and pulling them on hastily. Dog barked excitedly, running circles around him.

Christianna looked completely unruffled by his unease. She twirled a black ringlet thoughtfully around her finger and smiled at him.

"Has something happened?" Gareth asked, confused, working his damp feet into his boots.

"No. Come with me; I need to speak to you privately."

She took a few unsteady steps and offered her arm to him. "Shall we go away from the lake? I think I'm disturbing your brothers."

"I think that's an understatement. What in the hell is wrong with you? Aside from the fact that you're in your cups, I mean."

She smiled at him as he led her up the sloping path, up to the woodland trail, well out of sight of his brothers' prying eyes and ears. How handsome he was, even with his hair dripping over his collar, and that worried look in his eye.

"Here," she said, pointing to a small clearing, where a few fallen logs lay, mossy and with ferns growing out of them. "Shall we sit?"

"As you wish," Gareth answered, with more patience than he felt. He couldn't resist smiling as Christianna sat down, with the exaggerated care of someone trying to appear sober.

She looked at her lap and took a deep breath, and for a moment the only sound was the faint hum of the forest insects that passed by.

"You're going to say something unpleasant," Gareth predicted, after a moment of careful observation.

Christianna raised her eyes, wide and startled, to his. "What makes you think that?"

"Look at you. Every time you're going to have a deal with something unpleasant your face gets all pinched up and haughty, like a mask. Your going-to-tea-with-the-duke face. And, whatever it is you're going to say, you've obviously tried to bolster your courage with a bit of drink, and gone too far."

"Oh, you think you're clever, don't you?" Christianna retorted, sounding surly.

Gareth laughed softly, raking his wet hair off his forehead.

Christianna straightened her shoulders, remembering her intent.

"Monsieur Larkin," she said at last, trying not to hiccup, "it has become apparent to me, over the last few weeks, that there has been an affection developing between us."

"There certainly has," Gareth agreed, looking cheery.

Christianna ignored him. "And it is also true that though we knew my brother would send for me, it was not a prospect that gave either of us pleasure."

"No mistake about it," Gareth concurred.

"And I know that you are considered a man of great honor, a man to be trusted."

"Practically a saint," Gareth agreed.

"Oh, would you stop! I'm trying very hard to be serious."

"Where are you going with all this?" Gareth asked, sitting beside her on the mossy log. "Shouldn't you get straight to the point?"

Christianna sighed heavily, lifting her eyes to the green treetops and the brilliant blue sky beyond, and then to Gareth's face. His eyes were dancing with infuriating merriment.

"Ithinkweshouldgetmarried," she said, the words leaving her mouth on one breath. She stared down at her feet and the brown dirt of the forest floor, her heart beating rapidly. She was afraid to look at him, afraid of what he might say.

"Christianna," he began.

"If you laugh at me, I'll die," she warned him, her voice cracking. "I will. I'll lie right down here in the dirt and die. I have absolutely no pride left at this moment, and if you laugh at me, it will kill me."

"I have no intention of laughing at you, you little drunkard," he answered pleasantly, though he wanted to, very much. "I just want to know why."

"Why?" Christianna repeated, her cheeks burning. "What do you mean, why? After all, you . . . you ruined me."

"You asked me to," he pointed out reasonably.

Christianna hiccuped loudly, and thought about it. "You're right. Well, I do hate to travel, and it's a long way to New Orleans, isn't it? And

I would hate to leave my garden. And Dog. I'm very fond of Dog. And I like the weather here."

"You want to marry me because you like the weather?"

"You're not making this easy," Christianna cried. "What do you want me to say, for God's sake?"

Gareth took her face in his roughened fingers and turned it gently toward him. His eyes were pale green and bright in his golden face.

"The truth. That's all. Just the truth. I don't believe you'd marry me for a garden, or the weather, or my fat-assed dog. I want to hear the truth, and I want you always to tell me the truth, and trust me with it. I want no secrets between us."

Christianna felt a little dizzy, whether with the plum wine or his closeness, she wasn't sure.

His fingers stroked her cheek softly, just once, and then lay quiet in her hair.

"Very well," she said. "I love you. I love you so much that if I have to leave, I'll die. When I think of having to marry someone else I almost weep. I wouldn't care if he was as rich as Solomon. You are the kindest, gentlest, most wonderful man in all the world, and if I have to live without you, I'll weep for you every last day of my life. And that's the truth, and if you don't believe me," she finished, her voice strangled and tears in her eyes, "bugger you."

"Christianna?"

She hiccuped quietly, her eyes filling with tears.

"I love you too. You silly little drunkard."

For some reason, whether it was wine, emotion, or relief, she burst into tears.

Gareth, struggling not to laugh, gathered her into the circle of his arms, hiding his smile against the silky top of her dark head and letting her cry her relief and emotion against his shirtfront.

"When I'm fifty," he told her, "I'm going to remind you of this. I shall tell all our children that their mother proposed to me drunk, and crying like an infant."

"Don't you dare," Christianna choked. "Or I'll die of shame. Do you have any idea how difficult this was for me?"

His hand caressed her neck and slipped down her slender back. "Sweetheart. I'll marry you, and gladly. But you have to do one thing for me."

"Anything," she promised, still sniffling.

"Always tell me the truth. Let there be no secrets between us, ever."

For a moment the image of Raoul and Jean-Claude entered her mind, and she thought of telling him the whole ugly story, but his mouth was touching hers, hot and sweet and tender, and she tipped her face up to him gladly, pushing away the past.

The past, after all, was behind her, and there was no need to ruin a perfect moment like this. Later, when the time was right, she would tell him.

She leaned into his kiss, her hands reaching

up to tangle in his damp hair, losing herself in the heat and light of their embrace—until Dog announced her presence with a mournful howl and pushed her bulky body against their legs.

"You ass," Gareth muttered at the hound, as Christianna stumbled, laughing.

Dog barked at him, wriggling her black-and-brown body with excitement.

Christianna dropped to her knees, heedless of her lavender silk dress, the only frock she had that still looked presentable. She wrapped her arms around Dog's neck, hugging her, and looked up at Gareth with shining eyes.

"I love you. I love you so much. I can't believe that you asked me to marry you."

"I didn't," Gareth objected with a crooked grin. "You asked me."

"Never mind," Christianna answered, with a careless shrug and a brilliant smile.

"Never mind," muttered Gareth. "That's going too." He held out a hand and helped Christianna to her feet, trying not to laugh as she stumbled.

"Thank God that's over," she announced. She lifted her silk skirt and pulled the letter from Phillipe from beneath her beribboned garter. "Now I can read Phillipe's letter without crying. And then I can write him back and tell him to never mind. Won't he be surprised?"

Gareth stared at the letter in her hand. "I wondered what brought all this on," he commented as Christianna opened the letter and began to read. "What does he say?"

"Ma chere soeur—"

"In English, please."

Christianna laughed. Everything seemed so wonderful to her. "Let me see. They arrived safely and found a house—in the French quarter of the city, of course. The city is full of emigrants from France. . . . It seems that it was more than your brother James could bear, and he's moved to the Irish quarter of the city, which he likes very well. He's got a job breaking horses for a plantation owner outside the city, and he's doing well. Victoria is pregnant again, already!"

"Is she really?" Gareth asked, smiling.

"Yes. I wonder if she stands on her head? And business is well, and Phillipe is thinking of buying his own ship, and . . . oh, my God . . ."

"What?" Gareth asked, alarmed.

Christianna began to laugh. "It's not really funny, but listen—'There is presently an epidemic of yellow fever in the city. Under no circumstances are you to think of coming until all danger is past.' Oh, Gareth—I've been sick with misery all day, thinking that Phillipe had sent for me, and it was all for naught. I humiliated myself and proposed for nothing."

Gareth couldn't help but smile, even as a quick prayer flashed through his mind for the safety of his sister and brother. "Funny," he remarked, "the cards life deals us. Do you want to take back your proposal, now that you don't have to leave?"

Christianna smiled up at him, her eyes brilliant with emotion. "Not for all the world. Not ever. You're damned. And the sooner, the better. Marry me tomorrow, before you change your mind."

"Tomorrow?" Gareth asked. "Tomorrow we have to get the hay in. In these parts, people generally wait until after the harvest to get married. Would you mind? Unless, of course, there's another reason . . ."

"Another reason? Do you mean a baby? Oh, no. Though I was going to try that, if you said no. I would like one, very much. Not that I know much about them," Christianna confessed, blushing. "But I can learn. And it would be wonderful to try."

Gareth smiled his tranquil smile and drew her into his arms once again. "As you wish," he murmured, his breath hot against her ear, his lips seeking the tender hollow of her throat, where her pulse beat, warm and rapid. "Shall we begin trying?"

The letter from Phillipe fluttered forgotten to the forest floor, and Christianna gave herself over to the call of her body.

"I love you," Gareth whispered when he entered her body, and it seemed to her that sweeter words had never been spoken.

"Damned sudden, this marriage business," Stewart said to Geoffery. "Maybe I'll get married too."

"Go on," Geoffery exclaimed, staring down at

his brother from the top of the hayrack, where he was trampling the grass down. "Who'd marry you, you ugly lout?"

"Bugger you," Stewart exclaimed. He pitched another forkful of hay up at his brother, making sure that it landed on Geoffery's head. "Polly, maybe. She's pretty, and a good worker, and I bet she's a jolly good—"

"Forget it," Geoffery told him. "Polly's going to marry Daniel. Mark my words. It'll happen before the month is out."

"Oh, really?" Richard asked, wiping the sweat from his face and using his scarf to tie his hair out of his eyes, pirate-style. "When did you become the bloody local oracle?"

"Mark my words," Geoff repeated, jumping up and down on the hay, as if to punctuate his words.

"We'll see," Richard said in doubtful tones. He watched with interest as Daniel and Gareth approached across the shorn field, their identical auburn heads shining in the sunlight.

"Does Daniel know he's getting married? Or is this information exclusively yours?" Richard demanded.

Geoff shrugged.

"I heard a rumor that you'll be the next to wed, Daniel," Richard called across the field as his older brothers approached. "Any truth to that?"

Daniel looked baffled. *"Ad calendas graecas,"* he replied smoothly. "In short, when hell freezes over."

Geoffery raised a knowing brow. "Awfully cold, isn't it, for August?"

Gareth cast a suspicious glance at his youngest brother's knowing face. "Hell's going to freeze over by the time we get the hay in. Give me your pitchfork, Richard, and go help Geoffery pack it down."

"Somebody's awfully damned anxious for the harvest," Stewart commented. "The first of us to get caught. I never thought it'd happen."

"Caught, am I?" Gareth laughed. "Mayhap, but no man was ever caught by a sweeter hunter."

"Listen to him," Stewart cried. "Gone all soft. Fair makes me ill."

Gareth scarcely heard his brothers' laughter, or their teasing remarks. His eyes were fastened on the brilliant blue sky above the green horizon of wooded hills, and his mind was far away, thinking of the harvesttime.

Part 4
Harvest

I turn to thee as some green afternoon
turns to sunset, and is loath to die.
                    —Algernon Swinburne

Under the arch of life
I saw beauty enthroned,
And though her gaze struck awe,
I drew it in as simply as my breath.
                    —Dante Rossetti

My beloved spake, and said to me, rise up, my
beloved, my fair one, and come away. For lo, the
winter is past, the rain is over and gone.
                    —The Song of Solomon

Chapter Nineteen

"The world is coming to an end," Mrs. Hatton announced, laying a plump hand over her troublesome heart. "I'll not make old bones, not at this rate."

"You already have," pointed out Geoffery uncharitably. "And it's not the end of the world, Mrs. Hatton. Daniel got himself married, that's all."

Mrs. Hatton looked pained all over again. "And now I suppose That One will be in my kitchen, underfoot all the time."

"That One" was Polly, but Mrs. Hatton was far too upset to invoke her name.

"Maybe," Stewart said, sounding pleased. "And you thought you had it rough with Christianna about."

Christianna, sitting at the scarred oak table

with a mug of tea, made a face at Stewart.

"And it being harvesttime," the old woman continued in doleful tones, "and our Gareth getting himself wed in a week, and the sausages needing to be done, and the apples brought in, and the potatoes dug . . . my heart won't stand for it."

"Perhaps," Christianna suggested in honeyed tones, "you should go and stay with your sister until your heart is better."

Mrs. Hatton looked as if Christianna had suggested something indecent. "That's enough out of you," she said smartly. "Why don't you get yourself out to your garden and pick me some of that nice chamomile. That's all I need."

Christianna laughed and stood up from the table, almost tumbling over Dog. "Stupid thing. You just get bigger and more useless every day."

Dog rolled herself to her back, grateful for the attention, her tail thumping an ecstatic rhythm against the wood floor.

"I'm off too," Geoffery said. "Stew and I have some things to pick up in town."

"We do? Oh, yes, we do. Things."

Christianna rolled her eyes at them as she left the room and went out into the garden for Mrs. Hatton's chamomile.

The evenings were cooler now, and the sunsets had a hazy light. Blackberries were hanging on their thorny canes, full and heavy, and the grass in the fields was almost golden. The roses and violets in the garden were giving ground to the later-blooming marigolds and daisies. The peach tree had already yielded its fruit, and bees buzzed around the fallen ones that Christianna couldn't carry away fast enough.

The apples seemed never to end. Every day she helped to pick baskets full, and every day there were more. There was cider to make, and apple sausage, and dried apples for pies. It never failed to amaze her, the amount and variety of food produced by the farm. The work seemed never to stop, but nobody complained.

"Any work undertaken with love becomes a joy," Gareth explained to her. She understood this, felt the love of the land, and he looked at her with warm approval when she agreed.

And in a week she would be his wife. Whenever she went to the village she thrilled to the envy of the rosy-cheeked village girls, and tossed her braid and muslin skirts with more pride than she had ever flaunted her velvets and diamond earrings.

"I'm not leaving because I want to see Vienna, particularly," Artois had told her, on the sunny day when he made his au revoirs before sailing. "I'm leaving because you've become so insufferably smug."

They laughed together, and when Christianna kissed his cheek in farewell she thought of the last time she had bid him au revoir, the night that the revolutionaries took Paris. "I love you, my friend," she told him, repeating the words she had spoken that night, as if they were a good-luck charm that would assure his return.

"Do you?" he asked, his eyes sparkling with mischief. "Then perhaps you should come with me. After all, you really wouldn't miss Gareth *that* much, would you?"

She laughed at the memory of her horrified reaction, and was still laughing when she carried Mrs. Hatton's chamomile into the house. Not miss Gareth, indeed! No more than she would miss her eyes, if she was to suddenly lose them.

She went into the house with her heart singing. It had all been worth it—the lonely childhood, the empty, shallow years at Versailles, the cold, lonely months after the revolution—it was worth all the suffering, if it had led her here.

She was the luckiest woman in the world, she was going to marry the most beautiful man on earth, and she was sure that nobody had ever been as happy as she.

"I said we were picking something up in town and there it is," Geoffery said, settling himself at his favorite table at the Broken Bow and lifting his mug of beer.

"I'd better pick mine up too, then," Stewart said agreeably, raising his mug to his brother before drinking.

"What a couple of rats," Polly exclaimed. "Leaving the evening chores to your brothers."

"It's your last night at the Broken Bow, Poll. We could hardly let you finish off without us. And we can walk you home later." Stewart smiled up at Polly. "Protect you from wolves."

"Go on!" Polly laughed, tossing her golden braid. "The only wolves in these parts are sitting in this room. Any rate, Daniel's going to come get me later. And we won't need any company on the way home, if you get my drift."

Geoff and Stewart watched with admiration as Polly moved through the room, her capable hands deftly taking empty mugs and replacing them with full ones, moving chairs out of the way, wiping at a dirtied table. Someone said something that made her laugh, and her husky laughter rang across the room, her full breasts straining against her tight bodice.

"Damn," Stewart said in admiration. "Who'd have thought Daniel could get a girl like that? He's a sly one."

Geoffery looked a little worried. "I don't know, Stew. Things are changing. Gareth marrying; Daniel wed. And Polly's got a baby on the way, that's no secret. The house just won't be the same."

"What are you whining about? I'd much rather look at Polly or Christianna than you, you ugly little rat."

"Bugger you!" Geoffery exclaimed indignantly.

"Hey," Polly called from across the dark room, "did Christianna's French friend find her? I almost forgot to tell you; he was in here earlier. Ugly little grub."

"What, Artois?" Geoff asked. "He left for Vienna weeks ago."

Polly rolled her eyes and put her hand on her ample hip. "No, not Artois, you want-wit.

How come your brother's so smart and you're so thick? I know Artois, and he wouldn't have to look for Christianna, now would he? Just take himself to the door. I said an ugly little grub, didn't I? Artois's not ugly."

Stewart waved a languid wrist and affected a mincing air. "I don't know . . . he's just not my type."

"Give over," Polly said, disgusted. "Did he find Christianna?"

"Months ago," Geoff said, looking confused. "At the fair, remember?"

"Not Artois, you dolt! The ugly little Frenchman."

Geoff and Stewart shrugged in unison.

"Well, I don't like the looks of him," Polly said. "I told him to tell me where he was staying and I'd get word to Christianna. He didn't like that, I tell you. And then he went off with Giles Thornley. That's an odd pair, I thought."

"As odd as you and Daniel?" Stewart asked, his dimples showing.

"Oh, give *over!*" Polly cried, throwing her hands up in exasperation. "Drink your beer and go home, instead of hanging around here giving me grief."

"Be sweet, Poll. Give us another round," Geoff said, flashing a brilliant smile at her; and Polly, who had a weakness for auburn-haired men, hurried to comply.

"What are you reading, Matthew?" Christianna asked her soon-to-be father-in-law.

They were sitting in the quiet of the brick kitchen. Mrs. Hatton had finished the dinner dishes and gone back to her cottage for the night. Daniel, Richard, and Gareth were finishing the evening chores in the great barn, and Geoffery and Stewart had still not returned from their jaunt to the village.

Matthew looked up from his book, and his round, rosy face broke into a pleased smile. He always looked a little surprised when she spoke, Christianna thought, as if he had forgotten that she was there.

"Shakespeare," he answered, predictably. *"Twelfth Night."* He beamed across the table at her and pushed his spectacles farther up his nose. "What do you think of this? 'Love sought is good, but given unsought is better.'"

"I think it's divine, either way," Christianna replied practically. She picked up her violin and played a few notes. She cheered at the sound of them, bright and brassy and majestic, too grand for the homely, comfortable room.

"Handel, is it?" Matthew asked, glancing up from his book.

"Very good," Christianna told him, and sang out a line of "I know that my redeemer liveth."

She stopped as Gareth and Daniel came through the kitchen door, her cheeks warming at the sight of Gareth's tender smile.

"All in for the night," Gareth announced, taking the seat next to Christianna. Beneath the table, his hand slid onto her thigh and gave her a squeeze.

Dog, who had been sleeping on the warm bricks in front of the hearth, rose to her short, squat legs and came over to him, leaning heavily against his leg, her tail wagging furiously.

"Hello, stupid," Gareth murmured, tousling her long ears with a careless hand. "You just get fatter and more useless every day, don't you?"

"She does not," Christianna objected. "She's very sleek and beautiful."

Gareth choked back a laugh.

Daniel disappeared into the buttery and returned with two mugs of ale, offering one to his older brother. "I'm afraid with Christianna," he told Gareth, "it's a matter of *qui me amat, amat et canem meam.*"

"He who loves me, loves my dog," Christianna translated, laughing. "Do you love my dog, Gareth?"

He reached up to tug one of her shining black curls. The corners of his eyes crinkled as he smiled. "If I must. Anything to please you. But if your dog gets much bigger, the neighbors are likely to take her for a hog, and take her home and make her into sausages. Come to think of it," he added, "she already rather looks like a sausage."

Christianna raised a brow at Gareth, pretending indignation. She was about to speak when she was distracted by the sound of horses coming up the front drive.

"Funny," Daniel said, with a quick frown. "Who could that be?"

Dog began to bark as the front gate creaked,

and the low murmur of voices reached them.

"Oh, hush up, useless." Gareth rose to his feet and gave Christianna's shoulder a quick squeeze.

"I hope there's not been trouble with Geoff or Stewart," Matthew said, running a hand over his wispy gray hair. It looked no tidier than before.

"There's always trouble with Geoff and Stewart," Gareth told his father. "Nobody would bother coming to the door about it."

Christianna stood, taking off her apron and straightening her skirts as Daniel followed Gareth to the front of the house.

Dog resumed her frantic barking as a knock sounded on the door, and Christianna, knowing that she would get no peace, dragged her into the buttery and closed the door firmly. "Stupid thing," she muttered, walking back into the kitchen. She was about to follow Daniel out into the hall, but Matthew stopped her with an abruptly upraised hand, his face still and shocked.

Startled, Christianna paused, and listened to the voices that drifted back to the kitchen from the front door.

"You're mad, Thornley." Gareth's voice was dark with contempt, but calm and low as always.

"I tell you, I'm not. And with Father away, I'm acting as constable. You'll not harbor a known murderess in my village."

Christianna's heart gave a sickening lurch.

For a moment time seemed to stop. She was very aware of the sound of Dog scratching on the buttery door, the ticking of the old clock in the hall, the sound of a log popping in the fire.

Gareth's laugh floated back into the kitchen. "That's bloody rich. You're really reaching, Giles."

"There is a witness, you know."

"Is that so?" Gareth sounded completely unconcerned.

Christianna's heart began to pound, faster and faster in a sharp, hard rhythm. She glanced down and saw that Matthew was patting her hand with his chubby, ink-spotted fingers. She stared, strangely detached. It might have been somebody else's hand.

Silently, she began to move toward the door. She drew a deep, pained breath and, leaning against the wall, stared down the hallway at the front door.

Gareth stood in the open doorway, one strong arm barring it, as if he was holding the dark night out.

Beyond him stood Giles Thornley, his white face gleaming in the light of a lantern, his eyes sparkling with malevolent triumph. Next to him stood the miller, whom Christianna had spoken to a hundred times on errands to the village. Was his name Leigh? Something like that. And another man from town, whose face she couldn't quite place.

And beside him, Jean-Claude.

He stared up at Gareth with the cold, dark eyes of a reptile, his swarthy face set and bitter. He held some papers in his thin hands, and he was wearing a stiff new frock coat that didn't fit him well.

Christianna fought the panic and nausea that rose in her chest and pressed her hand to her mouth to suppress the cry that was struggling to escape.

The movement caught Daniel's eye, and he moved away from the wall where he stood, behind Gareth, trying to block the view of the stone step.

" . . . can believe this sort of crap from Giles," Gareth was saying, "but not from the rest of you. Surely, as members of the town council, you have better things to do with yourselves. Surely you can't believe this."

"We wouldn't want to doubt your word, Gareth," the miller said in apologetic tones, "but there is an awfully convincing case."

"There had better be," Gareth said impatiently, a muscle twitching in his jaw. "I haven't time for this nonsense."

"Pardon, monsieur." Christianna shuddered at the sound of Jean-Claude's voice, an echo of the nightmares that had ceased to haunt her. "But this is true. I 'av proof. I was in the room. She cut my *frere*'s—my brother's throat, as if 'e were a dog, a goat."

"You've got the wrong girl."

Giles grabbed the papers from Jean-Claude's hands and thrust them into Gareth's. "Read this then, Larkin. An order for her arrest."

"This is French," Gareth said gently. "It could say anything."

Giles grabbed the paper and pushed it at Daniel. "You then, Master Tutor, who is so clever with languages. Read that to your brother."

Daniel stood silently, the rumpled paper in his hand.

"Read it!" Giles insisted, his voice rising.

Gareth folded his arms and nodded to Daniel, a condescending smile on his generous mouth.

Daniel cleared his throat and took his spectacles from his pocket, settling them on his aquiline nose. "Wanted, for crimes against the state of France, for treason against the republic . . ." He heaved a quiet sigh, his glance flickering to his brother. " . . . and for the murder of Raoul Gerard, a loyal citizen. Christianna, the sister of the Marquis St. Sebastien. May be in the company of Artois du Valle. Of about eighteen years of age, slight height and slender build, with black hair and blue eyes. May attempt to flee to England. . . ."

Daniel handed the paper back to Giles. "What does this prove? It could be false."

"But it is not," Jean-Claude broke in, furiously. "Look, when she fled my 'ome, she left this, on my floor."

He held up the miniature portrait of Gabrielle St. Sebastien, Christianna's mother. The glass that had protected the delicate painting was gone, the pale, pastel-tinted picture darkened with grease.

Christianna's fist tightened against her mouth, she bit her knuckles.

Gareth took the picture from Jean-Claude and stared at it. "You could have stolen this."

"But why, Larkin?" Giles Thornley demanded. "Why would a man go to all this trouble to falsify documents and travel so far from his home for a falsehood? She murdered his brother rather than face questioning by the authorities."

Gareth appeared unmoved. "Balls," he answered simply. "Christianna couldn't hurt a fly. I don't know what your game is, Giles, but I won't play it. Get out of here, and take your friends."

"We have the orders—" Giles began.

"Is England even recognizing the authority of the revolutionary government?" Daniel asked abruptly.

Giles looked uncertain for a moment, and then took the offensive. "It doesn't signify. You've got a murderess under your roof, Larkin, and nobody in this village is safe."

Gareth tossed his head impatiently, then stopped as he caught sight of Christianna, tight against the wall, her eyes huge and frightened in her pale face.

He held out his hand to her and his voice softened.

"Come here, sweetheart."

Praying that her legs would carry her, Christianna moved forward slowly. She kept her eyes on Gareth's face, trying not to think of Jean-Claude at the door, only a few steps away from her. She felt Daniel's eyes on her, worried behind his spectacles.

"Don't be frightened." Gareth took her hand and pulled her comfortably to his side, his strong arm resting easily around her slender waist.

Daniel moved closer to her, and she felt his cool hand on her shoulder.

"Now we shall settle this, for once and all," Gareth said, and his voice was filled with quiet authority. He pressed the miniature of the Marquesse St. Sebastien into Christianna's hand. Her fingers curled around it tightly.

"Is this yours, sweeting?"

She nodded, and tried to speak. She couldn't lift her eyes, couldn't look at Jean-Claude, standing only three paces away from her. "Yes," she managed, at last. "It's my mother."

Gareth's hand was warm on the small of her back. "And how did this man get it, do you suppose?"

Christianna raised her eyes and met Jean-Claude's hate-filled stare.

For a long moment she thought she would faint. The details of the scene took on a dream-like quality—the flickering lantern light on the faces of the men at the door, the steady pressure of Gareth's hand on her waist, the cool touch of Daniel's fingers on her shoulder, the faint sound of Dog's whining from behind the closed door of the buttery.

Jean-Claude began to smile, his broken teeth showing in triumph.

Christianna looked at the portrait in her

hand, the delicate pink and white of her mother's face.

"It was stolen from me," she said, and her voice was clear and cool, "when I fled the revolution. This, and my jewelry, and my violin." She lifted her head and met Jean-Claude's gaze without flinching, a hard, cold smile on her mouth. "And I've never seen this man before in my life."

Beside her, she heard Daniel's sigh of relief.

"That's it," Gareth said, his voice finally showing his anger. "You've heard her. Anybody care to challenge her word?" He took a step forward, and his body seemed to swell with anger. The tendons in his arms showed; a muscle twitched in his jaw. "If anyone cares to disagree, let him speak, and we'll settle it now, when I rip his bloody head from his neck. Mr. Leigh? Thornley? Anybody else?"

Silence greeted him.

"Good. Get gone from my land. Especially you, Giles. God help you if I see you here again. And you . . ." He looked at Jean-Claude. "You'd better do more than get off my land. You'd do well to take your scrawny arse back to France. Do you hear?"

Jean-Claude's eyes blazed with helpless fury. The useless papers crumpled in his hand as he took a hasty step back from the reach of the redheaded giant advancing on him.

"Go!" Gareth's roar of fury startled even the horses tied out by the gate, and he slammed the heavy oak door with a strength that shook the sturdy house.

373

"Jesus Christ!" he swore, turning to face Christianna and Daniel. "What a crock of . . . my God, are you going to be ill?"

Christianna's legs had given out beneath her, she was shaking so wildly, and Daniel, who had caught her beneath her arms, was trying to steady her.

"Sweetheart . . ." Gareth lifted her easily, and she clung to him. "Silly thing. You've nothing to fear. I could never believe a pile of rot like that. The idea of you cutting a man's throat . . ." He stopped at the sight of Daniel's sharp glance. "What? What is it?"

Christianna buried her face in Gareth's neck, and the words she spoke were pained and bitter. "It's true. Every word. I did it, Gareth."

His breath left him in a long, low sigh.

"Why didn't you tell me?"

"She meant to," Daniel said, meaning to be helpful. "She keeps meaning to, but the time is never right. . . ."

"You knew of this?"

Christianna was afraid to look up. There was a coldness in Gareth's voice that terrified her.

"You knew, Dan? You knew, and kept it from me?"

Christianna clutched her mother's portrait in her hand, as if the miniature could give her strength.

"You told Dan?" Gareth asked. "You told him, and not me? You didn't trust me? Why?"

Christianna tried to explain, but the words sounded lame and inadequate. "You are so good . . . I couldn't bear it, if you thought ill of me . . . and I wanted it all to go away."

Gareth dumped her ungracefully into a battered armchair in the cool, dark sitting room.

"You did, did you? Well, guess again, your highness. Things like that don't go away. They tend to spring up at us when we least expect them. Did you really think you could pretend something of that magnitude away?"

His voice was tight and cold, and each word stabbed Christianna's heart.

She looked down at her hands, knotted into fists. It was happening, just as she had feared. He knew the worst about her and he despised her.

Already, she felt abandoned. Loneliness crept over her, like a cold rain soaking through her clothes.

"If you had told me," Gareth said, sounding pained. "If only you had told me . . ."

Christianna buried her face in her hands as she heard him stalk from the room. Daniel stood silently, a witness to her grief, and from her prison in the buttery, Dog gave a long, mournful howl.

Chapter Twenty

For a long time Christianna sat, her face buried in her hands. She would have cried, but it seemed that she had no tears. There was only a vast, empty void in her heart, blacker and more frightening than anything she had ever felt.

She had no idea how long she sat, alone in the quiet room. It seemed to be forever. She had lost Gareth. She had hesitated to tell him the truth; she had broken her promise to trust him, and now she would pay.

After a while she felt a light pressure on her shoulder.

"Please, don't cry, dear."

She looked up to see Matthew, his round face bleak with concern, his hair standing comically on end, and his neckcloth askew.

"I'm not crying," she said at last. Her voice

sounded very small and very cold. "Do you want me to leave?" she asked Matthew.

"Oh, dear, no. No. Why ever would you think such a thing?"

"I thought that since you knew . . ."

"Nonsense. Daniel explained everything to us. It was a matter of '*Mors tua, vita mea.*' Sometimes, someone has to die so that another person might live. That is one of the ugly realities of war. Unfortunately, we don't prepare pretty young things like you for war."

Matthew patted Christianna's hand awkwardly as he spoke, and his pale eyes were worried behind his crooked spectacles.

Somehow, his kindly tone made Christianna's heart ache even more.

"But Gareth . . ."

"Well. Well, Gareth behaved a little badly. He was hurt, you see, that you felt you could confide in Daniel and not him. And he was sorry that he couldn't protect you better, when your nemesis came knocking on the door."

Christianna had to smile a little at Matthew's figure of speech.

"He loves you, very, very much, you know."

"Still?" Christianna hardly dared believe it.

"Oh, yes," Matthew assured her. "He said so, right before he walked out the door."

Christianna sat for a moment, disbelief leaving her silent. And then joy; pure and perfect happiness flooded over her.

"Still?" she repeated, and her voice cracked, and the tears that she thought had deserted her flooded from her aching eyes. "Are you sure?"

At Matthew's nod, she threw her arms around his stocky neck and hugged him tightly. "Oh, thank you, Matthew. Oh, *merci*. How good you are, all of you! How kind you've been to me!"

"There, there," Matthew murmured, patting her shoulder awkwardly.

Christianna was already on her feet, her skirts flying around her ankles. "Where is Gareth, please?"

"I'm not sure. More than likely out in the barn, with the horses. . . ."

Christianna sped through the kitchen and out into the cool night, not even stopping to let Dog out of the buttery.

The long barn seemed dark and deserted. Only the horses, lined up in their stalls, stirred at her entrance.

"Gareth?"

From around the corner, where the long horse barn joined with the cow barn, Daniel answered her.

"Over here, Christianna."

She hurried past the horses and around the corner, where Daniel was carefully mending a broken harness in a circle of lantern light.

"Where is Gareth?"

Daniel smiled at her gently. "Gone. Oh, don't worry; he'll be back soon. He went to make sure nothing's amiss, and to get your things from the cottage. He says he'll not sleep well without you locked up in the house. At least not while Jean-Claude's still in the area."

Christianna pulled up a milking stool and sat next to Daniel in the circle of lantern light, listening to the warm, friendly sounds of the animals breathing.

"He's not angry anymore?"

"No, don't even think of it. He's heartsick that he dragged you to the door and made you face that bastard."

Christianna sagged with relief.

"How are you?" Daniel asked her. "I thought you were going to faint, when I saw you in the hall."

"I'm a little shaken," she admitted.

"A little?"

Her laugh was weak, but it was a laugh. "A lot," she confessed.

One of the horses nickered, and Daniel started. He leaned back and stared down the barn.

"I guess I'm a little jumpy too. I'll be glad when Gareth gets back in, and the boys. I've got to go to the Broken Bow and get Polly, but I'll stay until Gareth is here with you."

Christianna nodded. She didn't relish the idea of being left alone in the house with only Matthew for protection. "Perhaps we should go back to the house."

"Aye, if it will make you feel better. You've had a rough night."

Daniel stood, his tall shadow falling across the light, and walked across the barn. "Get the lantern, will you?" he asked, as he loaded his arms with the partly mended harnesses. "I'll put these in the toolroom and get to them

379

tomorrow. After all, there's no point. . . ."

His voice trailed off abruptly.

"What?" Christianna asked, picking up the lantern carefully. You could never be too careful in a barn, because of fire. Gareth had told her that, and she had listened. One stray spark, one careless move, and everything could go up in flames.

"What were you saying, Daniel?"

He didn't answer, and Christianna looked over at the door of the tool room.

Daniel was standing in the doorway, not moving, a peculiar expression on his face.

"What is it, Daniel?"

He opened his mouth, as if he was about to speak, but no sound came out. His face was very pale.

"Daniel?"

The harnesses fell from his arms and he swayed for a moment. His spectacles fell from his face and shattered on the hard floor. And then he pitched forward, his tall body falling with a resounding thud.

Christianna wanted to scream at the sight of the knife protruding from his back, the dark stain spreading over his shirt. She tried, but it was like a nightmare where no sound came out, only a strangled, dry noise.

Jean-Claude appeared from behind Daniel and pulled the knife from his back with an indifferent movement.

Terrified, Christianna sprang into rapid movement, her mind echoing with a silent scream of terror; but it was too late. He caught her easily, and the knife, stained with Daniel's blood, played at her throat, cold and deadly.

The lantern in her hand swayed dangerously, sending long, eerie shadows across the dark barn.

"Stupid, stupid bitch," he said in his vulgar French. "Did you think I would so easily be disposed of? Did you think that I followed you all this way to be frightened off by your hulking lover? That buffoon farmer?"

"Please," she whispered, the word tight and painful. "Daniel."

"Forget him, mademoiselle. You have greater things to worry about." Jean-Claude's breath was hot and fetid against her cheek, his grip around her waist cruel and hard, pushing the air out of her.

"Ah, you thought you were smart. 'I've never seen this man,' she says. Oh, Mademoiselle Aristocrat, you will regret the day you did see me. Do you know where you are going now?"

Christianna tried not to faint. *Think,* she told herself. Soon someone would come. Gareth. Gareth would come to find her. *Stall; play for time.*

"Where am I going?" she repeated, her voice high and quavering. "Let me think. Where am I going? To prison, perhaps?" *Please, please, let him say yes; don't let him kill me here.*

"Clever, aren't you? But not a nice, safe English prison. No, nothing that easy. I'm taking you back to France, where we know how to deal with your kind."

Christianna swayed, thinking of Gabrielle de Lambelle, the dark blood matting her golden hair. She forced herself to breathe and stared at the floor. Daniel's hand, white and still, lay half out of the doorway of the toolroom, as if reaching for his broken glasses. As she watched, it twitched. Alive? Silently, she offered up a prayer.

Jean-Claude was fumbling in his pocket, and out of the corner of her eye, Christianna saw him remove a small chemist's vial.

"Open your mouth and drink this." His rough fingers were shoving the bottle against her lips, bruising them. Instinctively, she resisted.

"Drink this, or I'll cut your throat. And when I'm done, everyone in the house."

Live, Christianna told herself. *Do whatever he says. You can't escape if you're dead.*

"What is it?" she asked, playing for time.

"Something to make you tired. It's a long way to the ship, and I won't have you making trouble on the way. Drink."

Christianna obeyed. The drug was bitter and cloying on her tongue, and she tried frantically to think of a way to spit it out, but the cold steel of the knife was close against the tender skin of her throat.

"*Bon.* You're learning to follow orders. In a moment you will walk out of the barn and get onto my horse. I'm anxious to get you back to Paris. It will be sweet to see you kneeling before Madame Guillotine."

Already the drug she had taken was making its way through her veins. She was feeling a little detached, a strange, floating sensation.

"I don't see how you can get me all the way to France against my will," she said, stalling.

"That's easy. When we reach the ship you will be asleep. Drugged. I will tell the crew that my poor wife is ill. That ought to keep them away."

The drug was dulling her mind. Her pulse was slowing down; her tongue felt slow and heavy in her mouth.

"And on the journey I can keep you amused, mademoiselle. I understand that you've developed a taste for peasants."

Far away, Christianna could hear Dog howling. Poor Dog, still locked in the buttery. Did she know something was wrong?

Her hands felt heavy, like lead weights. She hoped that the lantern wouldn't fall. Gareth would never forgive her if the barn started on fire.

At the thought of Gareth, tears began to slide from beneath her heavy eyelids. Gareth. He would curse her when he found Daniel dead or dying on the floor of the barn. Her eyes closed, and she could picture Mrs. Hatton shaking her head, her broad cheeks wobbling. "Trouble," Mrs. Hatton had said. "I always knew she was trouble."

Jean-Claude was forcing her to move, her legs stumbling and awkward in her opiated state. Her thoughts were jumbled and nonsensical.

Be careful of the lantern. Who would water the roses, next summer? Would Polly's baby be a boy or a girl?

Once, on a summer day in Paris, she and Artois and Gabrielle had gone to see a hot-air balloon launched and floating above the city. Her head felt like that now. Warm and floating. Perhaps her head would float away, and they wouldn't need to guillotine her. She laughed at the thought, and stumbled.

"Pay attention," Jean-Claude hissed in her ear.

The sound of singing reached her ears, toneless and strident.

> "Of all the girls that are so smart
> There's none like pretty Sally.
> She's the darling of me heart . . ."

Geoffery and Stewart, she thought, coming back from the Broken Bow. Think, think. How to get out of this.

She tried to focus. The barn seemed very long and dark. It was a very long way to the door. In a moment Geoffery and Stewart would come in and stable their horses.

"Bugger you," she said to Jean-Claude, her words slurring. "Now you've got some thinking to do."

"Shut up," he hissed. The knife at her throat moved and pressed into her back. "If they suspect anything, I'll run you through; do you understand?"

"Dead is dead," Christianna agreed. The words seemed very profound. Equal to Cicero or Virgil. How would Daniel say it in Latin? He wouldn't, she remembered. Daniel was lying on the floor, in a pool of blood.

The barn doors swung open, and Geoff and Stewart entered, leading their horses, laughing. They stopped short, surprised to see her.

"Hello," Stewart said agreeably. "What are you doing?"

"Nothing much," Christianna replied with great effort. *Standing with a knife pressing into my spine. Your brother is dead, around the corner. How do you do? This is the brother of the man I murdered.*

Geoffery belched loudly. "See your friend found you. Polly told us he was looking for you. She's right, 'e is ugly."

Stewart smacked Geoffery's arm with a loud thump. "Mind your manners, you drunk."

They were both drunk, Christianna realized. *They're no better off than I am—except for the knife in my back, of course.*

"Sorry," Geoffery apologized with a crooked smile. In a few years, Christianna thought, he would look like Gareth.

"Aren't you going to introduce us?" Stewart demanded, peering over the length of his crooked nose at Jean-Claude.

Jean-Claude's grip on Christianna's arm tightened painfully.

"Oh, yes. Yes, indeed. This is . . . John. John Smith, a friend from Paris."

Geoff and Stewart exchanged baffled glances. "Never heard of a Frenchman called Smith," Stewart pointed out.

"You haven't heard of much," Geoffery told him. "Do you think you know bloody all?"

"I think I know bloody more than you," Stewart announced. "And Smith is a bloody stupid name for a Frenchman, you idiot."

"Bugger you."

"You too."

They exchanged friendly blows.

The knife at Christianna's back pushed harder, and she felt a slow, warm trickle of blood.

"You know," she said, trying not to be sick, "John and I have a lot to talk about. Why don't you go away?"

"John," Stewart sang out in merry tones. "Would you like to come in the house? Have a beer?"

"That's a bloody good idea," Geoffery agreed. "Come have a pint with us."

"No, thank you." Jean-Claude's voice was tight and sharp, and Christianna had an almost hysterical urge to laugh.

"Pah'don me," Stewart said, in tones of exaggerated, pompous arrogance, "while I go to tea with the duke. We don't like beer; we're a grand Frenchman."

Geoffery laughed like an idiot. "Pahdon me," he echoed.

"Get rid of them," Jean-Claude hissed in Christianna's ear.

"Please go away," Christianna said, trying not

to slur. *Please don't leave,* she thought silently. *Not till Gareth gets here.*

"As her highness wishes," Stewart said with an affected bow. He and Geoffery were unsaddling their horses, laughing and murmuring between themselves.

Christianna tried to keep her legs steady and her eyes open. Geoffery's voice was making little sense. He and Stewart were laughing and walking to the large barn doors. In a moment they would be gone, and Jean-Claude would take her out into the night and far away from here.

She had to stay awake. She had to get Jean-Claude away from her long enough to alert Geoff and Stewart. They were pushing open the barn doors, and the cool night air rushed in. They were stepping outside.

Christianna's head dropped; the lantern in her hand was heavy against her thigh, the knife cold and sharp against her back. Jean-Claude's fingers were biting into her arm. In another moment she would be unable to think. . . .

Slowly, deliberately, she tipped the lantern against her skirts.

Fascinated, she stared at the flame as it flicked against the faded blue and white stripes, the edges curling brown and black, the flames of orange and yellow spreading over her legs, rapidly consuming the layers of fine white lawn petticoats.

Fast. She hadn't realized fire was so fast. Like a living thing, consuming her full, frothy skirts.

"Geoffery," she called.

It seemed that he turned very slowly in the barn door, his eyes widening.

Jean-Claude made a startled sound, and instinctively flung her away from him as the heat of the flames touched him. She knew that it should hurt, the way her body crashed against the wall, but it didn't. Flames danced before her eyes.

"My God!" Stewart's voice, from very far away, through a dark, thick fog.

" . . . a knife," Geoffery was saying. Far away. The sound of Dog barking. Cold, cold air. Was she in France?

And then darkness.

Her eyes were heavy, so heavy that she doubted she'd be able to lift them. Her tongue was dry, and she wanted a drink so badly. What had happened?

It came back in an awful flood of images. Daniel, with the knife in his back, his pale hand reaching toward his cracked spectacles. Jean-Claude, with the knife pressing against her back. Stewart and Geoffery, laughing and unaware, leaving the barn, and the awful sight of flames dancing around her, like a hellish ballgown.

She opened her eyes, afraid of what she might see.

She was lying in her old bed, upstairs at the house. Sunlight was streaming in the gabled window. There was a glass of fresh roses on the broad sill; brilliant, deep crimson next to the white curtains. There was a heavy weight near her feet and, looking down, she saw Dog, stretched comfortably across the bottom of her bed, sleeping peacefully, her breath coming and going in faint snores.

Christianna shifted and turned her head. Had it been a dream? Another nightmare?

She glanced down at her hair and saw that the ends were singed, pale brown hooks frizzled against the black. The acrid smell of burnt hair rose to her nostrils.

She struggled to sit up, and her legs throbbed with pain, searing, burning. She cried out, and Dog whined anxiously, opening her eyes and wagging her tail.

"Christianna?"

Gareth came charging through the door, his face pale and his eyes bright with fear. His breath left his chest in a relieved gasp when he saw her sitting up.

"Sweetheart . . ."

He enfolded her in the circle of his arms, and she wept on his shoulder. She was trying to speak, but the words wouldn't come. She clung to his strong shoulders, shaking with fear and relief. Delighted to be alive, terrified to ask about Daniel.

"Daniel . . ." The word came from her mouth at last, choked and almost inaudible.

"Alive. Alive. Poor Christianna . . ." Gareth's hands were in her hair, and she wept her relief against him.

"Don't cry, don't. It's all over. Everyone's fine."

Dog whined and dragged her bulky body to a sitting position. Christianna winced as the blankets dragged across her burnt legs.

"You little fool. Setting yourself afire." Gareth's voice was husky and low. His fingers wiped the tears from her face.

"Is Daniel alive? Truly?"

"Aye, he is. Wounded, but he'll live. Sitting up in bed, reading Cicero's *Rhetorica*."

Christianna sagged with relief. "Then he is alive."

"Would I lie to you?" Gareth asked, the hint of a smile playing around his mouth.

"No, never. That much, we can be sure of. Did . . . did I burn the barn down?"

"No. You little twit. As if I cared about a barn, when you were going up in flames."

"And . . . Jean-Claude?" She hated to ask. A superstitious shiver shook her at the mention of his name.

Gareth's face tightened. "Dead."

"How?" she whispered.

"Ah, sweetheart, you don't need to know. . . ."

"I do," Christianna insisted, her heart racing. "I do. After all, I'm responsible."

"Bull," Gareth informed her coolly. "And I'll hear no more of that. He chose his own path."

"How did he die?" Christianna repeated. It seemed important, necessary that she know.

"Stewart killed him. Took his head off with a scythe."

Horrified, Christianna stared, her eyes growing huge and round.

"A man does what he has to do, to survive," Gareth told her softly. "And a woman does too. Don't forget it."

He stroked her cheek and pulled her against him again. "I've been thanking God for your life every minute since I found you. Geoff threw you in the watering trough; do you remember?"

"No. Nothing beyond the fire."

"That's just as well. I was coming back to the house, and I heard Dog going wild, and I thought, funny, that you hadn't let her out. And then I had the most terrible feeling. I knew that something had gone wrong. I got there just as Geoff was pitching you in the water."

Christianna shuddered.

Gareth touched her face gently, and his lips pressed against her forehead and cheeks, softly, reverently.

"Get those legs better," he whispered.

Christianna nodded, smiling at last. "Dittany," she told him. "In the garden. The flower with the fuzzy green leaves and the lavender flowers? It's good for burns. And pennyroyal, from the mint patch. That should work, too."

Gareth raised his brows, impressed. "Yes, of course. If you say so."

"And for Daniel," Christianna went on, "we'll need burnet—Sanguisorba Minor. The short plant, almost thistly looking, with rose-colored blossoms. It will slow his bleeding inside."

Gareth stood slowly and reached out a golden hand to touch her cheek. "You know," he said, "could be I was wrong. You may make a fine farm woman, after all. Next thing you know, you'll be slaughtering chickens and slopping hogs. Mayhap even stuffing sausages."

Christianna made an appalled face and lay back against her pillows. "Oh, stop. Will you get me some tea?"

Gareth paused at the door and sent her a brilliant smile.

"As you wish."

From the journal of Gareth Larkin
September the tenth, 1790

The crops are in, at last. The London buyers have come and gone. A fine year. There has never been such a profit.

The thatcher came and rethatched the roof on the long barn, and that should last another twenty years. The cellars are full; the fields have been turned and are ready for next spring.

The rains have started, but it doesn't bother me like it usually does. There are worse things than being trapped in the house for the winter. At least I have Christianna trapped with me, and we are hoping for a child. Certainly we are making all possible efforts toward that end.

When the London buyers paid me I gave her a share of the profits—three whole pounds. It seemed fair, since she's been trying to pull her share of the work.

So there I am, thinking what a great

worker she's turning out to be, and how she's not at all the twit I thought she was when I first met her; and what does she do?

She takes the entire bloody three pounds and spends every last penny of it on a bonnet! One bonnet! "But, Gareth," she tells me, "it was the perfect bonnet, and those are very hard to find." For three bloody pounds, it had better be a perfect bonnet. It had better last her the rest of her life.

I was furious all that morning, but by night I was laughing along with everyone else.

"Omnia vincit amor," Daniel says. Love conquers all. How can we possibly doubt him?

HISTORICAL ROMANCE
WILD SUMMER ROSE
Amy Elizabeth Saunders

Torn from her carefree rustic life to become a proper city lady, Victoria Larkin bristles at the hypocrisy of the arrogant French aristocrat who wants to seduce her. But Phillipe St. Sebastian is determined to have her at any cost—even the loss of his beloved ancestral home. And as the flames of revolution threaten their very lives, Victoria and Phillipe find strength in the healing power of love.

_0-505-51902-X $4.99 US/$5.99 CAN

CONTEMPORARY ROMANCE
TWO OF A KIND
Lori Copeland
Bestselling Author of *Promise Me Today*

When her lively widowed mother starts chasing around town with seventy-year-old motorcycle enthusiast Clyde Merrill, Courtney Spenser is confronted by Clyde's angry son. Sensual and overbearing, Graham Merrill quickly gets under Courtney's skin—and she's not at all displeased.

_0-505-51903-8 $3.99 US/$4.99 CAN

LEISURE BOOKS
ATTN: Order Department
276 5th Avenue, New York, NY 10001

Please add $1.50 for shipping and handling for the first book and $.35 for each book thereafter. PA., N.Y.S. and N.Y.C. residents, please add appropriate sales tax. No cash, stamps, or C.O.D.s. All orders shipped within 6 weeks via postal service book rate. Canadian orders require $2.00 extra postage and must be paid in U.S. dollars through a U.S. banking facility.

Name_____

Address_____

City _____ State_____ Zip_____

I have enclosed $_____in payment for the checked book(s).

Payment <u>must</u> accompany all orders.☐ Please send a free catalog.

THE TIGER SLEEPS
FEIA DAWSON SCOTT

Bestselling author of *Ghost Dancer*

In India she roamed wild, a seductive creature as exotic as any jungle cat. Now, tangled in the snares of London society, Ariel Lockwood is betrothed to a ruthless predator who will ruin her family should she refuse to become his prize trophy.

A tawny minx not a proper English lady once aroused Dylan Christianson's burning desire. Years later, Ariel's image still lingers in the Earl of Crestwood's dreams. The only man who can save Ariel, he will forfeit all he has to awaken her sleeping passion and savor the sweet fury of her love.

___3529-4 $4.50 US/$5.50 CAN

Share the intrigue and passion of

A LEISURE GOTHIC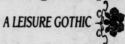

A Bitter Legacy by Jean Davidson. There are those who would kill to get the windswept estate Victoria Hunter has inherited from her grandfather. Saved from certain death by darkly handsome Jasper Thornley, Victoria seeks comfort in his arms. But an ominous foreboding warns her not to trust anyone until she unearths the long-buried lies that haunt her new home.
__3308-9 $4.50 US/$5.50 CAN

Mistress of the Muse by Suzanne Hoos. When young Ashley Canell returns to the Muse, her family home, she is faced with dark secrets—secrets that somehow involve her handsome stepcousin, Evan Prescott. And even as she finds herself falling in love with Evan, Ashley fears he might be the one who is willing to do anything to stop her from unraveling the mysteries of the Muse.
__3417-4 $4.50 US/$5.50 CAN

Darkness at Fair Winds by Charlotte Douglas. Sent to care for a young widower's son, Varina Cameron is captivated by Florida's Gulf Coast—and botanist Andrew McLaren. But the paradise of McLaren's plantation harbors dark secrets— not the least of which is whether Andrew's wife died of natural causes.
__3356-9 $4.50 US/$5.50 CAN

LEISURE BOOKS
ATTN: Order Department
276 5th Avenue, New York, NY 10001

Please add $1.50 for shipping and handling for the first book and $.35 for each book thereafter. PA., N.Y.S. and N.Y.C. residents, please add appropriate sales tax. No cash, stamps, or C.O.D.s. All orders shipped within 6 weeks via postal service book rate. Canadian orders require $2.00 extra postage and must be paid in U.S. dollars through a U.S. banking facility.

Name _____
Address _____
City _____ State _____ Zip _____
I have enclosed $_____in payment for the checked book(s).
Payment <u>must</u> accompany all orders.☐ Please send a free catalog.